Holiday Park Resort Ltd.

The Phoenix Agenda

• Ralph L. Cates •

IRON OAK PRESS
2012
San Diego, California

This novel is a work of fiction. Names, characters, and incidents are either the product of the author's imagination or are used fictitiously. Any resemblance to actual events or to any persons living or dead, except where noted, is purely coincidental and beyond the intent of either the author or the publisher.

Copyright © 2012
Ralph L. Cates

ISBN: 978-1-4675-1472-9

All Rights Reserved

No part of this book may be reproduced, stored in a retrieval system, or transmitted by any means — electronic— mechanical — photocopying — recording — or otherwise, without written permission from the author, except for review purposes.

Published by Iron Oak Press P. O. Box 2936, Ramona, CA 92065

ironoakpress.com

Dedicated to my wife, Sharon,
and my sons,
Christopher and Timothy

Holiday Park Resort Ltd.

Acknowledgments

Numerous people advised me in completing *The Phoenix Agenda*. First of all, let me thank both Will Greenway and his writing group, and the Ramona writing group. Margaret Harmon, Joan Oppenheimer, Annette Williams, Gaille Brennan, Pearl Ellis and my wife Sharon L. Cates, deserve special mention for their many tedious hours of editing.

During the writing of this book, I referred to my plentiful four-year journal entries and photos obtained while living in the Middle East for first-hand accounts of Dubai, Iran, Pakistan and Saudi Arabia. My previous book, *Black October*, was essential in this regard.

For research, the periodicals that stood out were: *The American Prospect, Barron's, The Economist, Foreign Affairs, Foreign Policy, National Geographic, The Nation, The New Yorker,* and *The New York Review of Books*.

Movies and research videos are very valuable also. Because of the vast corpus and multiplicity of media available, we live in fortunate times. My wife, Sharon, and I are avid movie buffs and critics. Of the videos, I find documentaries on PBS, National Geographic, Discovery, and occasionally The History Channel indispensible. Too abundant to mention are series specials. Recently *Homeland* on Showtime seemed very realistic.

Last, I thank the hundreds of Arabs, Indians, Iranians, and Pakistanis for their personal interactions, even when those interactions became unpleasant and sometimes dangerous.

Foreword

The Phoenix Agenda is a work of fiction. Except for al Qaeda leaders Osama bin Laden and Ayman al Zawahiri, all characters are a product of the author's imagination.

CIA contract agent Kurt Valdez, a former CIA non-official combatant or NOC, is a composite of three real persons: an adventurer, a CIA case officer who worked for the Directorate of Operations (the DO), and an analyst who worked for the Directorate of Intelligence (DI). Valdez' exploits are fictionalized.

The Phoenix Agenda is a story about the quest by Muslim terrorist organizations to inflict mortal wounds on the West.

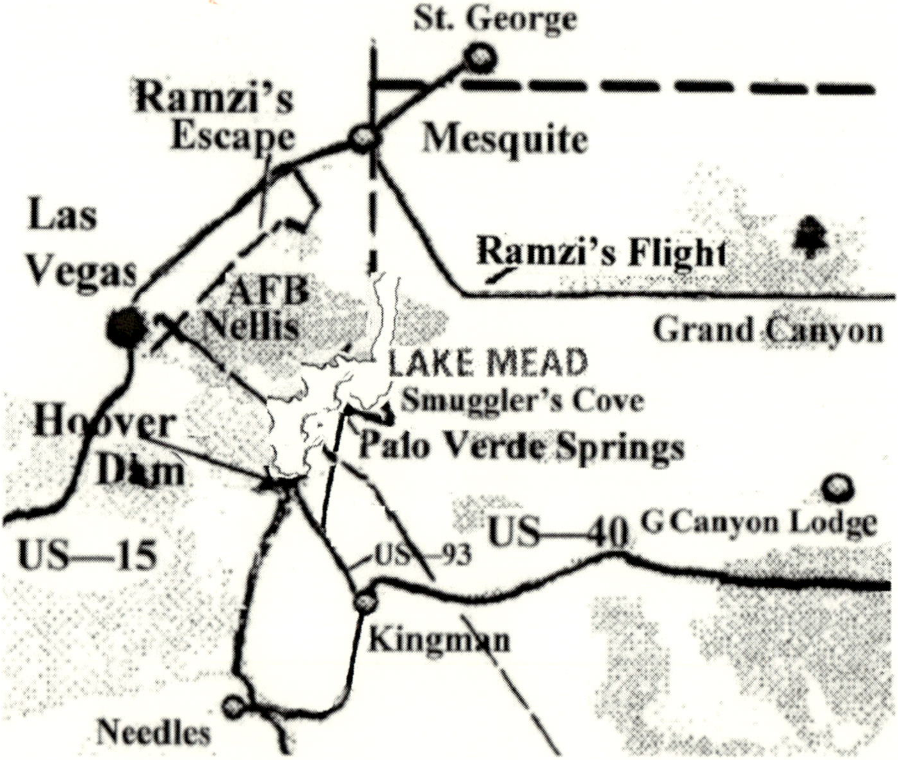
St. George
Ramzi's
Escape
Mesquite
Las
Vegas
Ramzi's Flight
AFB
Nellis
Grand Canyon
LAKE MEAD
Smuggler's Cove
Hoover
Dam
Palo Verde Springs
US—40
G Canyon Lodge
US—15
US—93
Kingman
Needles

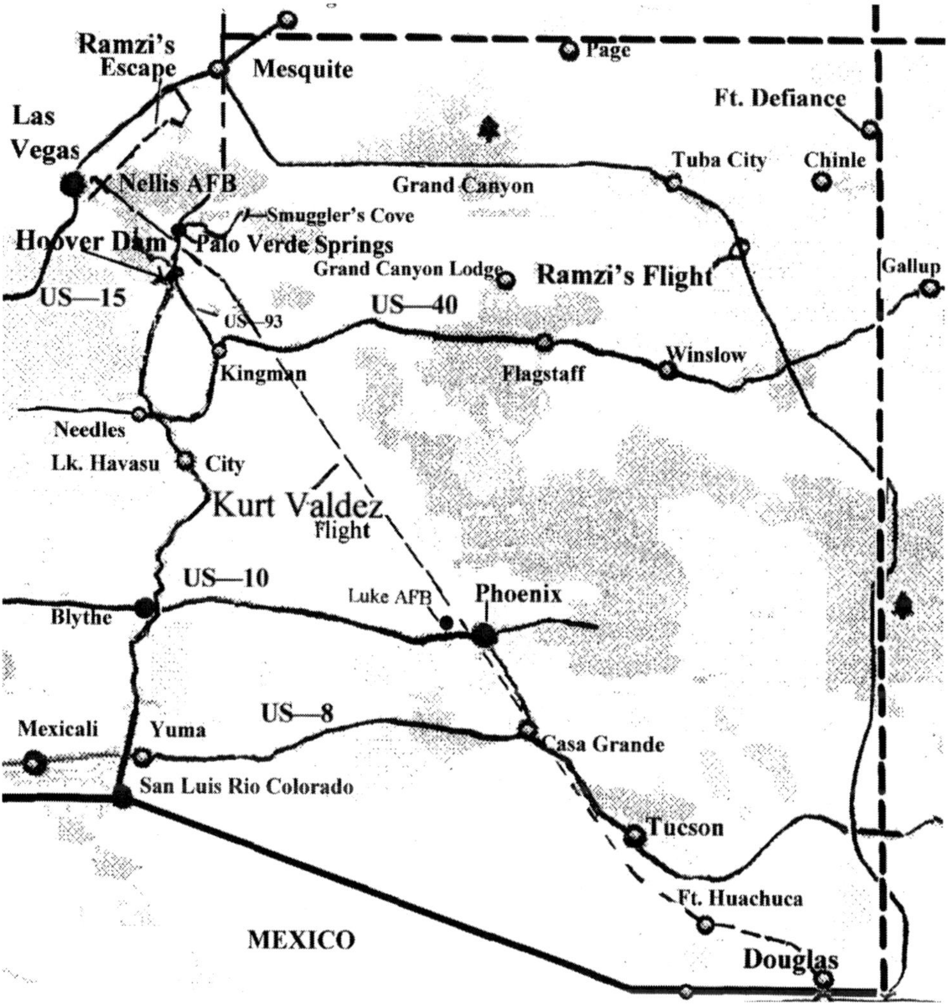

Ramzi's Escape
Mesquite
Page
Ft. Defiance
Las Vegas
Tuba City
Chinle
Nellis AFB
Grand Canyon
Smuggler's Cove
Hoover Dam
Palo Verde Springs
Grand Canyon Lodge
Ramzi's Flight
Gallup
US—15
US—40
US—93
Kingman
Flagstaff
Winslow
Needles
Lk. Havasu City
Kurt Valdez Flight
US—10
Luke AFB
Phoenix
Blythe
US—8
Mexicali
Yuma
Casa Grande
San Luis Rio Colorado
Tucson
Ft. Huachuca
MEXICO
Douglas

TURKMENISTAN
Caspian Sea
N
Mashhad
Tehran
MI
0
150
300
IRAN
Esfahan
Rafsanjan
Khafunabad
Ancient Village
Kerman
AFGHANISTAN
Sar-Cheshmeh
Murdan
Zahedan
PERSIAN GULF
PAKISTAN
Strait of Hormuz
Dubai
HALO Landing Zone
LZ – XL39

Fictional Characters

CIA
Kurt Valdez:: aka *Tiburon* (Shark): **Contract agent for D.O.**; former NOC (Non-Official Cover)
Don Berkley: Director of Operations (DO), Central Asia

NSA and Department of Homeland Security
Krysta Mazur, Former National Security Agency Translator: Middle East languages: Arabic, Pashto, Farsi. Now assigned by **DHS** to Northwest Arizona and Southwest Nevada.

Al Qaeda
Ramzi bin Omeri: aka The Snow Leopard. International Terrorist assigned to SWest, US

Mujahedeen:	Kareem abu Bakr	
	Ali bin Khalifa	
U.S. moles:	Abdul Bin Ibrahim	aka Ricardo Morales
	Zaki Bin Ibrahim	aka Jorge Morales
Shaheed	Mustafa Fakouri	(Suicide bomber):

Sheriff: Bob Stroman: Mojave County AZ: northwest, adjacent to Colorado river.
Deputies: Paul Davidson
Joe Zuniga
(Trainee)   Travis Williams

Sheriff Earl McGibbon: Sheriff of Clark County, Las Vegas, Nevada.

SEALS: Lieutenant Commander Menzies
Master Chief Gilbert Espinosa

(SAP) Special Access Program: (U.S., Attached to U.S. Customs and Border Protection)
Captain Brindle: Commander, SAP, Afghanistan and Waziristan
Captain Roberts: Commander, SAP, Southwest, U.S.

Chapter 1

Waziristan, Afghanistan-Pakistan border

Kurt Valdez plunged a boot into the deep snow and stopped to catch his breath. He inhaled several gulps from the small oxygen tank near his shoulder and allowed them to slowly flow out between his teeth. Sweat soaked his armpits and crotch despite the chill. Glancing at his altimeter, he read 6,330 meters—20,760 feet. *Almost there.*

A short, compact man with a large forehead, the former Non-Official-Cover—NOC—now a contract agent for the CIA, Valdez could almost match the mountain tribes people in endurance.

"Hold up, Hakim," he said to his guide. "The others are falling behind."

The Afghani stopped and leaned forward with one foot uphill, one hand on his thigh.

Kurt looked back below. SAPs in white camouflage and dark goggles stretched out for a half-mile behind the two men. They crunched through the snow and wound their way up the steep switchbacks. The SAPs—a Special Action Program that combined Special Forces from all branches of the military with paramilitary personnel from the CIA and FBI—periodically stopped to breathe from their oxygen tanks. They labored under heavy loads, heaving frosty exhalations. A trail, two feet deep, traced their path up the mountainside.

Afghani and Hazara porters behind the SAPs walked with steady, plodding gaits carrying 60- to 70-pound packs full of ammo and survival supplies.

As planned, the choppers dropped the group off below 10,000 feet on the side of the mountain before dark last night to keep from being spotted. Their destination was the saddle between two barren peaks up ahead where they could observe the valleys stretching toward Pakistan.

Valdez breathed slower. "Crystal clear today, Hakim. We can see Widowmaker." He gestured east toward the world's third-tallest peak on the western edge of the Himalayas.

Hakim grunted acknowledgment. "It's 140 klicks from here."

A tall, thin Pashtu from the Hindu Kush, Hakim Jamahalien had fair skin and a large, bulbous nose. The Company recruited him for his language abilities and skill in the terrain that al Qaeda and the Taliban inhabited. He was especially knowledgeable about the opium trade and the tribal areas of Waziristan, the unruly and ungovernable region between Afghanistan and Pakistan. The man was a goat in the mountains, earning him the moniker, *Shikar*—goat, in Farsi.

Valdez watched Hakim ease among rock outcroppings as the guide reached the pass. The Afghan lay still in place for several breaths, exhaling slowly to hide them. Finally, he spoke into his lip-mike. "Hostiles. Fourteen vehicles, fifty-plus Taliban, six dogs, eighteen pack animals."

Kurt winced. The animals' keen hearing and sense of smell made it next to impossible to approach the tribal warriors. He acknowledged and passed the message on to Captain Brindle. The captain would make sure the SAP didn't generate any metallic noises that animals could hear for miles in the mountains. Weapons, ammo, and other hard objects had been wrapped with cloth and taped.

Kurt heard the captain on his comm.

"Command post. Command post. Whiskey-November-158."

"CP. Go ahead, Viper."

"Prepare to release bird—1425 hours."

"Acknowledged."

Valdez listened to the comm exchanges. From 55,000 feet, a Global Hawk had spotted the Taliban massing two days ago. The SAPs' timing to arrive at the viewpoint was now perfect.

Reaching the outcropping, Valdez removed his backpack and eased down into soft snow next to Hakim. Then he slithered forward to view the terrain and warriors of the Taliban. Word was they were moving a large opium shipment and picking up a load of RPGs and explosives for IEDs.

Rocket propelled grenades—RPGs—had been the Taliban's weapon of choice for direct confrontation. But improvised explosive devices—IEDs—were responsible for the majority of deaths and serious maimings of American and coalition forces. Leadership wanted the supply stanched.

Kurt focused binoculars. Vast valleys spread out for hundreds of kilometers under a crystal-blue sky and white clouds scudded up the faces of peaks. Stark and jagged mountain ranges spread southward, one after another, as he scanned west. Tree line was 9,000 feet below them. Beyond the lush valleys, at the edge of visibility, the Indus River and its tributaries coursed through the verdant flood plain.

Valdez turned. Behind them was the western edge of the Hindu-Kush. Dozens of stark peaks rose above the two men. He crawled back, stood and slowly scanned the two peaks near them. His trained eye went over every indentation where explosives might have been placed. Making two slow passes, he suddenly stopped.

There! An antenna.

He wasn't sure at first. Focusing the binoculars, he zeroed in on the straight object.

Yes. It was wrapped with white cloth.

He signaled to Hakim indicating the find.

"We will have to take it out, comrade."

Kurt nodded and dropped back to the snow. Then rising to one knee, he retrieved the telescope from the backpack. A large, offset Questar refractor with a battery-powered rangefinder, it had a dull coating on the lens that would not reflect light.

Hakim crawled back and helped him set up the tripod. They attached the battery. Finally, they covered it with a white camouflage tarp and eased the scope to a position to survey the valleys.

Valdez put the pack under his chest, pulled off his dark goggles, and focused on the hostiles that Hakim pointed out. He read the rangefinder and mumbled, "1,967 yards." The magnetically-corrected compass on the instrument read 197 degrees off true north. With a glance at the Global Positioning System window, Valdez turned two dials and retrieved the precise location of the lead vehicle.

Hearing stealthy footsteps behind him, he turned to read Air Force Sergeant Rickman's name tag. Rickman carried a computer to direct the "bird," a Predator. The small remote-controlled aircraft would be their major weapon today. It carried no missiles, only another spotter scope controlled by the computer. Once the sergeant was ready, he would take control of it from Nellis Air Force Base near Las Vegas, Nevada.

Valdez heard the captain on his comm again.

"Command post. Whiskey-November-158."

"CP. Go ahead, Viper."

"Release control bird."

"Acknowledged."

Sergeant Rickman finished setting up and now spoke into his lip-mike, "Bird under control."

"Acknowledged," came the captain's comm message.

Valdez turned and frowned at the next three SAPs to reach the saddle, laboring to breathe off oxygen. He felt his stomach muscles tighten. The patrol was too casual. He signaled to keep the noise down, warning through his mike that the Taliban had placed explosives near one of the peaks above them.

In the pre-op meeting, the captain had warned everyone that if the enemy's animals detected the SAP, they could set off avalanches by remote control.

Captain Brindle was the next man to arrive. He leaned forward, his hand on his knee, and inhaled heavily off his oxygen tank. He nodded to Sergeant Rickman to bring the Predator around.

Hakim moved down and whispered to the porters, pointing to where they should set down their loads and cautioning them about the dogs' acute hearing abilities.

Kurt noted that the three marine sharpshooters arrived with 50-caliber sniper rifles. The weapons fired four-inch-long shells that were accurate at more than a mile. With frangible or spent uranium projectiles, they could blow an enemy's head off, or penetrate and explode a vehicle's fuel tank.

Their three spotters helped the respective shooters set up weapons on tripods and receive ammo belts from the porters. They covered the rifles with camouflage blankets and eased them into position, facing the valleys to the south and southwest.

Captain Brindle accepted the ranges, GPS locations and coordinates from Valdez. He fed this information to Sergeant Rickman, who controlled the Predator with a joystick.

"Get a move on," he said sharply.

Several minutes went by while the sergeant maneuvered the small aircraft into place. The plan called for him to set it on a high-altitude path directly into the wind, then allow it to lose elevation and glide silently toward enemy vehicles.

Hakim moved over beside Rickman on the computer. Kurt glanced at the Afghani and saw him pull his lip-mike into place. Hakim whispered into it and Kurt held a thumb up to indicate his voice was transmitting.

Shivering for the first time, Kurt realized that they had to work quickly. He scanned the peaks above them one more time, wondering where explosives might be. Captain Brindle's dark lenses turned in his direction.

Kurt pointed out the antenna on the side of the peak and conveyed the location. The officer nodded when he located it. Kurt saw the muscles on the side of his jaw knot.

Returning his attention to the telescope, Valdez adjusted it for the Taliban's most recent movements. They headed toward a road that turned south into Pakistan, one of dozens of opium highways. He gave updated information to the captain, who acknowledged with a thumb up.

The teams quickly slid under their white camouflage and made adjustments. Each marine position had a sharpshooter and spotter. While the spotter set up the range finders and determined the precise distance and wind speed—how much to correct for elevation and side-to-side drift—the shooter turned the adjusting knobs. The teams lined up left to right, facing the valleys so as not to fire across each other's shots.

Sergeant Rickman indicated that the Predator was now sending live images to the computer. He remotely focused the small aircraft's telescope.

Hakim scrutinized the Taliban from the images. "No Aces."

Captain Brindle said, "Acknowledged."

Valdez winced at the news. "Aces" were men they had been seeking for ten years, the top leaders of Al Qaeda and the Taliban. If they didn't encounter any Aces, the SAP had consent to take out secondary targets.

Hakim said, "Number three, Jack of Clubs. Number six, Ten of Diamonds. Number eight, Seven of Clubs. Number nine Five of Hearts."

The captain acknowledged on his lip-mike.

"Freeze!" Valdez rasped. "Those dogs are looking in our direction."

Not a man moved as Valdez scanned the Taliban. The dogs definitely detected something. Three of them, now four, stared in the SAPs general direction.

Hakim's voice came on the radio, "One of the Taliban has noticed the dogs. He raised his binoculars. Look," he said, "the last men are running for the vehicles."

Captain Brindle blurted, "Select your targets, shooters. Fire on my command."

From his left side Valdez heard the shooter nearest him say, "Range it."

The spotter replied, "Tertiary target, 1,912 yards. Wind three-quarter value. Push two left. Vehicle speed 23 miles per hour. Three mil lead. Four seconds to target."

"Got it," the shooter said. He turned his knobs.

Valdez said, "The Talib with the scope is pointing in our direction. He has a radio. They're setting up a mortar! The explosives, Captain!"

The shooter teams passed the message on to the captain that they were ready. A navy SEAL on Valdez' right finished adjusting his telescope and attached a video camera.

Captain Brindle's voice came over the radio, "Prepare to fire."

Valdez slid earmuff sound protectors over his earpieces. He inhaled a deep breath and swallowed. Balling his fists, he waited, hoping the concussions didn't set off the explosives.

The captain commanded, "On my mark: three, two, one."

Valdez flinched from the blasts. Even with the muffs, shots from the fifties were loud.

Within moments of the first rounds, the shooters fired again.

It took almost four seconds for the projectiles to arrive at the selected targets.

The SEAL with the video camera recorded images. Valdez stretched to look into the scope.

Uranium-alloyed projectiles found their mark. Three vehicles exploded. Gas tanks spewed orange flames. Bodies soared. Two more vehicles erupted. Before the Taliban could react, four small trucks flipped. Animals catapulted away and lay sprawled thirty meters from the caravan.

"Fire for effect," the captain commanded. He glanced at his sharpshooter. "Les, take out that antenna above us."

Within seconds, Kurt heard shots from a small caliber behind them. The marksman swore.

Get them, Les, before they blow us away.

Kurt flinched as every few seconds, the shooters blasted away. Surviving Taliban scrambled for cover.

Readjusting the telescope, Valdez searched for more enemy spotters and mortar positions.

Two more vehicles burst aflame. Then another. Surviving pack animals scattered. Three trucks turned downhill toward rock outcroppings.

Valdez heard Command on the comm. "Viper. Command post."

"Go ahead, CP."

"Larger hostile forces. Sector foxtrot. Truck mounted fifties. Mortars."

Valdez moved his telescope to assess the new threat. "Got them, Sir. Range 1,941 yards, 217 degrees true."

Sergeant Rickman redirected the Predator. "Coming about," he said.

The shooter, Les, finally yelled, "I got the antenna!"

Kurt exhaled and glanced at the captain. "Well done, Les!" he shouted.

Hakim watched the action on the computer as broadcast by the miniature aircraft.

The attached FBI operative shouted, "SAM missiles! Secondary vehicle."

Simultaneously, Hakim called out, "King of Spades, third vehicle from right."

Valdez jerked and adjusted the telescope. He focused the range finder on the Talib and knotted his jaw. Sure enough! *There he is. Nazir Fazlullah. The son-of-a-donkey who kidnaped Hakim's sisters! Stoned Kaleem because she was raped by a Talib.*

He grimaced and shook off the thoughts, read the GPS coordinates, and reset the range. In his lip-mike, he called out, "New position, Captain, 1,872 yards,—39-51-23 north, by 298-38-12 west.

The marines listened to Valdez' new coordinates and redirected their weapons. Shortly, the spotters indicated to the captain they were ready.

"Fire when ready," the officer said.

Valdez heard the muffled shots and felt the concussions. He watched as more than four seconds later Fazlullah's truck exploded. Flames burst from the vehicle. Five more vehicles blew in rapid succession. Mortars and missile launchers hurled away. Bodies flew in all directions from the blasts.

Surviving Taliban scattered to rock protection.

"Incoming!" a marine yelled. Valdez heard the scream of a mortar round.

The first blast erupted seventy yards below them on the side of the saddle.

The captain shouted, "Move out! Retrieve the Predator!"

SAP personnel grabbed packs and equipment and rushed down toward the chopper landing sites. The three shooter teams continued to pound the Taliban to cover the retreat.

Minutes later, hundreds of yards down the mountain, Valdez looked back up and saw the six marines and Sergeant Rickman running down, cutting across switchbacks.

A massive explosion erupted on the peak to the west. Valdez dodged rocks that fell around him. A cascade of boulders and ice plunged down the chute on their left. It roared, spreading out toward the personnel below.

The SAP now ran straight down the mountain. They plunged deep footsteps into the snow to slow their momentum. Valdez looked back at the peak directly above them and wondered why it hadn't exploded.

Choppers appeared in the distance. The marine sharpshooters caught up to Valdez and Hakim. Several mortars made it over the pass and exploded on the mountain, sending shallow waves of new snow cascading down behind the SAP.

More than an hour later, Valdez crowded into one of the helicopters taking on personnel. He set the pack with the Questar telescope between his legs, strapped himself in and tilted the seat back. The Chinook rose and hovered. It then banked in formation with the other helicopters and headed north.

Valdez closed his eyes and breathed deep—exhausted after the hard climb last night and this morning. Hakim was a good guide but difficult to keep up with. The Afghani reminded him of his former comrade Hassan.

Hassan and he had worked closely for five years before the man was killed. Kurt had watched helplessly as al Qaeda beheaded his friend one night in Karachi in 2004.

The two operatives discovered Osama bin Laden's lair in October 2001. An Egyptian, later apprehended in a snatch, told the CIA they nearly trapped the Number One terrorist himself. Bin Laden was ready to give the final word to his bodyguards to kill him, which included also making martyrs of the *jihadists*. The SAP was *that* close and never realized it. Valdez blinked merely thinking about it.

All this could be finished.

The chopper banked and hovered near its landing spot.

American Embassy, CIA station, Kabul, Afghanistan

Kurt sent an email to Langley informing the Deputy Director of Operations for Central Asia that they took out at least five top leaders of the Taliban, including Nazir Fazlullah. He attached a video transmission of the battle.

Glancing at his watch, he saw it was almost 1700 hours—8 a.m. in Langley, Virginia. He heaved a big breath. The climb to 21,000 feet had really done him in.

His satellite phone rang and he glanced at the readout.
Berkley?

He moved to a small office and answered, "You received my message, Top?"

"Yeah, *Tiburon*. Well done. Didn't lose anyone?"

"We were lucky this time." Kurt smiled at the use of his code name—*Tiburon*—shark in Spanish—and his involvement with a school of bull sharks that was behind the name.

"How's the family, Kurt? Misha'il over the measles?"

"They're fine. Yeah. He and Mohammad both came down with them. They quarantined the whole community. Baderi's pregnant again," Valdez said, referring to his second wife. "To keep the baby safe, she has to stay with my mother-in-law, Raisa."

"That's a good precaution."

"You didn't call to chat, Top. What's up?"

"I've been discussing you with the boss. The Company is planning to transfer three dozen agents with Middle Eastern language skills to the U.S. border areas."

"What about Waziristan?"

"You're half-Mexican, Kurt. Leaving you there is a waste of talent. The new battles are moving to North America."

There was a long silence while Kurt considered the drift of the conversation. He'd had thoughts about resigning and moving home before.

The chief must have taken his silence as a positive. "Fourteen years is a long time in Afghanistan and Pakistan. It's time to come home. Get your affairs in order. I'm working on a transfer."

Chapter 2

Mojave County, Arizona

Sheriff Bob Stroman floored the gas pedal to pass two 18-wheelers. The white SUV patrol vehicle sucked in a loud inrush of air and accelerated past the trucks. Stroman then swerved back into the northbound lane on Highway 93.

On his left, through gaps in the stark, barren mountains, he could see a view of the Colorado River, blue and placid, with trees and bushes along the banks. The turn-off to the lower end of the Grand Canyon came up on the right.

He narrowed his eyes and pressed *play* on his recorder once again.

The recording played.

"The Department of Homeland Security has infiltrated 17 Islamic terrorist cells on U.S. territory. This is highly classified information and doesn't get leaked to news agencies. Most of the cells are situated in densely populated areas of large American cities such as New York, Buffalo and Detroit. However, more and more, we are discovering them in remote areas near the Mexican border. We warn you to be especially alert for anyone who may have Middle Eastern connections. California, Arizona, New Mexico and Texas are prime territories for entry because of the large influx of immigrants through those regions of the porous border.

"To protect these border regions, the department is assigning contracts to private intelligence organizations. These firms have highly-trained personnel, some formerly employed by such government agencies as the Defense Intelligence Agency, or DIA, the National Security Agency, or NSA, and the CIA. The Department of Homeland Security will have one of these private firms assign one or more agents to your county law offices."

Stroman switched the machine off and mulled that statement around for the sixth time. A large man in his mid-forties, he had been sheriff of Mojave County, Arizona for 16 years. For the meeting, his wife Carrie insisted on having three of his uniforms professionally tailored and pressed. He'd also paid well to have a high military polish applied to both pair of boots. The sheriff was an outdoorsman—a hunter and fisherman—a good old boy—but Carrie had wanted him to be the epitome of the professional law officer for these meetings.

Appearance was not on his mind this morning, however. He and 127 other law enforcement officers in the state were summoned by Homeland Security to review the latest information on what was being done to combat infiltration into the United States. Terrorist groups such as al Qaeda, Iraqi mercenaries and the Muslim Brotherhood had recently begun using Mexico as a springboard. The presenters shared intelligence from computer databases and the latest information on surveillance equipment. They then distributed new computer interface hardware and software.

One of the displays that had so impressed Stroman was the satellite view of various Arizona counties. Officials demonstrated how they could zoom in on individual boats on Lake Mead. One speaker said that, if needed, they could provide aircraft or even drones to track vehicles, or search close or tight areas around buildings.

The mention of remote-controlled drones—Predators—caught Stroman's attention. Several big-city sheriffs expressed surprise with the borderline-invasive powers of the surveillance techniques.

Many participants from sparsely populated areas had received large amounts of money from the governmental department to upgrade their systems since 2002. Mojave County received seventy times as much assistance per resident as the government of New York City. However, because of the Iraq and Afghanistan wars, funds to rural areas had dwindled and were now channeled to large population centers.

The meeting was called to explain the tight budgets and therefore the agency's need for cooperation—as well as law enforcement agencies' input. They introduced several agents from private security firms—formerly with government agencies—who were being assigned to work with local Arizona and Nevada authorities.

The barren hills above Hoover Dam emerged in the distance and diverted Stroman's attention. Construction of the new Pat Tillman Bridge proceeded at a rapid pace.

He rewound the recorder and pressed *play* one more time to listen to the particular segment of the message that he thought might affect his county.

Chapter 3

Murdan, Iran

Ramzi bin Omeri brought his fist to his cheek and scowled at the computer screen. The crypto system transliterated the Arabic communication from al Qaeda's new leadership. He swallowed as the message he feared most emerged. Another mission, *The Phoenix Agenda*. As he read on, he realized it was boldest attack yet imagined on American soil, even *more* bold than the September 11 attacks of 2001, more audacious than the widespread attack on Saudi oil facilities four years ago.

That is why they have me working on the American slang and accent.

The Yemeni had disappeared since he'd masterminded the massive and successful attacks on Saudi Arabia. Every intelligence agency in the world listed him at the top of their Most Wanted List.

That's also why he was living and working in this remote, mountainous, copper-mining area of central Iran. He now had a low-profile position as an electrical engineer on the Sar-Cheshmeh copper mine's power plant and distribution system, a job for which he had been trained two decades ago. It was a good place to live discretely with his wife.

The high, arid mountains endured summer thunderstorms and winter snows. A sprawling suburb of pastel-colored masonry condominiums with asphalt streets and concrete sidewalks was now approaching 30 years old. However, it was well maintained by the national mining company. Ramzi and his wife enjoyed a standard of living as good as any engineer's family in Tehran.

He read down the screen once more, jotted several dates and locations, then deleted the message from the computer. Removing the memory stick, he went to the fireplace and burned it. Then he returned to the computer and rid it of all traces of the agenda.

This morning, his wife Shamci had shrieked and cut her hand with a butcher knife when she realized what the messenger left.

Wrapping a cloth around the cut, she said indignantly, "Will they ever leave us alone? Reza already died for the cause."

He hugged her and consoled her. "Reza was proud to die for Allah. He died fighting Americans. Besides, this is voluntary. They are asking me because we disappeared three years ago."

"We have responsibilities now."

Shamci had always been petite and attractive to him, with green eyes and dark red hair that she wore in fashionably styled hairdos. (She insisted on that one luxury.) She had slight eye folds and features that hinted of Mongolian bloodlines, not unusual for an Iranian.

In the Afghan War with the Russians, Ramzi served with dozens of Hazara, descendants of the mighty Khans. (Given his choice, he preferred them to Middle Eastern Arabs.) Shamci resembled some of the Hazaras. Ironically, he met her on an aircraft hijack mission. She was the first female al Qaeda terrorist.

"You can't let them activate you to take charge of another mission. You have an important job here as an engineer."

After Ramzi escaped from Waziristan, the mountains between Pakistan and Afghanistan, al Qaeda negotiated with Hezbollah to hide the former commander in these mountains near Sar-Cheshmeh, a day's drive from the ancient capital, Isfahan, Iran.

No one here suspected that Ramzi bin Omeri, the legendary *Snow Leopard* of the Afghan war with the Russians, lived in their midst. Certainly, no one in Iran knew he masterminded the massive and successful attack on the Saudi oil production facilities.

Ramzi rose and went to a mirror. He scanned his face to see if any scars were still visible, turning side to side for close examination. He no longer resembled a young Omar Sharif as he had two decades ago. Three operations changed his cheeks, chin, and eyelids. Al Qaeda showed him copies of poor-quality photos that French Intelligence circulated. It would be very difficult for western agencies to identify him now.

Running a bowl of steaming water, he dabbed shaving cream on his face and stropped a large straight razor, a hand-me-down from his father.

When he finished shaving, he slipped on the Aqualand eco-drive chronometer and dive calculator that Ayman al Zawahiri presented to him as a gift. It had a diamond bezel and depth gauge with decompression intervals easily set. The Number Two terrorist ordered it special for Ramzi in all black, instead of the more common and visible bright orange.

When he passed Shamci an hour later, now clean shaven, she gave him a look of dread and jerked the bandage on her cut hand tighter.

Chapter 4

Mojave County, Arizona • July 21, 2008

Sheriff Bob Stroman pointed at a butte strewn with the black remnants of an ancient lava flow. "Got a ram, a full curl, the other side of that ridge two years ago."

"How'd you manage that? I ain't been able to get close to 'em," Deputy Travis Williams said.

"I was on top looking down at Lake Mead after camping out all night. Beautiful daybreak coming over the Grand Canyon." He gestured to the east. "I was scanning with binoculars. Happened to see three rams raise their heads, right over a knoll. You know they have eight-power vision—like me with binoculars. I froze." Bob saw he had Williams' complete attention.

"They didn't move a hair for quite a while. Then the three of 'em ambled slowly over a ridge. That's when I bagged him." The sheriff pushed his shoulders back against the seat, both hands on the steering wheel. The story still made his heart race. "Clean shot, right through the neck with my Win 300 magnum. Stopped him dead in his tracks."

"Damn. I'd shore like to been there. Maybe we can go this fall." Williams moved a wad of Skoal around in his mouth. He was a husky young man with a haircut that still marked him as recently mustered out of the marines.

"Drew my tags already."

"I missed the draw. But I'd like to go watch."

"I try not to mix business and pleasure, but we might manage it once or twice." The sheriff brushed a bee off the reddish-blond hair on his arm and stared at what he thought was a new freckle.

Williams seemed reluctant to press the issue. "What do you know about this guy we're gonna see?"

"Ricardo Morales. Wife has a common name—Maria, I think. His brother Jorge and his family live in the back. Bunch of kids between 'em—seven or eight. Never figured out the arrangement."

The GMC "Jimmy" patrol vehicle rose on its springs as they came out of a dip. "They're Brazilian, wives are Mexican. They make big electric signs—mostly for Las Vegas casinos. Had three sections on the workbenches last time I was here."

"So what happened?" Williams spit juice into a Styrofoam cup.

"Last time, his torches were stolen. Tanks, too. The whole works. Probably some kids. Now it's his arc welder."

"Sounds like he needs a couple dogs."

"I told him to get an alarm system."

"You check out their papers? They clean?"

The sheriff shot the ex-marine a disgusted look.

"Just asking. We're not too far from the border."

"They had their green cards. Kids being bused to school with the Indian kids. And Walker's and Stufloten's grandkids."

They sat in silence for a few minutes while the sheriff pondered the previous investigation. He'd finally concluded that it wasn't worth his time for $550 worth of equipment, but he politely told Morales that he'd keep a lookout.

Stroman changed the subject. "So, how long have you known Alex?"

"Alex? Gunnery Sergeant Alessandro Peña. About six years. He trained us on the rifle ranges."

"He gave you high marks."

Williams grunted and spit tobacco juice in the cup. "Deputy Davidson seems a little wary of me."

"Ah, Paul's alright. He'll get used to you. Once he knows you're not his replacement."

"He reminds me of Barney Fife. Same build. Even the same mannerisms."

Stroman frowned at Williams.

"You know, on Mayberry, the old Andy Griffith shows."

The sheriff burst out laughing. "Now that you mention it, he does."

Williams smiled.

"Don't say anything to him. You'd hurt his feelings."

"I don't think Joe likes me," Williams said, referring to the other deputy, a huge Indian.

The sheriff was silent for a moment as he considered the Havasupai who always scowled. "I'll tell you one thing that nails him. I once asked Joe Zuniga, 'You know what a screw-up is?'"

Stroman paused for effect. "His answer was, 'Yeah, 1492.'" The sheriff laughed. "That captures Joe's personality perfectly. But he's excellent with our Indian problems. Since the casinos went in. I couldn't do without him."

They dropped into a broad valley. Barren hills of alkaline soil with sparse patches of creosote bushes, barrel cacti, and yuccas spread from both sides of the highway. Dark red, brown and black rocks from an ancient volcano lay strewn among the succulents.

They had left the office an hour ago and headed south away from Hoover Dam and the enormous new bridge being constructed across the Colorado River. There were several places where the river and Lake Mead were visible between the hills and buttes. The lower end of the Grand Canyon began 60 miles to the east of where they were now. Digital temperature read-out indicated 118 degrees.

The Jimmy bottomed its springs through another dip and the terrain changed to flash flood-cut gullies.

After a few minutes, Williams broke a long silence. Pointing to a road sign, he said, "Palo Verde Springs 13, Bonelli Landing 30. Almost there."

"Yeah. Few people want to live out here."

"Cheap," said Travis.

Stroman shook his head. "Retirees—few old miner types—poor Indians and Mexicans. The young Indians are working at the new Havasupai casino. Almost nobody on welfare, though."

"Government cleaned up that problem."

"Used to be a bunch of 'em out here," the sheriff said. He changed the subject. "You hunted much?"

"Got my first deer just before I went into the marines. Seventeen."

"Well, sheep take a lot more skill, 'cause of their eyesight."

Williams grunted and spit his wad into the cup. "Here comes Palo Verde Springs."

Gray cement-block buildings clustered on both sides of the highway. A curio shop on the right sold Indian artifacts and petrified wood.

Stufloten's store and gas station were on the left, an old white clapboard building.

Three-hundred yards beyond the last house in town, Stroman pulled the SUV down into a long graveled driveway and stopped before a metal building with a wide, segmented-metal door rolled open.

Ricardo Morales' grinder sent sparks flying off metal. A medium-height man with a slight build, his full head of wavy black hair bristled from under his welder's cap. He stopped, pushed up his faceplate and looked at the car.

The lawmen got out and stretched. Stroman scanned the premises. To the left of the shop, a small, pastel-blue masonry house had a neatly raked gravel yard and a few cacti aesthetically arranged behind a low parapet wall in front. The metal shop building contained drills, grinders, some machine tools, and several large fabricated structures on steel tables with roll-around wheels. Pipe and hardware were separated in vertical bins along the back wall, and in a long pipe rack near the right wall.

Stepping forward, the sheriff said, "Howdy, Ricardo. This here's my new deputy, Travis Williams."

Morales greeted them with a weak handshake. His brother came out to join them. "You know my brother, Jorge, from before."

The sheriff nodded, touching a finger to the bill of his cap then extending his hand. Looking around, he took in everything. He noted the usual sign work with coils of electric wire and light-fixture parts. There was a new steel table, and perhaps two or three more machine tools than he'd seen the previous time. "Business is good, Ricardo?"

"*Sí, Señor*. We get more big contract last week."

The sheriff looked at the slab floor that had sheets of plywood, edges fragmented, fitted around the work areas. He scanned the ceiling for signs of an alarm system. There were the usual shop lights. On the east side, a chain-and-hook assembly hung from a heavy-duty crane system, moveable north-and-south and east-and-west on two sets of tracks so it covered almost the whole inside of the structure.

The Brazilian gestured for them to come through the building to the back right and led the sheriff and deputy to the jimmied door. He showed them the bent hardware that appeared to have been pried open with a large bar. "They bend the bolt, *Señor*."

"What did they get this time?"

"Our electric welder. Cost 3,220 dollars."

"I don't see an alarm system."

"We no have time to buy one."

Stroman glared at him. He handed his pad to the deputy and told him to fill out the report while he dictated. Stepping out the door, he said, "No obvious footprints in the gravel. Door was jimmied with a large crowbar. Probably used gloves. How heavy was the welder and where was it?" The sheriff glanced at a small house in the back as he asked this. It had a large garden surrounded by a high plastered fence, with sunflowers, corn, and the tops of tomato plants showing. Ceramic owls rotated on small windmills and scarecrows stood up in four places.

Inside, Morales pointed to an empty spot four feet from the door. "Need two strong men to take."

"You got insurance?"

"No."

"No dogs yet, I see."

"No."

"I'm surprised that someone could break in and take a heavy welder without waking your families."

"I surprised, too."

"We will file a report and keep our ears open. I'll ask around if anyone has been selling used welding equipment. You gonna get a dog or alarm system now?"

"Oh, *sí, Señor, mañana*." Ricardo handed the sheriff a picture of the blue welder. "I get serial number later."

Stroman nodded as he looked at the picture. He faced the Latinos. "Your green cards still up to date?"

Morales turned to his brother and spoke in Spanish. Jorge hurried out the front and around the side.

The sheriff examined the floor for wheel marks toward the front, and noted a fresh scuff. "They took it out the front roll-up door. You must be sound sleepers, Morales."

The Brazilian tilted his head and frowned.

Jorge returned with the documents.

Stroman worked his mouth back and forth in deep thought, looking at the papers. "Appear okay." He regarded the Brazilians with a penetrating gaze. "Walker's got a couple of Australian shepherd pups. He might part with one."

"Dogs?"

"Yeah, dogs." The sheriff scowled.

"Thank you. I ask him."

"Sign this report, Mr. Morales."

The Brazilian signed his scrawl where the sheriff pointed.

The lawmen got in the SUV, the sheriff backed out and headed east on the highway.

After several minutes, Williams asked, "What do you think?"

"Ah, poor devils. Real hustlers. Just trying to make a living."

"I mean their accents. Didn't sound Latino to me. And, they had a weird smell. Maybe something on their clothes—something they eat—fluids they work with?"

"Yeah, now that you mention it. Passports were from Brazil. Perhaps a different diet there. Probably grew up speaking Portuguese, too."

After a few minutes, Travis said, "Three grand is a lot to lose."

"Hell, got about seven, eight kids, between 'em."

Chapter 5

Palo Verde Springs, Arizona

"What you think, Abdul? The sheriff not come again, ensha Allah?"
"The sheriff know we build signs. And your Arabic is getting bad, Zaki." Abdul flashed a sinister smile.
"We will report two more small break-ins and waste his time driving far out here. He has $40,000 trucks stolen and $50,000 drug raids. We are only trouble to him."
"We bring out other big sign for the diesel truck, my brother. So Americans in town can watch it go through. They believe that is all we do."
Abdul dragged a tin box out from under a shelf and handed Zaki some *qat* grass from it.
The younger brother grinned as he stuffed a wad of the mild narcotic in his mouth and tried to get his tongue around the golf-ball-sized mass.
Abdul laughed. In a half-hour, their minds would be perfectly sharp, but they would feel as if they had just had two glasses of liquor.

Three hours later after lunch and siestas, the two Palestinians, Abdul and Zaki bin Ibrahim, rolled the large sign they had just completed outside, in front of the electric sign shop, and lowered the door to set to work.
They piled 16 pieces of plywood from the concrete floor onto a lifting strap. Zaki lifted the load of wood with the large shop crane and the two brothers maneuvered it to the side where they set it down.
Abdul ran a water saw through four lines in the concrete floor in a rectangular shape twenty-eight feet by eight feet. He then made six cross cuts to expose the joints of the seven four-by-eight-foot sections. While he did the cutting, Zaki located the fourteen lifting bolts and chipped concrete out of them.
When he finished saw-cutting, Abdul turned the water off. He worked two lifting yokes into the now-exposed bolts of the first concrete section and hooked short cables to them. His brother brought the crane hook over and took up the load. The crane assembly squealed as Zaki tried to lift the first section. The brothers backed off, holding their arms in front of their faces in alarm and watched the crane groan. The cables went taut and appeared ready

to snap. Finally, the section came loose with a loud pop.

"*Ensha Allah.* There goes 4,000 kilos," Abdul said.

"*Caramba!*" Zaki said.

They maneuvered the concrete floor section to the side where Abdul disconnected the cables. Repeating the lifting operation on the next six sections that came out easier, they stacked them aside as quickly as possible.

When they had all the sections removed into three piles, Abdul glanced at his watch. "Three hours and twenty minutes. We were told we have to get it down to two-and-a-half hours."

"That will be hard, my brother."

The work now completely exposed the hidden basement below with a stair access on the eastern side. Two full-sized cars would fit within, end-to-end.

The eighteen-wheeler arrived that night after midnight. It was a black night, no moon. Abdul, as usual, let the Mexican driver sleep at his house.

They rolled open the shop door and, using both a large rental crane and the shop crane, they transferred the hardware and materials from the tractor-trailer to inside and rolled the door down. Then they relocated the load to the lower level.

Four hours later, they wrapped it up, replaced the concrete sections, and re-covered the floor with the plywood. Abdul exhaled. They had finished in time to have breakfast with their families and the driver.

Later that morning, Abdul motioned with hand signals to his younger brother operating the hydro-crane. Zaki maneuvered the large electric sign into the big-rig. After banging the load against the walls of the trailer for several minutes, with the driver and Abdul yelling, it stabilized. They lashed it down. Zaki eased off the hook, allowing them to disconnect it.

The driver left with the new sign. Zaki secured the boom and rigging and returned the crane to Dave's Rental Agency.

Chapter 6

Palo Verde Springs, Arizona

Abdul and Zaki bin Ibrahims' visitor arrived shortly after midnight two days after the big rig left. Abdul was notified of the plans by email. The man was Middle Eastern in appearance and about 50. He had a medium build, but looked solid under his khaki shirt and slacks. Abdul noted lighter skin where a beard was shaved off recently.

He introduced himself as Omar bin al Habib, an Egyptian. The man had the regal bearing of a higher-caste military officer. He spoke English with a British accent. Yet, he impressed Abdul with his lack of superior attitude.

By way of the stairs, the three went to the basement immediately to commence work. Zaki switched on the dozen lights. Omar began instructing the two Palestinians on how to assemble the materials.

The suave Arab first broke out a laptop computer case. He showed them how to defeat its self-destruct mechanism then reset it, to be activated any time the device wasn't used.

"If you forget and do not defeat the mechanism, white-hot metal will burst from the case in front of your face and melt through this table." Omar knocked twice on the metal for emphasis. "It will go through your body and kill you."

The brothers looked at each other with wide eyes.

Omar nodded, then had Abdul boot up and open several drawings in numerical order, one after another, so they were all available simultaneously. Once they were opened, Omar showed the brothers how to quickly switch from one drawing to another.

"A boat?" Abdul said, "for underwater."

"Yes," Omar said. "A submarine." He looked hard at the brothers. "This must be kept absolutely secret. The children must never see it. The women must never see it. You must work on it only at night. The mission could fail if anyone discovers this project."

Abdul raised his eyebrows and nodded that he understood. The hardware they had unpacked that so puzzled them now began to make sense: Four round bulkheads; one 21-foot length of 36-inch pipe; one 15-foot length of 48-inch pipe; various shafts, bearings, gauges, and seals; boxes of fittings; pipe and a wiring harness.

Omar looked directly into Abdul's eyes, then at Zaki. "You were schooled in English, Spanish and Portuguese for nine years. We paid to train you as mechanics and obtained residency visas to the United States. Al Qaeda expended much time and effort. This is your *jihad* for *Allah*."

The brothers nodded. Abdul knew they had been lucky. Everyone he knew when he was a child was either dead or barely existing on the West Bank.

Abdul turned and looked back and forth from the drawings to the hardware several times. He and Zaki had sold dozens of large electrified signs they had constructed. He felt that he and his brother were good enough at reading drawings and skilled enough as mechanics and welders to assemble this machine.

He smiled at Omar. "We can build it."

His younger brother agreed.

Again, Omar glared at the brothers. "I must emphasize, never—never let anyone see this. There is no hurry. You can take nine months. We will see that you have money in your account from your work. The trucks will keep delivering signs so that neighbors see what you do. Understand?"

"Yes, *Sheikh*," Abdul said. "We understand."

"The policeman you mentioned in your email?"

"We fooled him. He came to investigate our most recent welder theft. He thinks we are only trouble."

"Good." Omar took rolled plastic templates out of a box. "Place these on the pipes, mark them and make the cuts." Omar pointed, "Weld those rings into place." He pointed to two rings with round holes in them. Then he flipped to an isometric drawing on the computer that showed inside views of the submarine. "Weld those four labeled bulkheads where they are shown, aligning the numbered arrows. The drawings on the computer are in order. Open Number One, then Number Two, then the others in sequence. Finish *all* the work on one drawing before going to the next. This step is very important."

Abdul said, "It will be a fine boat when we are finished." He flashed a puzzled look. "What are the wheels for?"

"To roll it around on." Omar found the drawing that detailed how to weld the wheel assemblies to two support yokes. "It will be easy to move the submarine on those supports."

Abdul nodded that he understood.

Zaki pointed to a bag. "What is this, *Sheikh*?"

"*Qat*. To keep your minds clear while you work. There are new seeds to plant so you have a steady supply."

The brothers grinned at each other. A constant supply of the pleasant narcotic.

"What is the boat for?" Abdul asked.

The look Omar gave them this time caused Abdul's stomach to tighten.

The Egyptian snarled, "You will be out of here before it is used."

Abdul nodded, indicating he understood. *Do not ask questions.*

Omar looked at his watch. "My ride will be here in two hours. Until then, I will sleep on that bed you made. We will contact you the usual way when we are ready." Again, he gave them the piercing stare. "Do not contact us from here in the United States. Ever. In an emergency, you know what to do."

Abdul bin Ibrahim closed the computer programs and folded the machine into its case. Leaning over and holding a trigger, he held his breath and activated the incendiary device as he closed it.

Afterward, they went up the steps. They maneuvered the last concrete section into the frame in the floor. They slid the last two plywood sheets over the concrete. After the Egyptian declined a meal, the brothers departed out the back door to their homes.

The Arab, Omar bin al Habib, aka Ramzi bin Omeri, the *Snow Leopard*, set the alarm on his Aqualand eco-drive chronometer and lay down on the bed. His ride would arrive soon. Phase One of the Phoenix Agenda was ready to commence.

Chapter 7

American Embassy, CIA station, Kabul, Afghanistan

Kurt Valdez couldn't shake the thought that the assault on the Taliban three weeks ago, one of the most successful against their leadership, was going to come back to haunt NATO allies. It gnawed at him.

He and his comrade, Hakim Jamahalien knew the enemy well. They had discussed how the Taliban would certainly retaliate for these devastating assaults. The NATO forces and SAP—especially—were taking the battle right into their tribal homelands. Remote-controlled drones were now killing large numbers of tribal warriors and their leaders. However, the "collateral damage" inflicted, included the accidental killing of innocent tribesmen—*and* women and children.

Each time Valdez read field reports was a stab in his heart. He knew how much his wives and mother-in-law's families had suffered from the never-ending wars. Siamarra had lost four brothers and a sister. She was his mother-in-law Raisa's only surviving child.

Baderi, his second wife, lost her entire family when a suicide bomber attacked their bus. Later, at the age of seventeen, she was widowed.

As a result, Valdez had a short fuse when it came to dealing with the Taliban and al Qaeda. The warriors possessed few modern weapons, but they had other more insidious ways to strike back. They used vicious guerrilla tactics in areas where NATO and coalition forces, and the Afghani and Pakistani Armies had only meager control. More and more, they employed young suicide bombers, *shuhada'a*, to attack targets that resulted in killing civilians.

NATO forces and the Afghanistani and Pakistani populations lost growing numbers to these attacks. However, IEDs were a more serious concern. Improvised explosive devices, especially those buried in roads, and remotely triggered, took an ever-larger number of American and NATO lives. They also inflicted horrible, debilitating wounds. Coordinated attacks by tribal warriors, usually during the night, with RPGs—rocket-propelled grenades—added to the number of wounded and killed.

The *Haqqani* Network, a Mafia-like, Joint Chiefs of Staff and intelligence bulwark for the high-mountain tribes, directed the high-level planning for the attacks. Western sources of information understood that the Pakistani intelligence network, ISI, contained high-level alliances with the Haqqani families. Leaders of the other most powerful tribes in Waziristan and surrounding "tribal areas" commanded absolute allegiance.

Kurt and Hakim also knew that the Taliban, and what remained of al Qaeda, thought of themselves as freedom fighters. They defended *their* tribal lands. It was *their* duty to protect their soil and religion against the infidels. If they lost territory in Waziristan, the two CIA contract agents knew they would take over other areas.

The governments of Pakistan and Afghanistan were shaky at best. From safe havens in Kashmir, the Taliban and affiliated tribes attacked Pakistan's northeast provinces. They now controlled a large area there. They had in fact reached positions only sixty miles from the Pakistani capital, Islam-abad.

Young suicide bombers operated in the principal cities and recently set off numerous bombs in crowded marketplaces. They had also carried out several high-profile assassinations.

In Afghanistan, they went after high-value targets—the brother of the president—other relatives of local and national leaders.

Developments such as these caused many sleepless nights for Kurt. Worse, his wives and mother-in-law kept him posted on current news. One common occurrence in Kabul, young men, religious zealots, drove by and threw acid in the faces of women and girls who did not wear *burkas* or did not have their faces and entire bodies covered.

The situation had become serious enough that Kurt had moved his family.

As he entered the lab in the back of the office, Hakim was processing photos of tribal leaders and updating the most-wanted list.

"*Ala shoma koobai, Shikar.* What's up today?" He grinned because he had used Hakim's field-op name, "goat," in Farsi.

Hakim smiled back. "Good morning, *Tiburon.* I'm rearranging the hit list."

Kurt nodded. His satellite phone rang and he glanced at the readout.

Berkley?

He moved back to the office and answered, "What's up, Top?"

After greetings, Berkley said, "Take a look at your email and the four photographs beginning with Alpha-Whiskey-Tango-six-five-niner. Check out the man who's talking to the customs agent. Our contact in Tehran took these. Compare the four with the six old photos you have of the *Snow Leopard*."

Valdez flinched when the chief mentioned the leader who had managed to deliver two nuclear bombs to Saudi Arabia. Kurt had prevented the second one from going off by killing Mustafa al Khalawi, a terrorist he and the Company had located.

"Right away, Top."

"And, Kurt...."

"Yes?"

"We acquired you a property in Tecate, Mexico. Get your family ready to move."

Valdez swallowed hard. Even though he expected the order's approval, it still surprised him. "... Tecate?"

"I guarantee you will like it, Kurt. A lot."

"I'll look at the photos, Top." He signed off.

Tecate? His father's ancestors had come through Tecate to settle in San Diego. After several minutes of reflection, his thoughts returned to the Snow Leopard.

It had been three years since he returned from his battle with the man who ordered the beheading of his former comrade. Mustafa and his commander, the famed Snow Leopard, Ramzi bin Omeri, acquired two nuclear weapons from a Russian general. Ramzi then masterminded the attacks on the Saudi kingdom and vanished. None of their thousands of contacts had spotted him since.

When he returned to the office, Hakim asked, "Why the frown, Kurt?"

"I'm being transferred to Mexico." He glanced at Hakim's open-mouthed response. "And, the chief's sending me some more photographs to analyze."

Turning on his computer, he allowed Hakim to digest the news; they had become very close. Then he entered his password and logged onto the government net. It took him a moment to find the path and the numbers. While he waited for them to download, he brought up the best pictures he had of Ramzi bin Omeri, and printed new enlargements.

Hakim took them off the printer and brought them over. "Who is it?"

"A famous commander of the *mujahedeen* under General Massoud's Northern Alliance. Gave the Russians their worst-ever defeat in the Panjshir Valley in '88 with some sidewinders we supplied. Changed the course of the war."

"That was way before my time," said the 27-year-old Afghani.

The photos loaded. Valdez spent a few minutes enhancing and zooming in on them before sending the pictures to the printer. Hakim collected and clipped them on a display board to view.

They scrutinized them together. The man in the new photos had a close shave and faint scars on his forehead, face, and neck. He had a new discoloration like a birthmark on his left cheek. In addition, his nose, cheeks and chin were smaller than Ramzi's.

"Why are they sending his pictures to you?" Hakim asked.

"We've been trying to locate him for three years. His *mujahedeen* killed Hassan. He planned and orchestrated the nuclear attack on Saudi Arabia. Then he up and disappeared, the same as Osama bin Laden and Ayman al Zawahiri."

"I'm sorry about Hassan." Hakim obviously noted the pain in Valdez' eyes when he mentioned his former partner. "I didn't realize you were connected to those responsible for the nuclear attack on the Saudi refineries."

He didn't tell the Afghani that he had prevented one of the bombs from going off only seconds before it was set to blow. Few of the military people in this country knew that Valdez was one of those silent and unidentified patriots. If they were killed in action, they received only a star on the entry wall of the Central Intelligence Agency in Langley, Virginia.

The NOCs lived under that curse. That was precisely why they were Non-Official Cover or Combatants. Americans working for the State Department had no knowledge of their assignments. If they were caught stealing foreign government secrets, the U.S. could not give them diplomatic immunity.

NOCs were the wraiths of the intelligence world. They flitted in and out of dangerous situations and places. Even CIA personnel attached to embassies didn't know of their existence. And the Company sometimes kept information from them for their own protection. If caught and tortured, they would not know enough to reveal secrets. The inability to disclose detailed information under torture might even save their lives.

Valdez snapped out of his thoughts. After further consideration, he and Hakim decided that the man in the new photos might possibly be the Snow Leopard.

What's this?" Kurt pointed to a partial exposure of something on the suspect's wrist.

"Some kind of big watch."

"Huh. I'm going to see if I can enlarge it." Valdez went back to his computer. He zeroed in on the wrist and enhanced the picture. By changing the colors and contrast, he concluded that the edge of the instrument contained what looked like a diamond bezel. He printed the enlargement.

Hakim walked back in again with the photo. "Very fancy watch. It has dials and buttons. And isn't that a ring of diamonds?"

Kurt examined the device closely with a magnifying glass. He could make out an "A" at the beginning of the instrument. "I've seen these somewhere before. I'll think on it."

Valdez sent a concluding email that the suspect *could* be the Snow Leopard.

Later that afternoon, he received another communication from the Deputy Director of Operations for Central Asia. Berkley passed on the information that they had tracked the suspect's flights back to Madrid, Caracas, and Mexico City.

Valdez noted the latter with new interest. Buzz in the intelligence community the past year was that al Qaeda was planning another series of spectacular attacks on U.S. soil, even greater than September 11, possibly with small nuclear weapons.

In low-profile raids, Valdez learned, the FBI and Homeland Security units uncovered and broke up several attempts to organize terrorist cells. They thereby disrupted the plans against American targets. So far, authorities had discovered only individual attack concepts such as those that occurred weekly in Afghanistan. However, lately, the missions seemed more desperate and suicidal in scope. Individuals trained in the crucible of Iraq, and from dozens of Arab and predominantely-Muslim countries, had been detained trying to enter the United States at the Mexican and Canadian borders. The real questions, of course, were how many had they missed? And how many cells were now operating within the U.S?

Another disturbing trend was that many of the detainees were not connected to each other. Al Qaeda had fragmented under different leaders. That had good aspects and bad aspects. Smaller decentralized units would find it more difficult to pull off coordinated attacks at multiple sites and cities at the same moment due to lack of financing and organizing. On the other hand, the terrorists were getting more knowledgeable about the latest explosives and remote control devices. Homeland Security was worried about IED-type attacks on chemical trains, fuel storage facilities, and especially the older nuclear plants where a large amount of waste was stored.

The questions and challenge of returning to the United States intrigued Valdez. The next round of battles with terrorists would be staged near home, or what used to be home. He pondered this for several minutes. It was incredible to think that all his training and experience in the Middle East would lead him back to San Diego. Intelligence agencies and Homeland Security would need his services as someone who was expert in Middle Eastern languages and the customs of the region, and indeed, could even infiltrate terrorist cadres.

He ran with that line of thought for several minutes. *Mexico.* His two wives and children had finally settled into a routine over the last year outside Kabul. His mother-in-law was only 200 kilometers from her beloved family property. Their hope was that Afghanistan would finally stabilize after decades of war and terrorist acts to the point where Raisa could bring her brood "home."

If he received a new assignment in Mexico, it would mean pulling up stakes and moving his wives and children there. There was sure to be a family battle. Raisa would be the one to object most strenuously. However, his mother-in-law would not go against the wishes of the man of the family.

On two recent visits to the States, his wives and children—there were now four with one more on the way—had been ecstatic, especially twelve-year-old Mohammad and eight-year-old Misha'il. Even though the last visit was a sad one for Kurt—his father's funeral—his family had hardly been able to contain their excitement in his home country.

He had given hours of thought as to how to keep his two families in the U.S. without breaking the law there. In Afghanistan, where the population was predominantly Muslim, Valdez had converted in order to marry his first wife, Siamarra. It was not uncommon in the country for men to have two or more wives. Even his grandmother from Lebanon, who had raised him, had relatives who came from plural-wife marriages.

Siamarra persuaded him to take his second wife. Baderi was Siamarra's widowed cousin. Raisa took her in when she was 17 and intended to marry her to *her* cousin, a man 48 years old, as his *third* wife. Both young women strenuously argued against the idea, and Siamarra talked Kurt into the second marriage. As it turned out, all of them were happy together, very happy.

Nevertheless, his family situation could be an issue in America. Over time, Kurt read materials about the Mormons and how the few remaining polygamist sects dealt with the problem.

One thing that had troubled him on their recent visits to the States was his wives' attractiveness. The women, to their surprise, discovered makeup and stylish clothes such as they had only seen in magazines. There had been several incidents where men gaped at them, especially Baderi.

The CIA had obtained a visa for her as a widow and dependent of Raisa. From Kurt's point of view, it was a dicey situation in his business to have American men coming on to Baderi. Well, he would deal with that problem when it arose. For now, it was time to tell the family they were moving to North America.

CHAPTER 8

Mojave County, Arizona

Sheriff Bob Stroman turned left off Highway 93 South onto Temple Bar Road, heading toward Lake Mead and the lower end of the Grand Canyon. Argentine pampas grass by the side of the highway was turning the color of wheat, and creosote bushes on the hills behind the grass had changed from a dull green to dark gray. It was mid-morning and the temperature readout in the vehicle already read 122 degrees.

"What'd you do over the weekend, Sir?" Travis Williams asked. The deputy spit tobacco juice into his ever-present Styrofoam cup.

"Got twelve big stripers below Davis Dam. One of 'em weighed seventeen pounds."

"The hell, you say."

"Below Davis's got to be one of the best fly fishing holes in this here part of the country."

"I suspected you were out on the river. You got sunburned."

The sheriff glanced at the fine orange hairs on his arm and his slightly reddened skin. He grinned. "Probably got another hundred freckles, too."

After a few minutes, Williams asked, "You take Carrie and the kids?"

"Yeah. They picnicked and swam at the little beach below me. I used waders to get out there where the fishing's good."

"You sure know how to enjoy life, Sir."

"Got to live it while you can. We filleted the big bass. Kids won't eat much fish. But they liked this 'un. Carrie's a good cook."

"You all camped near the river?"

"Naw, a ways back, in the trailer park. Too many mosquitoes near the river. Roasted marshmallows on a campfire until late. Diane and Derrick's old friends were there. They've been camping together since the kids were little."

"Good looking kids."

"Yeah. Diane's 14, and I'm beatin' the boys off with stick already. Derrick likes to fly-fish. They're both athletic. Diane likes softball and soccer. Derrick plays Pop Warner football every chance he gets—over in Boulder City."

Travis grunted and spit tobacco juice in the cup.

Stroman noticed that the deputy had shaved his head over the weekend. "Say, you been workin' out? Look kinda buffed up."

"Yeah. I can clean jerk 440 pounds, now." Williams smiled, obviously proud of his new look. "Got a part-time job as a bouncer at the Cairo Hotel." He glanced away and pointed. "There. Isn't that the ridge where you got that full-curl ram?"

Stroman grinned. "Yeah. That was a good hunt."

An eighteen-wheel, semi-truck approached with an electric sign chained down in the trailer.

The sheriff gestured to the truck. "A Morales brothers' sign. Reminds me, I should stop by and tell 'em we haven't heard anything about their welder."

———

Abdul bin Ibrahim and his brother Zaki set the last heavy concrete floor section back in place with the overhead crane. "Okay, set plywood and move signs inside."

They shifted the pile of plywood sheets to the middle of the floor with the crane then quickly distributed them according to their numbers.

Abdul heard the dog bark. Zaki flashed him a panicked look.

"*Muy rapido.* You put hook to wall," Abdul said. "I stall, then open big door."

He rolled open the big metal door just as Sheriff Stroman pulled the patrol vehicle to a stop on the gravel in front. A twenty-foot electric sign on a roll-around table sat on the concrete in front of the shop.

The Australian shepherd pup inside a chain-linked fence on the side of the building barked.

The sheriff and deputy got out of the vehicle slowly. Stroman called out, "Looks like you're busy, Ricardo. No word on the welder."

Morales seemed to ponder this for a moment. Then he shouted, "I bought new Miller." He gestured to the bright new machine.

While the brothers wheeled the sign and table inside, the two lawmen followed.

"I see Walker sold you a dog."

"Nice man, he give him to me. We buy alarm, too." Morales scanned the shop. His head jerked and his gaze stopped on the open laptop computer with a blue screen showing. An isometric of the submarine was displayed.

The sheriff saw the device and Ricardo's reaction. He took two steps forward, staring at it.

Morales moved in the line of sight. "Jorge, could you get other serial number on stole welder?"

Jorge frowned. "I thought we—"

Ricardo glowered at his brother. "Remember? Sheriff no get number last time."

Jorge cocked his head, still frowning at Ricardo. As the man turned, his face blanched when he spotted the computer screen.

Abdul caught Stroman looking right at his brother, and back at him. The sheriff narrowed his eyes.

He moved over to see the screen better, but Ricardo moved with him, continuing to block his view. Jorge ducked under the crane hook and opened a file cabinet. He rifled through some file folders and took out a document. When he came back, he passed by and lowered the computer screen.

"That how you build the signs? From drawings on the computer?" the sheriff asked.

Ricardo reached for the paper from Jorge. "Sign companies send drawings. We build." He handed the document to Stroman. "This right model and serial number for stolen welder."

Stroman stared hard into the eyes of the Brazilian. Then he diverted his gaze to the paper. He handed it over to Williams, who had his arms crossed while studying the overhead crane and ceiling. "Record these numbers, Deputy."

Williams took the folder and produced a pen. He wrote the information on his hand.

The sheriff turned back to Ricardo. "I'd like to see some of those drawings."

The small man went around the workbench and deftly turned the computer so Stroman couldn't see the screen. He flipped it open and hit a few keys to bring up two drawings. Turning the computer so the sheriff could see it, he showed first one, then the other. "We make sign from these drawings."

Stroman tilted his head back and looked down his nose. "I see."

Williams handed the file back. "Thanks, Jorge."

The police radio blared out, "Base to Mobile One. Base to Mobile One."

Williams turned. "The radio, Sir."

Stroman frowned.

The loudspeaker said, "Serious injury boat accident and fire near the Bonelli landing marina. Life Flight helicopter has been dispatched."

Stroman said, "I heard it. Accident at the lake." His voice sounded annoyed.

"Let's go, Deputy." They jogged to the vehicle.

The brothers watched the sheriff's vehicle drive off.

Zaki said, "Sheriff see boat on computer."

"Yes. It on screen. The most bad mistake we make."

"*Muy malo*, Abdul. Sheriff be bad trouble for us."

Sheriff Stroman drove fast. It was only twenty minutes to the docks of the marina. They arrived as the helicopter was lifting off to head back to Las Vegas.

Travis pointed beyond the docks. "Over there. Radio said there were two badly injured boat occupants."

Stroman stopped the Jimmy next to the docks.

He approached a man with a bandaged hand and asked him, "Who was driving the boat?" He handed Travis the notebook to fill out a report.

A man in his thirties with a Fu-Man-Chu mustache wearing a faded tank top and cut-off Levis said, "I was." He held up his hand.

"I hit a stump in the shallows over there." He gestured across to where the river fed the lake.

It took the sheriff several minutes to finish questioning witnesses. Travis folded the report closed. They tended to other first aid chores, then headed to the office.

There was a long period of silence on the drive back.

Finally Stroman spoke. "The Morales brothers didn't want me to see what was on their computer."

"I didn't notice."

"You were looking at the overhead crane, the sign work and the building. The look on both their faces was one of serious alarm—panic." The sheriff rubbed his jaw. "I thought the drawing was a cigar-shaped sign. But their reactions make me wonder."

Williams frowned. "You suppose they have something illegal going on?"

"I can't imagine it. They seem so straight. They are such hard workers and good businessmen. I figure they crank out four or five signs a month."

"Well I sure don't picture them working with the Mexican cartels. Or selling drugs. Or hiding illegal aliens."

"No. Nothing like that." The sheriff rolled down the window a small amount to flick out a fly. "Puzzling. I'll have to think on it."

"The next time we're out here, you can ask them to show you the drawings again." Williams sounded bored by the subject.

Stroman blew air through his nose. *Have to file this in the back of my mind.*

Chapter 9

Palo Verde Springs, Arizona

Abdul bin Ibrahim motioned with hand signals. His brother Zaki operated the crane and took the weight of the electric sign. He swung the load to the back of the semi trailer.

When the apparatus was in place, Abdul lashed it down.

Easing the weight off the crane hook to disconnect it, Zaki returned it to its driving position. Abdul smiled. The Palestinians had become experts at maneuvering the heavy signs into the trucks.

The brothers had worked rapidly since the email they received yesterday from Omar bin al Habib. The leader sent an abort message.

The message came after they notified him about the sheriff's visit and the near discovery of the computer drawings of the submarine.

They stopped work on the craft immediately, and hid all evidence, tools and equipment. Sealing the joints between the floor sections with Rockcrete, a hard, quick setting substance that in a half-hour would match the surrounding concrete, they replaced the plywood over the concrete slab.

Omar's message also directed them to fill a new order for three large signs.

The truck driver of the big rig had dropped off a load of fabrication materials and iron. Now he pulled out with the last finished sign that read *Roaring Twenties Casino* and would meet the sign installation company in Henderson, Nevada.

As the brothers watched the dust settle from the truck, Abdul motioned with his head to the right and said, "Come to back."

Zaki knew by his look what he was implying. Since Omar left, they always had a good supply of qat, the narcotic from East Africa. They had planted a row in the rear of the garden.

At the back of the shop, Abdul slid open the compartment of a large tool crib, moved aside an empty drill box, and pulled out the tin with the weed. He offered it to his brother.

Zaki stuffed it into his mouth and before long had a wad the size of a golf ball rolling around in his cheek. They grinned at each other as they waited for the euphoric feeling of mild intoxication.

Chapter 10

Mojave County, Arizona

Deputy Travis Williams heard a car stop outside the sheriff's office. "Sheriff's back," he said to Deputy Paul Davidson.

Sheriff Stroman entered and shut the door behind him. "Afternoon, Paul, Travis."

"Afternoon, Bob." Deputy Davidson replied.

"Afternoon, Sir," said Travis. "How'd the meeting go?"

"You know, Travis. You don't have to keep calling me 'Sir'. Especially when we're alone in the office or vehicle. Just call me, Bob, like Paul and Joe do. It's okay."

"Habits are hard to break after the marines, Sir—er-Bob." He grinned.

"Anyway," the sheriff said, "I was impressed at the meeting with the presentations. Did you men know that Homeland Security now has unmanned drones—UAVs, Predators and Global Hawks—scanning the borders? They even use satellite surveillance to try to track terrorists entering the U.S."

A call came in on the office speaker about an accident. Deputy Davidson said, "I'll get it." He grabbed his hat and gunbelt and left.

"Border Protection needs to do something. Too many illegal aliens coming across the border. Having babies in the hospitals." The deputy was keeping his head shaved and his body buff.

Stroman furrowed his eyebrows as he looked at Travis. His wife, Carrie, easily became annoyed with all the attacks on poor Latinos. Said it was a political smoke screen.

But then she always had a cause. She didn't want the family to buy from Wallmart because of their labor policies; they didn't stop at Exxon or Mobil gas stations because the former hadn't entirely paid for the Exxon Valdez oil spill; They would not buy a foreign vehicle because it indirectly caused job losses in the Midwest.

Stroman growled, "They're worried about al Qaeda, not Mexicans." He plopped down photos and printed information from the meeting and set his recorder on the desk. "They told us to pay close attention to any possible suspects that might be Middle Eastern. They suspect trained terrorists from Iraq, Afghanistan, Yemen and Pakistan are filtering across the border."

"Damn. Iraq, Afghanistan, Yemen and Pakistan?" Williams rifled through the close-up photos of captured or dead terrorists. "They could pass as Mexicans, couldn't they?"

Stroman glanced at Williams and scratched his all-day stubble. "Yeah, they could." He opened a drawer, put away some files from his desk, and placed the photos and information materials on his in-basket. Turning, he said, "Say, Travis, on the way back from Phoenix I got to thinking about what you said about the Morales brothers being different somehow."

"Like you said … uh, Bob, they sure looked suspicious the other day about those computer drawings."

"The computer had something on it that both of the brothers were nervous about. Jorge's face turned almost white."

"Definitely."

After a long pause, the sheriff said, "At the meeting, we were told to investigate all leads. Well, we found an oxygen and acetylene set in the garage at that dope bust we made Monday."

"Yeah, the welder set?" Williams ran his hand over his shaved head.

"Why don't you take the Jimmy down to Bonelli Landing tomorrow for that routine boat license check? Take your bathing suit. Spend all day. Paul and I will hold the fort."

"Yes, Sir!"

"Take the welder set, stop by and see Ricardo Morales, ask him if it's his. I need time to review my current reports and the recording from today's meeting. Gonna have Carrie log them into the computer," he said, referring to his wife working as occasional secretary.

Williams beamed—picturing a drive to the marina and the beautiful women in bikinis at the lake.

"I'll call Alex," Stroman said. "The reserve sheriff lives in Boulder City, if I remember correctly. Is he Mexican?"

"Alex is actually South American, from Chile. Lived in Brazil for a while."

Stroman pushed the bill of his cap up with a finger. "He speaks fluent Spanish."

"Former Gunnery Sergeant, Alessandro Peña. Spanish is his native tongue. He speaks Portuguese, too."

"Excellent. And they speak Portuguese in Brazil. Have him talk to the brothers, see how their accents sound."

Travis, still grinning, said, "Yes, Sir…er, Bob."

Chapter 11

Mojave County, Arizona

Travis Williams pulled the sheriff department's SUV into the parking lot on the Arizona side of Hoover Dam. Glancing around, he spotted reserve sheriff Alessandro Peña and waved.

Peña was a dark-skinned, medium-sized man, with a wiry build and a full head of graying hair. There were deep creases on the sides of his mouth.

Deputy Williams stepped out of the car when Peña approached and handed him his deputy badge. "Alex, my friend. How goes it?"

Peña flashed a big smile. "Semper Fi, Mac." They banged fists together.

After a few minutes of small talk, they got into the patrol vehicle. Williams barreled out of the parking lot onto Highway 93 and up the winding road from Lake Mead into Arizona. The new bridge was still under construction over the river.

"You're looking good, Travis. Been lifting weights, huh? What's with the haircut?" Alex had only a trace of an accent left.

"I'm a bouncer at the Cairo Hotel in the evenings. Meet lots of women that way. Shaved head turns 'em on." He grinned. "You're lookin' good, too, Alex. How's the little wife? The grandkids?"

"They're fine, *Amigo*. You got a cushy job after the marines, eh?"

"I don't know about cushy. You know it doesn't pay much in Mojave County. I think the sheriff is a little uncomfortable with me so far. And the other deputies act like I want to take their jobs."

"No kidding."

The white GMC crested the hill above the lake, and the new Pat Tillman Bridge came into view.

"Wow, Travis! That is a big sucker. Be open in a year."

"It's amazing what they can build. We're the modern-day Romans."

After a few more hills, the broad desert spread out before them. Williams floored the throttle and kicked it up to eighty. There was a loud inrush of air to the intake.

The Chilean raised his eyebrows. "Guts, huh?"

"Yeah. Has the five-point-seven-liter engine."

"So, what's the latest news?"

"Sheriff Stroman went to a Homeland Security meeting in Phoenix yesterday. The experts think there are hidden terrorist cells all over the country—in Vegas, Los Angeles, Miami, New York. They're expecting more trouble." Williams mulled this for a moment. "They should be onto these guys like a pair of GI shorts, Alex."

"We have to be polite and ask other governments to *please* let us have their terrorists."

Williams mocked the ex-marine's sarcasm. "Please, Sir, can we come in and arrest the terrorists living in your country?"

Peña shook his head. "The hell's the world coming to. Fucking bureaucrats."

"They hold us back. Can't do our job. Then they send us in at the worst time to be shot up. 'You boys go in there and protect our embassies. Make it safe for Americans.'"

"That's the way it is, Travis." After a long silence, the old gunnery sergeant asked, "So, what's this little job Stroman has in mind for me?"

"Going to let these two guys from Brazil look at the welding set I have in the back. Theirs was stolen. They have Mexican wives and kids, but I have suspicions about 'em."

"Aw, come on, Travis. You're not picking on some poor Latinos, are you?"

Williams glanced sideways at Peña and frowned. "I don't believe they're who they say they are. And the sheriff says the government wants to know everything they can about foreigners. No offense, Alex."

Peña rubbed his jaw. "You have reason to be suspicious?"

"Not really. Call it a hunch. But I have a gut feeling—like something doesn't sit right with me. Sheriff said they had some suspicious drawings on their computer, too."

"I guess we have a right to be paranoid."

"I just want you to talk to them in Spanish *and* Portuguese. Check to see if they're legit."

There was a long pause. Williams scanned the horizon and the yellowing pampas grass alongside the highway. Canyons down to the west allowed brief glimpses of the Colorado River. The brilliant blue water contrasted with the stark, rocky hillsides. He stuck a wad of Skoal in his mouth.

"You still killing yourself with that shit?"

Williams grinned. "You sound like the sheriff."

The deputy accelerated and passed two 18-wheelers. The noise from the diesels' wheels sang on the asphalt.

After they slowed, Alex gestured with his palm. "So you mean you want me to see if their accents sound authentic?"

Williams looked at him and nodded. "Yeah, that's all. I'll be satisfied if you can talk to 'em and they sort of—you know—pass the language test. You pick up on anything else, let me know."

"Sounds reasonable, *Amigo*."

"Then I can get 'em out of my head. Clear 'em, once and for all." The deputy spit juice in the cup.

"Yeah, okay."

After a few minutes, Williams pointed to a road sign. "Here's our turn."

The sign indicated Palo Verde Springs 26; Bonelli Landing 43.

"Twenty-six miles to Palo Verde Springs." The deputy turned left and headed northeast. He moved the wad of Skoal around in his mouth. "Sheriff checked them out. Saw their green cards. Kids are being bused to school with the neighbor kids. Everything looked okay."

The butte where the sheriff shot the ram loomed on the left. They dropped into a valley of creosote bushes, barrel cacti, and yuccas stretching out on both sides of the highway. The barren hills of alkali soil were strewn with black and reddish rocks from an ancient volcano. Digital temperature readout said it was 102.

"So, what's the problem?"

"Like I said, a gut feeling. I suspect they're not really Latinos. Something about 'em."

The two men were silent for the half-hour it took to reach the small town.

"There's Palo Verde Springs comin' up now." Williams spit his wad into the cup.

Stufloten's old store and gas station was on the left, unpainted cinder block buildings surrounded by saguaro cacti on the right. The shop that advertised petrified wood and Indian artifacts had one car parked in front.

They passed through the small town quickly. Approximately 300 yards beyond the last house in town, Williams pulled the patrol vehicle down onto a long driveway. He stopped next to the workshop with the SUV's wheels on a concrete slab. Trash containers and a new fence were to the right. The Australian shepherd pup went wild.

Williams got out and lifted the lids.

"Hey, *Amigo*, what are you doing?"

Williams grinned. "Good investigators always go through a suspect's trash."

The shepherd pup raced along the fence, barking.

The trash barrels contained pieces of metal, residue from sweepings, welding rod stubs, and small, empty plastic trays that had contained flux and hardware. There were also soiled blue shop towels with grease and black smudges.

Williams wrinkled his nose and tore the printed label off a sack, folded it and stuck it in his pocket. When he moved the sack, he saw a ball of what looked like soggy grass. He took a shop towel and grabbed the wad. Opening the door of the Jimmy, he dropped it on the back floor.

Peña grinned and shook his head. The dog repeatedly charged the fence. The two men headed around the garage toward the house.

Ricardo Morales must have heard the dog barking. He rounded the corner to meet them.

The slightly-built man with a full head of curly black hair greeted them with a limp handshake. After a minute, his brother came out to join them, eating the remnant of a taquito. They both looked sleepy.

"You know my brother Jorge from before," said Ricardo.

"This is Deputy Peña," Williams said.

There was a long awkward silence while Ricardo looked quizzically at the two men. The dog repeatedly leaped at the fence.

Then Williams said, "Oh, the sheriff recovered a stolen welding set and he wanted you to look at it. See if it's yours."

Morales considered this for a moment, and made a hand motion at the dog. The animal whined and cowered to the ground. Then the small man followed Williams to the SUV. Jorge trailed behind.

The deputy opened the back.

Morales shook his head. "Our set no fit in the back of car. It was big."

The deputy nodded. They walked toward the workshop.

At least a minute passed. Then Williams asked, "Did you say you were from Brazil, Mr. Morales? Mr. Peña here is from Chile."

Morales looked at Williams with his intense black eyes. Then his gaze shifted to Peña. After an awkward moment, he smiled and said, "I live in Brazil before eight years ago."

Williams walked over toward the dog. The deputy was amazed at the growth spurt in the animal in the three weeks since his last visit. He reached over the fence, and slowly offered the back of his hand. The dog lunged and snarled ferociously, eyes blazing.

"Wow! Williams jerked back and said, "You got a good guard dog here, Mr. Morales."

When the deputy turned to look, Peña had already walked toward the house with the two men. He could barely hear them conversing in a foreign language. The deputy went over and got into the vehicle. He scrutinized the three Latinos talking, watching their body and hand movements, their facial gestures.

After several minutes, Peña walked around and slid into the SUV. Jorge had disappeared around the side of the building, and the shop door rolled open. Williams saw piles of fabrication metal, angle iron and plastic. A large, half-finished electric sign perched on a twenty-foot worktable. The inside appeared orderly, tools hung on pegs, machine tools on the back counter, cables and wire rolled on hooks, new particle board on the floor, pipes in long bins.

Williams started the engine. Morales smiled, waved, and flipped on the shop lights. The deputy backed around to head out onto the highway.

The two ex-marines didn't say a word for ten miles or so. Williams could tell Alex was thinking about the morning's business. The deputy rubbed his jaw and scanned the barren landscape.

Finally, he could no longer stand the silence. "So Alex. What do you think?"

Peña put his hand on Travis' arm as he spoke. The gesture caused the deputy to frown at his old friend, as if he were saying, "Men don't touch men."

"That was it," Peña said. "Morales kept putting his hand on my arm as we spoke. I felt nervous as he did it. It was very unusual for a stranger meeting me for the first time to do that. Like he was overdoing it. Trying to convince me."

"Put…putting his hand on your arm?" Williams frowned.

"Yeah, and leaning in my face each time he spoke, as if for emphasis. Eyeball-to-eyeball."

"That *is* an unusual trait."

"Yeah. Their accents were very good, both of them. Spanish and Portuguese. Only a few words mispronounced, especially in Portuguese. Other than that, the hand-on-the-arm, and the in-the-face gestures. He did that several times. And his breath had a strange odor."

"Interesting, Alex."

"Ricardo's skin is more yellowish than usual. But I saw Indians in Brazil who looked like that. I can imagine an Indian mispronouncing words. They said they moved to an area where they learned Portuguese later. I have no problem with that. They spoke Spanish very well."

Williams raised an eyebrow. The Chilean surprised him with his acute observations. "Anything else?"

"His hair. The second brother …."

"Jorge."

"Yeah, Jorge. Many people there have real curly hair like the first brother. But his hair was frizzy." Peña paused. "Like they may have a different father or mother. The people in that region have a lot of African blood—from the slaves brought over in the seventeenth to nineteenth centuries. Maybe one of Jorge's parents was part African. He was darker."

"That's good, Alex. You'd make a good detective."

"They seem to have good work skills, don't they? I mean, I got one quick glance in the shop as we left."

"Oh, yeah, sheriff says they're real hustlers and excellent mechanics."

"So the only things I can think of are the *very* unusual hand-on-the-arm, and the in-the-face conversation."

Williams considered this in silence for a few minutes, then stuck another wad of Skoal in his mouth.

Peña looked at the tobacco with disgust, shaking his head.

Williams went silent staring out the side window at the arid desert.

Before he dropped Peña off at the dam late that afternoon, they stopped at Home Depot. He showed a sales clerk the label from his pocket and asked what Rockcrete was used for.

"Plumbers use it in bathrooms after pipe repairs. It dries so hard in a half hour, you can lay floor tile."

The deputy nodded and thanked the clerk. He tapped his chin in thought.

"Anything else, Sir?"

"No that'll be all."

Back at the office, Williams gave Sheriff Stroman a complete report on Peña's observations.

Stroman narrowed his eyes and considered the remarks. "We may have to visit the Morales brothers occasionally and keep up with what they are doing."

"Yes, Sir. I think that would be a good idea."

"You did well, Travis."

Chapter 12

Mojave County, Arizona

Sheriff Bob Stroman motioned Travis Williams into his office. "Have a seat, Deputy. Close the door, please." The sheriff pulled a file drawer out and placed a folder in it, then slid the drawer closed. He sat down and straightened the stack of papers in the incoming basket on the right corner of his desk. Then he turned his desk calendar clockwise.

When Stroman looked at Travis, he asked, "Still got that job as a bouncer at the Macao?"

"Cairo Hotel, Sir."

"Ah, yes." Stroman cleared his throat. "I'm not good at this. Never had to do it before."

Williams frowned. The muscular young man's head glistened under the fluorescent lights. He rubbed his right biceps with his left hand. "Do what before, Sir?"

The sheriff shook his head. He looked down at the desk calendar.

"Damn it. You know about the state's deficit problems, all the budget cuts. This is the hardest part of a manager's responsibility. And you've been doing a good job." He lifted his gaze to the deputy.

"Oh, no. Don't tell me." Williams sat up straight in the chair and lowered his arms. "You have to furlough me."

The sheriff threw his hands out in front of him. "It may be temporary, Travis. I appealed to the county supervisor, but she said we have no choice for now."

"Damn, Sir! I was just gettin' the hang of the job."

"I know. Times are hard. Budgets all over the country are in trouble. Hell, you can do better at the Cairo. I've got friends making $80,000 a year in the casinos."

Tight-lipped, Travis sat looking stunned for several minutes. Then he reached down to remove his badge and slid it across the desk to Stroman.

The two men stood and shook hands.

"I'm really sorry, Deputy."

Williams swallowed, loosened his gun belt and wrapped it around the holster. Handing it to Stroman, he asked, "Any chance I'll be coming back—I mean, after the budget problems get corrected?"

"I'll keep your uniforms and equipment handy, Travis. Anything changes, I'll call you immediately."

The young man shuffled toward the front office and bid goodbye to deputies Davidson and Zuniga.

The thin deputy and the huge Indian expressed their sympathies for him.

Travis turned and said to the sheriff, "Thank you, Sir—for the patience and training." He closed the office door behind him as he left.

Chapter 13

Palo Verde Springs, Arizona

Abdul bin Ibrahim ran a cutting torch along a mark traced from a plastic template on a steel sheet. He had his back turned to an ultraviolet screen protecting him from the arc welder. His brother, Zaki, welded the first of three beads on the conning tower of the small submarine.

Bright, blue-white light flickered from Zaki's arc. An exhaust fan circulated the smoke out of the basement work area into a metal vent that passed through the ground floor above, and then through the roof.

It took the two Palestinians a week to set up the workshop again after receiving the signal and email from Omar the Egyptian. The al Qaeda leader directed the two brothers to resume work on the boat.

This was the first night back to work. They'd sawed and chipped one section of the concrete floor above where they'd sealed it, to make the access stair available again.

They also received two more orders for electric signs. Omar's instructions were to construct the signs during the daytime, with the shop doors open. They would then labor on the submarine secretly during the night, rationing their time between the two projects. The Palestinians knew they needed to work diligently to complete the boat.

Chapter 14

Persian Gulf, Port of Bandar 'Abbas, Iran

Ramzi bin Omeri wiped the sweat off his forehead and glanced at his watch. Twelve minutes after midnight. The Saudi, Kareem Abu Bakr, would be here with the truck in half-an-hour.

He pulled on rubber gloves and carefully disconnected the cables from the charger. The meter now indicated that the large capacitor held 20,000 volts, enough to kill a man.

See how long this holds.

He removed the gloves and turned to the nuclear bomb. Encompassed in a cylinder of stainless steel, it stood the height of his belt and as wide as his hips. Taking a small battery, he opened a cover and snapped it into the timing mechanism. He operated a switch. Red lights flashed indicating zero hours, minutes and seconds.

Ramzi set it for fifteen seconds and pressed the start button. The numbers counted down: 15 seconds … 14 … 13 … until it reached zero, then clicked. Even though he expected it, he flinched.

Still works.

All that was required now was to connect the charged capacitor and the wiring harness from the plug and jack assembly to the timer. When he received the key to defeat the safety features from al Qaeda, the bomb would be operational.

Twenty minutes had passed and the charge on the capacitor still held. Ramzi reconnected it to the charger to bleed the charge off to zero. Then he grasped the capacitor with both hands, lifted it, and swung it into the case on the side of the explosive device. There, he fastened straps, a shorting bar and metal caps with thick insulators onto its posts.

He nodded in satisfaction and fastened the cover on the initiating mechanisms. Operating the electric winch to lift the ordnance, he eased it over into its lead container with Styrofoam hollowed out to accommodate the weapon. After he inspected the O-ring seal, he bolted the lead cover onto the cylinder. The bomb itself weighed only 44 kilograms—97 pounds. However, inside the lead container, the whole assembly weighed 350 pounds.

Ramzi connected the hoist to the lifting eyes of the container and ran it up and over to a waterproof fiberglass vessel. He was amazed how snug the fit was as he lowered the heavy assembly into the container not much larger than a washing machine. Sliding and fastening the outer cover on it, he checked the time again.

Kareem will be here soon.

Upstairs, Ramzi went outside. He heard the diesel coming from several kilometers away. When the truck was close, he operated the roll-up door, closing it quickly after the driver backed inside. He recognized Kareem Abu Bakr when the Saudi climbed out. Kareem was a dark, thin man with a neatly-trimmed beard and he wore a gray *shalwar kameez*.

"*Hamdella alas-salameh*—thank God you have arrived safely," Ramzi said.

Kareem gave him a surprised smile. "I again work with the legendary Snow Leopard. It has been a long while since we Arabs fought the Russians in Afghanistan, my commander. I hardly recognize you." He pulled Ramzi toward him and kissed his cheeks.

Ramzi grinned and touched his face. "Surgery. I had to change my look. But I think maybe we are getting too old for this, my friend." He reached and tugged on Kareem's gray hair.

"Bah, I'm strong as a donkey."

Ramzi motioned, "Come, we must hurry."

The men went below and hoisted the bomb container to a pallet jack, then rolled it underneath the access hole to the first floor. Ramzi closed and locked the storage room, then went upstairs to operate the large hoist.

Pushing buttons on a control operator, he moved the hook into place, lowered it to the container, and Kareem attached it. Ramzi maneuvered the bomb up to the truck bed with the Saudi riding it and guided it into place. Kareem snapped the hold-downs.

Finally, they replaced the floor sections, installed tamper-proof bolts and sealed them. They moved a lathe back into place so the machine shop could continue fabricating oilfield equipment parts.

Ramzi held out his hand. "Where's the package from Ayman al Zawahiri?"

Kareem nodded, fetched a locked box from the cab, and handed it over.

"Move outside, my friend. I'll lock up."

While Kareem moved the large truck out, Ramzi rotated numbers on the lock and opened the box. The hair on the back of his neck stood on end. He stared for several breaths at the meticulously-ground, doubled-edged key that would defeat the safety features on the bomb.

Taking it, he rotated the heel of his boot ninety degrees, forced the key under a rubber hold-down strap, and then turned the heel back into place.

He read the accompanying directions from the box. Al Zawahiri and their close circle of leaders had two other keys, with instructions should they be killed. The Chechnyan mafia had managed to acquire the uranium-plutonium bomb, with a yield of 200-kilotons. Ramzi coughed when he realized its explosive power.

We now have the power to destroy the American and Jewish infidels.

Outside, it was already muggy. The commander's shirt and trousers stuck to his skin in the moist, salt-laden air.

He locked up and hopped in the passenger side of the truck. Glancing at his watch, he said, "We must hurry, Kareem. The tanker will be ready to load us at 0300 hours."

The Saudi revved the diesel and ground the gears on the two-and-a-half-ton Mercedes. It lurched as the two former *mujahedeen* comrades took off.

Ramzi blew out a big breath and squeezed his hands into fists. "This is the most dangerous part of the plan, my friend. If the Americans find out what we're doing, we will meet Allah."

Kareem shifted the deuce-and-a-half into a higher gear and accelerated. "It is only thirty minutes to the docks."

"Go slow," Ramzi said. "We don't want to lose this cargo after all the trouble."

The Saudi downshifted when they came to the end of the road and made a left turn toward the docks. For several minutes, he drove the truck through old, cracked streets constructed of individual tiles, with occasional sunken depressions. Finally, the docks came into view in the faint light. When he turned again, they both saw the policemen at the same time.

"Gendarmes!" Ramzi said. "Pull up to them and stop."

"What are they doing out at this time of morning?" Kareem sounded alarmed. He pulled the deuce-and-a-half up to within five meters of the police vehicle.

Ramzi got out and walked over to the policeman leaning on the car. "*Ala-shoma-koubai*—How are you?"

"*Kheili koubai. Kheili-maam-nun*—Fine, thank you."

Ramzi offered the officer a cigarette and light. The second patrolman got out and accepted a cigarette also.

After conversing for several minutes, Ramzi discovered that their car had stalled. He offered to connect a cable and pull it until it started.

The men declined, saying a tow vehicle was on the way.

Ramzi smiled and turned. "*Khoda-ha-fez*—good bye."

Back in the truck, he said, "Their car has stalled. Take off and pass them. Shift the truck when you come alongside."

Ramzi waved as they passed.

Kareem exhaled slowly. "You scare me, my friend."

"Remember, in America, it is much more difficult."

The Saudi was silent for a few minutes, apparently deep in thought. Finally, he asked, "How big is the bomb?"

"You mean yield. I asked our scientist the same question. He said this one bomb would destroy all of Los Angeles."

Kareem blinked. "A nuclear reaction?"

"Nothing will remain within 120 kilometers in all directions from Ground Zero. There are four kilograms of plutonium in the center. Two cylinders of highly enriched uranium are arranged on both sides of the core. High-explosive C-4 charges are set off at the same moment to drive the uranium into the core. In a blink, it initiates an explosion like the energy that powers the sun. The Crusaders will never again control the Arab world."

The Saudi pursed his lips and exhaled.

They had traveled another kilometer, when Ramzi pointed. "There's our boat."

When he saw the dilapidated, military-style landing craft, Kareem jerked his head. "Can we trust that old junk?"

"No one will suspect it."

A mobile crane waited alongside with an operator and tender. Popping noises from the boat's exhaust created bubbles in the water. An Indian pilot, wearing a black turban that matched his beard, motioned them closer.

Kareem, obeying the boatman's hand signals, pulled the truck alongside the craft. The crane operator swung a hook and cables to the cargo. Ramzi had already pulled the tarp back to expose the load and released the hold downs. He fastened cables to the container. Then he signaled for the operator to take in the slack. The rig easily lifted the bomb, paused for the load to stabilize, then gently swung it onto the small vessel. The Indian flashed a concerned look at Ramzi when the boat settled in the water.

Ramzi glanced at his watch as the pilot revved the engines on the craft. *Good. 0210 hours.*

Kareem retrieved a telescope and flashlights from the truck, along with their personal gear. He passed the keys to the crane operator's tender, with instructions where to park the vehicle. Finally, he paid the two men for assisting.

The Arabs boarded the vessel and waved to the operator. The noisy exhaust from the deuce-and-a-half and mobile-crane made loud sounds in the heavy, damp air of Bandar 'Abbas as they headed away from the wharf.

The Indian motored slowly away from the docks. Ramzi and Kareem examined the boat for leaks as it negotiated the harbor. It took forty minutes for the old military vessel to reach deep water.

Searching through the thin fog with the telescope Ramzi spotted the liquid propane gas tanker with its five gas spheres above deck. He focused in on a signal flag.

"It's them." He blinked a series of signals. The LPG tanker answered back. In a few minutes, the Indian pilot pulled alongside and matched the big ship's speed. The crew had already lowered a hook and Ramzi and Kareem hurriedly rigged cables to the bomb container. The small boat rose in the water as the crane took the load.

A ship's ladder unrolled down the side of the ship, the Arabs paid the Indian and bid him good-bye, then they climbed up to the deck of the huge vessel. Ramzi signaled the crane operator to guide the load into a hold, while Kareem went below with a crew member to lock down the valuable cargo.

Within minutes, the LPG gas tanker came about fifteen degrees to port and headed for the Strait of Hormuz. The Arabs settled into their cabin for the long trip to the Western Hemisphere.

Chapter 15

Las Vegas, Nevada

Travis Williams had worked as many hours as he could bear over the past month as a bouncer at the Cairo Hotel in Las Vegas. It was his way of overcoming his disappointment after he was furloughed from the sheriff's department.

The hotel expected an entourage of the Saudi royal family. Management prepared the staff for the onslaught, beefing up security, ordering food the Arabs liked, bringing in prostitutes.

The Saudis were also arriving to set up their own protection. After a past incident, they now reserved one entire floor, bringing their own security with them. One year ago, a Thai servant had escaped from the group. She started a scandal with sordid stories of rape and maltreatment, which the local press covered at length.

One member of the royal family had already arrived with two bodyguards. He caused quite a stir when he lost more than 72,000 dollars at the crap tables. The employees continuously talked about it. In his expensive Italian suit and Gucci shoes, he had consumed one drink of Chivas Regal after another. The hostesses plied him with liquor and let him fondle them, while accepting 100 dollar chips.

Williams saw the Arab at a roulette wheel earlier surrounded by a huge crowd. The man ran his winnings up to $200,000, before he began losing.

Freddie, a thin, pale-faced waiter, called out, "Hey, Travis! Go check out the Arab. He lost sixty grand!"

Williams hadn't located the Saudi when he received a message on his earphone, "Number three to table 44, near the wall."

As Williams approached, he saw a big man in a western hat and boots mouthing off at the Arab and his personal bodyguards. "You rag-heads are throwin' your money around to make up for the 9-11 attacks." In a hard southern accent, the words were loud enough for the people in a dozen of the nearby tables to hear. Two of the man's companions, also in hats and boots, turned and came back.

The Arab guards came forward and stood with their arms crossed. Williams wondered what kind of weapons they had.

He approached from behind and grabbed the big man's collar. Then Williams jerked his arm behind his back. Barry, the other bouncer arrived to help.

One of the companions yelled, "Turn him loose!"

Barry pulled out a Taser gun, and the two backed off.

Williams glared at the others while pushing his man ahead of him. "Out! Go get sober! Come back and you'll be arrested." Travis turned him loose. "The revolving doors are to the left at the top of the escalator."

The big guy turned and looked as if he were going to hit Barry. In a crouch, the black bouncer pointed the stun gun at the man, the other hand motioning him to come on.

The cowboy's lady-friend tugged on his belt, and his friends said, "Come on, Cliff. You need to sleep this off, before you get the shit beat outta you."

Barry followed them out.

Returning to the Arab's table, Williams asked, "Everything okay for you, Sir?" His stomach churned at having to be polite to the man. He believed that high oil prices and the soft economy had resulted in the state budget cuts, contributing to his furlough from the sheriff's department.

The Arab sized him up. "You're a good bouncer." He glanced at Travis' hard build and shaved head. He motioned for his bodyguards to relax.

Williams said, "That's what I do, protect people in the hotel."

"I had a friend at UCLA who worked as a bouncer." The Arab spoke flawless English. "Wound up playing for the Forty-niners," There was only a hint that the liquor had affected him. "I'm Khalil." He rose and offered his hand with a smile. The man was handsome, with light skin coloring, short curly hair, and a Van Dyke beard.

The Arab's comments and sincerity caught Williams off-guard. He accepted the handshake. "I'm Travis. I used to be a sheriff's deputy, but they had cutbacks. People are angry and sensitive toward Muslims." Williams turned his palm up. "The Iraq and Afghanistan Wars."

Khalil motioned Williams to pull up a chair. "The war has been a tragedy for the area. Saudi Arabia has certainly suffered its share of attacks from al Qaeda. They are a serious problem for us. We are remorseful about the attacks on the U.S. soldiers in Iraq, and we understand that many Americans would like to simply shoot *all* Arabs and get it over with." He assumed a disarming manner of speaking.

"Do you know any of the bin Ladens? I hear there are a lot of 'em."

"I'm acquainted with one of Osama's younger brothers. Most of them are businessmen, lots of interests in Texas. I actually met Osama once, when I was young. He's history now." He placed his hand on Travis' arm and leaned close to his face, as if for emphasis.

Williams glanced at the Arab's hand and sat straight in the chair. After a moment, he said, "Why do terrorists set off bombs in crowded marketplaces?

And, why do they hate America so much?"

"We have many religious fanatics in Arab countries. They don't want modern influences. There are also tens of millions who live in poverty, especially in Palestine, Jordan, Egypt and Iraq. It's easy to whip up hatred against America."

When he said this, Khalil again put his hand on Travis' arm and came close to his face.

Williams knotted his jaw.

Suddenly, it dawned on him. *Morales!* Alessandro Peña mentioned the hand-on-the-arm and in-his-face mannerism when the former marine questioned the two brothers at their business.

Williams paid closer attention to the conversation.

However, when Khalil put his hand on him again, Williams flared his nostrils. He needed to change the subject.

Remembering the wad of something he retrieved from the Morales' trash, he said, "You gonna be here for awhile, Khalil?"

"Until I finish eating."

"I want to get your opinion on something. I'll be back in a few minutes."

The Arab looked at him quizzically as a waiter brought his meal in covered dishes.

Williams moved as fast as he could through the crowded casino, up the escalator, and out to the parking garage. Employees parked on the fourth level.

When he arrived at his car, he unlocked the trunk. There it was, a wad of what looked like dried grass almost the size of a golf ball.

On his way back, he thought of several questions to ask that always puzzled him. At Khalil's table, he pointed to the booth seat.

The Arab said "Of course, my friend. Sit down." The man's guards watched them from a nearby table.

"I'd like your opinion on something, Sir."

"Don't call me Sir, call me Khalil."

Williams smiled, "Do you know what this is?"

The Arab looked at the wad of material on the napkin. Then he broke it open and smelled it. He squinted and thought about it at length, apparently trying to recall where he might have come across it.

Finally his face spread into a broad grin. He said emphatically, "*Qat!*"

"Qat. What's that?"

"It's a narcotic—like marijuana, only better. The great national pastime in Yemen is sitting around for an hour each afternoon, chewing this stuff. It gives you a mild high, yet sharpens your senses. Sort of like marijuana and coffee at the same time. Where'd you get it?"

Williams leaned back and tapped one finger on his chin. He flashed a smile. "I got it from some Arabs."

Williams watched Khalil fork chicken and rice into his mouth. The man had impeccable manners. Frowning, Williams asked, "One thing that really puzzles Americans about the suicide bombers is they actually blow themselves up. That doesn't make sense to us. How do they get people to kill themselves?"

"*Shuhada'a*," said Khalil. "It's a political tool." The Arab raised his voice. "Would you have gone to Iraq in the war?"

"I finished my military stint a year before the last war started."

"If you had been commanded to go to Iraq, would you have done it?"

Williams raised both hands, palms up. "Of course."

Khalil pointed with a fork. "Why? For money?"

"Ha! Marines are poorly paid."

"What then? Patriotism? How does a war in Iraq relate to patriotism?"

The comment made Williams angry. "Valor. And honor. Because we *are* Americans. We're protecting democracy."

"*Shaheed* believe they are dying for justice. They feel they have nothing to lose. It is their *only* advantage against the industrialized West. " Khalil took a drink of Chivas Regal. He looked pensive. "They usually grow up in poverty. They are soldiers. It is their one viable weapon against trillions of dollars of advanced military hardware and intelligence systems."

Williams tapped his chin with a finger, and then asked, "Is it true that they believe they'll meet virgins after they die?"

"Seventy virgins," the Arab corrected. "That's what they've been taught."

"Do you know Arabs who would die for this?"

"I grew up with friends and relatives who joined al Qaeda because of what they see as the Palestinian injustice and injustices against Arabs in particular. The most aggravating issue is the U.S. backing Israel with billions of dollars in weapons and aid each year. That allows the country to dominate its Arab neighbors and occupy their historical lands."

"That's what it's all about? The Palestinians!"

"Not all of it. There are fanatics, similar to your religious fanatics in the U.S., who want to set civilization back a thousand years. The most radical want a return to the day of the *Caliphate* when Islam ruled from Spain and Morocco to India and Indonesia. They fantasize they can return to that condition. It's stupidity."

The comparison to religious fanatics in the U.S. caused Williams to flinch. He felt his face flush. "But seventy virgins! That's ridiculous. And Mohammad flying to Jerusalem in a dream."

"Is that any more nonsensical than Moses talking to a burning bush? Or receiving stone tablets on a mountaintop? Twice! Or, Joshua destroying the walls of Jericho with trumpet blasts?" The Arab spoke freely, his tongue apparently loosened from the liquor.

For a moment, Williams was at a loss for words.

Khalil said, "Arabs don't understand the American people's *blanket* hatred after September 11. Americans here appear to hate any and all Arabs, all Muslims. We heard stories about Pakistani women being attacked in America for dressing differently or merely *looking* Arabic!"

"It's true that we're generally angry at all Arabs. Wouldn't you be, if you lost someone in the Iraq War, or in New York or the Pentagon on September 11?"

Khalil gestured with his hands out, frowning at Williams. "But Americans didn't want to kill all Kansans after McVeigh and Nichols blew up the Federal Building in Oklahoma City, did they?"

The conversation had taken a turn that angered Travis. He thought his face was red. Pointing to his earphone, he said, "I'd better get back to my duty. I'm on call if there's more trouble."

He slid out of the booth, rose and said, "Thank you, Khalil. You've been very helpful. I'll leave you to finish your meal."

The Arab smiled and forked another piece of chicken into his mouth.

Williams headed toward the escalator.

Ragheads.

Williams went to see his boss and asked her permission to take the rest of the day off.

Chapter 16

Palo Verde Springs, Arizona

It was dusk when Travis Williams arrived at Palo Verde Springs, Arizona. Beyond the town he stopped where the road widened at the approach to the Morales brothers' driveway. He grabbed his binoculars and got out of the car, not allowing the door to latch. Walking around the vehicle, he threw his empty Skoal can and the wad of tobacco from his mouth into the bushes. Then he leaned on the hood and brought the binoculars up.

He scanned the front of the closed workshop building, panning to the yard where the Australian shepherd pup was fenced. The dog stood and watched him between limbs, his tongue lolling out, but didn't bark. The full front of the house to the left of the shop building was not visible. Williams saw what was probably a living room with a light behind the curtains. Only the roof showed on the house in the rear.

He lowered the binoculars. It was a well-kept property. The brothers and their families took good care of the place. For a moment, he wondered why he bothered. Hell, he was no longer a deputy. This seemed silly, driving all the way out here.

So what if they were Arabs? His marine buddy and reserve deputy, Alex, was a Chilean. He considered him to be one of his best friends. He'd also had a black buddy in the marines, Josh. And there was Barry, the other bouncer.

Williams had protected an Arab today.

He reflected on that. He'd protected the guy because his employer told him to treat them with respect. They brought in lots of money. Would he have done it in a different situation? In a bar? After the 9-11 attacks? He didn't know.

Khalil had charmed him. Even with the insinuations that had pissed him off. The Arab certainly was no asshole like that drunken loudmouth cowboy.

As he thought about this, he saw a flash, a flickering blue light like an arc welder produces. He brought the binoculars back up.

The light came from a galvanized vent. He focused more precisely. Someone definitely was arc welding.

Those boys really are hustlers.

He noticed smoke coming out of the vent, too, probably from work. He had brought some small pieces of beef along just in case he felt brave enough to approach the building. He thought he might try an experiment. Going back to the car, he started the engine for a quick getaway, and then unwrapped the meat, taking one piece. He again closed the door without letting it latch.

He walked noisily down the driveway gravel. When he got to within sixty paces of the dog, it barked. He kept going.

The dog raged at the fence. Williams dropped the meat over, turned and went back to the car. He looked through the binoculars again. The flickering hadn't stopped.

Interesting. They can't hear the dog.

Going through the same routine again, he gave the animal a second morsel. Back at the car, he noticed the welding had stopped. He waited for at least twenty minutes. Finally, the blue flickering started again.

He picked up the last two pieces of meat and returned to the dog. This time the animal wagged its tail and didn't take its eyes off the treat. Williams tried to give it to him from his hand, but the dog snarled. He dropped one piece over the fence and walked around back. That was where they jimmied the door when he and Sheriff Stroman came out to investigate the welder theft.

From there, he had an angular view of Jorge's house. There was a light in a curtained window also. He listened at the back door of the shop. Standing there for several minutes, he was surprised that no noise came through the door. That puzzled him. He heard grinding, but it seemed to come from the roof, maybe the vent.

Passing the shepherd, he gave the dog one half of the remaining meat.

Williams returned to the car, shut off the engine and took the keys. He slammed the door. The arc light still flickered. He grabbed the binoculars and a flashlight, went to the fence again, and gave the animal the last morsel.

Then he walked 200 yards to the back of the property, beyond creosote bushes. He scouted a half-circle for a quarter-mile, then returned to the original point. Through the binoculars, he could see the blue light flashing from this side of the building, too.

A slight breeze kicked up as he waited. A three-quarter moon came up and rose half way to the zenith. Coyotes yelped in the distance. The temperature dropped.

He'd almost dozed when he heard the back door open. Glancing at his watch, he saw that five hours had passed since he arrived. He shivered and watched through the binoculars. It surprised him how clear and loud noises sounded in the dark. The men stepped out from the shop door and headed toward the houses.

He could hear them talking. Sounded like Spanish.

Workin' all night. Must be a rush job.

The voices stopped. One man walked back to a cactus patch and urinated. Then he disappeared around the edge of the building.

Williams waited for a long while, and then walked past the dog again. The animal, curled into a ball near its house, raised its head, looked at Williams and wagged its tail two strokes. It didn't bark.

The former deputy returned to the car and drove toward home.

On the way back to Las Vegas, he chided himself for being so suspicious. So what if they were Arabs? They're just making a living.

But he couldn't shake them from his thoughts. One thing didn't fit. The noises. He could hear grinding at the back door. But the noise seemed to come from the roof. Unless that back door had *very good* soundproofing, that was puzzling.

In addition, he remembered Sheriff Stroman's seeing the computer drawings.

Over the next couple of days, the incident at Palo Verde Springs crossed Williams' mind only a couple of times. However, when he saw the director of Homeland Security announce on the evening news that they had evidence there were terrorist cells operating in the United States, it started him thinking. He vowed he would follow up and pay another visit to the Morales brothers.

Chapter 17

Tecate, Mexico

Kurt Valdez sipped a coffee and surveyed the property from the veranda of the Spanish style hacienda.
Nice spread.
He hadn't imagined that any place like this existed near Tecate, Mexico. The dry, dusty border town, 70 miles southeast of San Diego, sported several main streets with small shops and stores, a Corona Beer factory, and outlets for farmers markets. Street vendors pushed carts hawking tacos and tamales. A large farm community supported by a few water wells and arable drainage creeks surrounded the town. The U.S. border crossing was 200-yards north of the main street.
To the south and east lay the cordillera of a mountain range that topped out at 4,500 feet—high enough for violent summer thunderstorms and snow in the winter. A north-south highway ran for 70 miles adjacent to the cordillera through farms and villages to Ensenada, a major seaport on the Pacific Ocean.
Kurt's hacienda was at the edge of a pine forest with two wet-weather creeks that supported oaks. The rectangular building, with rough, tan plaster and heavy wood columns and doors in the Spanish-Mexican style, lay 200 yards off the highway. A rock security wall surrounded it, with a wrought-iron, electric-powered gate. Rumors were that a *consigliore* of the U.S. Mafia used to own the place.
A small pool and Jacuzzi, along with picnic tables, a masonry barbecue and a kiln, occupied the area below a terrace in front of the building. Lower rock walls surrounded a large garden and orchard. Avocado trees, forty acres of them, grew downhill to the southwest. Uphill sat a large capacity galvanized water tank.
The Castenadas, caretakers, lived on the property in a smaller hacienda. They had three girls and two boys, and two grandparents lived with them. They harvested and sold avocados and crops in town.
The CIA moved Valdez here to follow a lead on Ramzi bin Omeri, the legendary Snow Leopard. The Company managed to trace the man's travels backward from Iran, from Madrid, Caracas, and Mexico City. Then, using an alias,

César Hernandez, Ramzi had traveled from Mexico City, to this small town in the mountains, where he apparently crossed into the United States. Kurt knew the area well. His father's family had lived here for three generations.

He heard a noise and turned. Siamarra, Baderi and the children came out from the pine trees.

Twelve-year-old Mohammad looked like Kurt's side of the family, olive complexion, curly black hair, and eyes dark as the night—the result of a Mexican-Lebanese ancestry. Misha'il, eight, had Siamarra's looks—thought to be derived from a British ancestor in Afghanistan during the 1880s—fair with gray eyes, and a slight build. He might grow taller than his older brother. Five-year-old Zoya also had Kurt's dark complexion. Baderi's daughter, Tahani, a three-year-old just walking well, scrambled to keep up with the older children. Already, she had her mother's wavy black hair, petite figure and olive complexion. Baderi was now pregnant again.

"It is beautiful, Papa," Mohammad said.

"We saw a deer!" Misha'il added.

Zoya piped up, "It had a baby with spots!"

Kurt laughed. "A fawn!" He could tell that the women and children were excited about the thought of staying here in this lovely, peaceful place for the next year. No more war, no more bombs going off.

Kurt even liked the idea of the Catholic school. The children would be exposed to a different culture and system and would learn a new language. The problem of two wives he would deal with later.

The women, cousins, left their *burkas* in Afghanistan and Kurt took them on a shopping spree. He'd frowned at several of the short skirts they picked out. In the end, he rejected them. The women giggled and said they were teasing him.

His mother-in-law, Raisa, Siamarra's mother, accompanied the last of her family reluctantly. Nevertheless, when she saw the estate, she had tears in her eyes. It reminded her of her family's property in Afghanistan—the rocky peaks, two small streams, the pine forests, garden and orchards, and all the animals.

Inside, Mohammad turned on the television. He fiddled with controls and searched the program offers of over 100 selections from the satellite system. Misha'il argued with him to stop on *Sesame Street* when it came up. Kurt smiled at Siamarra, laughing at the program he had loved as a child. The boys and Zoya discovered *Sesame Street* last year when they came to San Diego for his father's funeral.

Raisa gestured to the outdoor table and told the boys to turn off the television. She had ground some wheat berries, and cooked Afghan-style bread, *naan*, in the kiln. It was similar to those she'd used when she was a girl, she said. The children raved about the *naan*, on which they spread peanut butter mixed with honey.

Excitedly, they all ran outside to the table.

As Kurt bit into the delicious bread, he surveyed his family. He knew that they would never go back to Afghanistan, after settling in the West. That would be it. It wasn't the first time he thought like this. He had actually started planning to stay in the southland for some time.

Two hours later, the email from Berkley arrived. The CIA already had instructions for Kurt.

Chapter 18

Las Vegas, Nevada

The Saudi Royal family's visit lasted three weeks and kept most employees working overtime at the Cairo Hotel. The Arabs spent and gambled over ten million dollars. The hotel management was naturally thrilled with the visit, and fawning to the royal family's entourage.

Travis Williams' mixed feelings toward the Saudis caused him to swallow his seething anger. Since he was a marine at the time, he had never forgotten there were fifteen Saudis among the September 11 hijackers. Word amongst the hotel and casino staff was that many of the young princes, and their women and children, flaunted their wealth and treated hotel employees like lowly servants.

They kept the peace by lavishing everyone with big tips.

In charge of security, Williams and Barry, the former marine who worked with him, were called on several times to interrupt offensive threats and incidents. Looking back, it was good he'd met Khalil first. Otherwise, he wouldn't have had the stomach for the other members of Saudi royalty. The suave Arab warned him, "You're not going to like my cousins."

Monday morning, on his first day off in a while, the phone rang.

Sheriff Bob Stroman's voice came on the line. "Would you like to come back to work, Travis?"

Williams snapped to attention and gushed, "Yes, Sir."

"Well, Mojave County just obtained additional federal funds from Homeland Security. I'll see you at eight a.m. on March 15."

Williams smiled to himself when he hung up. *I can take four weeks off.*

It just dawned on him. He'd been too busy to follow up on his vow to pay another visit to the Morales brothers' property.

Chapter 19

Mojave County, Arizona

Heavy thunderstorm clouds and rain squalls left wet patches of road as Travis Williams traveled south from Hoover Dam. After he turned toward Lake Mead, he had to slow at dips partially filled with runoff.

Williams had enjoyed several days off after he quit his job as a bouncer. It would be three weeks before he started work at the sheriff's department. He had talked about a vacation to Mexico.

But early this morning, he donned his dress khaki marine uniform and pinned on a fake deputy badge. Noting how his bulging biceps filled the shirt sleeves, he smiled in the mirror, then removed the round marine hat.

He'd bought a black-and-white car from a friend awhile back who purchased it at a California Highway Patrol auction after the door symbols were sandblasted and painted. With a magnetic flashing light and Siren assembly for the top of the vehicle, he figured the Morales brothers would be fooled by appearances.

Now he would follow up on the clues he heard from the friendly Saudi, Khalil. The man who identified the qat Williams retrieved from the Morales brothers' trash as a narcotic many Arabs enjoyed. That suggested Arabic connections.

After the night of his six-hour visit to the sign fabrication facility, where he saw evidence of the brothers working late into the night, and the subsequent feeling that he was wasting his time playing detective, the call from the sheriff had re-stimulated his excitement.

This was a high stakes game. If his suspicions were true, that the Morales brothers were hiding the fact that they were Arabs, he would make solid points with Sheriff Stroman. Hell, he'd be on the fast track. They might be connected to a terrorist cell. That's what Homeland Security warned about in the meetings the sheriff attended. It was a stretch in this case maybe, but possible. If he were wrong, no one would have to know.

He lost that train of thought as he passed beyond Palo Verde Springs and came to the turnoff to the sign shop. Sliding the magnetically attached light onto the top of the vehicle, he turned down the muddy gravel driveway.

Ricardo Morales was grinding on a large sign in the front part of the workshop. The man wore a facemask and welder's cap. Dark red sparks flew from the metal.

The Australian shepherd dog barked as the car approached. Morales stopped work, removed the facemask, and looked at Williams as the black-and-white car crunched to a stop.

Williams glanced at his badge in the mirror and straightened his hat. Opening the car door, he grabbed a package of materials.

"Good morning, Mr. Morales."

The small man smiled weakly at Williams, looking at his marine clothes and the badge. He scrutinized the black-and-white vehicle. Then he frowned at the dog.

Williams saw the animal stop barking and put his paws up on the fence. It whined and wagged its tail, straining toward the deputy.

Morales gaped at the dog for a long moment. Slowly, he turned his gaze toward Williams. "Why you come to our business today, Sir?"

"Got some brochures Sheriff Stroman wants you to look at. Welders. I want you to show me your model." Williams opened the booklet he carried.

Morales' black eyes stared at him for a long moment, then he glanced at the pamphlets. He grabbed them, selected the Miller welders, and opened it to a Model 500, 225 amps. "That it." His tone was emphatic.

The ex-marine glared at the small, dark-skinned man for several seconds. Then he scanned the shop. "Got a couple of sign jobs goin', huh?" He took a step toward the building.

Morales turned with Travis, taking another hard look at the dog. The animal merely rested his paws on the fence, tongue lolling out, still looking at the deputy.

"Have you tested your burglar alarm system lately?" Williams asked. He made a once-over of the shop, then stopped to look at the vent that passed through the roof. It had two screened openings that allowed smoke from the shop to exhaust through the roof. An electrical cable was attached to an internal fan near the rafters. Williams walked a few steps and saw that wallboard covered the shaft down to floor level.

"Alarm company test it when they install. They give us number for six months."

Travis' gaze stopped on welding cables dropping through what looked like a threaded hole. He traced the cables back to their source: the welder. He pointed to the large sign resting on the 20-foot-long table. It hung over both ends and was at least two feet thick. "How long does it take you to build a sign like that?"

Morales widened his eyes. "That one?" He frowned as he watched Williams scrutinize the shop.

"Uh-huh." Williams nodded.

"Eighteen days."

Williams ran his hand over the sign that still smelled of fresh paint. He shot another glance at the cables passing through the hole, then at the plywood floor. "Good craftsmanship."

"What?" Morales asked.

"The sign. You guys do good work."

Morales glanced down. "You gun. You not have it. When you and Sheriff Stroman here before, you two have guns."

Williams sneered. "It's in the car. I don't have to wear it all the time. Where's your brother?"

Morales worked his mouth as if he were chewing seeds. After a few moments he said, "Jorge return crane."

Williams crossed his arms and circled the shop. He looked at the ceiling lights and the I-beam track that the overhead crane ran on. A hefty hook hung at eye-level on cables from the rig. He glanced at the work benches and tool bins against the back wall. "I don't want to take any more of your time, Morales. It looks like you're busy."

The small man reached for his face shield. "Is that all you want? For me pick out welder type?"

Williams put his hands on hips. "Yeah. You boys sure are hustlers. Crankin' out these signs the way you do." He pointed to a laptop computer folded closed on the back workbench. "That where you get your designs from?"

"Designs?"

"Yeah. Plans. Do they send you plans that you put on the computer?"

Morales glared at the deputy for several breaths. He walked around to the backbench and flipped open the computer. After it booted, he opened two drawings of the sign he was working on and flipped back and forth between them.

Williams studied the two drawings intensely, his mind considering several ideas. "So you create these huge signs from just these plans? Amazing."

Morales opened several detailed drawings, exploded views of complex corners and the structural joints near the base where the sign attached to the support column.

The former marine nodded his head. "Very interesting." He inhaled and tried to sort out the smells in the shop. There was a smell of burnt metal probably from the grinding. A faint smell of paint. And an odor that probably came from the small man's clothes or body. It had a sour tinge.

Morales closed the computer. He adjusted his welding cap and started to put on the shield. "I must work. We have rush job."

"Oh, by the way, have you got any more qat?" The deputy grinned as he asked the question.

Morales was clearly stunned. He opened his mouth to speak then looked down at the deputy's feet. "Qat? What that?"

"You know. That narcotic you boys chew. To get high."

"I not know what you talking about. I ... I ...."

Williams smiled wide. "Look. I don't care what you do. I don't think there's a law against chewing qat, Mr. Morales. Or, is it Morales?" He raised his eyebrows and tilted his head.

"Is it?"

"Or is it Mohammad? Or Ali?"

The small, dark man narrowed his eyes at Travis.

Williams laughed and said, "Relax. I have an Arab friend, Khalil. I don't care if you're an Arab."

Morales' nostrils flared wide. With his right hand, he held on to the crane hook as if for support. Finally, a wide smile spread on his face, too. He nodded and laughed two notes. "You right, Sir. Very smart. I am Palestinian. My father bring me to Brazil when I was boy. We take my stepmother name, Morales, when my father marry."

"No offense, Morales. Look, I told you I had an Arab friend. He knew what the qat was. And there's no law against it. What does it do for you?"

"We used to no sleep at night when we have rush jobs."

"It works that well, huh?"

Morales nodded. With his left, he raised his face shield toward his head again. "Now, I need get to work."

Williams smiled a disarming smile and cocked a finger at the small man. He squatted to look at the pipe sleeve where the welding cables passed through to the basement below. He followed the cables back to the welder. As he rose, he asked, "Is there a basement…?"

A sharp pain surged through his head. His ears rang. Opening his mouth to yell, he could make no sound. He plunged forward and saw his polished brass belt buckle fly before his eyes. His vision narrowed to a bright tunnel that grew narrower. Then it went black.

Chapter 20

Palo Verde Springs, Arizona

Abdul bin Ibrahim—Ricardo Morales—dropped his face shield and let the crane hook swing back. He shot a look at the road. No cars passed by on this stormy weekday morning. The children would not be home from school for at least two hours. He stared down at the deputy. A small pool of dark-red blood spread on the plywood.

He inhaled a large breath. Quickly moving to the wall, he pressed the button that rolled down the door. It seemed to take minutes for the big metal sections to close.

He placed two fingers on the deputy's throat. The man had a faint pulse. Bin Ibrahim cut a piece of rope and passed it around the deputy's neck. Winding one end of the rope around his foot, he grabbed the other end, stood up, and took in the slack. The Palestinian paused and knotted his jaw muscles. It had been eighteen years since he had seen a dead man. He was a child when he lived on the West Bank.

He started when he heard a car skid to a stop on the gravel in front of the shop. Shortly, his brother Zaki banged on the metal door.

"Go around to the back door!" Abdul shouted.

After a bit, he heard the back door open and Zaki said, "*Que pása, hombre? Porque esta aqui la policía?*"

"*Tenemos problemos.*"

Zaki glanced open-mouthed at the big deputy on the floor. "*Muerte?*"

"No." Abdul wrapped the end of the rope around his foot again and took up the slack. He grimaced as he pulled. Travis' body trembled and lurched as his air was shut off.

After awhile, the uniformed man on the floor ceased to move. Abdul gave the rope two extra pulls, then dropped it. "*Ahora, está*"—He is now.

Zaki stood gaping at his brother. He backed away from the body. "We die, my brother. There is police car at front."

Abdul snapped, "put the Toyota to the front of my house. And move the car around back. Hurry!"

Zaki ran out the back door.

Abdul slipped on mechanic's gloves and rolled off a piece of visqueen plastic, cut it, and spread it out on the floor next to the body. He heard the Toyota's motor, then the deputy's car started and moved to the back. Zaki opened the door and Abdul pointed. "Put that tarp over the car."

When Zaki returned, Abdul said, "Let's get him on this plastic and scatter lime on him."

They wrapped the body and bundled it tight with nylon ropes. Afterward, Abdul wiped blood and skin off the crane hook. "The children will be home in two hours. Let's replace this piece of plywood with the bloody spot. We'll burn it tonight."

Zaki said. "Are you thinking what I am thinking about the car?"

"Putting it below with the boat?"

Abdul nodded. "The children must not see anything."

The two brothers dragged Travis' body to the back of the shop.

After rolling the sign and workbench to the side, Zaki jockeyed the black-and-white car inside while Abdul watched for cars until the door rolled closed.

When he returned through the back door, Zaki had a twisted, angry look on his face. "Why did you have to kill him? That can bring attention to our *jihad*."

Abdul glared at him. "When the deputy arrived, Pancho didn't bark after he got out of his car. The dog wagged his tail. That deputy has been snooping around here."

Zaki flashed a horrified look.

"Then he got pushy," Abdul said. "He stepped by me and went further inside the shop. He saw the vent through the roof, and I am sure he realized it was for the basement. Then he walked around to where he could see the back wall."

"The cables!"

"That's right, my brother. He saw the welding cables passing through the pipe. He pretended not to notice it. But I saw his eyes follow them back to the welder. His eyes turned to slits when he returned to where they pass through the floor."

Zaki pressed his hands together in front of his mouth. He closed his eyes and shook his head slowly.

"He also knew about the qat!"

Abdul nodded at his brother's shocked look. "Come, my brother. I have seen hundreds of our people killed by the Zionists. His life is a small price for the glory of Allah. We must be calm when the children arrive. Let's wash and make sure we are clean."

"You are right, Abdul. We can dispose of this infidel late tonight when the women and children are asleep."

"We must plan carefully. We do not know if someone else knew he was coming here. The American police are smart."

Zaki nodded in agreement. "They look for everything."

That night after the women and children had gone to bed, the Palestinians entered the back door of the shop. With small lights, they moved the black-and-white car behind the shop and covered it. It was a dark night.

They dragged Travis' body to a back corner. Then they rolled the workbench with the nearly completed sign outside and closed the door.

Removing the flooring, they sawed joints on four concrete floor sections, and with the crane, moved them aside. Only three cars passed by on the road, and the dog had not barked.

They stared down at the nearly completed submarine, already primed black. All that remained to make it usable were wiring harnesses, the internal welding of the piping, and installation of water seals and other rubber components.

Zaki brought the car around through the open door and jockeyed it alongside the hole. As soon as possible, Abdul rolled down the steel door.

He removed the magnetic flashing light assembly from the top of the car and rigged two nylon straps around the vehicle. While Zaki took up the slack, he went below and rolled the submarine on its carriage toward the stairs. Back on the main floor, with the crane, they lifted and maneuvered the car into position. Abdul tugged on one of two tag lines, jockeying it into the hole.

The crane strained to its limit with the weight. The brothers grimaced as they held the tag lines and guided the black-and-white vehicle down front first into position in the pit with only three feet clearance. Abdul went below to remove the straps, and they eased Travis' body down between the car and submarine.

They re-installed the concrete floor sections and laid the plywood back in place. Finally, they opened the steel door and rolled the long workbench and sign inside.

Abdul said, "You burn the piece of plywood and the rag with the blood stains out near the back fence, and I will clean the four spots with paint thinner where I tracked blood."

Zaki nodded.

The next morning, Abdul slept late.

"*Que pasa?*" asked Maria. "*Estás enferma?*"

"No, Maria. I am not sick. We worked very late last night. *Yo quiero huevos rancheros éste mañana.*"

"*Sí.*" She served him his favorite, scrambled eggs with hot salsa and chicken strips. The recipe called for pork, but Maria could never get Abdul to eat that particular meat.

In the shop, the brothers discussed a plan. Zaki left in their four-wheel drive truck. Abdul locked the doors to the shop and lifted the small access door to the lower floor. He went below, covered the submarine and body, and spent the next four hours sandblasting the car. Then he primed it.

Zaki returned later with two newspapers. They looked through them, understanding only rudimentary English, but found no stories regarding a missing man, only two girls. Certainly, no police officer was missing.

They ate lunch and slept, telling their families they had to work late again.

Well after dark, they pulled Travis' body, already beginning to smell, from the lower floor, up through the access door. Loading it inside the camper shell in the back of the truck, they piled some scrap plywood on him.

Abdul saw the stress lines on Zaki's face. "Do not worry, my brother. Get the tools and nylon straps."

Fifteen minutes later, Zaki drove slowly through the still damp streets of Palo Verde Springs approaching the only gas station at the west end of town.

Abdul pointed. "There's Sheriff Stroman." A paramedic van parked alongside the sheriff's SUV with its light flashing. "Do we need gas?"

"No," Zaki said, alarmed. "I filled up today."

Stroman glanced at the brothers. Abdul's stomach knotted. He smiled and waved at the sheriff. "Pull over there."

"Are you stupid?"

"Come on, act relaxed."

Zaki pulled over and stopped. Abdul rolled down his window. "Any problems, sheriff?"

"We've got it under control," the lawman said. "Stufloten's wife had another heart attack. Paramedics are taking care of her."

"Anything we can do?"

"I gave her some aspirin half-hour ago. That held her 'till they arrived. Thanks for stopping."

Abdul waved. He had taken a good look at the sheriff's gun, clothes and car.

Zaki took off and jerked the wheel hard to the left. "What were you doing?"

"He looked right at us. What could I do? Watch how you drive! Don't get their attention."

"Don't get their attention! You can smell the body!" Zaki watched the rearview mirror. After several minutes, he said, "He's not coming after us."

There was a long silence. Zaki drove slowly watching for water runoff in the dips until they came up to US highway 93. He turned right toward Hoover Dam. Several travel trailers and eighteen-wheelers came into view in front of them.

"I pray to Allah there are no accidents tonight." Zaki said.

Abdul grunted acknowledgment. After awhile he said, "You know that deputy was not authorized to come to our business."

Zaki looked at him. Another long silence.

"He didn't have a gun. There was no radio in the car. Look at this." Abdul showed Zaki Travis' hat.

Zaki glanced at Abdul and scowled. "Are you saying that hat is a fake?"

"Yes. I don't know what's going on, but his uniform didn't match Sheriff Stroman's. The sheriff had on a dark shirt."

"But he came out with the sheriff, and with that man from South America the second time."

"We do not know how their police system works. But that deputy was not working for the sheriff yesterday."

Another long silence. Abdul pointed, "Milepost ten. We are looking for milepost eight."

"Yes, two miles." Zaki accelerated the truck to increase the distance between them and the eighteen-wheeler behind them. A mile further, he turned in a dip, bounced onto the dirt road, and after 200 yards, stopped. He turned off the lights and took his foot off the brake.

Shortly thereafter, the big-rig passed on the highway.

"It's really dark out here." Zaki's voice quivered.

"At least it's no longer wet."

Four hours later, Abdul smiled to himself as they headed home. After digging a deep hole about three miles off the dirt road, they stripped all clothes and a ring from the body before taking it out of the plastic. Abdul broke and pulled the deputy's teeth out and cut his fingers off before they buried the corpse. Dropping the teeth, fingers, a ring and pliers into a plastic bag, he sealed it. With their truck winch and nylon straps, they dragged a boulder over the grave. They then made several circles towing the straps to stir up the sand and erase the boulder tracks. It would appear as if a group had camped at the spot.

The brothers were silent all the way to the turnoff from Highway 93 and through several of the dips. Finally, Abdul said, "Now we finish painting the car blue. You drive it to San Luis, wipe off fingerprints, and park it in the barrios. You leave it unlocked with the keys inside. Three weeks later, it will be in Mexico City. It's that easy."

"The teeth?" Zaki made a face looking at the plastic bag.

"I will wash them in Muriatic acid and scatter them in the desert. We must burn the plastic and lime. These infidels underestimate us, do they not, my brother? We speak four languages, and read them fairly well, too. We can fabricate electric signs and build an undersea boat."

Zaki smiled weakly when he saw the entrance to their driveway.

Chapter 21

Palo Verde Springs, Arizona

Several days passed. Zaki drove the now-blue hemi to Mexico, left it with keys in the ignition, and returned by bus. Abdul cleaned up all evidence of the submarine. Omar bin al Habib emailed that he was delivering a package.

Zaki came into the shop and did a thorough inspection looking for evidence. "Now that boat finished, we seal floor."

"Permanently," Abdul said. "Until al Habib come."

He stared at the pipe their welding cables passed through to the floor below. He pointed, "Big deputy see welding cables pass in that hole. And he see vent pass through the roof. No one else must see."

Zaki stared at Abdul. "When Omar bin al Habib come?"

"Two weeks. I send him message we finished with undersea boat. We tell women we have rush job and take siesta. Tonight, we work late on floor. Seal with Rockcrete. And pipe hole for cables."

"What we do if they discover him?" Zaki said.

Abdul frowned at his brother. "Remember what Father say. 'Don't worry about things that haven't happened.'" He wagged a finger. "We never mention deputy again. Al Qaeda tell us about small microphones and cameras."

Zaki nodded. "Yes, they put anywhere."

Chapter 22

Davis Valley, California, five miles from Mexico

Kurt Valdez stared out the side window of the helicopter into the black night. The powerful thump-thump-thump of the rotors sent vibrations through his butt down to the soles of his feet. His stomach felt as if it were in his throat.

He pulled on two sets of gloves, slamming each fist into the opposite hand to tighten them.

Even though he expected it, he started when the command came to deploy. Hyperventilating several breaths, he called out to the pilot that he was ready.

Shawn Gunnison acknowledged.

Kurt adjusted his night-vision headgear then released his seat belt. He slid the chopper's side door open and the noise from the props changed to loud pops. A blast of cold air mixed with kerosene exhaust rushed in. He attached the two-inch rope and ran out the outrigger beam until it locked into place. Then, he kicked the coiled rope into the darkness.

Timothy Barfield slapped him on the shoulder.

Kurt grasped the rope, drew another breath, and plunged into the night. The rope burned as he alternately squeezed and released pressure on it. A narrow-beam spotlight above him allowed him to watch the ground below. Two hundred feet down from the chopper, he hit hard and rolled downhill to his right. Within seconds, Barfield and Sergeant Navarro landed nearby. Kurt reached to Barfield's chest to make sure he had the computer. Then, he stowed the burned-through gloves in his lower pants pockets.

The three men quickly took cover. Scanning the dark through the night vision, Kurt saw the other fourteen men of Echo Squad fanning out.

The stealth choppers veered off in formation and returned north. Sounds from their low-frequency thumps faded until they completely subsided. Squads formed into the preplanned groups.

Captain Roberts gave the command to proceed.

Kurt acknowledged and spoke softly into his lip-mike, "One hundred sixty degrees. The illegal aliens are beyond and below that ridge three klicks away."

"Got it," came the reply.

The SAP Units impressed Kurt. The Special Access Program, bolstered by FBI and CIA paramilitary units with former military Special Forces, now assisted the U.S. Customs and Border Protection department, the CBP.

For this mission Kurt was joined by two recently acquired CIA contract agents like himself. He met Sergeant Hector Navarro and Tim Barfield only two hours ago.

A part-Mescalero Apache from El Paso, Texas, Navarro sported a neatly-trimmed mustache and beard that contrasted nicely with his tan complexion and straight-black hair. The former Ranger went through jungle warfare training at Fort Benning, Georgia, and then got his ticket punched in the drug wars in Colombia.

Tim Barfield—Specialist Barfield—grew up in Inglewood, California, south of LA. Kurt found out that his father had been regular army. The man was a strict disciplinarian with Tim and his brother and sister, which was fortunate, because the family lived in a drug-immersed Crip neighborhood. Tim maintained good grades and entered the Army right out of high school. He met Navarro at Fort Benning and they became buddies throughout their tours.

"Valdez? Mexican Huh?" Navarro had asked when he and Kurt met.

"Also half Lebanese. My mother."

Captain Roberts' voice interrupted on the earphones.

Glancing at his watch, Kurt saw that a half-hour had passed. He turned to Barfield. "Get the computer ready, Tim."

The man opened the laptop. While it came on, Kurt peered up at the vast, star-filled desert sky. The Milky Way stretched wide across the horizon. Dark forms of mountains loomed in the distance, with shadowy sagebrush and lighter rocks on sand in the foreground.

He flipped the night-vision to high-power and searched for the Predator. One of the captain's men in Alpha Squad guided the small remote-controlled aircraft with another laptop. Kurt finally spotted it moving on the bearing he had given. The machine made almost no noise.

"Look at this," Barfield said.

Glancing at the green-tinted image on the screen, Kurt saw movement. The Predator picked up seventeen advancing shapes.

Echo squad progressed on a heading of 165 degrees.

It took the three groups of CBP more than an hour to reach a point overlooking the valley where they could cut off the escape route. During that time, Kurt, Navarro, and Barfield saw several additional movements on the screen.

On his earphones, Kurt heard the captain command the groups to fan out. After a few minutes, the officer said, "Charlie, Echo Squads, engage targets."

Kurt said, "Go! Go! Go!" Locking and loading, they sprung from their positions and charged. Illegal aliens ran in all directions.

"*Tenga cuidado!*" yelled Navarro.

Damn right! Watch for coyotes with Uzis. Kurt learned they had been hired by the cartels to bring Middle Easterners into the U.S. When surprised, the coyotes sometimes shot them.

Charlie and Echo squads dispersed the fleeing illegal aliens. Navarro shouted into the loudspeaker that they had them surrounded. *"Sientense! Manos arriba! En la cabeza."* Sit and put your hands on your heads.

Within a few heartbeats, Kurt counted eleven aliens obeying the order. Six took off running. Bravo squad cut off the escape route. The aliens were blind in the darkness. CBP had night vision.

A rapid burst from an automatic weapon erupted.

Barfield yelled, "I'm hit!"

"Two coyotes have guns!" a voice blurted in the darkness.

Return fire concentrated on the rifle bursts.

There was a scream and the weapons' blasts stopped.

"Cease fire," shouted Captain Roberts.

In the skirmish that followed, Kurt watched the CBP circulate among the intruders. He took a deep breath, held it and listened. Navarro with the computer now, watched the movements. The noise quieted to low voices, as everyone remained motionless and silent.

Finally, Captain Roberts relayed, "We got 'em all. Bring in the lights and choppers. Check those wounded men."

Kurt shined his light on Barfield's wound.

Sergeant Navarro stashed the computer. Kurt and the sergeant hoisted Barfield and called for medics.

"Minor leg wound," Kurt told the medic.

Barfield groaned.

After several minutes, helicopters arrived to pick up the aliens.

Kurt moved in with Echo Squad to look over the detainees, now cuffed with plastic ties and sitting in a circle. Poor Mexicans crossing into the U.S. weren't his interest. He searched for more important prey. The CIA estimated that more than several hundred Middle Easterners, many of them veterans of the Iraq War and sympathetic to al Qaeda, had already entered the country by way of the porous border.

Two hours later, the CBP agents brought in the coyotes and Mexicans one by one into a brightly lit room to be questioned and have their documents examined. Kurt listened carefully as Border Patrol agents Manuel Ramirez and José Cárbajal questioned the men in rapid Spanish.

The two interrogators pushed the envelope as far as rough treatment could go. It reminded Kurt of the al Qaeda detainees he had helped round up in the mountains of Waziristan. He himself had conducted 268 interrogation sessions in Afghanistan.

All but two of the Mexicans spoke good conversational Spanish. They drugged the two who had difficulty with the language and readied them for transport to the CIA's Camp Tango Interrogation Clinic.

Chapter 23

Ensenada, Mexico

The harbor was black when the LPG tanker arrived at Ensenada, Mexico. The ship anchored offshore. A myriad of twinkling lights danced on the oily surface water, creating a visible outline between the city and anchored vessels. Ramzi bin Omeri immediately began to worry that there was so much shipping traffic that his connection would miss him. There was no allowance for a mistake.

The dank, salty smell in the harbor suffused his lungs. Sea birds slept on the water and on rocky cliffs. Rotting, crushed barnacles and mussels added to the pungent odors. Bird droppings on the protruding rocks were barely visible in the faint reflections. A fresh breeze from the Pacific Ocean to the west stirred against the harbor smells.

Ramzi turned toward the open ocean and inhaled in a large breath. Customs would examine the manifest in the morning. The vessel could then discharge its liquid petroleum gas at the terminal forty miles to the north.

The Yemeni looked in awe at the outline of a large number of tankers and container ships anchored in, or just outside of the harbor. He scanned the shoreline with his telescope, making a slow visual inspection through the half-circle he could see. Completing it, he glanced at his watch. 0230 hours.

He swallowed hard. Sitting out here in the harbor was risky. If the authorities discovered the extra cargo they intended to deliver, he and Kareem were prepared the fight to the death. They would not allow themselves to be questioned.

He made another scan with the telescope and saw nothing of interest, only nightlights on other ships.

Late. Something must have happened.

He shivered in the morning chill. The sky over the mountains showed faint contrast. He could now distinguish a white band of cloud encircling a peak to the south. It was at least three hours before daylight. His stomach tightened. *Calm yourself.*

After a few more minutes, he began another scan. *There!* He spotted a strobe. He focused the instrument on the light. Then he blinked several quick flashes in its direction.

A light responded. He blew out a large breath. *Good.* He sent the pre-planned series of coded flashes.

It would take the boat a while to reach them. He awakened Kareem. They prepared to unload the cargo. While his comrade doused his face with cold water, Ramzi went to the bridge. He told one of the four watches that they were ready to leave. The dark complexioned man with a three-day beard blinked a few times and grunted. "I will wake up two deckhands and the crane operator."

The captain had received $200,000 dollars to ship contraband that he thought was opium. He had given his permission for them to unload it. But, he wanted to be asleep when that transpired.

Several minutes later, after the hatch was opened and the operator worked the crane controls, Ramzi guided a hook down into the hold. Kareem and the deckhands below unfastened holddowns to the cargo. Then they attached the hook.

A purse seiner, an eighty-foot fishing boat, motored alongside the ship. The operator hoisted and swung the load. He eased it into the hold of the nearby vessel, working with small red lights. He then returned the crane apparatus to its proper position.

A deckhand rolled the ship's ladder over the gunwale and the Ramzi thanked the crew. He and Kareem left the LPG tanker to board the smaller vessel.

Abdul bin Ibrahim — aka Ricardo Morales, greeted Ramzi as he dropped to the deck. Abdul smiled and gestured, "You remember my brother, Zaki?"

In Arabic, Ramzi said, "An honor to meet brother jihadists again." He reverted to his military poise and motioned, "My comrade, Kareem Abu Bakr. We fought together against the Russians in Afghanistan."

"*A Salaam alaikum,*" Kareem greeted them.

"*Alaikum salaam,*" the brothers answered back. They looked at the older man with awe.

A Mexican deckhand came out of the wheelhouse.

Abdul turned to him and switched to Spanish. "*Estamos listos, señor*" — We're ready. We are to meet another boat 160 kilometers to the south."

The Mexican rattled off Spanish to the pilot. The diesel engines revved and the fishing boat made an arc southward, heading toward the open sea and around Punta Banda, or Banded Point. The white cloud that ringed the peak emerged clearly in the pre-dawn light.

It was well after dark 15 hours later when the fishing boat motored alongside a vessel, the *Elena Fritz*, sporting an American flag. Abdul had discovered a couple, Bruce and Pamela Fowler, who owned the sailboat. They had suffered a serious financial setback and thought they were transporting a load of opium for $200,000, half paid now, the remaining paid upon arriving at their unknown destination.

The fishing vessel had stopped twice on the voyage down to allow Ramzi and Kareem to dive, showing the diver's flag to passing boats. The diving had been a stalling tactic to await nightfall.

They pulled alongside the *Elena Fritz* and rigged the purse-seiner's winch to transfer the load to the bait tank well of the smaller vessel. Ramzi was pleased that the submerged fiberglass container fit. No odors or radiation would escape now. The small bait tank was hoisted on top to conceal it. Finally, they loaded their diving and fishing gear.

At daylight, the successful transfer completed, the *Elena Fritz* weighed anchor. Abdul gave Ramzi American and Mexican tourist visas to go with their Saudi passports. Abdul also gave Ramzi a cell phone. Then, he and Zaki left with the seiner.

Bruce Fowler rigged sails and piloted the sailboat on a five-day voyage along the arid and multi-colored, rocky Mexican coastline past thirty or more islands. Pausing for at least two dives at almost a dozen locations, Ramzi and Kareem posed as rich Arabs.

Bruce constantly watched the shoreline and other boats for the Mexican law, or Fish and Game. An average sized man with a medium build, he kept his head shaved and wore a San Diego Padres baseball cap. He had scars from teenage acne. Pamela Fowler seldom came out on deck except when the Arabs dove, or when the winds were high and she helped sail the boat. She appeared sickly to Ramzi—thin and pale—and wore her black hair in a Cleopatra style.

It was a strange ocean for the Arabs. They constantly discussed the large amount of visible life. Sea lions covered the rocky islands. Pelicans and gulls cruised low over the water. Sport fishing boats caught popular fish. Dolphins played off the bow of the sailboat. Several times, the Arabs and Fowlers joined the other vessels to fish.

Chapter 24

Mojave County, Arizona

The sheriff picked up the ringing phone. "Sheriff Stroman here. What can I do for you?"

"Hey Bob, this is Earl McGibbon over at Clark County."

"Earl. Long time, no see. Vegas keeping you busy?"

"We're always busy. Say, you had a deputy, Travis Williams, used to work for you."

"Yeah, I hired him back. But he hasn't checked in."

"Interesting. He was reported missing two weeks ago."

A long pause. "Missing?"

"Yeah. The other bouncer at the Cairo noticed he didn't come in to pick up his paycheck and reported it. His family in North Carolina hasn't heard from him, either."

Stroman glanced at his desk calendar. "I offered him his job back on the morning of February 17. Jotted it down."

"The other bouncer, uhh . . . Barry Andrews, a big black guy and former marine like Travis—he said he thought Williams took off to Puerta Vallarta, Mexico. But he's overdue. You said the eighteenth?"

"Yes Sir. Noted it on my calendar."

"Eighteenth was the last day Andrews saw him. No one has seen or heard from him since. We haven't found his car either. Checked at the airport. Border patrol hasn't logged it coming back to the States.

"What kind of car?"

"A former California Highway Patrol black-and-white Dodge Hemi. I gave the complete story to the *Sun*, all the info from the Missing Persons Report. I'll fax copies to you. Number still the same?"

Stroman frowned. "Yeah."

He thanked McGibbon and hung up.

After several minutes, the fax machine ejected five pages. The sheriff organized them and opened a new file. The pages noted that Travis Williams was missing ten days when the other bouncer reported he hadn't picked up his check. The Cairo Hotel personnel department didn't give it too much thought, the newspaper said, because it was common for employees to take time off. This was especially true after all the overtime they'd worked recently during the Saudi royal family visit.

Barry Andrews finally became worried and reported it. Travis' check included a considerable amount of overtime pay, the bouncer told the newspaper.

Stroman leaned back in his chair and fastened the paperwork under a clasp. He narrowed his eyes as he completed the article.

They should have found the Hemi.

He glanced at his scrawled note underneath the February 18 on the calendar. *Eighteenth was the last day he was seen.*

A gnawing feeling in the pit of the sheriff's stomach suggested something wasn't right. He decided that if they hadn't heard from Williams in a week, he'd do some personal investigating.

Chapter 25

Mojave County, Arizona

Sheriff Stroman placed the phone back on the cradle and stared at the wall in thought. Eight days had passed since Sheriff McGibbon called and Travis Williams' family hadn't heard from him since February 18. It was now two weeks past March 15, the date that the young man was supposed to report for work. His friends and co-workers had heard nothing. He still hadn't picked up his paycheck. And, his car had not been recovered.

How in hell does a car vanish?

Stroman opened his file again. He added two more clippings from the newspapers, an email message informing Williams that his paycheck was ready, and his own handwritten notes. His memoranda included conversations with Travis and Patti, a woman Williams dated twice before he disappeared.

The sheriff learned that Williams frequented *Cheetah's* and *Little Darlin's*, a couple of strip clubs, or Gentleman's Clubs, as they were referred to in Las Vegas. He apparently had no interest in working at those establishments, and as far as anyone knew, had not dated any of the women. Williams attended the First Methodist Church, but so infrequently that few could remember him.

In mid-April, Stroman ran notices with the radio and television stations requesting information from anyone about Travis' whereabouts. Several routine calls yielded nothing.

Travis Williams had simply disappeared.

After thinking it over, Stroman couldn't believe that there wasn't something sinister going on. The mob used to control many of the Las Vegas casinos. Rumors circulated that there were, at the very least, dozens of bodies buried in the desert surrounding Vegas. However, a couple of decades ago, the mob had formed partnerships with Wall Street and lost a significant amount of their influence. They cleaned up their act and became respectable businessmen. Besides, the younger generation held ownership through front men, and rarely took out anyone these days. At least, that's what the conventional wisdom claimed.

When Stroman discussed that possibility with Sheriff Earl McGibbon, the officer was evasive about the mob. Nevertheless, McGibbon followed up on

Williams at the behest of the Arizona sheriff, and found no large gambling debts or immoral connections. All the Clark County office could determine was a hint that the young man had several sexual relationships with some of the cocktail waitresses at the Cairo. No one would admit to being paid; these were well-kept secrets in the gambling capitol. Otherwise, Williams seemed to be a straight young man who occasionally went to church.

Stroman leaned back in his chair. He had driven his wife nuts the last two weeks with the mysterious possibilities of Travis' disappearance. Carrie offered many suggestions and the sheriff had added a score of his own. None of the ideas panned out. In addition, he went through a considerable amount of his county budget. Carrie had finally become exasperated and talked him into going fishing.

That hadn't done any good either. In his waders, in one of the finest fishing holes on the Colorado River, he dwelled on the disappearance. His gut feeling was that Williams was dead.

The following Monday in the office, the phone rang. Deputy Joe Zuniga took the call.

"Bob, Alessandro Peña's on the phone about Travis."

Stroman took the call. The reserve sheriff, Alessandro Peña, Travis' old marine buddy, greeted him.

"Good morning, Alex. What's up?"

"No word about Travis?"

"Nothing. Absolutely nothing."

"Something's wrong, Sir. I know Travis. We were in the same marine unit. He simply wouldn't disappear without telling someone."

"I thought maybe he took off to Mexico with a lady. I expected him to come back to work on March 15. He hasn't even picked up his paycheck from the Cairo Hotel. And they also haven't found his car yet."

"Last time I heard from him was that day we went to visit those South Americans," Peña said.

"I have his report in the file for that. I reread it. Nothing special on that day."

"How about NSA? Will they check the satellite passes? See if they can pick out his car in photos?"

"Little chance of help there unless we have definite suspicions and dates. The satellites are all rescheduled over Afghanistan, Pakistan, and Iraq. They make a few daily passes over the U.S. But, do you know how many man-hours it would take to go over all the photos obtained with powerful stereographic lenses? Like trying to find a needle in a haystack."

"Even if they spotted his black-and-white car, I guess it would disappear from the satellite after a while." Peña said.

"Yeah. I would have to have some very good evidence to get NSA's assistance."

"It was just a thought, Sir."

"Thanks, Alex."

Stroman hung up and flipped the file back to his entries on the two days after they thought Williams disappeared, February 18 and 19. He had responded to two traffic accidents on the 18. On the 19, there was a boat accident at Lake Mead. On the way back from the lake, he'd stopped at Palo Verde Springs to assist with Mrs. Stufloten's heart attack. He gave her powdered aspirin and coaxed her into a coughing fit until the ambulance arrived. That was the extent of his reports for that day.

He replayed the events in his mind. He'd driven on Highway 93 several times those two days. If Williams had passed by, he would have honked and waved. Likewise, the sheriff knew he hadn't been at the lake. At least, not while he was there.

The only clue Sheriff McGibbon had was that one of Williams' neighbors reported seeing him leaving dressed in his marine uniform. That puzzled Stroman.

Why in the world would he be in his marine uniform? Unless there was some kind of a vets organization meeting.

But, that was it. No further contacts.

As the sheriff recalled the visit, Olé Stufloten was distraught and of no help with his wife's latest heart attack. Stroman's quick thinking regarding the aspirin and coughing fit saved her life.

The sheriff analyzed the incident. He remembered going outside with the paramedics. In the darkness, he saw a small truck swerve toward him. The Morales brothers stopped to ask if the sheriff needed any help.

The incident was so insignificant he hadn't even noted it in his daily report.

He shrugged it off, and merely added it to the report in pencil the next day. He scrawled it below the Stufloten entry, the last one on February 19. Then he didn't give it another thought.

Chapter 26

Offshore Avalon, Catalina Island, California

After seven days, Ramzi bin Omeri watched Bruce Fowler pull the *Elena Fritz* into Avalon, Catalina Island, California, for the U.S. Customs check. A radio call had advised Fowler that customs was running a temporary operation there. He felt that the timing was excellent. They would not have a full-staffed cadre of officials.

Drug sniffing dogs came on board and customs agents checked the Arabs' papers. Pamela Fowler had finally come alive in the calmer waters and barbecued a large Dorado and two lobsters.

The agents looked over the fish catch, the scuba and the fishing equipment. The Fowlers managed to pass themselves off as entertaining Middle Eastern guests. Ramzi spoke distinguished English with a British accent and carried a Saudi Military ID. Kareem, who feigned ignorance, was passed off as his uncle. Several photos of the two Arabs with sizable marlins were displayed.

Had it not been for the dive equipment, fishing gear, and the catch, U.S. Customs might have been suspicious. A thorough search of the boat turned up no drugs or weapons.

In addition, the Fowlers got to know the Arabs during the cruise. Ramzi, as a Saudi military officer, claimed he was a liaison with the American military. Unmentioned was the issue of why the Arabs would be bringing in a load of opium.

Cleared by customs, Bruce Fowler sailed on for Two Harbors. Ramzi and Kareem took his Zodiac inflatable raft on several dives along the coastline.

On the next day, in a different small cove, a larger boat, the *Island Hopper*, anchored about 200 feet from the *Elena Fritz*. Three other boats left after dark, and Ramzi signaled to transfer their cargo to the larger vessel.

The pilot of the *Island Hopper* out of San Pedro, Claude Bigelow, was a balding man, with gray muttonchops and a ponytail hanging down the middle of his back. He wore cutoff jeans and a sweatshirt, and had a belly that hung over his wide leather belt.

Ramzi paid the Fowlers their remaining $100,000 and thanked them for bringing in the load. The Arabs spent most of the next day casually diving along the shore, and then made the ninety-minute passage to the wharves in Wilmington, California.

The Middle Easterners made a big show on the docks with fish and game bags. They hauled out two carts of dive gear. Late that night, they had Claude pull the boat into a slip alongside shore, then leave. In the early morning hours, they unloaded the bomb container onto a Ryder rental truck with a winch from the *Island Hopper*.

A Mexican, Jose Sanchez, drove. His instructions were to head toward Las Vegas, turn east on Interstate 40 toward Needles, California and Kingman, Arizona, then head north on Highway 93 toward Lake Mead. They stopped at restaurants and stalled until nightfall. Ramzi contacted Abdul bin Ibrahim once from a pay phone to update progress and give the Brazilian an estimated time of arrival. He and Kareem dozed intermittently.

Ramzi awoke when the driver asked where the final turnoff was. Blinking, he said, "Toward Bonelli Landing and Palo Verde Springs." He glanced at a milepost. "Thirteen miles further."

A half-hour later, they passed 300 yards beyond Palo Verde Springs and as directed, Sanchez pulled the truck down the long driveway to the shop building.

Zaki rolled the door open, while Abdul directed the Mexican driver to back into the shop.

Ramzi checked his watch. *0250 hours. Good.*

While the Arabs unloaded the crate, Ramzi paid Jose Sanchez $2,000. He instructed the Mexican to drop off Kareem at the Amtrak terminal in Los Angeles headed for Mexico, before he returned the rental truck. "That is enough money for you and the rental."

Jose beamed, folded the money and slipped it into his pocket.

Ramzi drew Kareem aside and instructed him in Arabic to kill the Mexican with Abdul's *Jambiga*, his short Yemeni sword, with a thrust upward into the man's heart. "Dump his body into the big river with rocks to weigh him down."

Kareem blinked at Ramzi, as if thinking: *What has this man done to us?*

Ramzi caught the look. "He knows too much," he said, furrowing his eyebrows.

Minutes later, the Mexican eased the rental truck out of the driveway, with Kareem in the passenger seat.

The Arabs rolled down the door. They removed the bomb, and extracted it from its protective lead shield, then set it on the floor. Abdul and Zaki moved one floor section.

The Snow Leopard and Abdul went below while Zaki lowered the nuclear device. In a few minutes, they were all below examining the submarine and weapon.

Ramzi ran his hand over the vessel. He inspected the conning tower hatch cover gasket and latch, and the seals around the four thick-glass view windows. Peering inside the sub, he noted the minimal gauges and valves, and the fold-down seat.

He raised his eyebrows, nodded, and, with the Mexican gone, switched to Arabic. "I am impressed with your craftsmanship. You both did a professional job."

Abdul was obviously pleased with the praise. "We finished the wiring harnesses, seals, and stainless piping last so we could test the high-pressure air system. The assembly that holds the bomb up inside the submarine arrived three weeks ago along with a mock-up of the bomb."

Ramzi turned and removed the stainless cover from the top of the weapon. "Nothing was damaged during shipment," he said. "It's almost daylight. We must hurry." He replaced the top cover.

The three Arabs moved the ordnance under the boat on a creeper.

"I have to load the bomb so I know how the mechanism works." Ramzi eased down onto another creeper and rolled under the submarine. He unbolted the swing-open doors and operated a lever to release hooks and cables. Air escaped as he pulled down the lifting apparatus. Zaki pushed the weapon over to him, and he connected the hooks.

"Turn air valve same as clock to raise package," Abdul said. "Slow. Not to bend."

The Snow Leopard turned the valve and air noises entered to draw the cables up inside the submarine. Suddenly, loud clacking noises came from the vessel. The bomb lurched to the side.

"Get out!" shouted Abdul.

The air assembly growled. It made a squealing noise and jammed. Ramzi felt the brothers grab his legs. They jerked him. A cable snapped. The bottom of the weapon fell on his wrist.

He yelled. The Ibrahams yanked him to a standing position.

Ramzi swore and grabbed his wrist. Working his fingers, he shook his hand.

Zaki crawled under to inspect the damage. "Bomb went to the side, not straight. It snap cable. We buy new one."

Ramzi continued to move his fingers and massage the wound. "Does the cover look damaged?"

Zaki said. "It not bent too much."

He pushed up the hatch cover. "The cover no close."

Ramzi still grimaced and shook his arm. "Can you fix it?"

"I think we fix, Sheikh," Zaki said.

"Can you have it ready to move by next week?"

Abdul looked at his brother. "We try to rush job. I want to move it."

Zaki climbed out from under and nodded that he concurred with Abdul.

Back on the shop floor, Ramzi turned to the brothers. "Once we move the boat out, you both need to disappear from here. We have a property in Mexico City in a safe area for your families. I must send a message that we are ready. Your job here for Allah is finished. Bring me the computer."

Jorge opened a steel drawer and brought the briefcase to Ramzi.

The Snow Leopard motioned them to follow him out back. Ten paces from the building, he set the case on the ground and told them to step away several paces. He got into a crouched position, flipped open the lid without disarming the trigger, while simultaneously jumping back.

A brilliant shower of white molten metal sprayed from the computer accompanied by a cloud of smoke. Within a few seconds, a blob of red hot metal ran into depressions in the sand.

The brothers stood wide-eyed before the display.

"There," Ramzi said. "Get a shovel and hide the evidence."

He turned to the Ibrahims. "Tonight you can drive me to Kingman. Then get all your affairs together. Once you repair the submarine, be ready to move to Mexico for the last time."

"I have to make toilet," Kareem said to Jose Sanchez.

"Okay. I pull down that road." Jose pointed to a left turn that apparently went down to the Colorado River. "I must have *siesta*. Good time to stop."

A quarter mile further, down the small road that ran along the river, Jose pulled over.

Kareem got out of the Ryder truck, walked to bushes and pissed. As he did, he slipped the *Jambiga* out of his trousers.

Jose Sanchez finished urinating and zipped his pants. He turned to head toward the truck, taking three strides toward Kareem. "If you want to sleep in the truck, I will make a place on the sand by the river." A shocked look spread on Jose's face when he spotted the *Jambiga*.

Kareem jabbed the small sword up under Jose's ribs. The Arab yanked upward to jam the weapon into the Mexican's heart.

The small man gasped. He opened his mouth to scream. The only sound that came forth was a gurgling.

Kareem lowered the body to the ground, looking around to make sure no one saw them in the faint lights of the bridge. He went to the truck and got some rope. Removing and inflating the man's pants, he tied off the leg bottoms. Then he drew the Mexican into a tight fetal position and dragged him to the water. Kareem seized a good-sized rock and tied it to him. Then he waded far enough to get the body into the main current.

One more look around, and he let Jose go.

The Mexican's body floated away, barely buoyant. Kareem figured that the pants would take in enough water to sink in a few minutes, somewhere another kilometer down the river.

Twenty minutes later, the Arab filled the gas tank of the truck and studied the map Ramzi marked in Arabic characters. He needed to return the truck to Long Beach by dark or it would be reported as missing.

He pushed a wad of qat into his mouth and chewed it down.

It will keep me awake.

Chapter 27

July Fourth, Mojave County, Arizona

Sheriff Bob Stroman pulled the white SUV out of the parking lot on the Arizona side of Lake Mead and floored the accelerator. The big V-8 engine responded with a noisy inrush of air and surged out in front of an oncoming Ford truck.

"Radio said Bonelli Landing. How far is that, Sir?" Krysta Mazur asked.

"Almost eighty miles. The life flight helicopters will be long gone with the two children by the time we arrive."

"Does this happen often?"

"About twice a month during the summer."

While Krysta surveyed the new vehicle bridge over the Colorado River, he looked her over. A tall brunette in her late twenties, she had an athletic build and tanned features. She worked for a two-year-old intelligence firm subcontracted to Homeland Security. The government agency assigned McFadden Security, her employer, to work closely with law enforcement agencies in the northwestern Arizona county and southern Nevada. Mojave County would be her prime area for a year. She was to appear to be a deputy.

The sheriff had studied Krysta's résumé and learned that she graduated from the University of Virginia, having majored in Middle Eastern languages. She interned two summers with the National Security Agency, or NSA, as it was known in government parlance.

"Going to be an amazing bridge."

Out of the corner of his eye, Stroman glanced at Krysta's short khakis and long, tan legs. He remembered how nice they'd appeared in a skirt when he first met her. "Part of the new super-highway system to move imported goods from Mexico and Asia. Another one runs from Texas up into the Midwest."

"Homeland Security listed Hoover Dam as one of the most vulnerable targets for terrorists. The government wanted to get the big trucks off the structure."

"Yeah, said Stroman. "I remember that from the meetings."

The SUV crested the hill beyond the curves coming up from the lake, and Highway 93 opened up before them to the south. Stroman punched the accelerator again.

"Sounded like one of the children was in serious condition."

"Driver of that boat better hope the doc saves him."

"Las Vegas is still the nearest hospital? I've been away seven years."

"Yeah. Only takes the chopper 19 minutes to get there."

"And Bonelli Landing is a boat landing at the upper end of Lake Mead if I remember correctly?"

"Next to last boat landing before the Grand Canyon."

Krysta shifted in the seat. "I've never seen Lake Mead this low."

"The lake's the lowest it's been in more than sixty years. Did you smell it?"

"Yes. Algae bloom. Awful."

He changed the subject. "They trained you originally for the National Security Agency?

"Yes. NSA. Four years of college and a two-year internship. They privatized many functions and I wound up accepting a job with this newly formed company. With benefits, I make forty-percent more."

"And they're subcontracted to Homeland Security? Janet Napolitano's department?"

"That's right. The private company wanted me because of my language skills. My natural fluency in Arabic."

The sheriff smiled at her, looking into her large, soft brown eyes. "I met Napolitano last fall in a meeting. Intelligent lady."

"There's a lot of infighting in the government. It always amazes me how much they do accomplish."

"Carrie, my wife, gets angry when she hears about the government splitting and all the privatized companies. She says it's a way to make the government smaller. It's driven by the ideologues and actually costs the public a lot more—waste."

"Interesting. I'll have to think about that one."

"So, how'd you learn Arabic?"

"My grandfather was Syrian. He spoke Arabic around us all the time."

"Is it a hard language to understand?"

"The concepts are simpler than English. But the sentence structure is completely different. You would think it was turned backward. That's what makes it difficult for English speakers."

"I had a hard time with Spanish."

"Some Spanish language structure is similar to Arabic, a few of the words, too. The Arabs occupied Spain for several hundred years."

The sheriff nodded. "See that trail?" He pointed down to the right and stole a glance at Krysta's breasts. He couldn't help himself, but looked quickly back to the road.

"Yes, Sir."

"A great hike down to the river, and some hot springs a half mile to the south."

He grinned. "We used to go skinny-dipping there when I was a kid." He stepped on the accelerator to pass another eighteen-wheeler.

After a period of silence, he saw a sign that indicated a left turn onto Temple Bar Road. It read Palo Verde Springs 36, Bonelli Landing 53.

Stroman made the turn. He pushed the SUV up to 70, as fast as the desert road would allow with its dips and curves.

The Argentine pampas grass by the sides of the highway had turned the color of wheat. The creosote bushes on the arid hills beyond the grass had changed from a dull green to their dark gray of summer. Temperature readout indicated 116 degrees.

"So why didn't you stay in Washington?"

"I missed the West. I grew up in Henderson. Dad was an electrical engineer at Hoover Dam's hydroelectric facilities. He was excited when I received a scholarship to study government at the University of Virginia, my mom's *alma mater*. That's how I wound up in Washington. The private offer was a way out and back west."

Krysta looked around at the desert. "*Really* dry this year."

"It'll be green after the thunderstorms."

She said, "There's an amazing amount of water and greenery fifty miles up the Grand Canyon. I hiked to where the Havasupai Indians have some nice land with several waterfalls, pools, and pasture."

"Our deputy, Joe Zuniga, handles that area. He's a Hopi." He passed a slow car. "Your résumé said you liked outdoor activities."

"I hiked the eastern slope of the Sierras and the mountains north of Mount Charleston a lot."

"I figured you as an outdoor girl."

"I've been on top of Mount Charleston four times, Mount Whitney twice."

Stroman turned his attention back to the highway. "Palo Verde Springs is coming up. A few months ago I saved the life of a woman who was suffering from a heart attack. I fed her some aspirin and got her coughing. Kept her going 'til the ambulance arrived."

Krysta smiled and nodded. They passed through the town with several tiny houses. All of them were of natural gray cinder block or painted pastel colors. They passed two businesses and a curio shop with Indian pottery, blankets, and petrified rocks on display. She said, "I'm surprised at the number of people who live out here. It's hard to imagine how they can make a living."

"Indians mostly. They get stipends from the tribes' casinos."

The sheriff guided the car around a curve, and the upper end of Lake Mead came into view. A light-colored band lay above lake level, marking the former water level. Family groups picnicked and played along the beaches. Dozens of boats plied the deeper middle of the lake.

As the sheriff pulled the police car over to a congregation of people surrounding a beached boat, a uniformed man headed toward the white SUV.

"Patrick Townsend. He's the head park ranger for the lake area." The sheriff grabbed a clipboard and got out of the car.

"Hey, Pat. What happened?" The sheriff offered his hand. The ranger took it and glanced at Krysta with an arched eyebrow. "This's Krysta Mazur, with the government."

The ranger greeted her, then turned and gestured with his thumb. "That lunatic over there with the bloody bandage on his head lost control. Drove that boat right up on the beach. Hit two kids. Pretty serious."

"Yeah, heard one of 'em's in intensive care. Torn liver and busted ribs." said Stroman.

"I held him for you," said Townsend. "Found six empty beer bottles in the boat."

The sheriff handed Krysta a camera and asked her to take some digital photos. He donned gloves to retrieve the ice chest and beer bottles. Then he moved to the injured man while a tow truck backed up. The beached boat had a broken transom with a large black Mercury motor still attached by cables and a gas line.

After a few questions, Stroman led the man in plastic cuffs to the SUV, and pushed him into the back seat. He seemed dazed and remorseful.

The sheriff waved to Townsend as they pulled out. They drove in silence for more than twenty minutes and arrived at Palo Verde Springs. "You like a Coke?" Stroman asked.

"I don't drink sodas," Krysta said. "But I'll see what they have."

Stroman pulled into Stufloten's and they got out. He cinched the cuffed man to the screen separating the seats of the vehicle and left it running with the AC on.

Inside the small store, the sheriff said, "Hey, Olé, this's Ms. Mazur. She's with the government."

A thin, bland-looking man with blond hair, Olé Stufloten greeted the sheriff and acknowledged Krysta with a smile.

"How's Helga?" The sheriff asked.

"She's fine. She has to keep the nitroglycerin close by. Otherwise, everything's back to normal."

Stroman pushed the bill of his cap up with his index finger. The desert store and gas station was old–at least '50s vintage–with rough concrete floors. It smelled of spilled beer and dust and dried-out wood. New refrigerated cases filled the back wall and contained ice, alcoholic beverages and soft drinks. The cases on the sidewall had the frozen foods and ice cream.

As the sheriff turned toward the soft drinks unit, Ricardo Morales stepped out from behind the last shelves. "Oh, hi, Ricardo," he said. This is Ms. Mazur."

"Good morning, Sheriff." Morales smiled at Krysta. "A real pleasure to meet you."

Krysta greeted him.

The sheriff walked on, selecting a Coke for himself and a bottle of water for the arrested man. He noticed that Krysta picked out a bottle of Lipton tea, unsweetened. The sheriff followed her back toward the counter. Looking down the aisles as they moved toward the cash register, she suddenly stopped and stared.

Stroman saw that Ricardo Morales's brother, Jorge, faced them, but was looking toward a rack of cookies. Jorge turned his back as he moved along the shelves.

"*A salaam alaikum,*" Krysta said.

The sheriff had just looked back toward the Brazilian when he saw Jorge flinch. The man's hand froze for a moment in midair. With his back still toward Stroman and Krysta, he casually grasped a box of cookies, then continued around the end of the aisle.

Huh? Stroman wrinkled his forehead and paid for the drinks.

Outside, the sheriff cut the snap-tie for the prisoner and gave the man a bottle of water. Getting in the SUV, Stroman revved the engine to speed up the AC. They drove along in silence heading toward the hospital. There he had the prisoner treated and tested for blood-alcohol level. They then locked him in a cell while they awaited news regarding the injured children.

Two hours later, Stroman invited Krysta into his office. "Have a seat." He gestured to a chair.

She scooted it over toward his desk. "What's up, Sheriff?" She pushed a strand of hair behind her ear.

"I didn't want to say anything in front of the prisoner. But you spoke Arabic to Jorge Morales at Stufloten's, didn't you?"

Krysta crossed her arms in front of her. "I'm sorry if I insulted him ... I ... I ... mean—"

"Oh, no. There's nothing wrong," said Stroman. "It's just—"

"Well, Sir, the first one you greeted—"

Stroman frowned. "Ricardo Morales—in front of the cold cases."

"Yes. He looked Mexican. But the other man—with the frizzy hair, he looked Middle Eastern to me. I don't know—Palestinian. I worked with three of them in Washington." Krysta spoke in a defensive voice.

"Don't be apologetic. You're not the first one who's said that about the Morales brothers, especially Jorge, the one with the frizzy hair. It got me to thinking on the way back here. When I went to the meeting with the Homeland Security Department last year, they warned us about embedded Arabic cells within the United States."

The Phoenix Agenda

Krysta's eyes lit up. "When I interned with the NSA, the FBI discovered a cell in Utica, New York. It had received money and instructions from some of the suspects connected to Osama bin Laden. There are mosques throughout the United States," she made a circular gesture with her arms, "that funnel money to Middle Eastern students. Some of them were connected to Mohammad Atta, the leader of the attacks on September 11."

"Yeah," Stroman said. "The government told us about those."

"The FBI definitely knows there are. But trying to find individual suspects is extremely difficult. Those people may live in the U.S. for years, unnoticed. Suddenly, they are called to carry out a mission. If you remember, they contacted two men who lived quietly as college students in San Diego. They participated in the hijacking of the aircraft that hit the Pentagon." She spoke animatedly.

The sheriff nodded. "What I've read really puzzles me. There were some blatant clues, such as Middle Eastern men trying to take pilot lessons. The FBI and CIA never connected the dots."

"Huh!" Krysta muttered. "One summer in Washington would clear up that mystery for you. Every agency is swamped with what they call 'noise,' millions of routine conversations. There is simply too much information to process. They had me listening to recorded messages that NSA intercepted. I did this nearly every day for several months, with a break every two hours. It surprised me to discover how NSA could pick out certain messages to analyze. And how well they filtered out the static. The messages came from our satellites in space."

Stroman twisted in his chair, placed his elbow on the desk, and brought his hand up to his jaw. He was curious about details regarding the nation's capitol and listened intently to Krysta.

She paused for several seconds and pushed her hair behind her ear. "The languages that we heard had to be categorized, and we became proficient at identifying certain speakers' accents. I actually listened to a recording of Nazir Fazlullah's voice my first month at work. They killed him in Pakistan in 2009."

Stroman shook his head. "So what happens when you identify someone or single out a message?"

"It's called humit, human intelligence. They kick it up to an expert, maybe a CIA field-op who lived over there, with the thought that they might understand the inferences of the message."

"Sounds like tryin' to pick a needle out of a haystack."

"I had a difficult time keeping my attention focused. Almost fell asleep several times. That's why we were on for only two hours at a time."

"So how'd you wind up working for a private company?"

Her nostrils flared. "Washington wasn't what I expected! I didn't like the agencies' infighting and turf battles. My first summer was in 2006. The next summer, in 2007, the Bush people still didn't trust two of the Clinton administration holdovers. There were many conflicts like that in the NSA. They tried to hide it from us interns, but I constantly felt like a hand grenade was going to go off. There was so much tension and anger." She shrugged. "I heard things."

The sheriff frowned. "The Department of Homeland Security was supposed to tie everything together, stop some of the infighting."

Krysta looked straight at Stroman as if trying to read his thoughts. She remained silent.

"What?"

She paused, then said in a lowered voice, "The bureaucrats think DHS is a joke, a terrible sham perpetrated on the American people because of the September 11 failures."

Stroman felt his cheeks flush. "I... I...."

"Oh, don't get me wrong. There are some excellent and diligent people in the intelligence services. What Washington didn't need was another huge bureaucracy. For perspective, imagine combining AOL and Time-Warner, then magnifying their problems by several orders of magnitude. It takes years, sometimes decades, to organize a new department that size. The professionals believe DHS has merely drained top people from other agencies, a shifting of assets. It will have a disorganizing and demoralizing effect for years throughout Washington because of the turnover in the top slots."

The force with which Krysta said this stunned the sheriff. "You think Homeland Security is a bad idea?" Stroman thought his voice sounded meek.

"It's a cruel diversion. Covering up failure. What's more, they are privatizing everything. All that does is run up the costs for government—private bureaucratic inefficiency and waste. More than 2,000 companies subcontracting to DHS, like us."

Wow! She's feisty!

"That's what Carrie says." Stroman repressed his anger. He stared at the pencil and eraser as he poked the tabletop, then slid his fingers down it several more times. After a long awkward silence, he suggested, "Maybe you should run the Morales brothers' names through their computers. They told us they now share everything with the FBI also."

Krysta must have sensed his unease. After a moment, she said, "That would be a good place to start. The FBI could look at their bank accounts and business arrangements; see if they're receiving funds, and whether they're legitimate. They could also find out if there were any Muslim or Middle Eastern connections. The government's getting better at those skills now with all the new computer systems they rushed into service."

"My former deputy...."

"The one who's missing?"

"Yes, Travis Williams." Stroman swallowed. "Our reserve deputy Alessandro Peña and Travis were marine buddies. Maybe we should bring him in for a conversation. He went with Williams to visit the Morales brothers. Travis was suspicious, too. Maybe I'm missing something. Something they discussed."

Krysta shrugged.

That afternoon at five, Stroman heard Reserve Sheriff Peña come into the front office.

The sheriff saw the solid, medium-sized man with Indian features—brown skin and salt and pepper hair—introduce himself to Krysta Mazur.

Stroman had called Alex before noon, after the discussion. He found out Alex was in Las Vegas and would be happy to come by on his way home.

"Come in here, Alex," Stroman stood to shake hands.

He motioned Krysta into his office, also. "Pull up some chairs. Let's do a little brainstorming."

The sheriff filled Alex in on what had happened that morning, and Krysta glossed over what her government-related job was.

After she finished, Stroman said, "We ran into the Morales brothers at the store. When she spoke in Arabic to Jorge Morales, he almost jumped out of his boots."

The dark man ran a hand through his hair. His frown left a furrow between his eyebrows and deep creases on both sides of his mouth. "After Travis's disappearance, I wrote down everything I could remember about our contacts over the last year. The most time I spent with him was that day we went to visit the Morales brothers. I also saw him in the Cairo Hotel twice when my wife and I ate there."

The sheriff leaned back in his chair, elbows on the armrests. "Tell us what you can about that visit to the sign shop."

Peña looked up at the ceiling. After a few moments, he said, "As I recall, we went to the brothers' business to show them an oxygen and acetylene setup. Travis had a hunch that something wasn't right with them—their story. At least, that was the excuse to scrutinize them. The brother with the curly hair—"

"Ricardo Morales," the sheriff interrupted.

"Yeah. He came around from the house after the dog went wild. As I recall, I spoke Spanish and Portuguese with them. I had a sense they felt uncomfortable. As if they were being singled out."

Peña looked up at the ceiling again, fingering his top collar button.

After a bit, he continued, "I finished talking to them while Travis sat in the car. He felt they would be more relaxed that way. They spoke excellent Portuguese and okay Spanish. Ricardo told me that they had moved to Brazil eight years before. That would explain why their Spanish wasn't quite as good."

Stroman pushed back and made a tent with his fingers. "Was there anything else you remember from that day that might help us?"

"Travis and I continued driving to the lake afterward. I told him I remembered hearing some irregularities in the second brother's speech."

"Jorge," Stroman said.

"Yeah. He had some peculiar pronunciations." Peña looked at the floor and placed his thumb on his chin. "Jorge didn't pronounce some words correctly. I thought that was strange. Also, I noticed that Jorge had yellowed skin and frizzy hair."

Stroman nodded in satisfaction. "What was odd about that?"

"I just thought it was unusual and mentioned it to Travis. It was as if the two brothers had different fathers. Actually those traits are not *that* uncommon in South America."

Krysta asked, "Did you notice anything odd about the premises or their behavior?"

Peña thought for a minute. "I think Travis took something out of the trash. I didn't see what it was. Other than that, only that they had a great workshop."

"Yeah," Stroman said. "Them boys are really hustlers."

"Their dog was trying to reach Travis' throat."

The sheriff rose. "Thanks, Alex. We'll fill in the blanks."

Peña rose, shook the sheriff's hand and nodded to Krysta. "Nice meeting you, young lady."

He walked toward the door, then stopped and turned.

"Something else, Alex?" Stroman came out from behind his desk.

The man from Chile came back. "Ricardo had a strange habit that I mentioned to Travis." As he said this, he placed his hand on Stroman's arm and came close to his face.

The sheriff pulled his head back. Peña took his hand away, then after a few seconds did it again.

This time, Stroman felt annoyed.

"That's it. When Morales spoke to me, he put his hand on my arm and got right in my face. I told Travis I thought that was highly unusual. Almost...."

"Almost what?"

"Almost foreign."

"It is!" Krysta exclaimed. She pushed her hair behind her ear. "My grandfather used to do that. We grew up with it and didn't realize he had the unusual habit. But my friends from school made remarks about it. It's a Middle Eastern trait. He also used twigs as toothpicks. He was always chewing on a fragrant twig. His breath had a strange odor."

"Now that you mention it, Morales and his brother both had strong breath odors."

"I'll be damned!" said the sheriff. After a few moments, he said, "I wonder what Travis found in their trash?"

Peña shrugged. "I don't know. Hope I was of some help."

Stroman smiled as the man left.

He turned to Krysta, "I'm going to think on this for awhile. A contact I have in the FBI will tell us what they have on the Morales brothers. Well done, Ms. Mazur."

She gave him a wide smile.

Chapter 28

Mojave County, Arizona

Krysta Mazur entered the sheriff's office, headed to the back and handed a large envelope to Sheriff Stroman. He accepted the U.S. Express Mail, tore it open, and began reading: "FBI report on the Morales brothers."

"I thought so." She returned to the front desk.

After almost an hour, Stroman called her to the back. He handed her the correspondence in a new file jacket and said, "Since you were with the government, see what you think of this. Read between the lines."

She nodded and returned to the front, began reading and making notes on a pad. When she'd finished and thought about the contents, she rose and took her notes to the back.

"What do you think?" Stroman asked. "Anything there?"

"I saw what you saw. Their banking and business records are flawless. Looks like they have a clean and consistent history of business transactions. Their father emigrated from Palestine in 1973. But, there's no ties to any mosque or Arab charities. In fact, their families are Catholic."

The sheriff said, "The FBI doesn't feel any surveillance is warranted, though their assumed name became Morales and they're descended from a Palestinian."

She nodded. "The government's getting a bit more gun-shy. After all the random arrests of Arabs and Muslims the last eight years, there were a lot of complaints about the heavy-handedness. Lots of criticism of the Justice Department and former Attorney General Gonzales. The ACLU and large numbers of attorneys have been making noise about personal liberties. Some members of congress weighed in, too."

Stroman scowled. "Yeah, those idiots, tying our hands. But, there's one case I know about personally. Earl McGibbon, the Clark County sheriff in Las Vegas, was irate about a Pakistani woman beat up so bad she had to be hospitalized. Then, thinking she was Arabic, the nurses refused to treat her. The cities' liberals were outraged. McGibbon was also angry about the woman's treatment. He arrested the assailants."

After a long silence, Krysta said, "I worked with a whole group of Arab Americans in Washington. Most of them were with the intelligence agencies.

They are good patriots, Sir." She furrowed her forehead. "Many of them were upset about the stories of the arbitrary arrests after 9-11, and the treatment of Arab citizens—merely because they were Arabic."

Stroman stared at her.

Deputy Paul Davidson's voice came on the radio to announce that he and Joe Zuniga would return from lunch shortly.

After the interruption Krysta continued, "I naturally felt empathy for them. Several left the United States. I can assure you a few intended to join the *jihad* against America." She pushed her hair behind her ear.

The sheriff seemed to ponder this. "You know what, Paul and Joe should hear this. Wait a few minutes, I want to ask some questions for all of us. Since they'll be working with you, I'm sure they'll have questions, too."

Several minutes went by and the deputies arrived. Krysta greeted the two men she had only met yesterday.

Stroman said. "We were discussing the treatment of Arabs after 9-11 and I wanted to ask her some questions pertaining to intelligence and Arabic culture in general. I thought you two might benefit from hearing this."

The deputies pulled their chairs over.

Krysta said, "We were discussing the treatment of Muslims in general in the U.S. The sheriff referred to a Pakistani woman in Las Vegas, who was severely beaten after 9-11 because she wore a *hijab*, and the nurses refused to treat her."

"I remember that incident," Paul Davidson said.

Krysta continued, "It's important to realize that most of the inhabitants of Iran, Pakistan, Afghanistan and the surrounding countries are not Arabs, not Arabic at all. Most people in the West make that mistake. They think if they are Muslims, they're Arabs."

The sheriff asked, "What's a *jihad*? You hear that so much."

"A jihad is a struggle. Any struggle. It can mean overcoming a personal challenge. But in the international context, it means a holy war. Arabs think they're fighting a new Crusade with the West. A crusade they see as a spiritual war against Islam, with a strong religious connotation."

Stroman frowned and nodded. He had an intense look. The deputies asked some of the details about suicide bombers, 70 virgins, and Mohammad, which she answered in simple terms.

"The caliphate?" Joe asked. "What does that mean?"

"The caliphate is the maximum territory under Islamic control in the ninth to twelfth centuries, from Spain and Morocco, to Indonesia and India. Think the Roman or Mongol Empires at their peak. There are a few Muslims who dream that they could re-achieve that religious empire. Some of the megalomaniacs of the Muslim Brotherhood think that way.

"In its heyday," Krysta continued, "Islam swept right through the Byzantine Empire, the descendant of the Roman Empire, like a hot knife through butter." She smiled at the simile and pushed her hair behind her ear. "It did somewhat the same to much of the Hindu and Buddhist areas of Indonesia and India. India at the time included Pakistan, Afghanistan and countries up into the old Soviet Union such as Tajikistan and Uzbekistan."

Joe Zuniga frowned. "How did Europe fit into this picture? And Genghis Kahn?"

"Genghis Khan's forces clashed with the empire down into Persia in the 1200s. They gained control of most of the territory almost to Iraq, to the Arabian-Persian Gulf and to northern India. Europe was largely barbarian. Twelve Islamic intellectuals of the time are considered some of the great thinkers of all time, on a level with Aristotle, Plato, and Archimedes."

A 9-11 call came in on the radio and the sheriff nodded to Davidson and Zuniga to take care of it. They rose and thanked Krysta for the history. Joe Zuniga didn't smile and looked down his nose at her.

She told them it was a pleasure to be working with them, and that her father was very proud of his heritage. He was an amateur historian. He had told her family stories as they grew up.

After the men left, and a long silence, while Krysta studied her notes, Stroman said, "It appears the FBI doesn't consider the Morales brothers worth investigating."

"It would appear so, Sir."

Chapter 29

Boulder City, Nevada

For the next four days, Stroman discussed the brothers with his wife, and occasionally asked himself questions. Other than that, he didn't have much time to think about them.

Carrie was sympathetic toward the Latinos. "They just want to make a living and be left alone."

The fifth day was a slow morning, so he suggested that he and Krysta pay a visit to the Morales brothers.

He left Deputy Davidson with the office.

The sheriff and Krysta were mostly silent on the way to Palo Verde Springs. Then, as they approached the Morales' driveway, the sheriff pulled over and stopped alongside the road.

Stroman turned toward Krysta and said, "Pay close attention to them, if you will, when I confront them about their Arabic ancestry. Watch their body language. A law officer can tell a lot by the way a person acts—no eye contact, looking down, their nervous tics. Stuttering. You know what I mean?"

"I understand. What are you going to do, tell them right out that we know they're Arabic?"

"Yes." As he answered, the sheriff caught a glimpse of something green in the bushes. It startled him.

Krysta saw the expression on his face. "What's wrong?"

Stroman got out and went around the vehicle. He retrieved a small, round green can. Returning toward the SUV, he glanced down and saw that the roll-up door on the building was shut. When he closed his car door, he showed her the can. "Skoal. My deputy used to chew this brand."

"What does it mean?"

He dropped the box in a plastic sample baggy and sealed it. "Probably nothing. Anyway, the shop doors are closed. They may not be here."

He started the car and pulled down to the front of the shop. The Australian shepherd dog barked loudly and jumped at the fence.

They got out and Stroman looked into the trash cans. "I always check the suspect's trash. See what they throw away."

There was nothing of interest: small pieces of fragmented metal; sweepings of ground metal and paint chips; some blue shop towels with purple grease on them; worn grinding disks.

Huh-oh, what's this?

It looked like a wad of grass. There were no other clippings and Stroman didn't remember any grass in the yards, only cacti.

He took a piece of soiled paper towel and picked up the wad. There was another one in the bottom of the container.

Interesting.

He put one in a sample baggy, grabbed the other sample, and set the baggies on the floor behind his car seat. Then he and Krysta went to the front door. After three rings and no answer, they returned to the shop where the dog, still in a frenzy, followed them along the fence, lunging. Stroman scanned the premises toward the back, where the door had been jimmied a year ago. Gravel covered the ground to where the dirt was neatly raked around a cactus garden. Jorge's small house was over to the left.

Behind and beyond Jorge's house there was a large garden. The sheriff noticed it when he and Travis investigated the theft of the welder. It had a high plastered wall around it with a ceramic owl and three scarecrows visible above the fence. Several plants protruded above the wall.

"I'll bet they have those kids working all the time on this property—raking, cleaning up. Place is neat as a pin."

Stroman tried the back door, which was locked.

"Are you allowed to do this?"

"Not really. Supposed to have a warrant. But I know 'em well. We investigated a couple of thefts for them awhile back. Let's go."

Two hours later, back at the office, the sheriff said, "Would you take these samples over to the lab in Vegas, Ms. Mazur, on your way home? There's a guy named Herb who will check them out. My note and the address are in the envelope."

She nodded and accepted the package. "Why don't you just call me Krysta, Sheriff?"

He smiled. "You can call me, Bob, but only in the office and inside the vehicle."

Chapter 30

Mojave County, Arizona

The following Friday, Krysta picked up the results from the lab. When she returned to the office, she saw Alex Peña in the back office talking to the sheriff. Deputies Davidson and Zuniga were there, too.

"Back here, Krysta," the sheriff motioned. "You remember Alex?"

"Of course." She offered her hand to the man from Chile and greeted the other deputies.

"I called Herb at the lab before you picked up the results. They found two of Travis' fingerprints on the Skoal can. He definitely stopped at that spot and threw it out. The question is when?"

Krysta flashed them a puzzled look.

"Then I called Alex. He was on his way to Las Vegas, so he stopped by. He tells me that he and Travis did *not* stop on the highway when they went to visit the Morales brothers."

"That means Travis must have pulled over there some other time," she said. "What was the other stuff in the package that you sent to the lab?"

The sheriff shrugged. "They don't know yet."

"Does the Skoal can have a manufacturing date on it?" Deputy Zuniga asked. He looked at Krysta with squinted eyes, his jaw set, and flared nose.

Stroman raised his eyebrows, "Good question."

She handed the sheriff the package from the lab. He cut the tape on the box, and set the two specimen envelopes on his desk. Then he brought out a magnifying glass. Turning over the baggy with the Skoal can, Stroman inspected it.

"The only thing here is a stamped number on the tin bottom. Would you go online, Krysta? See if you can find out what that number means?"

Leaning over, she took the glass and examined the box. She sensed Stroman looking at her breasts, straightened quickly, and went back to her computer.

After several minutes she logged online and retrieved information. Stroman stood and bid Peña goodbye. Then the ex-marine walked by her desk and said politely, "Good luck, young lady."

She flashed him a smile. Thank you, Mr. Peña.

Shortly, she gave Stroman the 800 number of the tobacco manufacturer who produced Skoal.

He was on the telephone for at least twenty minutes. She heard him grumbling.

Finally, he came out from behind the desk with his calendar and said, "It was manufactured in late December. Skoal has a fast product turnover in Vegas, the man said. It only remains on the shelf about six weeks."

"What does that mean, sheriff?"

Stroman drew his finger along the calendar. "It was mid-September when Travis and Alex went to see Morales, and I furloughed him on November 17."

She nodded. "So, that means Williams visited the Morales' place well after he was no longer a deputy."

"Yes. Sometime during late winter. I called Travis on February 17, and told him to return to work beginning March 15. He disappeared shortly after that. A friend of his from work told me Travis was headed to Mexico for a vacation."

Deputy Davidson was listening. "So that Skoal can must have been deposited there at the earliest in late January or February," he said.

"Right before or after the time I called him," the sheriff said.

Stroman glanced at his watch. He handed Krysta the calendar and said, "Why don't we take a ride and see if the brothers are home."

He turned to Davidson. "You hold down the fort, Paul."

Zuniga said, "I'm due at the reservation."

"Right, Joe."

On the drive out they discussed how they would question the men. Krysta noted that Stroman had added a penciled entry on the calendar on February 19. "It was the night of Mrs. Stufloten's heart attack. You added it later. Why?"

"Yeah, I was outside the store. The Morales brothers merely stopped to ask if anything was wrong. I thought it was routine, but later noted it."

When the sheriff turned into Morales' driveway, he said, "I'll do most of the talking. When I signal, you speak Arabic. I want to see their reactions."

The dog barked loudly and stood with his paws on the fence. Ricardo Morales was twisting wires together and shoving them into a box. He turned up from his work when they came toward the building. As the two law officers approached him, he said, "Good afternoon, sheriff." He smiled and nodded at Krysta. "*A salaam alaikum.*"

Krysta flinched. "*Alaikum salaam.*"

Stroman frowned.

"Are you Arabic?" Morales asked. "I hear you speak Arabic in market."

She glanced at the sheriff. He nodded.

"Yes. My father is Syrian."

Morales straightened. "My father was Palestinian. After my mother killed on West Bank, he emigrated to Brazil to escape all war. When he marry his second wife, he take her name, Morales, because they treat us like Africans." The small man walked over to the Australian shepherd dog and pointed his finger, then made a down motion. The dog whined and lay down behind the doghouse.

Krysta widened her eyes, seeing the control he had over the dog.

Morales turned toward Stroman. "What I can do for you today, sheriff?"

The officer obviously caught off guard by Morales' quick response, took several awkward seconds to respond. "My other deputy, Travis Williams, is missing. We wondered if he came out here."

Ricardo squinted at Stroman and worked his mouth as if he were chewing seeds. Finally, he answered, "The big man? He come here show us acetylene welder set. It not our stole set."

Stroman glared at Morales. "You sure that was the last time?"

Morales frowned. He placed his hands in his back pockets. "There was dark-skin man with him. He look Indian. He speak good Spanish and Portuguese. I surprised."

Stroman rubbed his chin. "I know the man you're talking about. Where's your brother today?"

"Jorge deliver sign to Las Vegas. And he pick up load of steel."

"You don't remember the deputy coming out here again?"

Morales cocked his head. "No, that last time."

At that moment, Jorge turned into the driveway and pulled down alongside the dog fence. Backing the truck, he stopped where they could unload the steel. He got out of the vehicle looking warily at the law officers.

Before anyone could say anything, Ricardo spoke up. "Jorge my half-brother. His mother Brazilian." He said this loud enough for his brother to hear.

Jorge frowned at Ricardo, then at the sheriff and at Krysta.

"*A salaam alaikum,*" Krysta said.

Jorge stared at her wide-eyed. "What go on here?"

Stroman held a hand up to Ricardo, indicating silence. He turned to Jorge. "When was the last time you saw my deputy Travis Williams?"

Jorge, still looking stunned, was silent for several seconds. His eyes darted from one person to another. Finally, he said, "South American with him. Show welding tanks."

Stroman looked at Ricardo and nodded. Then the lawman folded his arms across his chest, turned, and scanned inside the shop.

Finally, he motioned for Krysta to head for the car. He touched his finger to his hat. "Thank you, gentlemen."

"We happy to help, sheriff," Ricardo replied. Then he turned to his brother, "We unload steel."

They began sliding off long angles of the metal and loudly dropping them inside the shop.

Stroman opened the car door.

"The weed," Krysta said.

Stroman nodded, "Ah, yes."

He picked up a piece of the grass-like stuff he had taken out of the trash. Walking back to Ricardo, he asked, "What's this?"

Ricardo looked at the broken wad. He turned it over in his hands, examining it. He broke it in half and smelled it. Then he nodded. "*Qat*. Where did you get it?"

Stroman's cheeks reddened. "Uh … it was here in the driveway the last time we were here."

Ricardo looked back at him with lowered eyebrows. After a long pause, his expression changed. He asked, "It is legal, no?"

"Uh. I've never heard of it."

"We use to stay awake, when work at night."

"Where'd you get it?"

The small man narrowed his eyes. "We grow in garden." He and Jorge lifted, then dropped another piece of steel with a clang.

"Now, is finished, sheriff? We have rush job."

"Sure. We'll leave you alone." Stroman motioned with his head to Krysta.

They got in the car and the sheriff backed out. Down the road several minutes, Krysta said, "I watched Jorge carefully while you asked Ricardo questions, especially about the weed—qat. Jorge was trembling. They're dirty, Sir."

The sheriff looked out the side window as they passed creosote bushes. "Ricardo is very cool under fire, confident. But, you're right, Jorge would break under pressure."

He remained silent until they reached the area where the pampas grass grew alongside the road. "When Jorge got out of the truck, Ricardo warned him. That's precisely when he said, 'Jorge's mother was Brazilian.' That was a tip-off."

"I see." She nodded. "Very clever."

Stroman made the turn north onto Highway 93. He looked down toward the Colorado River. "They rehearsed everything except the qat. Ricardo wasn't ready for that. But, did you see how cool he played it? He broke it. He smelled it. He turned it over in his hands. All the time he was thinking. Finally, he came right out with it. Smart."

"They speak four languages, Sir. And read those drawings from the computer. Then, they manufacture signs from them."

There was another long silence. Stroman finally said, "I wonder if Travis discovered something. Alex said he took something out of the trash. Suppose he picked up the qat, and later found out it was a narcotic—an Arabic narcotic. That could have happened in Las Vegas while the Saudi Royal family was there. What would he do?"

"He would have come to you, Sir, just like I would. By itself, the qat means nothing."

Stroman rubbed his jaw. "You're probably right."

"We'll sleep on this," he said. His voice sounded tired. Indeed, he looked tired.

"Still, Jorge looked guilty," Krysta added again.

"Definitely."

Chapter 31

Palo Verde Springs, Arizona

The brothers dropped the last piece of steel. Abdul bin Ibrahim — Ricardo — motioned for Zaki to come into the shop.

"They suspicious, my brother. New woman deputy knew we Arabic." He watched Zaki closely.

"They know we chew qat. They arrest us." Zaki's face muscles looked drawn.

Abdul flicked his hand. "I not worried about qat. We make sure no sign of submarine, if they come again. They not find out big deputy here." As Abdul spoke, he wiped off the big hook that he'd used to hit Travis on the head.

"Now we fix cable and finish boat, we put back all floor." Zaki said.

Abdul stared at the pipe their welding cables passed through to the floor below. He pointed, "Big deputy see welding cables go into that hole. He see vent go through roof. We no allow sheriff to see these."

"We tell *mujares* we have rush job and sleep. At night, we work late get boat repaired." Abdul slid open a bin and took out the new piece of stainless cable. "Soon as we fix, we seal floor, and pipe hole."

"What if sheriff find him?" Zaki asked.

"Remember what Father say. 'No worry about things that no happen yet.' We send Omar bin al Habib message. Need to take out submarine fast. We never speak deputy again. Al Qaeda say small microphones easy to hide."

Zaki nodded. "Yes, they put anywhere."

Chapter 32

Camp Tango, 25 miles west of Calexico, California

With binoculars, Kurt Valdez scanned the detention center from the helicopter. The office in Langley referred to the site and the surrounding premises as the "Clinic."

"This wasn't finished the last time I flew over it," he said to the pilot. "It does look like Aqaba, in Jordan."

The chopper pilot, Shawn Gunnison, said, "It certainly does look like something near the Red Sea." He banked the aircraft toward the north end of the parking area where a helipad was marked.

Kurt took one last look from the air. The buildings were situated in the middle of a low bowl, with all of the visible terrain rising away from them. Sand hills with sparse shrubs and clusters of olive and almond trees flayed away in three directions.

Kurt laughed. "They even brought in camels."

"Yeah, I heard they were wild ones from the United Arab Emirates."

The animals grazed on the higher elevations. A high, razor-wire fence beyond eyesight from the buildings kept them in the vicinity.

Three wings connected by corridors to a central square building. Its entrance faced north. The middle wing, the largest, ran perpendicular from the south wall of the main building and ended in a "T" shape.

Gunnison obviously noticed Kurt scanning the buildings. He said, "I hear that southern section, the Tee, is referred to as *"Halawa."* All the cells face south toward the sand hills. They process new detainees there first. What does halawa mean in Arabic?"

Kurt smiled. "*Halawa*" is the Arabic process of painfully removing *all* body hair. Much worse than a wax job."

Gunnison laughed two notes.

"Those two other wings connected at 45 degree angles to opposite corners of the south wall of the main building contain holding cells," Kurt gestured. "Those sand humps with shrubs between the wings make it so they're not directly visible from each other. They weren't there when I was last here."

"That's right," the pilot said.

Kurt said, "With the wings not visible, the new detainees from the Middle

East are taken down the middle to halawa after they're processed. They keep them in individual concrete cells. There's only a twelve-inch window in the door. They can talk loud to each other. When microphones pick up discussions, loudspeakers drowned them out by playing recorded tapes of real torture sessions from Jordan and Egypt. Guards are from Arabic countries also. They have to speak those regional languages.

Gunnison hovered and landed.

Kurt grabbed his backpack and thanked the pilot. In the building, he flashed his ID at the front desk where he underwent a thumb and eye scan.

He remembered on his first visit, before the building was finished, all signs throughout the southern half of the main building and in the wings were written in Arabic—green with the white script. Even writing imprinted on doors and hardware, and on labels on light fixtures, were in script.

Kurt had seen all this on his last inspection visit. Only the outside shrubs, camels, and fence had been added since then.

Eight interrogation rooms in the back half of the main building were set up with one-way glass and video and audio recording equipment. They contained chains with manacles hung from walls along with "tools"—various pliers, metal rods, and swords—and a gas-fired foundry with blackened firebrick. A waterboarding tank and small kennel occupied the opposite corners. IV equipment, electrical shock paddles, and electronic monitoring equipment sat on small shelves behind the headboard of a strap-down operating table. When Kurt walked into the room two days ago, anesthetics stung his nostrils.

Since the northern half of the main building was typical offices, with a large parking area out front, all detainees came in during the night with eyes taped and wearing hoods. Heavily sedated and flown to confuse them about the passage of time, what sometimes required only a four-hour flight from Texas might seem like days.

Kurt was impressed with Camp Tango and with the attention to details. When he walked into the interrogation room, he *felt* like he was in Aqaba. Detainees would believe they were in an Arab country, a true "false-flag" operation. It was even better than the facility the Special Forces used near Kandahar, Afghanistan.

He had personally participated in the capture of Abu Zubaydah, the September 11 leader, and later in his interrogation at that location. He later bristled when it was suggested that the terrorist had been waterboarded. Kurt was adamant against waterboarding and that treatment had not been necessary because the terrorist almost died from the wounds he received during capture.

No actual torture would take place in this facility, he was reassured, merely the appearance of it.

Two Arab interrogators, Fawwaf and Mansoor, had arrived two weeks ago from Aqaba, Jordan, where they'd interrogated Hamas and Hezbollah prisoners. The U.S. cooperated with Jordan with information and exchange of detainees occasionally, but looked the other way on the country's severe treatment methods.

"Give us about a half hour to get the first guy ready," Fawwaf told Kurt. The guard was robust and dark for an Arab, with a *fu-man-chu* mustache.

Mansoor, also well built, was honeyed-colored. He, too, sported an intimidating beard.

Fawwaf and Mansoor had already interrogated the latest 41 detainees that Kurt and Rex rounded up. Rex, the SAP agent in Del Rio connected to the CIA, selected four more that might have information the U.S. wanted.

To soften them up for interrogation, guards marched in six new Jordanian prisoners just recovering from drugs and a trans-Atlantic flight. The prisoners had major facial and head wounds, burned spots and missing fingernails. After recuperating for a few hours, they were roughed up to get them moaning, then noisily ushered into the Halawa Wing two days ago to make sure the new detainees heard and saw their wounds and condition.

Kurt watched through the one-way glass as they brought in Rahman al Talal, one of Rex's catches. As they approached the room with Rahman in tow, a stretcher bearing one of the worst wounded of the Jordanian prisoners was wheeled out. Rahman's eyes went wide when he saw the man.

Fawwaf and Mansoor manipulated Rahman in a half-circle so he spotted the tools, manacles and waterboarding tank. Mansoor turned on a valve and a fire burst forth in the foundry. He set a round poker on a brick ledge with its tip in the fire. They stripped Rahman naked, shoved and strapped him into a steel chair, and jerked his legs apart.

Fawwaf returned shortly with an enormous black German shepherd. The dog lunged for the detainee. Fawwaf shouted and jerked it back. The animal lunged again, for the detainee's throat this time. It required both guards to force the dog to its chain anchor.

Fawwaf flipped a switch and placed his hand on a glass globe that buzzed loudly and sizzled with electrical discharges. He held up two paddles and a bolt flashed between them.

Mansoor noisily rattled the poker in the foundry flame. He removed it and held the dark red poker up so the detainee could see it. Rahman trembled and began crying.

Kurt watched through the one-way glass for his moment.

Fawwaf got into the prisoner's face. He snarled, "What we want to know is, who is your contact?" Fawwaf began displaying photographs in front of Rahman, allowing several breaths for the detainee to study them before bringing up the next.

Rahman, sobbing, blubbered and refused to acknowledge any of the al Qaeda, Hamas or Hezbollah leaders in the photos. He merely shook his head and cried louder. The seventh picture they showed Rahman was the terrorist who crossed into the U.S. with him. Fawwaf held it before the prisoner's face for several seconds longer.

When he started to bring forth another picture, Mansoor slammed the metal poker on the table. He thrust the red-hot end toward Rahman's groin. The black shepherd raged to the length of his chain. Rahman shit. He screamed and wept louder.

For the next few minutes, Kurt watched various intimidating thrusts of the poker and lunges by the dog. When the interrogators returned to the picture of the terrorist who entered the U.S. with Rahman, this time he nodded and mumbled an Arab name.

Kurt opened the door and entered. He shouted, "What are you doing? We don't treat our prisoners this way!" He got into the interrogators' faces and gave them a good dressing down. Finally, he demanded that they release the man and give him his clothes.

Obeying orders, Mansoor and Fawwaf released Rahman. They wrestled the dog under control and left the room.

Kurt took Rahman to a restroom to clean himself and get dressed. Afterward they went to an office. Kurt gestured to a chair in front of a desk.

Earlier, Kurt and Rex had set it up so the two interrogators from Jordan would move to another interrogation room and replay the torture scenario with the dog and implements again. Rex would interrupt that supposed torture at the right moment, exactly as Kurt did.

Kurt now sat at the desk and plopped the photographs on the desk. He took his phone, dialed some numbers, and then said in Arabic, "We are ready, connect us."

He gestured with the phone to Rahman and said, "Your mother is coming on the phone. Tell her you are in prison here in Jordan."

Rahman burst out weeping and blubbered, "No, not like this."

Kurt glowered at him. "You will talk to her or go back to that room. We have people who know where she lives. We know you have two brothers. You wouldn't want anything to happen to your family? Would you Rahman al Talal de Ajloun?"

Rahman flinched when Kurt named his home village.

A female voice on the phone said, "A salaam alaikum."

Kurt handed it to Rahman. The detainee choked as he spoke to his mother. He told her he was okay and that he was not in serious trouble.

Kurt could tell that she scolded him for associating with those who make trouble for all Arabs.

Large tears ran down Rahman's face when he finally handed the phone to Kurt.

Kurt laid a series of photographs of terrorists in front of the young man. He cited their names and aliases, their families and nationalities. He detailed what plots they had been involved in and their history with al Qaeda, Hamas and Hezbollah.

"None of these men are with al Qaeda or Hamas or Hezbollah now. They are working for us. We pay them to get information and infiltrate those organizations. Many of them have families of their own and earn a decent living. They are living safely in Canada and the United States. Their families are protected in their home countries."

Kurt flipped over to a picture. "This is Nazir Bedehan. He is a Pakistani who helped us catch Mahmood Fhazlula. Fhazlula set up an attack that killed eight CIA intelligence experts near Kabul. Nazir located Mahmood near Islamabad, Pakistan, where they trapped him and five other top leaders."

Kurt flipped over another picture. "This is Nazir today with his family. They live in Canada. He is an engineer." The photograph showed a man in a brown tweed suit with an attractive wife and a boy and girl. Kurt showed the young man three more pictures of other former terrorists.

Rahman blinked and stared hard at the photos.

Kurt went back to the original shots. "These terrorists were all caught and are in prisons in Saudi Arabia, Jordan, Egypt and Yemen." Kurt tapped two pictures. "These two died there at young ages." He let that information sink in.

"I am a Muslim. I have two wives. Here are photographs of them with my five children." Kurt showed Rahman two pictures of his children and wives in burkas. "We live in a Muslim country."

Now Kurt took out several more of infiltrators who had crossed into the U.S. recently. He pointed to two of them. "They were with you when you crossed." Kurt told Rahman who they were, where they came from and their associations.

The detainee blinked in surprise.

Flipping to others, Kurt said, "What I want you to do is tell us who these others are, and whether they entered the United States or Canada."

Chapter 33

Boulder City, Nevada

Sheriff Bob Stroman pulled out a chair at the breakfast table and opened the newspaper.

Carrie Stroman handed the sheriff his favorite breakfast, a ham and cheddar omelet with onions, bell peppers and garlic. She wore tight denim shorts and sandals, and had her hair in rollers. To the sheriff, his wife was sexy. Her nice figure was the result of almost daily two-mile runs and aerobic exercises. She fixed her hair to match her daughter's.

"You snored like an old bear last night."

He grinned. "Drank too many beers."

"You'll have to change your whole schedule next year after the new Pat Tillman Bridge and sheriff's office opens."

"Yeah. Twenty minutes less driving."

"That new bridge looks scary. Hard to believe they'll drive semi-trucks over it."

Stroman nodded. "An engineering miracle."

"Well good morning, sleepyhead," Carrie said as she turned. Fourteen-year-old Diane plopped her backpack on a chair and gave her father a peck on the cheek.

"Got any more of that omelet mix left, mom?" Diane looked over the contents on the kitchen counter.

Stroman glowered at his daughter's short skirt. When the girl turned side on, he inspected her legs, butt, curled blond hair and budding breasts. He swallowed hard.

"That's an awfully short skirt, Honey."

"Oh, Dad. That's the style!"

"Well, I don't like it. It's … dangerous."

Carrie looked at the girl and they burst out laughing. "He's getting to be an old man," Carrie said.

The sheriff growled. "I'm the one who investigates crimes against girls and women. If you saw what I have, you would be more cautious."

"Sure, Dad."

Stroman heard the sliding glass door open and the dog come in. He reached and scratched the Lab's head. "Good boy, Shadow. That's the way. Stay down." The dog wagged his tail so hard his whole rear end went back and forth.

"I've got some omelet ready for you, too, Derrick." Carrie handed the boy a plate. "Your game is at 3:30, right?"

"Yes, Mom. We play Henderson today. They're tough. They beat North Las Vegas last week."

"Just keep catching those passes like you did last week, Derrick."

"Awe, Freddie exaggerates, Pop. Quinton hit me right on the hands four times."

"Well, you still caught 'em. Put the dog back outside while we eat, son. Before you sit down."

Derrick said, "Come on Shadow. Outside."

"Next soccer game is Thursday? Right Diane?"

"Yeah, Dad. You're really going to have to make one of them before the season's over."

"You know your dad can't leave work that early." Carrie frowned at Diane.

"You know what I'd like?" Stroman asked.

"What's that darling?"

"All of you should come over to the office Saturday and meet Krysta."

"She's a woman, huh Dad?"

The sheriff smiled at his son. "Yeah, she worked for the government in Washington."

Diane forked a piece of omelet into her mouth. "How did she get a job like that? She must be *really* smart."

"Yes, she is."

Diane glanced up at the clock. "We're gonna be late, Mom, we don't get going."

"Okay. Brush your teeth, kids."

Stroman stood and kissed Carrie and the kids. Both of them turned their heads down.

Chapter 34

Mojave County, Arizona

"Can you see what it is?" the younger boy said.

The wiry sixteen-year-old with sand-colored hair adjusted the scope on his rifle and opened his eyes wide to get a better look. "Can't make out what they're digging."

"Coyotes never hang around people, Danny. They looked right at us and they're not runnin'. Why don't you shoot nearby, chase 'em off?"

Danny aimed the rifle and pulled off a shot. Dust kicked up to the right of the animals from the .22-short. They ran from the diggings, but stopped and kept vigilant eyes on the two boys.

"Come on, Joey. Let's check it out." The older boy chambered another round and grasped the rifle by the middle of the stock. He rose and moved toward the four coyotes.

The animals still seemed reluctant to leave the spot. They backed away, but circled warily.

The boys came out into the open now, where the coyotes could fully view them. Three animals loped away toward a canyon opening. A large, mostly-black male lingered. He stood obliquely to the boys, head held low, tongue lolling.

"What is it?" The younger boy hurried to keep up. Joey, nearly as tall as his brother, weighed a third less. His red hair stood in sweaty tufts.

Danny strode toward the holes. After twenty or more paces, he stopped and brought the rifle up to his shoulder again. He squeezed off one last shot. A spatter of dust kicked up, off to the side of the big male. Finally convinced, the coyote turned and ran into the canyon, and out of sight.

Danny went forward then stopped again. He focused his scope on the diggings. His eyes grew wide as he peered through it. "Shit!"

"What is it? Come on, let me look." Joey reached for the rifle.

"It's a human arm, sticking out of the dirt."

"Let's get out of here!"

The older boy continued walking toward the digging, fascinated.

"Come on, Danny!" Joey shouted.

Danny shuffled slowly toward the arm sticking out of the ground. "Don't be afraid. The dead can't hurt you." After another fifty feet, he turned to his brother and said, "We need to call the sheriff, Joey."

"Call Mom on the cell phone."

The older boy stopped where he could now see the arm clearly, curving upward, definitely a woman–slender fingers with long fingernails painted red. He took out his cell phone and rotated it to a signal connection.

His younger brother held back, staring down at his sibling from a ridge.

His mother answered after four rings. Danny exclaimed, "Mom, Joey and I found coyotes digging up a body! You need to call the sheriff!"

After a few moments of excited questions, she told them not to leave the spot.

Danny said, "Okay, we won't leave. I'm holding the coyotes off with my .22."

"Exactly where are you?"

"Off Highway 93. A dirt road near Mile Marker 7. We walked an hour."

"So that's about three miles east of 93. Where your dad took us in the dune buggy on the Fourth?"

"Yeah, Mom, the signal's breaking up!"

Danny clicked off the phone and walked gingerly toward the hand sticking out of the ground. It appeared stiff and white, with tooth marks on the torn skin, but no blood.

Chapter 35

Mojave County, Arizona

Krysta Mazur picked up the phone on the second ring. Sheriff Earl McGibbon from Las Vegas asked for Sheriff Stroman.

"They're all off today, Sir. I volunteered to hold down the fort."

"See if you can run him down. They may have found the three young women who've been missing for two weeks."

Krysta snapped to attention. "When . . . where?"

"Down off 93. Four miles east of Mile Marker 7. Find Bob. Tell him I'm bringing in some cadaver dogs."

Krysta acknowledged and hung up. She immediately dialed the sheriff's home number. After five rings, his answering machine came on. She hung up and tried his cell phone. He had told her emphatically not to call him this Sunday unless it was a real emergency. This qualified. She listened to four rings, then the recording. Apparently, he was out of range.

She left a brief message explaining Sheriff McGibbon's call. She added that she would call Reserve Sheriff Peña to fill in, take her cell phone, a camera and recorder, and head for the site. From there, she would relay the GPS coordinates.

Locking the office, she headed out in the SUV, barreling toward Highway 93, where she turned south. As the vehicle crested the hill above Lake Mead, the desert opened up before her. The blue water of the Colorado River came into view in several places far down to the right.

As she drove, she went through the particulars of the report in her mind, psyching herself for dead bodies . . . decaying dead bodies.

Two weeks ago, three young women who worked at the Spotted Leopard, a topless nightclub in Vegas, had disappeared. The story dominated the news. Investigators found out the women had engaged in room-service prostitution as a sideline. Authorities temporarily held two men, previous bodyguards, for questioning.

Krysta passed Mile Marker 7, went over two knolls, and then saw the turnoff coming up on the left. She heard a ring.

Sheriff Stroman's voice boomed. "If I understood the message correctly, Earl thinks he's found those missing women."

"Sounds like it, Sheriff."

"I'll drop Carrie and the kids off at the house. Take me at least a half-hour to get to the site. Take lots of photos and recordings till I get there."

"Yes, Sir. I'm approaching the turnoff now."

"See you there."

Swerving across the middle line, Krysta slowed almost to a stop at the turnoff. Numerous tire tracks led away on a bumpy, hard-crusted road. The SUV bounced over potholes as she followed a twisting jeep trail up a rise. The tracks crested a knoll and headed downhill. As the road headed into a valley, she saw several vehicles.

Sheriff McGibbon followed two black German shepherds on leashes. Three deputies, shaded by a makeshift awning, dug around what she could see were bodies. Everyone wore surgical gloves, masks and dark glasses.

She pulled to a stop, waved to Malcomb Johnson and Randy Hammond, two Las Vegas deputies she had met previously. The well-built men, along with a slender deputy she didn't know, were digging. She winced and coughed when she exited the SUV, donned a mask, and made her presence known to the sheriff.

The sheriff was a medium-sized man with a potbelly and a brush mustache that matched the blended colors of his graying brown hair and sideburns.

Sheriff McGibbon said, "There's no doubt it's the three women from the Spotted Leopard. Tattoos and navel jewels match descriptions." He pointed to two boys sitting back on a nearby ridge, watching the work. "Those boys found the bodies. Coyotes were digging 'em up when they arrived with their target rifle."

Nearly gagging, Krysta began taking photos of the cadavers and held a microphone close to her mouth entering observations into a recorder. She said, "Three Caucasian women approximately 25 to 32. No obvious marks indicating strangulation or beatings. Pubic hair shaved on the two blondes. The dark-haired woman has a thin black strip remaining with a multi-colored bird tattooed above it. Light blonde has a chain tattoo around her right ankle, and a small red devil on her left shoulder. The dark blonde also has several chain tattoos, and a gold ring with a pearl in her navel.

Deputy Malcomb Johnson moved away from the bodies and vomited. He held his stomach as he retched.

Krysta felt bile rise but managed to hold it back. She continued, "Both blondes have incisions for breast enlargements. Dark-haired person appears natural, with medium sized breasts. Latter also has stretch marks indicating she bore a child or children."

Turning when she heard the whine of a SUV, she saw it coming over the ridge. "Here comes the sheriff now."

McGibbon waved to the vehicle.

Sheriff Stroman guided the vehicle to a stop and got out. Krysta saw him wince when he caught the full force of the overpowering smell. Pulling on a mask, he greeted the other sheriff.

"Hey, Bob." Sheriff McGibbon offered his hand. "Sorry to encroach, but I thought you'd need the cadaver dogs."

"No problem, Earl." Stroman stared at the bodies. "These the missing women?"

"Yep. Description and tattoos match."

For the next half hour, the sheriffs, deputies, and dogs scoured the area. Stroman, coughing from the stench, told Krysta to take additional close-ups of the white, stiffened bodies now lying on elevated pedestals of dirt. She recorded that no buried articles were found with them.

"Better get 'em outta the heat, into the body bags and over to the lab," McGibbon said.

"Yeah, lemme sign that release, Earl." Stroman leaned over and signed off on the bodies, which would allow the Las Vegas sheriff to take them to their lab facilities.

Two ambulances arrived, and Krysta watched the men pull on surgical gloves, bag the bodies and slide them into the back. Then she took photos of the imprints in the soil where the bodies had lain. The vehicles took off, the slender deputy with one of them. Malcomb and Randy took fine rakes and went through the remaining soil. Finding nothing, the sheriffs looked at each other, acknowledging that the job was complete.

McGibbon allowed the large male German shepherd to go to a boulder because he was acting as if he needed to urinate. Krysta watched the dog sniff the rock then pause for a long moment. The other dog, obviously interested, joined the first. Now both dogs started sniffing around.

The two sheriffs had diverted their attention, discussing the murder of the three women.

"Why are the dogs acting like that?" Krysta asked.

McGibbon looked back, startled. "Well, I'll be damned! Might be another body. Judging by the dogs, it's been there awhile. Scent's about gone. See how Rex's goin' all the way around that boulder?"

"Lemme get a chain outta the SUV," Stroman said. See if we can move it." He went to the vehicle and backed it up, swerving to miss the freshly dug holes.

Krysta joined the deputies and helped wrap the chain around the big rock. She backed off as Stroman put the vehicle in low four-wheel-drive, eased forward and dragged it several feet. She photographed the flat-bottomed boulder as it slid, and noted it on the recorder.

With the soil now exposed, the dogs sniffed and pawed the ground.

"There definitely *was* a body here," McGibbon said. He turned to the deputies. "Work slowly on this one. Don't destroy any evidence."

Krysta pulled on surgical gloves and took Randy's place with a shovel. She and Malcomb dug and threw shovelfuls of dirt onto a screen. After several minutes, there were only some plant seeds and a few small, irregular rocks on it, with a pyramid shaped pile of sand underneath.

They had dug nearly three feet down when McGibbon asked them to back off. "May be a false alarm."

The male dog lunged back into the hole and pawed at one spot.

"Huh! Try that spot there, Malcomb," Sheriff McGibbon said.

The deputy acknowledged and probed a rod into the ground. He hit something solid.

Everyone's attention now focused on the deputies digging with hand trowels, poking, hitting solid material, then scraping dirt away. Finally, a bone appeared.

"I'll be damned," Stroman said. "Skeleton. Old, no flesh left."

Sheriff McGibbon winced. "Something was still decaying. Wasn't buried *that* long ago."

Krysta stared as the skeleton emerged into view. It had been buried about four feet deep, apparently naked, for there were no clothing fragments, buttons or zippers. When the skull appeared, she was surprised that there was no hair, only stubble.

The experienced deputies dug a large hole around the bones and then picked away, sometimes with awls, to remove the debris from the skeleton. Underneath, near the spine, there was apparently still matter decaying.

"Two or three years in the ground, I'd judge," McGibbon said. "Some decaying. Big, robust man. Shaved head . . . see, a little stubble shows after his skin dried!" McGibbon pointed to the now emerging skull.

"Shaved his head?" Stroman said this as he eased in closer for a better look. "Big ... man."

"I'd say six-two," McGibbon said. "See the biceps bone? Imprint of muscles. This guy lifted heavy weights."

Stroman got down on his knees as the face emerged. He jerked back.

Krysta saw that the teeth were missing. It was obvious the teeth had been knocked out with force, probably with a hammer. She looked at Sheriff Stroman's blanched face.

"No fingertips, either," Malcomb said. "Someone didn't want this guy identified. But, his pubic hair is still intact. We can do a DNA on him."

"Uncover his left knee!"

Krysta jerked at the sharpness of Stroman's voice. Now it dawned on her that this might be Deputy Travis Williams.

Bob Stroman straightened when the left kneecap emerged from the soil.

His face grew dark red. He swallowed and said, "Bullet wound on the knee cap from the marines."

Krysta spotted the chipped spot on the bone. She brought her hand up to the mask.

Sheriff McGibbon, now realizing this must be Deputy Williams, put his hand on Stroman's shoulder, "I'm sorry, Bob. We'll do forensics on him first. See what the details are."

Everyone was silent as Stroman stared at the skeleton, his cheek twitching, muscles in his jaw repeatedly knotting. After a few moments, he said, "Broke his teeth out, cut his fingers off, dumped him naked, and then dragged that boulder over him." Stroman's eyes moistened.

The other officers stared down at the emerging skeleton.

"Don't beat yourself up, Bob," McGibbon finally said. "Our labs can do all the work. Boys'll scour everything here ... even check the boulder for prints. I'll get you a full report."

Stroman took one long, last look at the skeleton. Then he turned to Krysta, "I'll meet you back at the office."

As he got into the vehicle to leave, Krysta saw the two boys, sitting on the hill rise. They had taken bottled drinks out of their backpacks.

She glanced over her shoulder and saw Sheriff McGibbon guiding the two dogs into the backseat of the Clark County sheriff's car. The deputies continued to trowel dirt onto the screen, which she now sifted for small objects.

When the deputies had the skeleton completely uncovered, they slid it onto a fiberglass board and weighted it down with blankets.

She said goodbye to Randy and Malcomb as they transferred it into their SUV.

Twice she had locked eyes with Randy for several heartbeats. She noticed him checking her out while they worked—glancing at her legs. But, in moments, the two deputies were gone.

Several minutes later, Krysta left the valley and headed toward Highway 93 with the two boys. She asked them for particulars while recording their responses. Danny, the sixteen-year-old, drove an old Toyota that couldn't make it over the high-centered roads. She returned them to their car, thanked and complimented them on doing a good job reporting the discovery. Then, she took a few photos of them for the record.

Chapter 36

Palo Verde Springs, Arizona

"They find body!" Abdul bin Ibraham looked at his brother and widened his eyes. He plopped down a newspaper.

Zaki blanched. "Sheriff take us away."

"We make ready go to Mexico. The families, *todos*."

"We die in prison, my brother."

"We not caught, yet. Omar bin al Habib have to move submarine before they find. I send him emergency email on new computer fast."

Zaki's hand shook as he looked at the photograph of Deputy Travis Williams.

"Stop! We have time. We make plans before move."

Abdul thought for a moment. He reached into the bottom drawer of the file cabinet, pulled the files forward, and took out a packet. "Remember al Habib give us DZ-41 pills. Al Qaeda use when this happen." He said, "We not be take alive."

"The death pills?" Zaki swallowed.

Abdul removed two small envelopes from the packet. Holding a flap open, the two brothers looked inside at the pink capsules. He recalled the grave look al Habib had given them. "'If they know you make killing, and come, you have to kill you.'"

Chapter 37

Mojave County, Arizona

On Monday morning, Krysta came into the office ten minutes early. Deputy Davidson was in the front and Sheriff Stroman sat at his desk in the back room.

She greeted Davidson and approached the sheriff carefully. "Have you heard anything yet?" She pushed her hair behind her ear.

He leaned back in his chair with a grim look on his face. "Just talked to Earl. Only thing they found out about the skeleton, other than the missing teeth and fingertips, was a bump on the back of the skull. A large, curved blunt object made it." Stroman spoke in a low monotone. "The blow was probably not enough to kill him."

Krysta hadn't seen him this grave before. She watched him turn over Travis' Skoal can in his hands. "They're preparing to ship the remains to North Carolina for burial."

"We should wire some flowers."

Stroman squeezed his lips together. "That's a good idea."

"I studied your notes again," she said. "The dates you narrowed down the disappearance to. We might be able to get the National Security Agency to send us pictures from the satellite flyovers for those two weeks. I mean, now that we know there was foul play."

He studied her with a lethargic look.

"I could call a former associate with NSA and say there is a homicide investigation ongoing. Ask him to fast-track it."

"It would be a real long shot—with the hunt for the heads of al Qaeda and the Afghanistan war going on."

"I think they would do it, now, Bob."

"We would need flyover photos beginning February 18, 2009, the day after I called Travis."

Krysta nodded and returned to her desk. She and the sheriff had discussed Sunday's incidents for two hours after they returned to the office yesterday. Even with the shock of discovering Travis' remains, the find was not unexpected. Stroman was convinced there had been foul play all along. But a brutal murder? That was a shock. The teeth knocked out, the fingers cut off!

Krysta felt a queasy feeling in her stomach all evening after the brainstorming. They reviewed several of the earlier conclusions from the 2009 investigation. One contingency that they kept returning to was that Travis had somehow discovered something sinister about the Morales brothers.

At four o'clock, Sheriff Stroman said, "I'm gonna take off early."

Krysta looked up from her desk at the officer. He appeared weary and depressed. His eyes were red.

"Would you finish that email and send it? Paul will return again later for the night shift. I'll see you in the morning."

"Okay, Bob."

Sheriff Stroman didn't look back. He merely slouched through the door to the vehicles.

Chapter 38

Camp Tango, Near Calexico, California

Kurt Valdez tidied his office, stacking piles of papers on the 'in-basket', inserting loose sheaves into their proper files, and then filing them away. He took out his favorite family photographs, one with Siamarra and him, with their two boys and girl, and one with his second wife, Baderi and him with their daughter. Finally, there was a picture of them all together, with his mother-in-law, Raisa, included.

There was a rapping on the door, and Kurt said, "come in." The interrogator Fawwaf brought in Rahman al Talal. Kurt thanked Fawwaf and the Jordanian closed the door behind him.

Kurt smiled at the Palestinian and pointed to the chair in front of his desk.

Kurt pressed an intercom button and said in Arabic, "We are ready, connect us."

After a moment, he handed the phone to Rahman.

Rahman beamed and said, "*A salaam alaikum, Mama.*"

Her voice boomed from the speaker.

Kurt flashed five with his hand and wound a timer. He left the office.

When Kurt returned, Rahman bid his mother and brother goodbye. He had tears of joy in his eyes. He wiped them from his face unashamed.

Kurt asked, "They are well?"

"Yes! *Shukran a saddique*—Thank you very much, my friend."

Kurt again reminded Rahman he was a Muslim, also. He glanced at the calendar. "Fifteenth day. We have made much progress."

Gesturing to the picture of Nazir Bedehan and his family, the Pakistani engineer wearing a brown tweed suit, Kurt said, "We are flying him here to talk to you and some of your fellow detainees."

For the next several minutes they engaged in easy conservation about Palestine. Then, taking out several more photos of infiltrators who had crossed into the U.S. recently, Kurt pointed to two of them, the same two they discussed fifteen days ago. "They were with you when you crossed." He told Rahman their names, where they came from, and their associations.

As he had done during their first conversations, the detainee blinked surprise that Americans had this information.

Laying out a larger group of photographs, Kurt said, "Could you identify any of these others? We want to know if they are in the United States or Canada?"

He included two pictures of Ramzi bin Omeri in the group. Kurt excused himself while Rahman studied them. "Take your time. I am going to pray and bring us some eats."

After twenty minutes or so, after a prayer session, Kurt returned with two trays of food.

The two men conversed freely again during the meal and Kurt learned several new things about growing up in the refugee camps of the West Bank. He had not heard the expression the "Swiss Cheese Solution," before.

Rahman told him that all Palestinians used it in reference to how the Jews carved up their lands. "The Palestinians get the deserts and the holes in the cheese. The Jews get the good farmland, the water sources, the sewage treatment facilities and valuable minerals."

Kurt scrutinized the young man as he spoke and noted his anger and his pain. During an earlier session, the Palestinian had spoke reverently of Hanadi Jaradat.

Every intelligence officer in the Middle East knew Hanadi's story. A twenty-nine-year-old law student who lived in Janin on the West Bank, not far from the cosmopolitan Israeli Mediterranean city of Haifa, she had lost a brother and her fiancé in "targeted killings" by the Israeli military. She was standing next to her brother when died.

She put on a *hijab*, strapped on explosives and calmly rode a taxi through the Israeli security barrier to Maxim's restaurant in Haifa, at the end of a jetty the extended into the sea. Maxims was an elegant restaurant that catered to both Jews and Arabs, a symbol of the new attitude.

On the Jewish Shabbat, October 4, 2003, Hanadi calmly watched two Israeli Jewish families, three generations, laughing and enjoying their Shabbat dinner. She commented on how cute the children were, frolicking and running around the table.

Finally, she told the driver he should leave. Then she stood up, walked calmly between the families and pulled the pin on her suicide vest. She killed 29 people, including both families, and herself.

After the meal and more tea, Kurt plied Rahman for four more hours, coercing and showing the detainee the families of two more terrorists who had been turned.

That afternoon, Rahman finally put his finger on the photo of Ramzi bin Omeri. The detainee pointed at two more pictures of Ramzi from the group of photos.

Kurt's heart beat faster. He focused on Rahman.

Several more minutes of careful questioning ensued before Kurt extracted the information he needed. The Palestinian leaked intelligence that a large group of terrorists would infiltrate into the United States.

Rahman revealed that they were supposed to meet Ramzi bin Omeri south of Las Vegas, Nevada. Another group was coming across near El Paso, Texas, from across the Rio Grande River. The approximate date was eight weeks from now.

Kurt felt a surge of satisfaction. It was extremely rare to find a low-level jihadist who knew any detailed plans. He logged the information. This would earn him a much needed break to visit his family for at least six weeks before confronting the Snow Leopard.

Chapter 39

Mojave County, Arizona

Krysta looked up as the door to the office opened. Several days had passed since the body discovery. Sheriff Stroman appeared completely perplexed. "Guess what!" he said.

Krysta pushed her hair behind her ear. "What?"

"The Morales brothers up and moved!"

"Moved?"

"That's right. I was in Stufloten's this afternoon. Olé told me they closed up shop and went back to Mexico. The owner of the building installed a hydraulic lift and a mechanic rents the place now."

Krysta looked at the sheriff open mouthed for several seconds.

"They told Olé Ricardo's wife's father was dying. And they decided to return to the old country to be near him. They left during the night."

"Huh! Well, that's an odd end to that story."

"I guess so," the sheriff said. "Olé said the mechanic's family is poor. Appear to be barely making it. Children in dirty, ragged clothes. Says he wonders if they'll be able to pay the family bills."

Stroman took his gunbelt off as he headed to his back office. "I guess we can forget them."

Krysta typed questions into the computer: Check owner of property, and where did the Morales brothers go?

Chapter 40

Mojave County, Arizona

Krysta Mazur entered the sheriff's office a half hour early, surprised to see Sheriff Bob Stroman already at his desk.

Walking to the back she asked, "What's up, sheriff?"

He scanned a topographical map with his magnifying glass, tilting a light on it. "NSA sent the microfilms for the dates we requested." He gestured at a government envelope. "One photo was taken every eleven minutes of the area we're interested in. The photos have the time and grid numbers on 'em. This topo map matches the numbers to locations that we can use to find the squares we need to examine more closely. Like in Palo Verde Springs."

"We don't have viewing equipment, Sir."

"There's a science lab in Las Vegas. Randy Hammond's going with you to help."

Her stomach tightened when he mentioned Randy. "From the Clark County office?"

"Yeah. Sheriff McGibbon has an interest in the case now, too. Since *they* found the body."

"So where do I meet Randy?"

"Scientific Technologies. Five blocks from the trade show. You know where Koval Street ends on the east side?"

"Near the Vienna."

"Right. The lab is located three blocks south from there on Howard Hughes Parkway, near the financial area–banks, et cetera."

"What're we looking for?"

"Start with February 18, 2009–say eight o'clock a.m. Find the grid square that is east of Palo Verde Springs, where the Morales Brother's shop is located."

Krysta still appeared puzzled. "We find twenty microfilms of a satellite looking down on their shop, then what?"

Stroman flashed her a disgusted look. "We're looking for his car!"

"Oh!" She pushed her hair behind her ear. The light bulb went on in her brain.

The sheriff said, "He owned a used highway patrol car sold at auction. An old black-and-white. Shouldn't be too hard to spot. That's the one thing we have going for us."

Krysta smiled and reached for the government package.

Stroman threw her the car keys. "Take the Jimmy. Randy will meet you at eight-thirty, when the place opens. Park near Charles Schwab's parking garage. Short walk from there."

Krysta turned and walked to the front office. She stopped and bent down to check a band-aid on her calf where a thorn bush had gouged her. When she looked up at the sheriff, he glanced at her cleavage. She straightened quickly. "February ...?"

"February 18, 2009 — 8 a.m. That's shortly after he was last seen."

She turned and smiled to herself as she exited the building. That was the first time since they found Travis' body that Stroman had shown any response to her. The sheriff moped around the office, lethargic and depressed, since they confirmed the body's ID.

An hour later, Krysta Mazur parked in the multi-level garage. She picked up the office briefcase that contained her notebook and the government envelope with the microfilms, and got out of the sheriff's vehicle.

"Kyrsta?"

Turning, she saw him. "Hey, Randy."

"What've you got?" He smiled and raised his eyebrows as he scanned her short khaki uniform that had the Arizona Sheriff's office insignia on her shirt sleeve.

"Microfilms from NSA. They have views taken on the dates Travis Williams disappeared. The sheriff wants to start with the last morning he was seen."

Randy pointed to a building a block past the Wells Fargo bank. "Science labs are over there."

The two deputies entered through a glass door. An Oriental secretary glanced at their uniforms. She gestured to soft-cushioned chairs.

In a couple of minutes, a heavy-set, middle-aged man with thick glasses, flaky skin, and dandruff on his shoulders came out wearing a lab apron. He introduced himself as Kevin Dunn and motioned the two to follow him. Passing through three doors, they entered the lab. A strong chemical smell came from an area where a machine printed lines and moved rapidly around in quick lurches.

Several other men and women viewed images and operated copying machines. The machines moved flatbeds around and made whirring and clacking noises while they printed.

Dunn pointed to several viewing scopes. Two were in use. "You can use numbers 111 and 112. Hand me a sheet of microfilm."

Krysta opened one envelope and handed him the other. Dunn loaded it in the machine, and turned on its light. He turned two knobs to focus an image. "Aerial photos?"

"Yes," Krysta said. "Of Arizona, where we suspect a murder was committed." She unfolded the map of Palo Verde Springs. "Here are the grids we're looking for. We want February 18 and 19, 2009."

Dunn looked through the view glasses and adjusted the viewing plate. "Look in here and you can see the grid coordinates and dates and the photo ID number under each photo." He moved aside so the two deputies could see how the machine worked.

"When you find photos that you want, jot down their numbers. We'll blow 'em up and print them for you." Dunn gestured to another machine that made copies from the microfilm.

Krysta and Randy thanked the man.

Krysta counted out and handed Randy six microfilm sheets. "Might as well start with these." She took out six for herself.

Randy grimaced and shook his head.

She pulled a stool over to the viewer and scrutinized the first image. Adjusting the lens, she worked two knobs to locate the ID information for an individual photo. She was surprised how much she had to magnify the mostly black negative to make out any details. It took her several minutes to figure out how the photos were laid out on the sheet, and how the indexing system worked. She heard Randy grumbling under his breath.

Three hours later, Dunn returned. "Ready for a break?" He signaled for them to follow.

Krysta straightened, twisted her torso back and forth, and rolled her shoulders.

In the lunch room, Dunn handed them each a cup of coffee. Passing beyond a microwave and refrigerator, he gestured to a box of doughnuts and paper plates. A roll of paper towels stood upright on the table.

"Tedious work," Randy complained. He reached for the coffee and took two chocolate-covered doughnuts out of the box. He placed them on a paper plate and ripped off two paper towels, handing one to Krysta.

She selected a plain, unglazed doughnut. "Find anything interesting?"

Randy dropped a sugar cube in his coffee. "Frigging negatives. Took me almost a half hour to figure out how to find the turnoff to Palo Verde Springs."

"I know. I finally figured how to find the town. Sheet moves the wrong way when you turn the knobs." She glanced around the brightly lit eating area. A short heavyset woman in a lab coat pressed buttons on the microwave and it growled. An electric cook-top rested on a counter alongside the humming refrigerator.

After their break was over, including stretching and walking around on the advice of one of the employees, they went back to work. It was more than an hour afterward, when Krysta blurted, "Randy, look at this!"

The other deputy moved over to her stool and adjusted the focus. "Outstanding! A black-and-white car!"

"Guess where it is? At our primary suspect's workshop!"

The other deputy looked at Krsyta with widened eyes. Looking back at the photo, he read the time and date, "10:21, 2-18-09. That the date you're looking for?"

"That's the day after Travis talked to the sheriff. Last morning he was seen."

Randy moved one screen right and left. "Nothing on either side of the picture?"

"The satellite moves the lens one-half degree before each photo," Krysta said. "You can join the pictures to make a mosaic. Let me back in there."

Randy slid off the stool.

"The images take eleven minutes to return to the same grid," she said.

"I knew that," he said gruffly.

"I'm going to look that far back, then that far ahead." She moved the images back and said, "Nothing back there." Moving ahead, the sheet ran out. Krysta replaced the microfilm sheet with the next in sequence. It took her several minutes to focus and locate the grid she wanted. "Bingo! Look at this!"

Randy once again slid onto her stool and adjusted the focus. "What?"

"Look behind the building."

The man turned the knobs and chastised himself, "The other way, dummy." After a moment, he exclaimed, "A covered car!"

"What's the time?" Krysta asked.

"Ten-forty-two."

"I bet something happened between 10:21 and 10:42. Someone moved the *black-and-white* car behind the building and covered it." Randy frowned.

"Move forward eleven minutes," she said.

Randy worked the knobs and moved the microfilm around. "Nothing."

"Let me look." She studied the image then advanced the sheet another eleven minutes. Adjusting the focus and zooming in further on the building, she turned the knobs slowly. "There! Take a look."

Randy slid back in and adjusted the knobs. After a moment, he said, "I'll be damned! They moved the car inside the building."

Krysta looked again. The back end of the car barely protruded at a 45-degree angle from the Morales brothers' garage. It was enough for the viewer to make out the trunk and one taillight. She moved the microfilm. To the east of the building, she saw the brothers' Toyota pickup parked on the gravel. She remembered it from her visit to the premises.

Randy returned with Dunn. The lab manager took the numbers of eight photos covering 88 minutes. It took him several minutes to feed them into a printer. While Dunn adjusted the machine, Krysta said, "So, within 54 minutes, on February 18, 2009, something happened. It caused the people in that building to hide Travis' car behind the garage, then move it inside." She pushed her hair behind her ear on the right side.

"It looks that way," agreed Randy.

Dunn turned around. "These are glossy, black-and-white prints. They'll take about a half hour. Why don't we have lunch?"

Randy turned to Krysta, "You like P. F. Chang's—Chinese?"

"Sounds good to me."

Dunn said, "I'll go with you. Let's leave now and beat the noon crowd."

At one o'clock, Krysta, Randy, and Dunn looked at three sets of glossy pictures. The black-and-white photos clearly indicated what they saw in the viewer. A black-and-white former police car pulled into the driveway at the Morales Brothers' shop on the morning of February 18, 2009. Sometime within the next 21 minutes, they moved it behind the building and covered it. In 32 additional minutes, a small portion of the car showed at an angle from the front of the building. No cars or trucks passed on the highway in those photos.

Krysta wrote this information in her notebook. She thanked Dunn and Randy for their help, and handed one set of the photos to Randy. "For Sheriff McGibbon."

Turning to Dunn, she said, "Could you fax these to Sheriff Stroman. Then send him the bill."

Dunn nodded, took the photos and left.

To the other deputy, she said, "It's okay if you want to leave, Randy. I'm going to go through the microfilms for the whole day, every eleven minutes until dark. I want to see if the Morales brothers drove away at any time."

"You seen the Terry Fator show at the Mirage?" Randy asked.

She blinked at him. "You asking me out?"

"Yes." He looked surprised at her reaction. "Absolutely."

There was a long awkward pause. Finally, Krysta wrote her phone number on a sticky pad, and handed it to him. "Call me after seven." Thinking she might have sounded harsh, she added, "I'd love to see the show."

"Fine. I'll call you tonight."

As he walked away, Krysta returned to the viewer. It took her a couple of hours to go through the remainder of the microfilms. She found there was a two-hour gap while storm clouds covered the area. Finally, she came to the last photo, taken shortly before dark through a break in the clouds. Except for two vehicles on the highway, there was no further activity near the Morales property. The Toyota hadn't been moved.

Krysta glanced at her watch: 3:15. She put the map, the remaining microfilms, and the photos in her briefcase. She thanked Kevin Dunn a second time and headed toward the SUV.

On the way back to the sheriff's office, Krysta radioed ahead and asked Sheriff Stroman if he had seen the faxed copies. He said he was reviewing them as they spoke.

Chapter 41

Mojave County, Arizona

Sheriff Bob Stroman examined the three faxed copies of the photos under his magnifying glass. Afterward, he read the transcripts that Deputy Davidson logged into the computer for February 19, 2009, the night of Mrs. Stufloten's heart attack. He noted the entry, first penciled-in by him, about the Morales brothers stopping to offer help.

Now he paced back and forth, talking aloud to himself. For several minutes, he recounted everything from early morning until he arrived home late that night.

The one thing that stood out beside the heart attack was the Morales brothers pulling over to offer help.

Notebook.

He remembered it was in the glove compartment of the SUV.

He got on the radio. "Base to Number Two. How close are you, Krysta?"

"Pulling in the driveway, Bob."

"Could you bring in the notebook from my glove compartment?"

"Sure will."

When she arrived, she handed him the notebook and laid the glossy photos on Stroman's desk.

He quickly looked at the three more-detailed photos, two with the black-and-white car in the rear of the shop, and one with the vehicle partially inside, but visible from the front of the shop. "Amazing what they can do."

Since he'd already seen the faxed copies, he flipped open the notebook to February 19, 2009. There was the penciled-in entry: Ricardo Morales had asked about the heart attack and offered assistance.

Stroman scratched his head. Krysta started to say something, but he held up his hand.

What were they driving? The Toyota? Now he remembered.

He said, "The Morales brothers pulled in by Stufloten's gas pumps that same night in their brown Toyota pickup. It had rained and the sky was overcast."

"The same day the NSA photos were taken? There was a two-hour break in them after five."

"Exactly. Sons-a-bitches are cool. Ricardo was on the passenger side. He asked if there was anything they could do."

"They may have had Travis's body in the truck then, Sheriff?"

Stroman narrowed his eyes. "Are the camera and flash charged?"

"Always."

"You got plans for tonight?"

"No, Sir. Except I need to make a phone call."

"Bring the camera, we're going to pay a visit. Let's take the biggest crowbar we have in the toolshed. I have to call Joe."

While Krysta put the equipment in the SUV, Stroman called Deputy Zuniga.

"Joe, Bob here. We have urgent business and I need you to answer the phones while we're gone. We're goin' to pay a visit to Travis Williams' killers. I'll leave you instructions."

Zuniga protested for a moment, saying he was just finishing dinner with Havasupai Chief Daniel Birdsong.

"Get dessert and bring him here. And, hurry!" He hung up.

The sheriff scribbled a note of instructions for his deputy and locked the office.

Krysta Mazur studied the photos with Stroman's magnifying glass while the sheriff drove. Several times, the car rose over the rises and bottomed out on dips. The wind and road noise were loud.

She'd been unable to scrutinize the photos in the science lab, so now she zoomed in on the car shots with the big glass. Glancing up once, she caught a glimpse of the Colorado River far below on the right. Her watch said it was six. One hour of daylight left.

"Government can watch everything we do," she said.

Stroman shot a quick look at her.

A long silence.

Finally, he said, "That's both good and bad. Good for the law, bad for those up to no good."

Another long silence.

Krysta flipped to another photo. "The creators of the Bill of Rights were certainly wary of who makes those decisions, who decides who the bad guys are."

The sheriff glanced over at her and grunted.

Returning to the third photo, she moved the glass closer. "There's a guy in this one! She blurted. "You can just see the edge of him!"

The sheriff slowed down to make a left on Temple Bar Road. Then, he pulled over, took the glass and focused on the photo. "You must have good eyes. I don't see anything." He passed the photo and magnifying glass back to her and pushed the accelerator to the floor. The SUV made a groaning sound, sucked in air, and accelerated.

It was almost dusk when they pulled down the graveled driveway to the Morales brothers' shop. The premises looked the same in the dim light, except for a layer of dust on everything, a reminder that no one had lived there for awhile.

"Let's walk around the premises, Stroman said. "Check everything—I mean everything. We'll allow it to get fully dark."

Krysta took one flashlight and looked up at the few stars that were beginning to show. "No moon tonight."

"Good. Douse your light when cars pass."

The sheriff told Krysta to go around the houses. He said he would check around the shop on the west side of the property. "Watch for snakes in the back."

She turned when she came to the east side of the shop building. The house where Ricardo Morales had lived with his family was a light-green cinder block building. It had white trim around the door and windows and an old evaporator air-conditioner on the flat roof. A block wall enclosed a yard of cactus that lined the small walkway to the front door. White curtains Krysta remembered from when she was here before still hung in the windows. She thought back. The place looked about as good as it could, considering the location, dust storms, and low cost of the place. And Ricardo's family were neat and clean.

Krysta scoured around both houses, finally going all the way around Jorge's house. Obviously, his wife was less tidy than Ricardo's was. There were no curtains inside the back of the house. She saw empty rooms with vinyl floors in her light beam. The screen door was falling apart. The wood on the back door was split.

A garden with a high fence was barely visible in the waning light. Flicking her light over the fence, plants appeared dark green. She heard a car on the road and turned off the flashlight.

Stroman came around from the other side. "There's nothing here," he said. "Let's head to the back door of the shop."

At the door, Stroman tried the lock. By now, it was almost fully dark.

"Are you going in without a warrant?"

"Wait here," he said.

He came back in a couple of minutes with the large crowbar. It took only two stabs to wedge the bar into the doorjamb. He gave it a powerful heave. The door sprung open, and the alarm went off.

"Let's take a ride," Stroman said. Back at the car, he threw the bar in the trunk and slammed it.

A quarter-mile toward the lake, Krysta said, "I don't believe what we just did. *That* requires a warrant." She pushed her hair behind her ear.

"We gonna get into a pissing contest? There are times when you have to do what you have to do."

"Huh," she huffed.

The SUV came to a wide place in the road and the sheriff turned around. He stopped and switched off the lights.

Ten minutes passed. The radio blared, "Base to Number One."

Krysta widened her eyes.

"Number One. Go ahead," Stroman said.

"There's been a burglary at 909 Temple Bar Road."

"Copy that. That in Palo Verde Springs?"

"Just east of Palo Verde Springs."

"We're a few minutes toward Lake Mead from there. We're on our way. Number One out."

"Base out."

Stroman smiled and punched the accelerator.

"Shouldn't we wait to get a warrant now, sheriff?"

"We're responding to a burglar alarm call. Got it on the recorder." Now there was anger in his voice.

Krysta remained silent for the few minutes it took to arrive at the property. As they pulled down into the driveway, Stroman turned on the flashing lights and left the headlights on with the engine running.

"Grab the camera. Get both close-up and wide-angle photos, 360 degrees around the room. Floor, ceiling, everything you can think of."

They exited the car and hurried around to the back door. Stroman pushed it open, found a switch with his flashlight and flipped it up. "No power."

Krysta followed him in. "Alarm system must have its own power. You want to open the roll-up door manually?"

"Not yet. Pictures come out better with flash in the dark. I'll hold the light on the floor. You take the photos we discussed."

"Okay, Bob." To herself, she sounded miffed. However, she started shooting pictures, walking around to get better angles.

"Watch that hydraulic lift. Don't trip."

Krysta edged around it and worked quickly. She took pictures of the back wall. Then she turned to the east wall. With no equipment, both walls had only empty bins. After several minutes, she said, "Got it all, Sir."

"Okay. I'm going to roll up the big door. When the car's bright lights flood in, let's see if we can find anything important." It took Stroman several moments to unlatch the power drive. When he rolled the door up manually, the room flooded with light.

They searched the room in the bright lights. Except for stationary and roll-around bins, it was nearly empty. The only big items remaining were the two long, roll-around tables, stand up bins still containing pipe, and a large bin on the west side with several large pipes in it.

"Ceiling looks the same," the sheriff said. "The crane assembly. The lights. The alarm system."

"Here's the electrical box."

Krysta switched on the breakers one by one, noting the bottom one was already on — the alarm system. The lights were the top breaker. They now came on, full brightness. The crane made a clacking noise when she switched on its power. Next, the exhaust fan came on with a loud rush.

With all the lights on, Krysta noticed the sheriff studying the vents opening into a shaft going through the roof. She couldn't see anything to examine. All the back shelves were bare, as were the large metal roll-around bins. The floor was covered with plywood, as it had been when she accompanied Stroman the first time, although, now soiled with grease spots. The sheriff rolled the tables in half-circles to the walls. He placed his hands on his hips and scanned the filthy floor, the bins against back wall, and the ceiling again.

"They installed that hydraulic lift after the brothers left. That mechanic didn't keep the place as clean as the Ibrahims did."

"Got the floor greasy near the front. Nothing much else to see, is there, sheriff?"

Stroman nodded. "Pretty bare." He pointed. "You know, those metal bins in the back don't come cheap. They *did* leave in a hurry."

She crossed her arms and thought about what he said.

He took the controller for the crane that was hanging from the roller assembly. Pushing buttons, he ran the hook up and down, the carriage east and west, then the whole bridge north and south, along heavy railroad-like tracks. Looking puzzled, he scrutinized the columns supporting the crane.

"Why are you frowning?"

"Why such a heavy crane? You could lift a diesel with this. I remember when they first built this shop, I thought the piers and columns were for a much larger building. They were for this crane."

Krysta said, "It's sure suspicious that the brothers left a shop like this? The FBI report indicated they had a great business here, making plenty of money."

The sheriff knotted his jaw. "We're missing something, Krysta. I can't put my finger on it."

She shrugged. "Doesn't make sense."

"It's almost nine. I need to get you back. Kill the power and go out the front. I'll roll the door closed and go out the back.

"Oh," he added, "don't kill the alarm power."

Chapter 42

Mexico City, Mexico

Ramzi bin Omeri glared at the computer screen in disbelief. He had suspected the encrypted memory stick that arrived from al Qaeda this morning would bring bad news.

Indeed it did.

The Snow Leopard frowned as he read the entire message: *Accelerate the Phoenix Agenda. The building where the submarine and nuclear bomb are stored in the United States has been broken into.*

Ramzi clenched his jaw. Discovery by American authorities could undo years of work and training. They could disrupt al Qaeda's plans.

The message further notified him that the other cells were ready to begin crossing the American border.

For several minutes, he studied the remainder of the message in deep thought. He started when he heard Shamci's sandals slap and drag on the tile floor.

She handed him a cup of tea. "What's wrong, Darling? You look like you've seen a ghost."

"Oh—it's nothing, Love."

She furrowed her brows. "It's not '*nothing*'. The stick had a message that has you disturbed."

Ramzi flashed an angry scowl at his wife, then he relaxed his face muscles.

Her round face and auburn hair enhanced her rosy complexion, derived from some distant Mongolian ancestor. Two creases formed around her mouth as she said, "My brother gave his life for their cause. We took great risks. You are no longer young, my love."

He remained silent for several seconds, studying his wife's features.

How much could he tell her? After all, she had worked with his cell when they hijacked an aircraft in Uganda. She and her brother, Reza, were major players in bringing two nuclear bombs from Waziristan to Bandar 'Abbas, Iran in order to attack Saudi Arabia. Her brother had died in a firefight with American Navy SEALS when al Qaeda attempted to set off a nuclear bomb near the Kuwaiti ship loading facilities.

She was disturbed when she learned they were now operating on U.S. soil. Only five al Qaeda leaders knew of the plans Ramzi was working on.

By her look, she appeared to understand. "You are my husband. I will submit to your wishes. But, we have given so much."

Ramzi stared at her, started to speak, then again changed his mind.

She seemed to sense that he could say nothing. After a long silence, she returned to the kitchen.

He turned back to the computer.

He typed in a message and encrypted it on a memory stick. Then, erasing all the files that pertained to the Phoenix Agenda, he went through the laborious task of deleting the encryption files. He de-fragmented his hard drive, to make it difficult for any foreign intelligence agency to retrieve useful information.

Finally, he tossed the memory stick into the cast-iron stove. The plastic and rubber burst into flame and a black, oily puff of smoke went up the exhaust vent. He winced at the acrid smell.

Chapter 43

Las Vegas, Nevada

Krysta Mazur parked her Prius Hybrid on the third level of the *Mirage* parking lot. She got out of the small car and heard a man's whistle.

Randy Hammond came out from between two parked cars and smiled broadly. "Wow! I've never seen you in a dress before. You should get out more often."

She returned the smile and felt her cheeks flush. "You, too, Randy. Nice shirt. What time does the show start?"

"Terry Fator comes on at nine. I got us good seats. We'll miss some of the preliminary entertainment." He pushed the elevator call button.

"Sorry, I couldn't get here sooner. Sheriff Stroman didn't return from the opening of the new Pat Tilman Bridge until six."

"You had to miss the bridge opening?"

"I volunteered. The three lawmen pleaded with me to watch the office so they could all attend. I met Sheriff Stroman's family today, also. His kids skipped school. Bridge opening was a big event in Boulder City."

"I can't believe you passed on the opening."

"I'm not the type who rejoices over public events. I'll drive over it tomorrow, and from now on when I go to Arizona."

Randy grinned and nodded. They stepped into a mirrored elevator and went down. He turned to answer a passenger's question about the show, and Krysta studied him in the mirror. She hadn't seen him since they examined the NSA satellite slides.

Slightly taller than she was in her low heels, he was probably six-two, with auburn hair and a nice tan. The slim-fit shirt accentuated his lanky build, that of a distance runner, which she'd discovered he was. But, he wasn't obsessed with running, a plus in her mind. Not one of those jocks who runs eight miles a day and can tell you the dates of the next three marathons.

He smiled politely at the gentleman and she saw he had sea-green eyes and a dimple in one cheek. She guessed he was Scots-Irish.

The elevator bell dinged and the door slid open. They hurried to the moving conveyor to speed them toward the theater.

She'd tried to reimburse him for the tickets, but he said, "Please allow me. You mentioned you hadn't seen Terry Fator yet."

She smiled at him and a warm feeling came over her. Randy was exactly what she needed now, after her last unsettling relationship with Patrick Donnegan, which she'd broken off in D.C. eighteen months ago.

It turned out Patrick was married, and she didn't discover it for five months. She was furious and firm when she called off the romance.

Patrick wept. He played the part of the desperately conflicted lover—too Catholic, and too attached to his three children to leave his loveless marriage.

Livid, she quit the job in Washington and swore off men. The decision was a good one. McFadden Security hired her. They subcontracted to Homeland Security, allowing her to remain in the intelligence profession, but to escape Washington.

Randy guided her to the line, which interrupted her train of thought. An usher then escorted them to their seats.

Three hours later, after the stunning and delightful performance, Randy invited her to his apartment.

She begged off. "I'd better not have a third glass of wine. I still have to drive back to Boulder City."

Randy definitely had charm. He smiled, showing his dimple, and hinted that she shouldn't drive home this late.

"Ah, ha. You men are all alike. First date and you want to jump in bed."

Frowning, he held his hand over his heart. "I'll sleep on my couch and you can have the bedroom."

She smiled and shook her head.

Chapter 44

Mexico City, Mexico

Abdul bin Ibrahim, aka Ricardo Morales, and his brother turned the corner in this pleasant suburb and headed back home.

"So that is it, *Hermano*. They delivered an encryption stick. I am waiting for the message."

Zaki exclaimed, "We cannot go back to *El Norte*. They will catch us."

"We are too smart for them."

Zaki frowned.

From the hill they were on, Abdul scanned the city. They'd been lucky so far. For their contributions—building the submarine and helping to load the nuclear bomb—al Qaeda had moved them to a safe, upscale, middle-class neighborhood. The only catch was that the separate three-story condominiums they lived in served as halfway houses for trained *jihadists* infiltrating the big neighbor to the north. Both their wives had complained about doing laundry and providing baths, beds and food for several score of frightening Middle Easterners that slipped in during the early morning hours.

Because of the brothers' years of training, they hid them temporily, then delivered the *jihadists* in modified SUVs to the next handlers. Abdul castigated his wife for her complaining. After all, they lived a fine lifestyle, their children attended good schools, and the filthy characters that arrived at the basements in the night never interacted with their families.

"*Buenos tardes, Señores.*" The Alvarez couple called out from across the street.

The brothers flashed big smiles and crossed over to converse with their neighbors.

Jaime Alvarez was a high school teacher with a light complexion and a paunch. He wore old-fashioned horn-rimmed glasses. His wife, Sonia, a real beauty with wavy black hair, worked for a television studio. She sported expensive clothes and professionally applied make-up. The three couples had visited each other in their homes, shared meals, and watched special TV programs together.

After the friendly exchanges, Abdul and Zaki returned to their separate condominiums in the same building. Abdul powered up his computer as he did at least six times a week. The machine went through the booting process and he signed onto the Internet. The message came up. He knew something serious was coming after the courier had brought him the encryption disc one week ago. Grimacing, he read the instructions and swallowed hard.

It had been a peaceful year after the two brothers left Arizona. Abdul had no desire to put his life in danger again. He understood why he had the DZ 41 capsules, and why he kept them close at all times. His friend with la Policía saw a warrant for his extradition and warned him that it meant life imprisonment if detained by them or U.S. Border Protection.

Two days passed before Abdul got up the nerve to go to the post office to retrieve the mail. As instructed, he continuously carried a DZ-41 capsule in his shirt pocket in case anything went wrong. He made sure no one noticed him as he opened his personal box. Even though he was expecting it, the sight of the memory stick made him cringe.

He sucked in a deep breath, retrieved the device, and locked the box. Scanning the people in the post office, he was satisfied no one followed him.

Back at the condominium, he turned on the computer and booted up. He went through the detailed processes of downloading the encryption disc then, when prompted, he inserted the stick.

His jaw knotted as he stared at the message. The al Qaeda leader that he and his brother knew as Omar bin al Habib informed him there had been a burglary in the electric sign shop in Arizona.

Abdul's heartbeats pounded in his head. What if the authorities discovered the submarine?

Al Qaeda was asking him to go to Arizona and investigate. He swallowed hard. The Palestinian fingered the packet with the capsules.

He glared at the screen for at least five minutes, thinking. The computer finally sounded a warning. Jerked out of his thoughts, he sent the simple five-word response to the network. Then, he went through the laborious process of ridding the machine of all traces of the message and sophisticated cryptography.

I will have to tell Zaki.

Chapter 45

Las Vegas, Nevada

Krysta Mazur pulled into a parking space next to Randy Hammond at the Mirage and shut the ignition off. She opened the car door revealing a bit of thigh.

He opened the car door all the way and looked away as her split-in-the-front skirt opened.

He pursed his lips then smiled broadly. "You look good enough to...."

She arched a warning eyebrow. "You better not say what I think you're about to, *Deputy*."

"You truly are stunning, Krysta. What a find."

She fingered her hair and pushed it over her ear. "You look striking in that sweater too, Randy." She ran her tongue over her lips, grabbed her purse and asked, "What time does Lord of the Dance start?"

"In a half hour."

As they walked toward the elevator, he said, "We have time for a drink."

"Sounds good. Get your heartbeats back to normal."

He laughed two notes. "What's the sheriff up to these days? Routine?"

She noted the abrupt change in topic. "Sheriff Stroman's still obsessing about Deputy Travis Williams. I've tried to say things to get his mind off the subject. We've had two accidents near the Tillman Bridge the last three weeks. One was a bad semi-truck jackknife accident. Sent four people to the Emergency Room at Sunrise Hospital. But he keeps returning to the photos and hard copies from NSA. He's examined them at least a dozen times. He thinks I don't notice."

Randy nodded that he understood. The elevator opened. There was no one inside, and as it started down, he turned her head gently and kissed her. Not a long, passionate, wet-tongue kiss. Merely a nice, soft, slightly-open-mouth-kiss. One that made her lips tingle with excitement. The kind that said "I like you a lot."

The elevator stopped to pick up more passengers and they quickly acted nonchalant.

On the way down, Krysta took the time to consider herself in the mirror. She felt her face flush when she scrutinized the split skirt and low-cut blouse.

They *did* show off her thighs, curves, and ample bust. For a brief moment, she thought it was too risqué, too soon. Then the elevator opened onto the casino floor.

During the break in the spectacular and mesmerizing show featuring Irish dancers and musicians, Randy suggested that she not drive back to Boulder City afterward. "I swear that I will sleep on the couch and respect your wishes."

"Let me think about it. I can't rush this."

More than three hours later, after the show, and two additional glasses of Chablis with the satisfying Italian dinner, she obviously surprised Randy when she said, "I will stay over if you promise me that you'll stay on the couch. I'm an old-fashioned girl and I need time to adjust to this new relationship."

He gave her a sincere look, "Promise."

She smiled her consent.

Chapter 46

*Davis Valley, California,
eight miles from the Mexican border*

Abdul bin Ibrahim, aka Ricardo Morales, started to move and Carlos seized his wrist.

"Listen! Don't move. I hear choppers."

After several moments of silence, Abdul heard them, too, faintly, way in the distance. In the near darkness, he watched as the Mexican-American adjusted his night-vision gear. Several minutes went by in total silence. The helicopter sounds faded.

Carlos gestured to the northwest. "I knew it. There it is. A Predator." He slipped off the headgear and said, "Pull your jacket over your face and bow down between these boulders. Hide your hands and make like a rock. They have powerful lenses and night vision gear."

Abdul obeyed. Several minutes passed in total silence. The Palestinian listened. Wind whistled through the weeds nearby, kicking up the dry, alkaline dust. After awhile, he heard the barely audible sound of what sounded like a model airplane motor.

For the past two weeks, Abdul had agonized over the decision for him to return to Arizona. He knew there was a warrant out for him for the murder of that deputy. He'd finally received a message to meet Carlos. The Snow Leopard had briefed him for the mission and told him Carlos' story.

The coyote guided illegal aliens from Mexico for several years for a syndicate. Al Qaeda made connections, and without the coyote's knowledge of who he was bringing in, sent two dozen high-value operatives into the U.S. Ramzi heard he was the best.

Born in Arizona and a former American marine, Carlos understood the country's best military equipment. The stout, light-skinned Mexican-American in his early thirties severed his connections with a large Mexican drug-smuggling syndicate in favor of running illegal aliens.

The businessmen moving illegal aliens paid quickly and well. If Carlos were caught, which he hadn't been for over six years, the U.S. authorities would slap his wrists with a small fine. The infraction would be a far different order of magnitude from helping to smuggle cocaine.

Abdul heard voices on the wind and knew that American authorities had rounded up the Latinos he had briefly glimpsed in the valley below them before dark. The sound of vehicles came over the ridge and the patrol herded the poor Mexican farm workers into them. It took less than an hour, then Abdul heard the vehicles pass back over the ridge.

Carlos finally sighed and said, "Okay, they're gone. We can move."

"How far to the road?" Abdul rose and took off his gloves and jacket, then stowed them in his small backpack.

"A three-hour walk."

The stout Mexican-American hoisted his backpack and flipped on his night-vision headgear. "Follow me closely and I'll miss the rocks and snakes, *amigo*."

Chapter 47

Mojave County, Arizona

Sheriff Bob Stroman furrowed his brow and focused the magnifying glass of Krysta Mazur's detailed photos of the Morales brothers' shop. The crystal clear pictures revealed the crane, lights, shelves and the floor covering. The back door hung from its hinges, and the hydraulic lift that was installed after the brothers left rested on the floor.

He repeatedly studied all photos, including the NSA flyover photos. Scratching his jaw, he frowned again.

The door to the front office opened, and he quickly shoved the photos and glass into his drawer. "Hey Krysta, I'm in the back."

Krysta entered and asked, "What's up for the day?"

"Same ol', same ol'. I must attend that meeting with Homeland Security in Vegas at ten. Can you hold the fort until Deputy Davidson arrives at about 9:30?"

She nodded. "I see you have a report on that accident on the Tillman Bridge to fill out for the insurance companies. I'll finish and send it."

He studied her for a long moment, then said, "Hum, you have an aura about you lately, a rosy glow to your cheeks. Better watch out for that Las Vegas deputy."

She blushed. Her gaze darted away for a few seconds then returned to the sheriff. "Randy's nice. I like him. Did you know that he runs five miles almost every day?"

"I think Earl told me about that," Stroman said, referring to the Clark County sheriff. "Looks like love to me." He grinned broadly.

She turned toward her desk and computer.

Stroman brought his fist up to his chin once again. His thoughts returned to the pictures of the Morales brothers' shop. *Got to be something we're missing.*

Early this morning, he'd searched old records and discovered an entry regarding an accident that happened a hundred yards from the property. He vaguely remembered that the building was nearing completion at the time. It had taken only four months to construct the commercial property, then an additional five months to add the two houses.

It hadn't registered on him immediately, but he now realized that a piece of the puzzle might be right there.

Rising, he went to Krysta's desk.

"I had a thought about the Morales brothers' shop. About when it was constructed. Would you make another request from your former associate at NSA for satellite photos: August, 1 through November, 2005 of the Palo Verde Springs grid square."

Krysta frowned, and gave him a look that said, *Let it go, Sheriff.*

After a few moments, she asked, "The request would be under the auspices of the murder investigation?"

"Of, course, the ongoing investigation."

She jotted some notes, and said, "I'll give it a try."

Chapter 48

Las Vegas, Nevada

Krysta Mazur pulled her Prius into a visitor's space at Randy Hammond's condominium. A few seconds later, she rang and the tall deputy opened the door.

He looked her up and down. "Whew! You're a stunner, Krysta. I'm a lucky guy."

She eased toward him and they embraced. Turning to face him, she smiled seductively.

He put his arms around her and pulled her close. They kissed. For the first time since they'd started dating, she moved her body hard against him. She had decided that this was the night. *The* night.

He pulled her into him and parted his lips. Her head swam and a tingle ran up her back. His lips felt warm and moist. His tongue felt hot and soft as it slid across hers.

After more embracing, he backed off and said, "Whoa! We're going to be late for the impersonators." He inhaled. "What's the perfume, Obsession?"

"Chanel Number Five. You like it?"

"Grrrrrr. I'll ravish you, you keep doing this to me."

She grinned broadly and pulled his arm toward the door.

They got in his Ford F-150 truck, and he headed toward the Golden Nugget. She caught him taking a quick glance at her legs, looked away and smiled.

"Have you seen this show before?" She deliberately changed the subject, still feeling a warm glow from the caressing.

"No. And they've been in Vegas for a while." He raised the sun visor. "But I didn't take in many shows before I met you. Too busy with the running and college."

Randy turned right onto the strip and headed east.

"Now all I want to do is snuggle up to you and smell the Chanel. Drink your sweet wine."

She blushed recalling the earlier thoughts.

―∾∾―

Krista's heartbeats raced as Randy parked at his condominium. The great show and two glasses of wine had made her head light. She shivered with anticipation.

Inside, he took out two wineglasses and opened a small refrigerator. He glanced at her as he poured from a decanter.

She held up a thumb and forefinger indicating a small amount.

Randy sat next to her, their knees touching, and handed her the glass. He smiled. "You have the most beautiful eyes."

She closed and opened them slowly.

The wine went down easily. It felt silky in her throat. "Oh, wow! This vintage stuff has a quick effect."

He set the two glasses on the table. Raising his eyebrows, he said, "We don't want to ruin the evening."

She leaned close to him and took several deep breaths, letting them out slowly. Her cheeks felt flushed.

He said, "I could take advantage of you."

"I won't resist." The blood seemed to drain from her body. Her fingertips tingled. With her eyes half closed, she said, "I want you."

He lifted her chin and pressed his lips to hers.

His mouth felt warm and soft and wet. As she put her arms around his neck, his hand slid to the middle of her back.

She pushed her body firmly against hiym.

He said, "If you want, we can stop now, and I'll sleep on the couch?"

"Turn off the lights." She took his hand and pulled him toward the bedroom.

As he took off his clothes, her eyes adjusted to the dark. His silhouette showed in the faint light entering through the small, high bedroom window. It revealed his perfectly formed abs. As her eyes adjusted further, she marveled at how radiant he looked. Like a classic Greek athlete. She wanted all of him. He was now her passion, her life.

He eased her onto the bed. She flipped her hair as he slid off her dress. Unfastening her bra while he slipped off his remaining clothes, she pulled him down.

Their naked bodies came together. She trembled under his touch.

She parted her lips for a lingering kiss. Her pulse pounded, loving the feel of his firm body against her.

He pressed his mouth on her neck and moved down to her nipples.

As he sucked gently on them, she felt her last bit of anxiety release. She flinched with excitement as they came together.

They consumed each other.

Her body surged in waves. She moaned and took the rhythmic thrusts that left her shaking.

Randy trembled, spent. After several final thrusts, he rolled to his side, and lay still.

Krysta gasped. After resuming normal breathing, her heartbeats slowed. She moved to caress his chest.

He inhaled one last deep breath, and slipping his arm under her neck, said softly, "I love you."

"Me, too."

The last thing she remembered was the sound of his rhythmic breathing as she drifted off.

Chapter 49

Palo Verde Springs, Arizona

Abdul bin Ibrahim said, "Drive by building slowly for first look, Carlos. We can turn around and come back."

The coyote grunted acknowledgment. "They may have surveillance cameras if they're watching the property."

Abdul swallowed. "Maybe." After a moment of silence, he pointed. "There a dirt road half-mile up there. Take it. We come around back. We park other side of little hill from shop."

Carlos slowed the vehicle when the headlights revealed the turn. The truck jostled onto a dirt road.

After awhile, Abdul asked, "Can you tell with headlight if anything they watch us with?"

Carlos considered this for a few moments. "It's possible. But they also might have trip mechanisms or silent alarms that start video equipment. Sometimes they automatically notify the law."

"They give me a key and the new alarm codes." Abdul said.

"But the law might have a deal with the company to report *any* intrusion, even if the alarm is deactivated."

Abdul gestured right. "That way." He kept opening and squeezing his fists.

Carlos made the turn. The pickup bounced over holes. He speeded up and a dust cloud billowed up behind the truck in the pale moonlight.

"Al Habib say check building and property. We leave fast as we get good look and see they not tear building apart."

It took them several minutes to arrive at the back of the hill. They got out and Carlos took the lead with his night vision. He carried a device to scan for electronic sensors. Constantly stopping and holding up a hand, he surveyed the premises for cameras.

Abdul heard coyotes yipping in the total silence. He inhaled the strong odors of sage and creosote bushes. When they finally arrived at the back door, he slipped on mechanic's rubber gloves, inserted the new key, and opened the door. Stepping into the familiar shop, he went to the alarm and punched in the new numbers Ramzi had given him. A red blinking light turned to green and Abdul exhaled a large breath.

"*Bueno.*" He now flipped on a circuit breaker for two dim nightlights.

"Hurry, *amigo*," Carlos whispered.

Abdul scanned the room, noting the shelves, the vent through the roof, and the sealed hole near the back wall where welding cables had passed through to the floor below. He quickly flashed his small light on the hydraulic jack that had not been there when he and Zaki used the premises. He examined the floor sheets. The clear tape between them was not torn. Only the back door, where it had been jimmied with a bar, showed any sign of human disturbance.

He sighed and motioned to Carlos for them to get out of the place. After the coyote passed through the door, Abdul turned off the small nightlights and reset the alarm.

Chapter 50

Mojave County, Arizona

The phone at the office rang at eight sharp.

"Mojave County Sheriff's office, Sheriff Stroman here. How can I help you?"

"This is Ampex Alarm Company. The building you're watching had visitors last night, Sir. You asked us to notify you of any entries."

Stroman's stomach tightened. He immediately snapped to attention. "Yes-Sir. Give me the time please."

"Three-thirty in the morning. They had the security code numbers and deactivated the system. But we have a video. Thought you'd like to know."

"Can you One-Day the video to me?"

"We can do better than that. It's only 93 seconds long. You can download it off-line from www.ampexalarm.com. Add a forward slash after com, with no spaces, then Palo VerdeSprings/0331hours at the end."

"Thank you very much," said Stroman, jotting the information.

He switched off the phone and scratched his jaw in thought. He dialed Krysta Mazur's cell phone. When she answered, he asked, "How close are you?"

"About a mile."

"Good. We have an urgent job."

Only Abdul and Zaki had the alarm codes.

A half-hour later, Krysta had downloaded the file from the Internet. She and the sheriff viewed the video of the inside of the garage and shop.

"Look at that," said Stroman. "He went right to the alarm and silenced it. Turned on the circuit breaker for only two dim lights. He knew exactly where everything was."

They both watched the screen fascinated, as Krysta replayed it over several times.

"The first guy is small and thin like Abdul," she said. "He never looked up. Kept his chin down."

"Yeah. Definitely knew what he was doing. Second guy was cautious, too.

Strong looking. Mexican, I'd bet. Did you notice, he scanned with an electronic device."

Krysta tapped her teeth with a fingernail. "Now that you mention it, there he goes." She replayed a sequence that showed the second man making a quick scan of the room in the near darkness.

"Can you enhance and come in close?"

Krysta zoomed in. But the lighting was poor. The images of the two men were purplish-gray and grainy.

Stroman glanced at his watch. "Eight-twenty. If that's Abdul, he's headed for the border." The sheriff went to a big map on the wall with numbered red, green, and yellow pins sticking in it that revealed past accidents. He ran his finger down the highways. "The only chance we have of stopping them is at the border. Calexico, San Luis, or one of the small villages toward Nogales."

"Most likely San Luis, the closest place," Krysta said.

"I'll call the sheriff's office in Yuma. Have them alert the inspectors," said Stroman. "You call the border patrol."

"The only description we have is that old driver's license picture from 2005, and the sketch we had made from it. Nothing more recent."

"That'll have to do. Fax it to Rollie Jenkins in the El Centro office, too. He'll get it out to all points in California. Look up his number in my old Rolodex."

Krysta grimaced. "I put all that information in the computer." She clicked a few keys, and the phone number came up. "Here it is on the screen."

The sheriff knotted his eyebrows and shrugged as Krysta dialed Rollie's number. In one continuous fluid motion, she pulled Ricardo's file out of the cabinet and handed the photo and sketch to the sheriff. He picked up the phone to dial Yuma.

"I'm going to call Lieutenant Markam at Nellis Air force base. I met him last week. He's in charge of the surveillance aircraft—the Predators and Global Hawks in the whole southwest. See if he can locate anyone speeding toward the border."

Chapter 51

El Centro, California

"Slow down!" blurted Abdul bin Ibrahim. "They have helicopters flying today." He pointed to the small aircraft crossing over Federal Highway 8.

Carlos dipped his head to peer under the sun visor. Then he glared at Abdul. "They looking for you? You into drugs, man?"

"Drugs? Absolutely not. I have good business in sign shop. There was accident."

Carlos shot Abdul a concerned look. "Accident? I don't want to know—can't know. Cops might have out an APB."

Abdul frowned at the Mexican-American. "APB?"

"All Points Bulletin. Border patrol. Sheriffs. CHP—uh, California and Arizona Highway Patrols."

Abdul leaned forward to see the side mirror. The chopper continued on away from them toward El Centro.

Carlos must have noticed something in the Arab's mannerisms. "They said take care of you. Paid a bunch of money to get you back. If there was some kind of silent alarm in that building …" As his voice trailed off, he pulled onto the off-ramp to Dunn Bar Road. "I'm going with the follow-up plan."

"What's that?"

"You'll see."

The robust ex-marine drove along a frontage road for another few miles back toward El Centro. Then he slowed and turned into a driveway. "We get a change of disguise. Or I don't get paid."

As Carlos backed toward a garage, he operated a remote. He got out of the truck as the door slid open. Pointing to two quad runners inside, he said, "Get the blue one. I'll take the gray." He grabbed one of two loading ramp rails and dropped the tailgate of the truck.

Abdul said, "I never ride motorcycle."

"Four wheels are easy. Blue one is automatic. Pop it into gear. Go and stop. That's it. Chicks can ride 'em."

Abdul swallowed.

Once the quads were loaded and strapped into place in the bed of the black crew-cab pickup, Carlos backed up to the hitch of a new white trailer. "This toy-hauler will be a good disguise. Has a generator and AC unit."

A tall, thin Latino with a shaved head and thick brush mustache came out of the house. "This is Albert. We call him *Pelon*." Carlos gestured toward Abdul. "Ricardo."

The two men acknowledged each other.

In a few minutes, they were back on Highway 8 headed toward Plaster City, Pelon sitting in the back seat of the truck.

Abdul said, "Good plan. They think we just riding motorcycles in desert."

Carlos nodded and ducked to see if there were any more aircraft.

After several miles, the Mexican-American took an offramp where a sign read Ocotillo, then turned south where another small one said Davis Valley. Pulling off the road 600 yards beyond State Highway 98 and a Chevron gas station, he said, "We'll leave the truck here. Pelon and I will check out the valley."

Carlos got out and stretched. Pelon went around back to unhook the trailer.

When the jack rose and the trailer popped loose, Carlos moved the truck forward far enough to unload the quads.

"What about me?" asked Abdul.

"You hide in the trailer. I'll run the generator for the AC to keep it cool. I'll get you later when it's all clear."

"Then what?" Abdul frowned. "What if cops come?"

"You stay hidden. Do not open the door until I come back with the key."

Abdul swallowed again. For the first time, he saw Carlos smile. Abdul blew out a large breath. "How far to border?"

"About a half-hour if you go straight." Carlos zipped his leathers. "The Feds fly over, they will just think we're white guys playing. Don't open that door for anyone."

Abdul nodded.

The former marine said, "We'll make like we're having fun. Ride around over the dunes. Wave to the choppers if they go over. Soon as it's clear, I'll come back for you."

Abdul squinted. "You only take me to border?"

"Another coyote will meet us on the Mexican side with my money." Carlos donned his red helmet, fastened the chinstrap and raised his leg to get on the quad.

Chapter 52

U.S.-Mexican Border south of El Centro, California

Kurt Valdez looked south toward the Mexican border. The helicopter had just passed over Calexico, California and Camp Tango detention Center returning from the "Devil's Highway" area of Southern Arizona. "How many undocumented aliens cross near here each week?" Kurt asked the pilot.

Shawn Gunnison gestured with a sweep of his arm toward the border. "Probably 300 to 500 pass through just this crossing alone, the bold ones with borrowed or faked passports, or Social Security cards belonging to someone else."

"That's another point I've wondered about," Kurt asked. "With the technology we have today, why don't they just issue more work visas along with Social Security cards that work like our ATMs and credit cards? They don't have a proper card, fingerprint and eye scan, and the proper PIN number, they don't cross. We need millions of laborers to clean up the fire-hazard zones in the high-risk areas all the way from San Diego to Del Rio, Texas. Hell, over large areas of the Southwest states like California, Colorado, and New Mexico, and even up to Idaho. Make them legal with high-tech cards, the word would get around, and they wouldn't have to sneak across. If the now-illegal aliens knew they could cross easily to work, and their pay was guaranteed and protected, and they could take their money and goods to their families, they wouldn't have to stay in the states for years, in hiding."

"Ah, but that would eliminate the political issue," Rich Newsome said, "In the 2004 election year, the sting of the Abortion Issue, the Gay-Marriage and Gay-Rights issues, and the Assault-Gun ownership issue were fading. Reactionaries needed another hot-button problem. A barbarian horde flooding into the U.S. from the south, swamping our hospitals and schools, overloading our social services. Serves to keep Americans in the southwest states looking in the wrong direction, while Wall Street casino operators siphon off annual incomes in the millions, their corporations saddle the country with successive financial crises requiring hundreds-of-billions in taxpayer bailouts, and the same criminals write the new pseudo-regulations to "correct" the problem they created and "prevent" further occurrences of their larceny. The elite and their puppets in Washington need to keep people looking the other way." There was a note of sarcasm in his voice.

Shawn snarled, "Well what do Liberals give you? Amnesty. Gun control. Cut and run from Iraq. Fags getting married. Unlimited abortion. Attacks on religion. Evolution instead of Intelligent Design."

Newsome grinned at Kurt, gestured with a thumb towards Gunnison, and said, "Huh. Those issues and the Iraq and Afghanistan Wars are what the authorities use to keep people's focus off the real important issues—who's stealing the country into poverty. If they wanted to fix the illegal immigrant problem, they would issue the high-tech cards and arrest the managements of big corporations and big farmers who are using illegal aliens. But, that would begin to correct the problem. And the hot-button political issue would go away."

Shawn snorted and guided the helicopter over an arid range of hills and another strip of desert. The morning sun beat down on the rocks and sand and sparse vegetation. The Pacific Ocean came into view in the distance.

There was a long silence. Kurt pondered the conversation. Then scanning the ground again, and adjusting the focus of the binoculars, he zeroed in on two quads. One of the riders apparently spotted the low-flying aircraft with INS insignia on the sides and stopped to wave.

After a while, Kurt lowered the glasses. "Those two guys on the quads are pretty good. They keep circling and going over several jumps. Fast."

Gunnison said, "White guys. Or a guy and a girl. Did you see him wave?" He still sounded angry. "Thousands of them all over the desert. You should fly over on Thanksgiving. Looks like cities. All the way from the Mexican border to the Salton Sea, sometimes 50,000 trailers and RVs. Bikes and dune-buggies like ants on honey."

Kurt brought the powerful glasses up to his face again and watched the riders. The chopper flew over the eastern foothills of San Diego County, with the higher mountain ranges to the north leading to the Santa Rosa Mountains.

Chapter 53

Davis Valley, California, eight miles from the Mexican border

Abdul bin Ibrahim, aka Ricardo Morales, heard the sound of engines and opened a window a slit to look out.

Carlos the Coyote and Pelon pulled the quads up to the trailer.

Abdul heard the lock unlatch.

Carlos poked his head in and said, "The roads are clear. Hurry and get into Pelon's riding clothes and helmet. I can take you to the crossing."

Pelon came into the trailer and took off his boots and riding leathers.

As he shed them, Abdul put them on.

In a few minutes, Carlos ducked into the trailer, and looked at his watch. He said, "Hurry, the contact will meet us in 45 minutes."

Abdul frowned and slipped on the boots. "Is this part dangerous in the daylight?"

Carlos shrugged. "There's always a risk. But an INS chopper flew over and I waved to them. We probably have an hour to get you safely across."

Pelon handed Abdul a small backpack. "This is a camelback. It has a water pouch built in. Put the tubing in your mouth." He showed Abdul the mouthpiece and thin tube.

Abdul took quick breaths. "What's the chance they might catch us?"

"It's always possible," the Coyote said. "But with the quads, they probably won't bother. And there was no one else riding today."

Abdul thought for a moment. He reached to his vest pocket and took out the packet containing two DZ-41 capsules. He recalled the look the Snow Leopard had given him. It said it all. *You cannot be taken alive.*

The Palestinian grimaced as he tore off a short strip across the top of the small envelope. Two pink pills lay in the bottom. He carefully tucked the envelope in the upper jacket pocket for quick access.

Turning toward Carlos, he raised the helmet and nodded.

The Mexican-American opened his jacket and pulled out a Sig Sauer 1911 pistol. He checked for ammunition and made sure the safety was on. Handing it to Abdul, he grinned, "In case you run into trouble. I added it to the bill."

The Palestinian stared at the weapon for a moment. He nodded, and, handling the gun gingerly, thrust it into his jacket.

Carlos mounted his quad and plunked it into gear. He spun a half-circle and took off.

Abdul revved the engine on the second machine and followed.

As they sped over several humps and headed into a wash with deep ripples and soft sand, the Arab fumed. He struggled to control the four-wheeler. He had to hang on to remain seated. After several miles, his arms, wrists and hands ached.

Carlos glided along easily, setting himself up for the jumps and flying over them. He obviously enjoyed the ride, even the deep sand with ripples. The man scanned from right to left as if watching for any sign of other people or aircraft.

Abdul cursed and struggled to keep up.

Chapter 54

Laguna Mountains, California

Kurt Valdez surveyed the Laguna Mountains ahead through the side window of the INS helicopter. With the binoculars focused, he noted that snow patches remained on the higher peaks. The Santa Rosa Mountains far to the northwest had a whole line of white peaks. He figured visibility was 70 miles.

Suddenly the radio speaker came on, "Got a copy there, Air Six?"

Shawn Gunnison answered into his mouthpiece, "Go ahead, base."

"What's your twenty?"

"Heading two-six-five. Coming up on Jacumba."

"Got an APB on a suspect that might be trying to cross the border. The Global Hawks have four possibles. One is in the area you just flew over, Davis Valley."

"Roger, that. I'll head back on zero-eight-five," said the pilot.

Kurt leaned forward with interest. "What's the APB about?"

Shawn adjusted and tapped a screen. "A picture will come up shortly."

Rich Newsome turned to Kurt and asked, "Global Hawks are the weird-looking ones that fly above 50,000 feet?"

"Right. High-altitude, remote-controlled, surveillance aircraft. Operators guide them from a computer. They use them a lot in Iraq and Afghanistan for high-res scanning. Using them more for the border areas now, too."

"Huh."

Shawn had made a large circle and pushed the joystick forward and exited the hills at a low elevation. The sand wash of Davis Valley came into view ahead.

Kurt focused the binoculars again. He panned across the vast area between U.S. Highway 8 and the Mexican border.

After a moment, he said, "There are the guys on the quads again." He clicked the field-glasses on higher power.

The pilot veered the helicopter to starboard and headed toward the riders. As it closed the distance, Kurt said, "Yep, same quads."

Shawn now banked the aircraft in a turn for a better look.

"Different rider on the second motorcycle. See how he took that jump? He can't ride as good as that other one could."

"Or someone running from the law never rode a bike before," said the pilot.

Kurt held the glasses on the small, slim rider in the rear.

The two riders looked up at the chopper. The one in front waved again. He was obviously the same one they had seen before.

"Take it up and give them some slack until they get to that open space over there to the right," Kurt said.

Shawn said into his mouthpiece, "Air Six to base."

"Go ahead, Air Six."

"We're going to land and check out two motorcycle riders."

"Copy that. Give us your GPS readings."

Shawn read off the coordinates. Then he remained behind the small motorcycles as they came to the large bowl.

Kurt asked, "Can you make a half-circle to port and come down in front of them so my door is facing them?"

"Sure." The pilot banked and made a large sweep.

Rich said, "That lead rider is not waving now. He's looking right at us."

Kurt slipped out his Uzi, the silenced pistol given to him by a Navy SEAL Captain. He racked the slide, tightened the silencer, and slid the safety off, then back on.

Rich looked at him with wide eyes.

"You never know," Kurt said.

Gunnison swung the chopper around and set down a safe distance in front of the quads. Kurt didn't take his eyes off the riders. The front rider stopped. The small one in the back slowed then stopped a ways back. Kurt slid the weapon into the back of his pants as he eased out of the aircraft.

The closer rider took off his helmet. He lifted his leg and got off the motorcycle, turning the engine off as he did. Kurt watched him closely. The man hung the protective headpiece on the quad's handlebars, and Kurt thought he reached to the front of the gas tank.

He whipped out the Uzi and shouted, "Immigration and Naturalization Service. Step away from the bike. Keep your hands where I can see them."

There was a long pause. Kurt inhaled two deep breaths. The man was dark-skinned and appeared to be Mexican. He had a robust build. "*Ahora, hombre!*"

"Easy, man." He spoke un-accented English. He held up both palms and started to step away from the machine.

At that moment the other rider revved his bike, circled, and took off north.

The man by the quad made a quick movement to see the other quad leaving.

Kurt shouted, "Put your hands on your head and turn around."

The robust man looked at his bike's handlebars for several seconds.

Valdez cocked his head. "Don't even try it."

Several moments passed. Kurt raised his Uzi to the man's head.

He was totally calm. He didn't blink or cower, staring right down the barrel of Kurt's gun.

Glaring at Kurt for a few moments, he then slowly raised his hands to his head. "Okay, you got me."

Kurt shuffled forward, reaching for a plastic tie from his back pocket. When he approached closer, he slid the gun in the back of his pants. "Hands behind you!"

He turned him, cinched his wrists, then slid a hunting knife out of a scabbard. Frisking him further, Kurt make sure the man had no more weapons.

Then Kurt checked for ID. There was no wallet or papers. He studied him closely, eyeball to eyeball. "Coyote?"

"No, man. I'm just enjoying the desert on my motorcycle."

"Then why did you resist?"

"Sorry, it was just a natural reaction."

"What's your name?"

"Carlos."

"Carlos what?"

"Carlos Alvares."

Kurt pushed him forward. He reached and took a pistol from a holster on the handle bars of the quad. "What's this for, Carlos Alvares? Shooting rattlesnakes?"

"Rabbits," said the man.

"So you're a smart ass, too." Go. Kurt shoved him toward the chopper. By this time the pilot had set up the back seat to accept the detainee.

As Shawn Gunnison and Kurt wrestled Carlos into the chopper, Rich Newsome snapped a good close-up picture. The pilot locked him in the seat.

Rich slipped the memory stick out of the camera and plugged it into the computer port. He sent pictures to the office."

Kurt said, "Why don't you take her up a few hundred feet, Shawn. So we can locate the other rider."

Turning the monitor so Carlos could see the image of Abdul broadcast by the APB, Neusome said, "That the man on the other quad?"

Carlos hesitated for several seconds. Finally, he rolled his lips inward and nodded.

"He's wanted for murder one." Kurt stared hard into Carlos' eyes.

The man blanched and swallowed. "Hey—hey man, I didn't know anything about him. It was just a delivery."

"Well, you're connected now. Aiding and harboring a fugitive."

Shawn revved the rotors and the aircraft lifted off. For a few minutes it was too noisy to talk.

The computers at INS returned a mug shot of Carlos. It scrolled the man's record.

Kurt turned again. Well, Carlos de la Villa, Coyote, it looks like you're in a lot of trouble."

Carlos tilted his head downward, staring out the window.

Kurt took up the binoculars again. After scanning a wide arc ahead of them, he gestured right. "There. The motorcycle's upside down."

"He won't get far," Shawn said. He guided the joystick and made a circle with the chopper for a hundred yards around the wrecked quad.

After a couple of minutes, Kurt said, "Set me down in that clear spot. I'll find some tracks."

"Careful man, he's wanted for murder. No telling what he'll do in desperation."

Kurt slid out the Uzi again. "No problem." He asked Carlos de la Villa, "Does he have a gun?"

Carlos was silent and sullen. Finally, he said, "He has a Sig Sauer .38."

The chopper landed. The pilot turned and said, "Here, take this drug gun. It has six darts. Get him alive." Shawn handed Kurt a rifle.

Kurt went to the quad. Cautiously checking it out, he noted a set of footprints heading south. Gasoline trickled out of the gas tank of the motorcycle. The exhaust system made pinging and ticking noises as it cooled. Oil leaked from a cap.

Kurt looked up to the chopper now hovering above him and gestured in the direction of the tracks. Then he scanned every boulder large enough to hide behind. He had searched about a hundred yards, when he heard a noise and saw a bush move. He shouted, "Come on out, Abdul, or, I'll have to shoot you." He fired one round into the sand.

Kurt heard some rocks rattle and the little man took off. Smiling, Kurt walked quickly in the same direction, looking up to make sure Shawn saw them. The helicopter stayed above.

Three times Kurt got to within shouting distance of Abdul. Each time the man managed to elude him.

The tracks headed up and to the left of a small knoll, so Kurt ran and eased around the far left side.

He quickly peeked around a rock and brought his head back. Abdul fired. The shot ricocheted off a rock.

Kurt lurched to another rock and fired a shot at the man hiding beyond the top of the hill.

The fugitive fired five quick shots at the chopper. Kurt heard impact noises. The pilot took the aircraft up several hundred yards.

Kurt took out the rifle and inserted a dart.

Get him alive.

He jumped around another group of rocks as the Arab fired two more shots at the helicopter.

One shot left, sucker. Kurt caught a glimpse of the fugitive and fired twice from the Uzi, kicking up chunks of rock in Abdul's face.

The chopper ejected a large net. Kurt chanced another look and saw the small man struggling to pull it off.

Kurt aimed the drug gun and fired.

The Arab jerked and tried to reach his neck.

Kurt watched Abdul's hand shake as he dropped his gun. He kept his eyes trained on the man while he advanced.

Twenty steps closer, he saw him working his mouth, his faced blanched.

Advancing cautiously, Kurt came to within ten paces. It was then that Kurt realized something else was happening.

The Arab looked like a fish out of water. He struggled violently to gasp air. His face turned dark red. By the time Kurt arrived, his arms seized his chest. His lips turned gray.

It took a few seconds for Kurt to realize what was going on. This was no normal reaction to the drug dart. He rushed to the man and saw him jerking violently and working his jaw. White foam now gushed from his mouth.

Kurt unzipped his collar, patted him down and found a packet in his jacket. He drew it out and saw the pink pill inside.

Fucking cyanide!

Abdul's eyes bugged wide.

Kurt recognized the effects of the suicide pill. He watched helplessly, trying to think of a way to save the fugitive.

Fuck! No antidote.

The Arab shook violently for a few moments. Then he lay quietly, his eyes and mouth open, his face muscles taught, foam on his chin and chest.

Kurt felt for a pulse. He shook his head, stood, and signaled the chopper with a hand across his throat. He motioned to take up the net.

As the aircraft reeled it in, Kurt untangled it from the dead man. The chest harness was lowered. The chopper drew the harness up with the corpse.

Kurt called Langley. He dialed his 11-digit international code then punched in his personal ID.

Berkley came on the line. "What's up *Tiburon*?"

"Got a dead Arab here, Top. He was trying to get to the border. We cornered him and he bit a DZ-41 capsule."

"A DZ-41! Al Qaeda!"

"Exactly. He was wanted for murder."

There was a long silence. Berkley asked, "Where do you go from here?"

"I'm going to track down the source of the APB."

"Good thinking. Keep me informed."

"Okay, Top. Out." Kurt put the phone away as the empty harness came down from the chopper to lift him up.

Chapter 55

Mojave County, Arizona

Kurt Valdez pointed "So there's the new Pat Tillman bridge."
"Second-highest one in the U.S. now," Rich Newsome said. "After the Royal Gorge."
"That a fact?" Shawn Gunnison asked.
The chopper passed over the concrete arch. "It's a beauty," Kurt said, as he waved his arm in an arc. "Damn! Look how low Lake Mead is."
Shawn Gunnison banked the helicopter to port.
Rich said, "Haven't had a good rainfall or snowpack in eighteen years. Even the last *El Niño* and *La Niña* seven and eight years ago didn't fill it up."
"It must be fifty feet lower!" Kurt shook his head.
"More like seventy," the pilot said. He eased the chopper forward. "There's the helipad next to the dam's parking lot. I'll set 'er down."
"Your ride's waiting, Kurt," Rich Newsome pointed to a white SUV with Sheriff's Department decals. "Bet you're gonna miss turkey this year."
"Again," Kurt said.
The aircraft eased gently onto the white cross marks and Kurt opened the door as the props and engine wound down to idle. A female approached, leaned in and offered her hand. Kurt noted her name tag, Mazur. He unzipped the body bag and she took a glance at the face of the dead man.
"That's him," she said loudly, making a face. She shot a quick look at the man in handcuffs on the opposite seat. "Coyote?"
Kurt nodded and shut the door. They moved from under the props. The chopper rose, banked, and took off toward the south to deliver the corpse.
In the SUV, Kurt flashed a badge. "I'm with the government," he added.
She offered her hand. "Krysta Mazur, assigned to Mojave County, Arizona Sheriff's Department for Homeland Security."
"Mazur? You must be part Arabic?"
"One-half Syrian. My father." Her eyes were hazel and she wore her black, wavy hair shoulder length. She was attractive with an olive complexion.
Kurt flashed a smile. "I'm half Lebanese." He handed her a jar in a plastic bag. "Has the suspect's finger prints on it, while he was still warm."
Krysta set the baggy in the middle tray and pulled the SUV out onto the

bridge over Hoover Dam. She pointed, "Our office is in Arizona." The SUV scooted between two more trucks. She said, "Government, huh? I used to work for NSA as a translator."

He started to comment. She held a hand up to quiet him while she maneuvered through two semi-trucks, then pulled into a parking lot.

Kurt followed her through a door into a satellite sheriff's office. He noticed that she was taller than he was and the short khaki uniform revealed tan legs.

Inside, a well-built, middle-aged man with auburn hair and a ruddy complexion came out from the back office. Krysta introduced Kurt to Sheriff Stroman. "He's with the government, Sheriff. They got Ricardo Morales."

"I was surprised to hear he was dead," Stroman said. "We've been trying to locate him for a year on a Murder One charge. Mexican authorities were supposed to be working with us."

"What we're interested in," Kurt said, "is the *way* he died. With a DZ-41 capsule. Al Qaeda uses them."

The sheriff went wide-eyed. "Al Qaeda. We've had suspicions about those guys for a couple of years. They're Palestinians."

"I saw the APB." Kurt said.

Stroman brought a hand on his chin. "We could never get enough evidence for a search warrant. When we finally did, they had disappeared."

"Do you have time to give me details?" Kurt looked from one to the other.

Krysta said, "I'll set up the PowerPoint." She pushed her hair behind her ear

She rolled out the chairs for them to sit. Then she turned on a projector and clicked some keys on the desk computer. A map came up on the screen on the opposite wall.

Kurt watched as they went through the slides and the story of the Morales brothers, Deputy Travis Williams' murder, and their subsequent discovery that Travis had visited the brothers on the day they suspected he died. Kurt raised his eyebrows when he heard that someone had knocked out the deputy's teeth and cut off his fingers.

Aerial photos from NSA showed a black-and-white car behind the brothers' shop building and part-way inside.

"He owned that former black-and-white California Highway Patrol car."

"Did you find out where they took the car?" Kurt asked.

Krysta said, "No. There were thunderstorms on and off that day. Those are the only three photos the satellites got of the car." She went to the next screen, a large view showing the whole area on the east side of Palo Verde Springs. Lake Mead was barely visible on the upper edge of the slide.

The sheriff said, "We found Travis' Skoal chewing tobacco can next to the road. Had his fingerprints on it. It was bought sometime during the month he disappeared."

Krysta used a light pointer to indicate where the can was found.

The next series of slides were taken inside the workshop during nighttime. "We investigated a burglary and took those photos," the sheriff said. "Show the alarm company's clip, Krysta."

Kurt watched as a very dark scene unfolded where two men came through the back door. They used flashlights and kept their covered heads down. One went straight to key in the alarm codes and turned on the small shop lights. The clip ended.

"We're certain that was Ricardo Morales—er—Abdul bin Ibrahim," Stroman said. "That clip was received last night. We put out the APB this morning."

"And he died trying to get across the desert into Mexico." Kurt said.

There was a long silence. He tapped his chin with his index finger. "Can you run that clip again? Freeze it on the second guy."

Krysta ran the show backwards.

"There," Kurt said.

She stopped the motion. Then she zoomed and tried to enhance the frame. It merely turned grainy with less contrast.

"That could be the Coyote who was taking him across the border—Carlos de la Villa." Kurt turned to look at the sheriff. "The question is what was the Palestinians' connection to Al Qaeda? Is the building empty now?"

Krysta answered, "Yes. A mechanic rented it for awhile. We could get a search warrant." She looked at the sheriff as she said this.

"There's nothing to find," Stroman said. "We have it roped off as a crime scene. Nothing but dust on the lights, overhead crane, and workbenches. Plywood over concrete floor with grease smudges, and a hydraulic lift. Turds in the dog pen. Houses were abandoned with rotting screens coming off."

Kurt looked at the sheriff. "How about the brother?"

"Zaki. aka Jorge." Krysta said. "He's thought to be hiding out in Mexico."

"Could I visit the shop?"

Stroman nodded to Krysta. "Don't touch anything. Treat it like a crime scene."

She switched off the slide show, rose and took a key from a hook. Turning, she said to Kurt, "I'll drive you out there."

Chapter 56

Mojave County, Arizona

Krysta drove the sheriff's white SUV up the curves leaving Hoover Dam and crested the hill. Kurt watched as the wide expanse of desert opened before them, with a view of the Colorado River on the right. Jagged mountains of black, reddish, and tan outcroppings lay to the east.

"I haven't seen this view since the 1980s."

"Where have you been?"

"I was in the Army during Gulf War One. They found out I could speak fluent Arabic, so I got special treatment as a translator for American officers."

Krysta stepped on the accelerator and passed two vehicles. "When I worked for NSA, I translated several conversations of Abu Zubayda to Ayman Zawahiri."

Kurt smiled. "I was in Pakistan when they got Khalid Sheikh Mohammad."

Now Krysta smiled. "KSM. Did they waterboard him like the news said?"

There was a long, uncomfortable silence.

Finally, Krysta said, "I'm sorry, I didn't mean to imply ...."

"There are things I can't talk about. It's a disaster over there now—with the drugs."

She accelerated around another car. "I quit and got another job in the private sector in '08. But I heard plenty."

"I had trouble sleeping sometimes." He said. "That whole area is a narco area. I sometimes wish we could just take the women out of the country for forty years and they would go extinct." Kurt glanced at her and saw her nod in agreement. Again he went silent.

The SUV went around an 18-wheeler. Mile post 12 came up on the right. He got a glimpse of the river. "My wife is Afghani. I really missed the states. Thought I'd never come back."

"I'm sorry—I didn't mean ...."

"That's okay. My wife, her cousin and mother-in-law came here with me. They are happy to be away from all the violence and destitution."

"Do you have children?"

"Two boys and two girls. One more on the way."

Krysta pointed. "The turnoff is four more miles."

Another long silence. Since Kurt had seen the slides this morning he was continuously analyzing. He cleared his throat. "So these Palestinians built electric signs? Like, for gas stations and markets?"

"Big signs. Casinos. Some in three large sections. They moved them on semi-trucks."

"Huh. That must take a lot of skills."

"Oh, yeah. I saw their accounting records. They had a booming business. Did everything, too—cutting and grinding metal and plastic, sophisticated welding, electrical. They have ninety-mile-per-hour winds in Vegas. Some of the support pipes were three feet in diameter."

"What made the sheriff suspicious in the first place?"

"They reported that their welder was stolen. Big electric arc-welder. Cost $3,000." Krysta appeared to be thinking this over. Finally, she said, "A few months after that Travis Williams …."

"The deputy who was murdered?"

"Yeah. He disappeared."

The vehicle slowed and Krysta turned left. Kurt saw the sign: Palo Verde Springs 26; Bonelli Landing 43. "What's at Bonelli Landing?"

"Boat ramps to launch small boats."

"Buildings?"

"Only a small ranger station, a ways from the landing. Toilets. Well above high-water mark."

"Huh." Kurt rubbed his jaw. After a moment he asked, "So these guys were good mechanics. They could build things."

"Oh, yeah. Bob—the sheriff said they were very smart. They spoke four languages and I think they read them quite well."

"Four languages? So, the sheriff *was* suspicious?"

"At that time, no one knew Travis was dead. You didn't have the satellite photos with the black-and-white vehicle."

"That's right. He was only reported as missing. And they thought he took a vacation to Mexico after he quit his job at the Cairo."

"And they never found the black and white?"

"No. The sheriff in Las Vegas investigated every lead—drugs, prostitution, even the Mafia. Travis was a fairly upstanding citizen. Even donated money to his church. The only thing they could think of, based on his buddy at work, was that he might have had a run in with drug gangs in Mexico—because of the car."

"That would explain a disappearance."

"The sheriff and I both believed they were dirty. We realized they were very nervous—especially Jorge. I told the sheriff that he would break under questioning. We discussed that further for weeks. Then the sheriff came back to the office one day after Travis' body was discovered and told me that they had suddenly moved back to Mexico."

Kurt went wide-eyed again. "They *were* guilty."

Krysta nodded.

"The sheriff contacted the Mexican police for help?" Kurt's mind worked furiously while he assimilated all this information.

"Yes. They have warrants and pictures posted everywhere."

There was several minutes of silence. Krysta slowed as they arrived at Palo Verde Springs. Kurt scrutinized the gray-block buildings and the curio shop on the right of the highway that sold Indian artifacts and petrified wood.

Krysta pointed. "That's Stufloten's store and gas station on the left. The shop is another quarter-mile."

Further on, as they approached the property, she said, "We found the Skoal tobacco can right there at the wide place in the road."

She turned down the driveway. Gravel crunched under the tires.

"Big place," Kurt said.

"Some of the signs they made were sixty feet wide."

Kurt scanned the premises and took in the house on the left which looked dry and rundown, with a layer of dust on the roof. Yellow plastic tape was wrapped around the shop and a sign noted the suspected crime scene.

"Wait here," she said. She got out and walked around the back. The large metal door rolled up.

Kurt noted the dog pen. "They had a dog."

"Yes, they got it after the welder went missing. That's also when they installed the alarm system."

Walking around inside the shop, Kurt looked out back. A low fence surrounded a cactus garden. Prickly pear apples reddened on the ears. Beyond the fenced-in area, waist-high bushes sparsely covered the terrain that rose at a gradual slope for at least several miles. When he returned to the front and looked east, he could see the entrance to the lower end of the Grand Canyon.

Krysta motioned him back inside. "They used these big roll-around tables to maneuver the signs around to work on them. This is virtually the way the inside of the building looked the last time I saw it. Only a little dustier."

Kurt looked at the walls and shelves, the ceiling lights and bridge crane, and the floor. He studied the back door and the vent that passed through the roof. The plywood covering the floor was warped up on the edges. A few of the laminations were frayed.

"The sheriff said they replaced the plywood frequently. It now has these oil spots from the mechanic."

"What's under the plywood?"

"Concrete, like near the walls." She answered.

"You have keys to the houses?"

"Yes. I've never been inside them."

They opened and walked through the front house. It smelled of urine, dirty diapers and rotted fruit. Kurt opened the refrigerator and slammed it shut. "Damn! That's what abandoned smells like."

The kitchen cabinets had a few mouse droppings. In the bathroom, the only objects were a bottle of child's Aspirin and two rubber baby-bottle nipples.

"Do you want to check out Jorge's house? They said it was totally empty."

"I'll take a quick look." Kurt hurried through the smaller building in the back, and went out the rear door.

He blinked as the back yard contained a surprise: a green garden. Good, plastered, high-fences kept out most of the smaller rodents and deer and goats.

Krysta said, "Huh. I didn't see this before in the dark. I heard the owner left the utilities turned on. It must have its own watering system. Those plastic owls and small windmills on the poles must keep away most of the birds."

Kurt opened a gate and walked to the end of the rows, then on along the side of the garden. Weeds grew around the bases of the plants. Rotted tomatoes, chili peppers and squash hung on vines. A row of grapes was visible near the back fence. After he passed the seventh row, he said, "Huh. They grew *qat*."

Krysta, following along behind, asked, "Where?"

"There." Kurt pointed. "Chewing *qat* is the national pastime in Yemen. Nearly all the men take an afternoon siesta and chew a golf-ball-sized wad every day except the Sabbath."

She went over and pulled some of the weed smelled it. "This stuff was in the sheriff's report. Stroman took a sample out the Morales' trash. He wondered if Travis had also found some."

"And perhaps paid a visit to the brothers on his own, to confront them?"

"That's what the sheriff said also."

"This stuff has to be fresh, very fresh. The armies fighting each other in Somalia stop their shooting momentarily to allow the trucks carrying *qat* to pass through their lines. It's that popular.

Kurt added, "I'll bet their al Qaeda contact brought the brothers some early on."

"Interesting." Krysta studied Kurt for a few seconds. Then she asked, "Have you seen everything you need to see?"

"I'd like to go inside the shop once more."

Actually, he was stalling for time. His mind raced. They headed out of the garden, crossed behind the shop and all the way around to the front again.

Walking inside, Kurt lifted a plywood sheet about 18-inches, then let it drop. He looked under two more.

"Concrete floor is spotless for a mechanic's shop, huh?" Krysta said.

Kurt grunted acknowledgment. He rose and walked around near the three inside walls, examining the floor, looking under shelves, moving metal bins on their wheels. "I'm amazed how clean everything is."

"Oh, yeah. The brothers were neat. I saw the inside twice while they manufactured signs. Wire was neatly coiled on hooks. Screws and bolts in bins or plastic containers. Tools hung on peg-board sheets with metal clips. Pipes were either stood on end in vertical bins or bigger ones were in that long bin next to the wall." She pointed. "There were kegs with big items like long bent bolts, washers and nuts. The welder always had its cables rolled on hooks when they were not using it. Torches had safety chains around them. Grinder even had plastic ties on the electric cord so it didn't hang."

"Empty now," Kurt said, nodding. "I guess there's nothing more to see. You ready to leave?"

"Yes. You go out through the roll-up door. I'll close it and turn the power off."

Heading out front, Kurt walked out onto the concrete slab, then turned for one last look inside. Just as the metal sections started to roll down, he caught sight of something under one of the metal bins.

"Hold it!"

Krysta stopped the door half way.

He ducked back inside and went to the back. Kneeling down he used his knife and dragged out a piece of metal.

Krysta bent over him. "A belt buckle. With a marine insignia!"

They looked at each other and said at the same time, "Travis!"

"Let me get a sample bag," Krysta said.

While she went to the vehicle, Kurt scanned the floor again and saw an imprint. It was faint and round, and about three-inches in diameter. He stared at it for several seconds. She returned and he carefully dropped the buckle into the specimen bag.

"Look at this." He pointed to the circle, took his knife by the blade end and tapped on the middle of the spot with the handle. A hollow sound came from the floor.

"Might be an old plumbing pipe that was capped off and sealed." She said.

"Yeah, could be." He tapped around the hole and the floor sounded solid. Remaining squatted, he did a once-around, looking under all the bins. "Nothing more here."

She went back to the door control and he returned to the vehicle.

Back on the highway, Krysta asked, "You like something to drink?"

"Sounds good."

She pulled into Stufloten's store and gas station. Inside, Krysta greeted the white-haired man, introduced Kurt, and asked, "How's Helga?"

While the two spoke, Kurt got two unsweetened Lipton teas out of the cool cases.

Moments later, Krysta followed him to the drinks.

"Looks like we have the same tastes."

He smiled and nodded. "Arabs."

Outside, Krysta got in the SUV and closed the door. Kurt walked several feet away. He took out his satellite phone and dialed the CIA.

Berkley came on the line. "What did you find out, *Tiburon*?"

"The dead guy had a brother. We need him, *now*. Yesterday! Get a picture, description and information from the Arizona sheriff. Here's his office number."

"Isn't there already an APB on him, too?"

"Yes. He's in Mexico," Kurt said. "Find out if our contacts can get anything from la policía."

"They're using extreme measures on the Coyote as we speak. A chopper is headed your way. Give me some GPS coordinates."

"Right. We're twenty minutes from Highway 93."

Kurt stepped over to the sheriff's vehicle. "Krysta, can you give me the coordinates of that turn on Highway 93?"

Krysta advanced the small screen on the GPS and read off the numbers while Kurt passed them on.

Berkley acknowledged and asked, "You awake, Kurt?"

"Barely. I caught some zees in Arizona."

"Okay, have the pilot take you to your vehicle. Catch some shut-eye at home. Keep your satellite phone nearby. I'll get back to you."

Kurt signed off and closed the phone.

On the road a few minutes later, Krysta held up the specimen bag with the buckle that had a marine insignia on it. "If this proves to be Travis' and it has Ricardo's—er—Abdul's fingerprints, we'll have our first definite piece of evidence."

"Yeah, too bad the man's dead."

"His brother probably isn't," she said. "With solid evidence, maybe the *federales* will get serious about Jorge."

"I want to find him first."

Krysta started to say something, then gave him a look that said, "I don't want to touch that one."

Chapter 57

Mexico City

Ramzi bin Omeri glanced at his satellite phone. It buzzed on silent ring and indicated the call was from the contact that was sent to pick up Carlos the Coyote and Abdul bin Ibrahim.

He stepped out of the SUV and scanned around. The lights over Mexico City were beginning to blink on. The sky showed dull red on the horizon through the ever-present smog.

Ramzi said, "*Sí.*"

"*Sobre las tortillas, Señor?*"

"*Las tortillas? Sí,*" Ramzi answered.

"*Lo siento, pero no hay maize.*"

There was a long silence. *No corn—they're missing.* Ramzi swallowed. "No maize?"

"*De verdad.*"

Answer him—not important. "*No importa. Te llamaré en la proxima semana.*"

Ramzi pressed the off button on the phone.

There was no mistaking the message: the bad-news signal. Carlos the Coyote and Abdul were late and missing—five hours late.

The Snow Leopard got back in the vehicle and said to the driver, "Take me back to the house as fast as possible. Don't alert the police."

At Zaki's condominium, Ramzi rang the basement buzzer. It took over a minute for the Palestinian to open the door. Ramzi's expression said it all.

The small man's face contorted. "Bad news?"

Ramzi grunted. "Get that briefcase you always keep ready. Come with us. Don't alert your family."

A few minutes later the driver sped away. After several stops and curves through residential sections of the city, they halted at a small shop for a make-up technician to disguise Zaki, then changed to another vehicle.

Ramzi had been silent until now. Now he spoke Arabic. "*Sadiqque*—friend, we must be prepared to make the supreme sacrifice. Abdul may have been captured, or if he bit his capsule, he is dead."

The force of his words obviously made a deep impression on the small Palestinian. He blinked back tears.

The driver, already briefed, turned onto the toll highway that led to the airport.

Chapter 58

Tecate, Mexico near the California border

Zaki bin Ibrahim examined his new Mexican passport and work visa that the Snow Leopard handed him. "The document makers are very good? These even have wear."

Ramzi bin Omeri nodded. "Yes, they are good." In Mexico City, the make-up technician had stuck on a thick brush mustache and curly wig.

Zaki said, "I am now Julian Padilla. And I have lived in San Bernardino for six years."

The Snow Leopard spoke in a serious tone. "When you arrive at the border crossing, have the DZ-41 capsule ready. If they recognize you, bite it."

Zaki squeezed his lips together and swallowed. He blinked back tears as he thought about his brother. Donning the motorcycle leathers and helmet, he slipped the suicide pill into his unzipped jacket pocket. He pushed the start button on the motorcycle and heard the engine come to life.

Ramzi patted his helmet and the Palestinian took off through the town of Tecate, Mexico headed toward California.

After six blocks, Zaki turned north and stopped in the traffic line. It was less than 100 yards to the International border. He edged forward. When he came to within six vehicles of the Border Patrol agents' booths, he lifted his face-shield and slipped the pill into his mouth. He pushed it up along the gum line with his tongue. He had one quick thought. It was a good thing that Ramzi had him take the beta blocker. The man told him it would keep his heart from racing. He felt calm as he approached the booths.

The border agent turned out to be a woman. "Good morning, Sir."

"Good morning," he said, in the best English he could muster. He handed her the passport and visa.

"What was the purpose of your visit to Mexico, Mr. Padilla?"

"My daughter was sick. They live in San Ignacio."

The agent twisted her mouth pensively. "And where are you headed?"

"I live in San Bernardino. I work in a body shop there."

She considered this for a moment. "Could I see your hands?"

Zaki shut off the motor and removed his gloves. He held his palms forward. She rubbed the hard calluses. "You should take off the helmet, too."

He put the kickstand down and removed his helmet.

She held up the passport photo and compared it to his face.

The woman then stepped back in the booth and compared him to a series of photos. She stopped once and glanced back and forth several times at one photo, tilting her head as she looked at him. He touched the DZ-41 capsule with his tongue.

"Okay, Mr. Padilla. It looks like you can proceed."

Zaki eased the helmet over his head and fastened the chinstrap. He put on his gloves, and pressed the electric starter. The engine came to life.

"Oh, just a minute." She put her hand on his arm.

"Yes?"

He felt his pulse pound at his temples.

"You almost forgot your work visa." She handed him the document.

"Oh … thank you," he said.

Slipping the document into his jacket pocket, he dropped the motorcycle into gear. He took off slowly, then shifted and accelerated.

After several cars went by, he spit the pill into his hand and placed it back into his pocket. Then he sucked in a large breath and exhaled slowly.

Six hours later, Zaki turned right off Highway 93 toward Palo Verde Springs. He had traveled through Yuma, Arizona, then alongside the Colorado River. Several times he'd thought about Abdul and blinked back tears. He filled up with gasoline at Kingman where he connected with Ali bin Khalifa. He recognized the Arab's red Honda motorcycle, and riding clothes identical to his. As planned, Ali joined him.

The two Arabs approached Palo Verde Springs at dusk. Zaki saw Stufloten's store and gas station on the left. The old man collected money from a customer.

Just as they passed through town, a sheriff's white SUV zoomed over a dip and roared by them. Zaki got a quick look at Sheriff Stroman.

He coughed as he thought about how risky this operation was.

Going by the sign shop at dusk, he could barely make out the yellow police tape around the building. He went on another mile and flipped on the right signal to alert Ali, then turned on the dirt road that swung on around a quarter-mile behind the property. They proceeded further with the lights out, dodging the barely visible creosote bushes, to arrive within 100 yards of the structures. Shutting off their engines, they put kick-stands down. Zaki told the other Arab to sit tight while he checked out the premises. He crunched through the gravel inside the cactus garden and on around to the back and side of the main building.

On the east side of the shop, Zaki put on mechanic's rubber gloves. He pulled slack on the telephone wires, skinned back the insulation and cut them. Then after pushing the slack back down into the conduit and snapping the cover shut, he backtracked to the motorcycle and waited.

At least a half hour passed when Mr. Stufloten pulled down the driveway, left his engine running, and walked around the property beaming a powerful flashlight. The old man shined his light into the houses, the walled garden in back, checked the back door of the shop, and left.

"Good," Zaki said. "That means they have lost the alarm system. The sheriff we passed earlier must have asked that old man to check the premises for him. That means the sheriff won't return. I figure we have eight hours."

Grabbing a cooler and tools off the back of the motorcycle, Zaki motioned for bin Khalifa to follow him to the back door. He took the lock-pick set Ramzi had given him, and worked on the lock. It took more than several minutes to finally open the door.

"Wait here."

Zaki kept his head down and flashed his tiny light around inside. At the circuit breakers, he cut off the alarm power first. Opening the alarm cabinet, he silenced the trouble buzzer. Then he erased the intrusion memory. After unplugging the back-up battery, he watched the LED lights go off.

Now he turned on a nightlight and crane power. He heard the relays make a clacking noise and exhaled.

Stepping outside, he raised the satellite phone. When a voice answered, he said, "Your order is ready, Sir."

The Snow Leopard's voice acknowledged and his satellite phone turned off.

"Follow me," Zaki said to Ali.

In the walled-in garden, Zaki shoveled sand aside and exposed a lift door to a small tool cellar. Inside it there were lifting hardware and cables for the crane, a water hose, and a concrete saw. He jumped down and handed the cables, shackles and hose up to Ali.

"Give me a hand with this saw. It weighs 100 kilos."

Ali climbed down and they strained to get the saw up and onto the gravel outside the garden.

Back inside the shop, they piled 16 pieces of plywood on a lifting strap. Zaki maneuvered the wood aside with the crane. He began running the water saw through four lines of pour rock in a rectangular shape twenty-eight by eight feet. He made one cross-cut at four feet to make a rectangle. Pausing the saw work to locate lifting bolts in the middle of the section, he showed Ali how to chip concrete out of them. The Arab chipped while he finished cutting the larger area. He then sawed the cross-cuts to expose the joints in concrete lift-out sections.

Completing that task, he turned off the water, vacuumed the excess water, and glanced at his watch. Two hours had passed.

Ali continued chipping concrete out of the lifting eyes while Zaki hammered two lifting yokes into the bolts of the first concrete section. He connected short cables to them, ran the crane hook over and took up the load.

The overhead assembly squealed as it lifted the first four-foot by eight-foot section. Ali backed off his work and looked at him with wide eyes.

"It weighs 4,000 kilos," Zaki said.

The whites of Ali's eye's showed as he looked up at the crane apparatus.

Zaki maneuvered the concrete floor section to the side and repeated the operation on the next five sections as quick as Ali could chip them out.

"A boat. An undersea boat!" Ali said, as soon as he could see below.

"Yes. It is very secret. We must get it away from here. But for now, let us eat, my friend."

From the cooler, Zaki split three tacos each and two large colas with the Arab.

After they ate and rested, he lowered Ali down and had him fasten the crane hook and cables to the lifting eyes of the submarine.

Several minutes passed as he jockeyed the load up to the first floor while Ali rode it up to help. The support cradles came up with the vessel. Finally, they maneuvered it to the side of the shop and set it down. They both stared at it in satisfaction. It was an elegant boat, with a conning tower, thick, round glass windows and a prop on the back.

"I built this with my brother. There are eight air tanks in this front compartment." Zaki gestured to a conical-shaped nose. "We hooked them to the 3,000 pound system that will keep a man alive for five days. The air makes the submarine run, and go up and down. And it has an extra motor."

Ali bin Khalifa was obviously impressed. "What is it for?"

"They never told us." Zaki didn't say anything about the bomb mounted inside the submarine.

He opened the cooler again. "Come my friend. I have Moroccan sweet cakes and more soda."

Ali reached for the treats.

They rested again for several minutes.

"What do we do now?"

Zaki gestured. "Set the floor sections back in place and seal the floor."

When they had set the sixth section in place and taken off the lifting yokes, Zaki showed Ali how to mix the Pour-Rock and fill in the saw-cut joints. After they finished sealing the floor, they put the saw and hardware away and covered the tool cellar with sand.

They took another break and drank more soda while the quick-setting cement dried.

The drink gave Zaki a boost and the two Arabs moved the plywood with the crane. From the central pile, they slid each sheet off to its proper place.

Zaki looked at his watch. "Six hours. They will be here at three. We can sleep on those workbenches."

Chapter 59

Arizona Highway 93,
Colorado River near Kingman

Ramzi bin Omeri shifted the green one-ton truck into third and accelerated past an eighteen-wheeler. After several hundred yards, he swerved the Ford F-350 and large fiberglass boat back into the right lane.

"Mile-post 22," he pointed. "I'm going to gain distance on that truck, Abu. Our turn is six miles ahead."

Kareem Abu Bakr grunted acknowledgment, smiling at the use of his affectionate name. Abu meant father in Arabic.

Several minutes later, Ramzi glanced in the mirror and flipped on the turn signal. "Here it is." He made the turn and accelerated. "The turn signal on the boat trailer works. I can see it in the mirror."

It was almost three in the morning when they arrived at Palo Verde Springs and the shop.

Zaki was expecting them and the roll-up door came open. Ramzi swerved around on the gravel and backed the boat and trailer inside.

Zaki and Ali were ready with lifting straps. They threw them around the boat while Kareem unfastened hold-downs. When the man signaled he was ready, Zaki lifted the large fiberglass boat off the trailer. Ramzi pulled forward.

Zaki maneuvered the big boat with the crane to the side of the shop where he set it on stands.

He then moved the crane assembly to the submarine, lifted it, and Kareem and Ali jarred the support yokes loose. Zaki maneuvered the undersea boat to the middle of the shop.

While all this was going on, Ramzi straightened the trailer out, all the while watching the men in his mirrors. Then, he watched Kareem's hand signals and eased the trailer under the vessel. Finally, as it came into position, Zaki lowered the submarine into its fitted cradle on the trailer.

Ramzi jockeyed the trailer and submarine out of the shop. Once the others had the large fiberglass boat situated, he backed under the vessel and watched the other Arabs position its large designed cavity over the submarine. He heard a solid clunk as the two vessels came together indicating a perfect fit.

"Connect the lights again, Kareem. I'll pull out."

He heard the slap on the truck when the men were ready, placed the truck in first gear and inched forward until he was out of the shop. While he did that, Zaki and Ali prepared to repair the alarm system and lock the shop for the last time.

Ramzi handed a folded paper to Kareem. In Arabic, he said, "Give it to Ali while Zaki is busy."

Kareem gave him that look. The one he presented when Ramzi told him to kill that Mexican driver. He rolled his lips in tightly and nodded that he understood.

Ramzi watched in the mirror as Kareem feigned helping the two men in the shop. Finally, Kareem slipped the paper to Ali and whispered to him. He glanced at Ramzi momentarily.

Kareem then hurried up to the road to make sure no vehicles were coming. Ramzi pulled out onto the main highway and Kareem got into the truck.

"Did the signals and brake lights work, Abu?"

"Yes," Kareem looked solemn.

"Okay we'll head for the storage." Ramzi took one glance back and, in the faint moonlight, saw Zaki and Ali in their black motorcycle garb heading south in the desert. He would meet them again in Mexico.

It was almost daylight when Ramzi and Kareem reached Kingman, Arizona and the parking garage that they had rented for the boat.

"Here is the key for the padlock and the remote control for the door. You have to hold the door all the way open to clear the big boat."

Ramzi pulled ahead, then backed and jockeyed the trailer into the tight space while Kareem signaled him.

Once inside, Kareem unhitched the trailer and ran the power jack up. Ramzi felt the load come off the truck. He watched in relief as Kareem locked the roll-up door.

"What did the paper say?" Kareem had a stern look.

Ramzi glared at him for several breaths. "I worked with Zaki long enough to know he will not bite the capsule if he is caught. The man will not be with Ali when we meet again in Mexico."

Kareem, the old soldier who had seen hundreds of Afghan-Arabs die in Afghanistan, narrowed his eyes. They flickered. He looked away for a moment. Then he said, "*Ensha Allah.*"

Ramzi repeated it and exhaled. *Made it with the submarine.*

As Kareem got into the truck, Ramzi made his phone call.

Then he said, "Now we have to make it safely into Mexico, Abu. But first, we need something to eat."

Chapter 60

Mojave County, Arizona

Sheriff Bob Stroman heard the front door close and signaled Krysta Mazur back to his office. After just returning from the processing lab in Las Vegas, she slid the NSA photographs onto his desk.

He spread them out in date sequence. "One hundred seventy photos of the sign shop with construction in progress."

"What are we going to do with them?"

"A friend is on his way to give us some expert advice."

"Expert advice?" Krysta looked puzzled.

"You'll see," the sheriff said. "Go ahead and arrange the digital versions in a PowerPoint display by number and date. Make a duplicate file so we can remove the unnecessary ones. Could you insert the sixteen slides we took first?"

Krysta returned to the front office desk and computer while Stroman studied the printouts, deciding which ones were not pertinent. As he examined them with his big magnifying glass, he kept the desired ones in a file, stacking the others aside face down.

After the sheriff sorted three-quarters of the photos. He gave Krysta the numbers of 27 slides to be removed.

She looked at the list and nodded. He went to the back office to finish culling them.

The phone rang. "I'll take it," he called out.

He answered, and then asked, "Thadius, how close are you?"

Thadius Daley, Stroman's construction expert, told the sheriff that he was 30 minutes away because a large semi was blocking the 215-515 junction.

"No problem, Thad. We're not quite ready anyway."

Krysta called out, "If you set up the projector, I'll take these last few discards out."

Stroman finished the list of slides to be removed and handed them to her. He brought out the projector and plugged it in, while she connected it to the computer.

Returning to the back office, he finished filing the photos to a cabinet and straightening his desk so there would be no interruptions. He heard voices out front.

"I have a 24-foot boat down at the marina. If you like to water ski, we could make it a Saturday. I'll bet you're a Chablis girl."

"Oh, Jesus. Here we go," Stroman said, walking in and interrupting. "I see you've met Thadius Daley, Krysta. You gotta watch him."

She stood. The color rose in her cheeks.

Daley held his hand over his heart. "Don't pay any attention to him. I'm harmless."

"She's engaged, Thadius." Stroman grinned and held out his hand. "Hey, old buddy, you look like Mr. Clean, without the big earring. Buffed out, too."

Daley shook it vigorously. "How goes it, Old Man?" he said in his low-raspy voice.

"Old Man, hell. I can hunt circles around you." He grabbed Daley and drew him in for a hug, slapping his back and laughing.

"Krysta? The new woman I heard so much about." He winked at Stroman. "A real looker."

Stroman said, "Hands off, *Buddy*."

She smiled wide. "And, you're the construction expert."

Turning to her, the sheriff said, "Thad has five younger sisters and a daughter. He reminds me of that movie Mel Gibson was in, where Mel could hear what women were thinking. Watch out for this guy, Krysta."

Daley laughed four vigorous notes.

"How's the daughter, Thad?"

"She's growing into a beauty. Look." He pulled out several pictures. "Nineteen now. First year in college. She wanted to come work for me, but I told her no way, get four more years of education behind you first."

Stroman looked at the pictures with surprise. "Wow! Look how she's grown up. Last time I saw her, she was 13, with braces. Good thing she got her mother's looks." He passed the pictures to Krysta.

She scrutinized them and said, "Huh. She looks just like him."

Daley gushed as he took the pictures back. "Business major at Oregon State."

"So she doesn't live with you?"

"No, her mom and I agreed to disagree." Daley laughed and put the pictures back. "You both gonna have time for lunch?"

"I think we can manage that," the sheriff answered. "The picture presentation will take about an hour or so."

Daley cleared his throat. "So what was it you wanted me to look at?"

"We've received some satellite photos."

"This about that deputy that was murdered?"

Stroman winced. "Right. Travis Williams. We have an APB out on a Palestinian. His brother killed himself with a suicide pill—the kind al Qaeda uses." Stroman paused to let that news sink in and noted Daley's shocked look.

"That's right, al Qaeda. The government and Homeland Security are involved. They've got the federáles looking everywhere for him in Mexico."

Krysta spun in her chair, pulled out an evidence tray, and showed Daley the contents. "We found Williams' marine belt buckle in the suspects' shop. Had his fingerprints on it."

Daley frowned. "I don't understand."

Stroman said, "Just past Palo Verde Springs, there's a sign shop."

Daley's face brightened. "The little Mexicans."

"They weren't Mexicans. They were Palestinians."

"Incredible. They made the big signs for Vegas. Had to slow down for the big rigs to pull out onto the highway once or twice. You mean they're involved with Travis' murder?"

Stroman nodded.

Krysta said, "It's a long story." She pushed her hair behind her ear.

"Bottom line is," Stroman said, "we have pretty good circumstantial evidence that they killed Williams."

Daley still looked puzzled. "So how can I help?"

"We need an expert," Stroman said. "The government wonders about the al Qaeda connection.

There was another long pause. Daley narrowed his eyes and pinched his eyebrows together. "So you think they were doing something else? Besides building signs?"

"Why don't we show him the slides, Krysta? See if you can tell from the photos, Thadius." Stroman pulled chairs over for Daley and himself.

Krysta handed Daley a light pointer, then turned on the presentation. "The sheriff and I took the first 16 pictures."

The screen lit up with two overhead shots of the whole property. The outside and inside of the sign shop building were the next sequence.

"Big crane," Daley noted.

Stroman agreed. "Some of the signs they constructed were over sixty feet wide, and fabricated in three or four sections."

"Run the NSA pictures, Krysta."

"NSA—the National Security Agency?" Daley asked, surprised.

Krysta said, "That's right. I used to work there." She switched to the next series. The first was a satellite shot that showed Palo Verde Springs and the south edge of Lake Mead.

Daley said, "You can almost see my boat."

The next NSA slide zoomed down on the shop property. Each successive picture showed grading, trenching for a septic system and tank, sewer pipes being laid, and electric and water utilities' conduits up to where the buildings would be constructed.

"What's the extra conduits heading off to the east for?" Daley asked.

"There were two small houses on the property, too." Stroman was fascinated by how systematic all the construction proceeded.

The photos displayed the rectangle of the shop laid out with lime. Then, a large drilling vehicle with an augur on the back arrived. "Hold it there," Daley said. "Can you zoom in on the rig?"

"Sure," Krysta clicked a few keys and the camera view closed in.

"There," Daley said, sounding incredulous. "My god, that's a wide augur. One-third the width of the rig."

"Really?" Stroman tapped his chin.

The truck drilled eight caissons. "The building was a single story, if I remember," Daley said.

"Yes," the sheriff answered. "A large machine shop. Like you said, Thad, the crane inside was big, ran on tracks like a railroad."

"Those caissons are big enough for a six story building. Who did the construction?"

Krysta answered, "Albert Kahn Construction out of Minneapolis,"

Daley looked pensive. "A Pakistani family owns that company. They did the Cairo Hotel."

As Krysta proceeded with the slides, they revealed a backhoe digging grade beams and pushing the dirt around. A load of rebar and steel arrived.

"Man, that's a lot of steel for a building that size!" Daley commented.

Krysta continued a rapid sequence of rebar being installed and a hydrocrane lifting the caisson steel into place.

"Hold it again," Daley said. "Can you back up one slide? Zoom in on the crane lifting that set of steel." Daley got up and went to the screen. He stretched his tape measure along the crane.

"Forty-two inches." Moving over, he said, "The rebar cage is 22 inches. That's a Bucyrus-Erie crane—about 70 feet long."

Krysta did some calculations on the computer. "That works out to about 37 feet of reinforcing steel."

"A 38-foot caisson!" He shook his head. "What does four-and-one-quarter inches work out to?"

"Eight feet," She said.

"Whew. Eight-foot column bolts. Probably an inch-and-a-half in diameter. You could put the Caesar's Palace sign on those eight columns. It was built for 120 mile-per-hour winds."

"Jesus!" Stroman exclaimed.

There was a gap in the slides.

The satellite has a 92-minute gap in coverage," Krysta said.

The screen came to a series showing concrete trucks pouring the caissons and grade beams. A small tractor spread sand. Carpenters then set wood forms for the outside perimeter. Electricians and plumbers installed pipe.

Daley said, "The electrical panel is on the east wall. See all the conduits leaving it? Bathroom is in the southeast corner." He shined the light pointer onto the screen indicating the locations.

Another picture gap occurred, then a loaded flat-bed truck arrived with a crew. The crew erected the structural steel for the building crane.

"That is a *huge* crane for the inside of such a small building. You could easily lift a 20-ton load with it, maybe more."

"Some of the signs they built must have weighed as much as a big truck," Stroman said.

A crane came. "That's a 75-ton rig," Daley said. "They need the jib, that extension on top, to reach the middle of the building."

The big rig lifted the building overhead crane mechanisms in place in three slides. Then another gap in time passed.

Krysta said, "This is really interesting. I would never have believed all the complex processes and the number of workers involved."

"They're definitely professionals," Daley said.

Next, a semi with siding and roofing metal was unloaded with a smaller crane. A crew installed the roof, complete with large metal ventilators and an exhaust fan. Partial shots of the bridge crane inside the shop in different positions, right to left and north and south, were visible until the roof was covered.

"They haven't finished the cement floor," Krysta said.

Daley said, "That was in August. You would want to pour concrete under a roof, beginning before daylight, so it didn't dry or cure too fast. The building crane inside would be used for the pour, with a big bucket."

As the show proceeded, they saw overhead shots of a fork lift offloading rolls of clear plastic, a tractor dumping sand, and a large flatbed with reinforcing steel and wire.

Daley said, "Those wire rolls go over the rebar throughout the whole building. Gives the concrete slab extra strength."

A night photo came up next and revealed a heavy duty fork lift. It had dual wheels on the load end, with something positioned on the forks. Krysta went to the next slide.

"Hold it," Daley said. "Back up one slide?"

She reversed the PowerPoint program.

"Could you zoom in on that fork lift?"

Krysta pushed her hair behind her ear and clicked the keys on the computer. The screen zoomed. The picture became grainy and purplish.

"Can you brighten and enhance it right on the load?"

"Slide 137," she said. "Let me switch over to the actual digital pictures." A photo display software showed on the screen. She selected *Go To*, and typed 137. The night shot came up. Krysta did several manipulations trying to brighten and enhance the picture.

"What's that on the forks under the edge of the roof?"

"Looks like the edge of a square object," Stroman said. "You can just see the corner of it. Show the original slides before it and after it, Krysta."

She went back two slides, then forward. "Only number 138 is another night time shot."

It displayed the fork lift loading a pallet onto the truck.

"Can you zoom that picture, too?"

"What do you see, Thad?" The sheriff asked.

Once again, Daley walked to the screen and measured with his tape. "Twenty-five inches."

"About forty-feet," Krysta said. "Notice it's one o'clock, Mr. Daley."

"Call me Thad; you make me sound old." He turned and winked at her, then continued. "So, that adds an interesting question. What did they bring at one o'clock in the morning that required a 40-foot trailer and a dual-wheeled forklift to unload? I'll have to think on that one."

"You're the expert," the sheriff said. "Would you enhance and print those two pictures for Thad, Krysta?"

"Okay, Bob."

She ran the printer then returned to number 138 on the PowerPoint program. Concrete trucks arrived.

"The concrete trucks unload into the three-yard bucket-chute that the inside crane moves and dumps, starting from the farthest corners, finally completing the pour near the trucks. See the cement finishers leveling in the back with long poles."

Finally the outside metal walls went on and a large roll-up door arrived. Another dual-wheeled forklift raised it near the entry.

The next group was the housing construction.

Stroman said, "We can go through the rest pretty fast."

Krysta went through 40-or-so slides quickly. After the houses were finished, and the outside concrete slabs and walkways materialized, gravel trucks dumped four loads of small rocks and a tractor spread them around the shop building and up the driveway to the highway.

Semi-trucks arrived with materials. The first trucks left with big signs. A night-vision slide displayed the lights of a flat-bed diesel arriving with a load of sign construction materials.

"Okay. That's enough. Let's go eat, Thadius."

"Sounds good to me. How about the *Goldcoast*? Across the dam?"

Stroman raised a thumb and nodded. "You ready, young lady?" Krysta exited PowerPoint and grabbed her fanny pack.

At lunch, they discussed the whole situation with the building and construction. Daley still expressed amazement at the size of the caissons.

The sheriff asked, "Any guesses as to what that forklift took off a forty-foot flatbed and set during the night just before the concrete pour?"

Daley looked at the dark, grainy picture Krysta printed for him. "Wish there had been more preceding and following pictures. But, I'll sleep on it."

CHAPTER 61

Boulder City, Nevada

It was black outside, and a chilly wind howled off the snow-covered mountains to the west. The gusts bore the last bite of winter and rattled the windows. That was unusual for Boulder City, this normally hot city south of Las Vegas, not too far from the Colorado River. Ramzi bin Omeri organized his cadre on the first floor of the masonry building. The *Snow Leopard*, for the first time since his attacks on the Saudi oil facilities four years ago, felt pressure from the Americans.

The developments over the last two years worried him. Al Qaeda was on the run in Waziristan. They were now striking in Pakistan—suicide attacks, *Shuhada'a*, against the Pakistani population. He felt this was a losing tactic in the long run. It would turn Muslims against them. And why were Muslims killing other Muslims?

They had just received the shocking news that Osama bin Laden was dead. Killed by Navy SEALs in Pakistan.

Ayman Zawahiri, Osama bin Laden's number two man, had given Ramzi this assignment in apparent desperation. Fifty-six battle-seasoned *Taliban* trained in Waziristan were now embedded with his forces in the United States.

But assaults on American soil bothered the Snow Leopard at the moment. They might jeopardize his complex plans contrived over the last two years.

He glanced at the satellite phone and awaited the signal to proceed. Inhaling deeply, he shook his head. His plans with the nuclear bomb would be much more significant in bringing down American power.

Checking his watch once again, he thought, *Kareem is late.*

Ramzi felt in his gut that something wasn't right. He had just learned of this new assignment three days ago from a computer disk, brought by a courier and now destroyed. It was only a day after Osama's death. The new information had caused his adrenaline and blood pressure to soar to the point that frequent and severe headaches began.

His watch now said it was nine minutes past midnight. What happened? No satellite phone call.

Members of his cadre were bedded down and Ramzi had posted guards. But the uneasy feeling hadn't subsided. No doubt about it, something wasn't right. His heart raced.

Ramzi's satellite phone vibrated and jarred him awake. He glanced at his watch: 0107 hours. Clicking the phone on, he heard Kareem's voice, "*Los pescados estan aqui.*"—Your fish have arrived.

Ramzi blew a large breath. "*Bueno.*"—good. He carefully recited a string of instructions giving Kareem his location. Then he said, "*Tenga cuidado, amigo.*"—be careful, my friend.

"*Siempre.*"—always.

Ramzi heard the signal disconnect as Kareem switched off. They had used the airwaves for no more than thirty seconds.

Kurt Valdez' heartbeat pounded in his temples. Inserting drug darts into his rifle, he locked and loaded. He glanced at his comrade-in-arms, Hector Navarro, to try to read the man's thoughts. Navarro worked with Kurt on several of the SAP border raids and had just come up from Brownsville, Texas for the joint operation. A former NOC like Kurt, and part Apache, he also spoke both Arabic and Spanish. He had a history of working in Colombia in the drug wars.

Navarro was sturdily built with a hard body. His striking black Indian pupils and coarse black hair were intimidating.

Neither of them had originally welcomed the idea of joining the SAP Units with U.S. Border Protection.

But both had come to trust Captain Roberts' competence and leadership over his special forces, especially after the two accompanied the captain on another raid. Berkley had assured his former NOCs that Captain Roberts was hand-picked for this mission.

These thoughts were going through Kurt's mind when he saw the signal. The officer motioned that the go-ahead had been received from CIA headquarters in Langley. Kurt sucked in a deep breath and steeled himself. He and Navarro moved forward with the micro-cameras. Four more teams like theirs were to set up surveillance points outside the building, feeding video images to Langley, who would direct the operation by way of a National Security Agency satellite. The NSA had intercepted, monitored, and pinpointed the two-story structure as a source of al Qaeda satellite phone conversations. Intelligence had confirmed that Ramzi bin Omeri, the Snow Leopard, was a voice they'd intercepted. But they had not been able to pinpoint the communications.

Now, signal-jamming equipment was activated by the FBI, and all electronic signals in the area were inoperative. Command left no possibilities of failure.

Ramzi's satellite phone vibrated and again jarred him awake. He glanced at his watch: 0321 hours. He heard Kareem's voice say, *"Estoy listo."*—I'm here.

Ramzi exhaled. *"Bueno."*

Ramzi twice flicked a small, red light through the blinds, the signal. Kareem's cadre began entering the building, three and four men at a time. They took up positions, placing their mats on the floor. The Muslims appeared tired.

Kareem pulled Ramzi aside and said, "There is much activity tonight, my friend." The look in his eyes told Ramzi that he was uneasy also.

Ramzi said, "I feel the same as I did before a major battle with the Russians."

Kareem nodded. Two experienced commanders obviously had similar jitters.

"Sleep, my friend. I will remain alert," Ramzi moved to a window and scanned through the blinds with his night-vision.

At 0347 hours, Ramzi's Aqualand buzzed. He made his pre-designated call, as instructed from the computer disk.

A voice had just said, *"Estamos listos,"* when Ramzi heard a screech on his satellite phone.

He shouted. "Get up! Get out of here."

The men of the cadre jerked awake. Kareem yelled and slapped two men to get their attention. They grabbed their weapons and headed for the windows and doors.

"Lock and load!" Ramzi grabbed an AK-47 and the laptop computer. He jerked a cord, unplugging a fax machine to kill what little light it emitted into the room. Kareem and the forward men, who had night-vision, signaled and flung open the door. Several soldiers rolled through and came to their feet. They ran out, surging past one another to form a perimeter. Kareem signaled and pointed he would head north. Ramzi nodded.

The warriors bounded one and two at a time out of the rooms in different directions. Once outside, Ramzi and his three bodyguards headed to their alternate designated safe house. His cadre would split and hide at designated hideouts.

Kurt Valdez peered through the blinds and saw a man sitting on a cot. Several others were asleep on mats on the floor. A fax machine gave off a faint green light that barely illuminated the room. Kurt counted ten then activated the micro-lens.

A few moments later, Captain Roberts gave him a thumb-up. Langley was operational.

Another nearby team peered into the room with night-vision.

At 0359 hours, Captain Roberts signaled for the paramilitary teams to get into position. The men inside would be forced to use the stairway and windows for their escape routes. The captain started counting . . . one finger . . . two. . . .

At 0400 hours, when the captain signaled with the third finger, more than twenty paramilitary personnel broke into the doors, smashed in the windows and rushed inside the building. They shouted and threw small concussion stun grenades. Kurt and Navarro jumped inside just as the terrorists grabbed their guns and knives. In rapid succession, Kurt quickly picked out and shot four warriors with drug darts.

At the same time, Navarro shot three men and they collapsed.

Kurt swung his rifle as a man jumped up from a cot to try to dive through the back door. An FBI agent shot him. Kurt saw splotches of blood gush from the man's thigh, groin and stomach. He lay on the floor.

Kurt spun as another jihadist came at him with a knife. Kurt twisted, parrying the man's thrust, and brought his rifle butt to the man's chin. He crumpled to the floor.

"Look out!" he yelled at Roy. His comrade dodged a thrust from a man wielding a *jambiga*.

Kurt whipped out his Uzi and stopped the jihadist in mid-air. He slumped to the floor screaming. The small Yemeni sword flopped out of his hands. Writhing, he seized his thigh.

The shooting stopped and the SAP unit poured into the room to gather prisoners.

Kurt saw that two team members had been wounded. To his lip-mike he said, "Get some medics in here, quick!"

The jihadist who tried to dive out the window lay moaning on the floor, blood gushing.

Kurt and Navarro went to him, along with an FBI agent. The agent had already examined each prisoner, lifting their heads so he could see their faces. "One eye. It's him. Umar Mohammad."

Kurt shouted and motioned to the medics, "Over here! We've gotta save this guy!" He keyed his lip-mike, "We got one of 'em, Captain."

"Roger that."

The sporadic shots coming from upstairs subsided. The last rapid-fire bursts from M-17s stopped. Captain Roberts came on the earphones, "Cease fire. Bring all prisoners out."

Kurt made sure that Mohammad's bleeding had stopped. Then he and Navarro grabbed two of the drugged men, now handcuffed with snap-ties, and dragged them out. Armored vans, manned by the Border Protection Units, settled low as they took on prisoners.

After the commotion stopped and the last handcuffed prisoners were shoved into vans, Kurt approached the captain.

"It was over in fewer than twenty minutes," said the officer, smiling for the first time tonight as the adrenaline rush obviously abated. "Forty-two terrorists captured and wounded. Only one of them dead. The best showing yet."

Kurt looked around as they finished loading the warriors into the vans. Paramedics attended to the four wounded captives.

"How are the wounded guys?"

"Not too serious," The captain was jubilant. "Flesh wounds."

Medics passed by with a man on a stretcher. The FBI agent with them said, "Captain Roberts, I present to you, Umar Mohammad."

The captain looked at the now unconscious man and saw the bloody clothes.

"Three serious wounds. He might die." The officer frowned.

Turning to the paramedics, he said, "We must save this man. Get him to an operating room as fast as possible."

"Guard the prisoners," Kurt blurted.

Concurring, Captain Roberts shouted at his Special Forces commander, "Bravo One, send a squad to protect and transport that prisoner! ASAP!"

"Affirmative."

The force of the captain's command left no doubt that Umar Mohammad was the most important catch of the night. They had to keep him alive.

The officer moved away and conversed with Langley by satellite phone. After a few minutes he returned to Kurt and Navarro and the other Special Forces' leaders.

Captain Roberts brought the others up to date. "Four other successful raids were carried in Henderson tonight. That's the gunfire we heard."

Kurt asked, "Umar Mohammad?"

"They want to airlift him to Summerlin Hospital in Las Vegas as soon as possible."

"No sign of the Snow Leopard?"

The captain shook his head.

Kurt frowned in disappointment. The main target was supposed to be here.

Ramzi bin Omeri, the *Snow Leopard,* heard shots from automatic weapons across the city from them. Helicopters with searchlights approached from a distance. Dogs barked and howled to Sirens. His cadre made their way, using well-practiced stealth tactics toward designated hideouts. He was furious about the lapse in security. He had split forces with Kareem and each group dispersed. The automatic rifle fire intensified, and he knew that somewhere in Henderson, Nevada warriors were dying. Or, worse, they were being captured. He also knew that his and Kareem's cadres had to get out of the country immediately.

Captain Roberts answered his radio and immediately motioned Kurt over. "Echo squad has detained fourteen suspects. Sergeant Wakefield here will take you in a Humvee to sector November. See if your target is among the detainees. If he's not in that group, Lieutenant Michaels and Bravo company have seventeen more to examine." The captain showed the sergeant the two locations on a map.

Kurt nodded and headed toward the Humvee.

Sergeant Wakefield started the engine and dropped the vehicle into gear as Kurt climbed in and buckled up. The non-com removed his night-vision headgear and typed the coordinates into the GPS. He took off and made a left onto the next street.

"This guy we're looking for," Wakefield asked, "He's an Arab?"

Kurt paused before he answered, deciding how much to tell the sergeant. "We've been after this terrorist for a long time. He's a high-level Taliban commander."

"You mean like al Qaeda?"

"Yeah." Kurt scanned the road and the residential community for activity. "He's connected right to the top. Like to Osama, who's dead now, and they are desperate."

"Holy shit!" Wakefield tapped the GPS and made a right. "I didn't realize so many were coming into the U.S."

"All the time," Kurt said. "We just detained a small group in Del Rio, Texas."

The sergeant made a right and the Humvee illuminated a group of captives lined up under bright quartz light stands. The vehicle skidded to a stop and Kurt swung out.

He went down the line of men, again pulling face coverings off and turning heads to different angles.

"He's not here," Kurt said.

"Okay, The sergeant said. "Let's go check out Lieutenant Michael's detainees in Sector Lima."

Back in the Humvee, Wakefield set the GPS again and took off in a hurry. "About two klicks from here." He notified Captain Roberts on the radio of the new destination.

Kurt growled, "Don't use the radio. The Taliban had sophisticated signal locating equipment in Afghanistan."

They made two turns, passed under a street light, and the sergeant accelerated through an intersection.

Kurt saw a bright flash.

"RPG!"

The blast sent the Humvee skidding on its side. Kurt seized a bar. Wakefield screamed. A shower of sparks flew away from the vehicle. It slammed into a curb, bounced and screeched to a stop. Kurt felt a massive pain when his head whacked something.

—*∾*—

Kurt heard voices speaking Arabic. He blinked. Wincing, he felt throbbing in his head. Damp, coagulated blood soaked his jacket.

He blinked twice more. He could see dirty combat boots … and sandals … the kind the Taliban wore. The hair on the back of his neck stood. He tightened his fists.

Suddenly he heard someone say in Farsi, "He is awake."

Two pairs of hands seized his arms, lifted him and dragged him across a room. "Beesh inja!" Sit here.

They slammed him down onto a hard chair.

Slowly, Kurt took in the surroundings, stopping with a jerk. A man's wrist caught his attention, a black Aqualand dive computer with a diamond bezel. He lifted his gaze to lock eyes with Ramzi bin Omeri, the Snow Leopard. Kurt swallowed.

Ramzi commanded the men to hold him and clean his face. One Talib roughly wiped off the camouflage grease and dried blood with a strong smelling solution. Then they flashed several photos. A chip was popped out of the camera and inserted into a computer.

Ramzi glanced at his Aqualand. In Farsi he said, "Don't go online yet. The satellite will be past this area in twelve minutes."

Kurt stole glances at the assembled men. He checked the surroundings. Out of the corner of his eye, he saw the body, with camouflage pants. Sergeant Wakefield was obviously dead.

His head hurt. Fresh blood still dripped onto his chest. His mind raced. It must have been a grenade from an RPG, exploding near the Hummer. They crashed and Wakefield was injured badly or died right there.

He wondered how far away Lieutenant Michael's Bravo Company was from here.

They hear the blast? They don't come quick, I'm dead.

Ramzi gave the signal. "Okay the satellite has passed."

A clean shaven Talib in khaki shirt and pants with new combat boots sent an email message.

For the next several minutes, the group checked the periphery of the house, peeking through windows, using night-vision gear to scan the street surrounding the property. The hair on the back of Kurt's neck stood when two huge Russian bear dogs were led through the back door of the masonry house. He shivered. Both behemoths must have weighed over two hundred pounds. They strained at their leashes toward Kurt. He sat stiff, didn't lock eyes with the beasts.

"Here comes the reply," the Talib on the computer said, still speaking Farsi.

Ramzi walked around to see the screen. After a minute, he sneered, "Kurt Valdez. CIA. *Tiburon*." He translated into Arabic and Farsi, "Shark! We will get our revenge for Osama."

Ramzi roared, "Strip him." He continued to read the report. His eyes narrowed. He glared at the screen.

Three Taliban grabbed Kurt and stripped his clothes off.

"I think Tiburon killed Mustafa al Khalawi and disabled a bomb I sent to Kuwait," Ramzi sneered. "He may have killed three Saudi princes who helped us."

Kurt's stomach seized when he heard this. Icy water splashed onto his backside. Hands wrenched him onto a block of ice. He yelled when his butt and testicles hit the frigid cold.

"We are going to sit you there for awhile so you can think, Tiburon," Ramzi said. "You are going to give us some information."

After several more minutes, with Ramzi still reading the computer, the commander said, "Where does a Muslim live in America, Tiburon?"

Kurt began to shake. His teeth rattled. Shivers ran through his body. His testicles burned.

Ramzi studied his prisoner. "He looks part Egyptian. It says he speaks Arabic fluently. And Farsi. And Pashtun. And Punjabi. My guess is he is from western Arabian blood, mixed with what? Italian? Spaniard? The black hair. The large forehead. The tan skin and dark eye circles."

Kurt shook violently. He glared at the Snow Leopard.

"How many al Qaeda, Taliban, and Pashtuns have you killed, Tiburon? How many tribal leaders in Waziristan?"

Kurt's teeth rattled loudly now.

"Get the weapon," Ramzi said.

Kurt's gaze followed one of the Taliban as the man unsheathed a classic Arabic sword, wide and triangular near the bottom of the blade, jewels in the handle. The same kind they beheaded alleged adulteresses with. The same kind they killed Ali with, while Kurt crouched in the dark helplessly watching as his comrade's head was lopped off.

For a moment, the shivering stopped. Kurt almost welcomed the blade. Put him out of this misery.

A window burst. Then another exploded. Taliban yelled. Automatic gunfire flashed. Glass flew. Devastating gunfire. Three stun grenades in quick succession. Five Taliban slammed to the floor. The dogs yelped. Silenced. Ramzi ran out the back door. A shotgun blast. The front door flew off its hinges. Tear gas and cordite filled the room. Guns went quiet.

"Christ, Kurt. We thought you were a goner." Captain Roberts' voice boomed. "Get him off that ice, men! Bring in the stretcher. Treat him for severe shock."

"Sergeant Wakefield's dead, Sir." A man said, kneeling by the corpse.

The officer said, "Shit! Get him in a vehicle."

Chapter 62

Palo Verde Springs, Arizona

Sheriff Stroman and Krysta Mazur stopped at Stufloten's store in Palo Verde Springs to buy drinks on the way to the Ibrahims' sign shop. Daley called last night and asked them to meet him. Said he had an idea.

The big story this morning was that Osama bin Laden was dead. It was all over the news. Everyone was talking about how brave the SEALs were.

As the sheriff pulled out, Krysta said, "They finally got him. It was only a matter of time.

"Yeah. But look where. One kilometer from Pakistan's West Point."

"I'm not surprised. The leadership and military of Pakistan are pathological liars."

"And they have 100 nuclear bombs."

"Pakistan is the most dangerous country in the world. Not only the nuclear bombs. But their connections to al Qaeda and the Haqqani network."

"The Haqqani network?" Stroman frowned.

"The Taliban's intelligence source," Krysta said. "They are like a mafia in Pakistan. ISI, Pakistan's intelligence agency, caters to them."

"I don't think I want to know more. The sheriff pulled down the gravel driveway to the sign shop.

Thadius Daley came out from the left side of the building, which was still wrapped with yellow plastic, crime-scene tape.

Krysta got out of the Jimmy and greeted him.

He beamed. "They finally nailed that murdering Arab bastard."

"Yes," she said. "They killed him."

She went around back. In a moment, the large roll-up door in front went up. She flipped on the bright overhead lights.

Daley stepped inside. He said, "Wow! That is a big crane."

"What have you got there, Thad?" Stroman stepped forward and asked.

"A powerful magnet and some tools. I have a hunch." He held an eight- or ten-pound magnet suspended from a thin rope. "I studied those dark photos repeatedly with a magnifying glass. I asked myself questions about them, and the large caissons, two dozen times before I went to bed the last two nights. Finally got a brain storm."

"What was that?"

"You'll see." He glanced around and frowned. "Why all the plywood?"

Stroman answered, "The brothers built their signs on those roll-around tables. Guess the wood was easy on their feet."

"That is *very* unusual for a shop. It would make it difficult to operate a cutting torch above it."

The sheriff squinted.

Daley said, "Get those nylon straps from the wall hook and set them in the middle of the floor." Daley went to the overhead crane as the sheriff and Krysta retrieved the straps. The construction specialist operated the button assembly that hung from the unit. He played with the controls for a few minutes, running the hook up and down and the carriage assembly right and left and back and forth. He then steered the hook over to the straps.

"Pile all the plywood on them."

"I've got it," Stroman said. "We'll set all the flooring aside."

Daley smiled. They moved the plywood over. Daley fastened the hook and lifted the load. He ran the crane assembly to the front west side and set the flooring down.

Next, starting under the roll-up door, he walked toward the back, holding the magnet an inch off the concrete. He stopped several times where it dipped. "Too weak. Probably rebar."

He traversed two-thirds of the floor, when the magnet clamped down. He turned and grinned. With the spray-paint can in his left hand, he painted a black dot on the slab.

"What happened," Krysta asked.

"There's a steel frame there." He grimaced and pulled the magnet up. Moving toward the rear, he walked three paces when the magnet clamped again. "It's a block-out—eight-feet wide." He sprayed another dot. "Now let's see how long it is. Judging by that 40-foot flatbed truck and heavy-duty forklift in the slides, I'd say 28 or 32 feet."

Sheriff Stroman was fascinated. "We should've had you a year ago, Thad."

Daley handed Stroman a measuring tape. "Measure how far those dots are from the back wall."

While the sheriff measured, Daley went to the west wall. He walked five paces and the magnet clamped down again. "Yep. Thirty-two feet." He put another dot, raised the magnet and walked 12 paces. The magnet clamped again and he sprayed another mark.

For the next few minutes, Daley helped Krysta find the corners and they struck chalk lines in a large rectangle.

Sheriff Stroman frowned. "So what does all that mean?"

"We're not finished." This time Daley walked slower and swung the magnet. It indicated steel, but not as strong a force as the main rails. He found and painted three joints. "Just as I thought, four feet apart." He handed Krysta the paint can and she followed him, painting four more dots. After the last one, he jumped up and down. "Solid."

"There are seven pieces of what appear to be very heavy concrete lift-out sections."

Stroman frowned, "How do you get them out?"

Daley held up a finger for patience. With the tape measure and chalk box, they struck seven more chalk lines.

"That's where we saw cut. Now watch this." He moved over and swung the magnet.

To Stroman's surprise, there were two strong forces four feet apart in the middle of the first four-by-eight floor section. Krysta put a dot on them.

"Hand me that hammer and chisel, Bob."

Daley took the tools and chipped away the concrete, exposing the bolt of an embed.

"There's your answer. Two lifting inserts."

Stroman wrinkled his forehead. "I'll be damned."

"Are you allowed to give me the keys? Daley asked. "I'll have a saw cutter brought out. We'll cut all the joints, and hopefully we can lift these sections out."

"How much do you think they weigh?" Stroman took two keys off his ring and handed them over.

"Plenty. Four or five tons each. But that crane will handle them, trust me." Daley got on his cell phone and made two calls.

"Saw-cutter will be here at one o'clock. Give him three hours. Meet me back here at four, and we'll see how well that crane works."

He stepped back to the entry and squatted, looking back and forth across the floor. "You can't see where the joints are. They sure sealed it good."

Late that afternoon, Sheriff Stroman and Krysta Mazur arrived ahead of Daley.

The saw-cutter glanced up as they came in the shop holding their ears. He looked Latin, with thick arms and shoulders. He sported a beard.

The man turned off the saw and let it wind down. When the noise eased, he took off his ear protection and said, "Thad will be back at 4:15."

Stroman glanced at his watch and nodded.

Daley showed up after the saw-cutter finished cutting, shut off the water to the saw, and put the equipment away. The man finished chipping out the remainder of the lifting bolts.

Paying him Daley said, "Thanks Enrique." The man smiled and drove up the driveway pulling the concrete saw. He turned onto the highway.

Then, Daley worked two yokes over the bolts of the first slab and fastened the crane hook to connecting cables. He gestured for the sheriff and Krysta to stand back and took tension on the assembly.

The cables went taut and twisted with the strain. A squealing noise came from the crane. Daley stopped and looked up. "Both of you get toward the front for safety. Something could give way."

When he operated the buttons again, he grimaced and held his arm in front of his face. Finally the concrete section snapped loose with a loud pop. Daley blew out a breath of relief, raised the piece of slab and eased it over to the side. He looked at Stroman and Krysta. "Whew! At least five tons."

Stroman, followed by Krysta, went over and gaped at the large area below. "Who would've known?" he said. "They sure were keeping this a secret."

Krysta pushed her hair behind her ear. "They sure were. And why? That's the million dollar question."

Daley raised his voice. "Let's get the other seven pieces of floor out. Maybe the answer to that question will be obvious.

It was nearly six o'clock when the last section came out. Stroman was amazed at the size of the work area and the fact that no one ever suspected it was there.

They turned the lower lights on and, using the stairway on the east end, went below.

Arriving at the bottom step, Stroman stopped. The hair on his neck stood. He shivered.

Daley pointed upward along the wall. "Bright wall lights and an exhaust fan. You could build anything."

As they scoured the area, Daley noted that there were blue and black paint overspray shadows on the wall and floor.

"It's big enough that they could have painted a car down here," Krysta said.

As soon as she said it, Stroman looked at her and gaped. "The black and white," they said together.

Daley asked, "What?"

"They never found Williams' black-and-white used patrol car, Thadius."

"It would have been a piece-of-cake to paint and lift a car in and out of here."

Stroman worked his jaw. He felt chills go through his body. "What else is down here?" he asked, perplexed by his reaction.

After a thorough survey, all they found were some old gouges in the concrete walls and floor.

Krysta pointed up to a round metal circle near the back wall.

"A pipe sleeve," Daley said. "Probably to pass cables, air lines or a water hose through."

"Kurt found that!" Krysta blurted. "Next to the belt buckle."

"Huh," Stroman grunted, staring up at it for several breaths. He scanned around one more time, then said, "Let's button it up."

On the main floor, the sheriff turned to Daley. "You think of anything else, Thad, give me a call. We'll notify Homeland Security. They're gonna want to investigate this."

As the men walked out front, Krysta set the alarm, turned off the lights, and locked the premises. Daley waved goodbye from his truck.

Stroman pulled out on Temple Bar Road and accelerated. He honked at Stufloten as they passed his gas station. On the way back to the office, both officers were silent until they came to the first dips in the highway.

"Stroman said, "When we went below, down those steps, I felt a strong reaction. The hair on the back of my neck stood up. Shivers ran through my body."

There was a long pause. Krysta said, "The body! Travis' body was down there."

"Damn. There it goes again, the chills. You could be right." He took several deep breaths and tightened his grip on the steering wheel.

Through several more dips and a few miles further, he said, "One day when Travis and I were out here, I caught a glimpse of the brothers' computer screen. They definitely didn't want me to see what was on it and were very nervous. Ricardo — I mean Abdul — kept moving in front of me and got Zaki to sneak by and close it. I pressed Abdul about the image. He turned the screen away from me and opened the computer. Then he brought up a couple of sign construction drawings."

She asked, "What do you think was on the display, Sir?"

"I'll swear it was round and cigar-shaped. But I thought a lot about it, and it could have been a sign. Still, they were very nervous when I saw the figure. Moments after Abdul showed me the two sign drawings, we got a call for an accident at the lake. Left in a hurry."

Stroman looked both ways when they reached Highway 93, then turned north.

After a few moments, he said, "I sure would've liked to have seen that first drawing again."

The telephone rang and Krysta picked it up.

"Good morning, Krysta," Thad said. "How's the lovely lady this morning?"

"Okay, Thadius. What are you up to this morning?" She pushed her hair behind her ear.

"Call me Thad. I've got an idea to run by Bob. But, first, I wanted to ask you. You sure you wouldn't like to go skiing this Saturday? I'm gonna have the boat out on the lake. Two couples with me."

"Randy and I are hiking the Mount Charleston area this weekend. Crossing over the ridgeline to Lee Canyon."

"Randy? That your fiancé? Water skiing is much more fun. Bring him along."

"Thanks again, Thad. We planned this trip for a month. Two deputies and a firefighter are going along also, with two wives."

"You know, there's something I've always wondered about. When you're out with a group like that, how do you do your business? You know body functions, with people around?"

She laughed. "I find a rock. Here's the sheriff."

Krysta smiled and shook her head. She could hear Stroman talking on the telephone in the back. After awhile, he hung up and came out front.

Thad says the Morales ... I mean Ibrahims dug the hole after they were in business. They could have dug it with a small backhoe tractor inside and moved the dirt around with a Bobcat tractor to scoop the dirt out.

"He said, it would have taken about eight dump trucks to take all the dirt away, and six concrete trucks to construct that lower work area. Someone would notice *that*. And I didn't see them doing it."

"That's a lot of trucks, Bob. They must have done that at night."

"What time is Homeland Security gonna be here?"

Krysta answered, "Two hours."

"Trucks can be brought in from long distances. But concrete has to be mixed fairly close-by. Why don't you call the concrete companies starting in Boulder City and Vegas. Find out if any of the dispatchers remember a good-sized pour going on all night in Palo Verde Springs?"

Almost an hour later, Krysta said, "I found the source of the concrete. It was supplied by a batch plant in Las Vegas, Bob. Seven truckloads."

"Excellent. Now we know."

Chapter 63

Palo Verde Springs, Arizona

Krysta Mazur unlocked the Ibrahim brothers sign shop, now a crime scene. She turned on power and rolled open the metal door on the front.

All 21 investigators entered the building. DHS was there with scientific analytical equipment. Casey Walinski held a Geiger counter, adjusting it for sensitivity.

Earl McGibbon led two black German shepherd cadaver dogs on leashes. Various crime scene lab technicians wearing surgical gloves swept small brushes on counters and desks. Others vacuumed under bins.

The groups went over every square inch of the shop. There was some talk about Osama bin Laden's death. There was also mention of the new bridge and how convenient it was.

Krysta peered down into the lower work area, still amazed at its size. Casey Walinski stopped in the middle of the floor, apparently certain that he was getting faint readings of evidence of radioactivity. She watched him go over the entire area, then come back to that one spot in the middle. But he seemed unsure about the finding. He kept tampering with adjustments.

Earl McGibbon, after going over the shop floor, now led the cadaver dogs down into the pit. She watched them sniff over the area and finally stop near the foot of the stair. The dogs lingered at that location for some time. But they never exhibited the definite signal McGibbon awaited.

Kurt Valdez asked her to forward to him the final investigative report due out in three weeks. He was still recovering from his ordeal and had mentioned that he was worried that the brothers could be connected to al Qaeda and might have handled nuclear ordnance.

After several hours, she noted that crime lab personnel ultimately took paint samples from the walls of the pit. That seemed like a stretch.

At the end of the two day affair, Krysta felt that they found precious little. The brothers, always neat, had left the place near-spotless. The marine belt buckle was one rare find.

Chapter 64

Las Vegas, Nevada

Kareem Abu Bakr switched off the video recorder equipment after the seventh *shuhada'a* completed his CD. The young men, all Arabs except one, finished giving instructions for their families and friends for their funeral commemorations and property distributions.

Over the last two weeks, the men gathered into the Consulate Suites one at a time, the reservations having been made for them ahead of time. They'd remained out of sight during daylight hours, sleeping, reading the Koran, and praying. At about three o'clock each morning, however, they could sit in the Jacuzzis and relax until almost daylight. Kareem even allowed two of the group a few alcoholic drinks as requested.

There was much discussion about avenging Osama bin Laden's death.

Several months ago Kareem and other al Qaeda leaders had chosen Las Vegas as an ideal location to mount widespread attacks because of its ethnic diversity. More than 50 different nationalities, many of them barely able to speak any of the local language, resided and worked in the city. Each of the Muslims attended a crash course in English before their arrivals.

As the day for their missions grew near, Kareem analyzed the young men. There was no allowance for mistakes at this point.

The Palestinian, the Yemeni, and the Somali had watched a dozen DVD movies between them. The group met each evening and practiced the American idioms, learned mostly from the films. The Somali, Abdul, a very dark man, had especially liked the American movies with blond women.

Before Jacuzzi time, most of the group chewed qat. Rasool, second-in-command, provided them with an ample supply of the fresh narcotic continuously.

The other four *shuhada'a* were very devout, reading the Koran and praying to Mecca six times every day. A successful mission on their part would be to avenge the Caliphate by dealing a crippling blow to the Crusaders and Zionists, reaching Heaven and obtaining their seventy virgins. Kareem brought a repertoire of indoctrination DVDs with political-religious themes to share.

Now, however, the time had come. The Snow Leopard sent detailed directions by courier to Kareem for their missions.

Kareem signaled to Rasool and had him bring out the harnesses for a demonstration. The new explosives he smuggled in the last three nights were stunning, much more powerful, more condensed, and lighter than cumbersome C-4 or Semtex. Video displays showed inanimate objects vaporized by small amounts of the chemical mixes. Explosives that a single *shaheed* carried on a harness could destroy three stories of a concrete building. A harness could be hidden under a bulky sweatshirt and detonated with any one of several hidden switches. New-style fuses were impressive, too. A fuse the size of a small wooden match, ignited by a tiny striker, could set off enough explosives to severely damage a high-rise building.

The Arabs took their shirts off and put on the equipment with various western clothes. Kareem judged them, noting where their bodies looked too bulky. Each man was selectively chosen because of his build—stocky—to be able to carry and hide as much destructive power as possible.

Glancing at his watch after two days of practice runs, the leader noted that it was approaching the time to send the *shuhada'a* on their way. From what little he knew of other details, he judged the Snow Leopard would be coordinating his end of the offensive to make the largest impact possible. The young Arabs' suicide diversions would draw attention away from Ramzi's mission—al Qaeda's principal attack—the one that would make history.

The imam Kareem had summoned came by and the Arabs held group prayer. Even though the religious man was obviously disturbed by the assemblage, Kareem knew he wouldn't report it until it was too late.

Pizza and Chinese take-out, their favorites, arrived after the holy man left. When they finished eating, the young men acknowledged with a look and a nod that they understood the moment had arrived.

The final plans called for them to leave in two groups. Kareem would drive the taxi himself. He would take the first group to the Macao Bay, Hadrian's Palace, and the Tuscan, then return for the second group. Rasool handed out fresh qat.

"You each have surveyed your target locations several times, gambled, and familiarized yourselves with the casinos. You know where to be positioned for the most effective attack.

Looking at his watch, Kareem said, "When I count down, set your watches for 11:55. He waited until the Arabs made adjustments, then counted, "Five … four … three … two … now.

The men synchronized their watches.

Chapter 65

Kingman, Arizona

Using a garage creeper, Ramzi bin Omeri rolled underneath the fiberglass boat, trailer and submarine. He reached up with the air wrench and spun the bolts loose on the sub's watertight compartment. It took him only a few minutes and the cover swung down exposing the nuclear bomb.

"Roll that cradle under the trailer," he said to Mustafa.

The young Jordanian moved the bomb carriage to where Ramzi could grasp it.

Ramzi pulled it into position, stretched and depressed a lever up inside the submarine. The sound of escaping air accompanied the lowering weapon. After disconnecting two hooks, he shoved the carriage and bomb to where Mustafa could pull it.

The Snow Leopard scooted out from under the trailer, stood and exhaled. "We have to hurry. Ali will be here with the truck in two hours. Help me stand up the bomb, Mustafa."

They grasped the top of the weapon and lifted, raising it onto its flat bottom. The stainless steel device was round and narrower than Ramzi's hips. It reached his belt. "It weighs forty kilos," he said.

Mustafa Fakouri's eyes widened. "Forty kilos! That is all?"

"Yes." For a few breaths, they stood in awe that a weapon this small could obliterate a city the size of Las Vegas or New York City.

Mustafa twisted his mouth to the side. "We will avenge Osama bin Laden."

The *shaheed* had recently arrived from Yemen, where he trained for three months on how to operate the submarine with the bomb. He'd already made his CD to give instructions to his family for his funeral commemoration and the distribution of his worldly goods. The young Jordanian was there only for this mission. Ramzi lost count of how many young Arabs he'd sent to meet Allah, surely more than fifty.

"Okay, let's remove the top cover."

With the top off, the bomb smelled new, like sliding into a vehicle for the first time and inhaling the odor of plastic and rubber and metal.

Ramzi slipped on rubber gloves and unscrewed the insulated protective caps from the large capacitor nested alongside the bomb's firing mechanisms. He touched a screwdriver across its terminals raising a small blue spark.

Mustafa flinched.

"That is for safety. The capacitor has to be fully discharged to connect it to the charger."

The Jordanian watched wide-eyed as Ramzi unlatched a hold-down clamp and set the device alongside the charger and wall outlet. Connecting the cables to the capacitor, the Snow Leopard removed the cumbersome gloves and switched power on. A red LED indicator blinked.

"When it turns green, it has a lethal charge, enough to set off the bomb."

"All my training was on what to do after I sat inside the submarine. How to arm the bomb, and explode it."

Ramzi nodded. While the capacitor charged, they turned to examine the bomb components. "Mohammad Agah Khan, gave me the original instructions to arm and set off the weapon. If you miss one step—if one of those devices fails—there would be no explosion."

Mustafa's eyes brightened at the mention of Pakistan's great nuclear scientist, whom all Muslims had heard of and held in esteem.

"Watch closely." Ramzi wound the timer assembly to twenty seconds and pressed the initiate button. Red numbers flashed and started counting down. They both jerked when the loud snap of a relay went off.

"With safety features overridden, that would have set off the bomb's initiation circuits."

"But, I would need the key."

Ramzi smiled that the Arab remembered it. He pulled the lanyard out of his shirt. It held the key that Ayman al Zawahiri, al Qaeda's number two man, had sent him. "This defeats the safety features. When the moment comes, I will give it to you."

"And the *only* lock is in the cockpit of the submarine," the Jordanian said.

"That's correct." Ramzi glanced over and pointed to the green LED on the charger blinking, indicating full charge. Mustafa took the cue and pressed the test button. The pointer on the meter flipped to 20,000-volts.

"They trained you well, Mustafa. But the next step is the dangerous one. That capacitor can kill you now."

Mustafa watched as Ramzi again slipped on the rubber gloves and disconnected the leads from the charger. Grasping the black capacitor firmly with both hands, he swung it to its perch on the bomb. It took both of them to fasten the hold-down strap. He then connected two thick cables to the terminals of the charged capacitor, screwing on protective caps afterward. He removed the rubber gloves. "Do you remember the instructions?"

"I memorized all the lessons.

Ramzi raised his eyebrows. The zeal with which the Jordanian spoke reminded him of former *shuhada'a*, long since dead.

"You have been trained well, my comrade."

The Snow Leopard unplugged the timer. "Put this in your pocket until we need it." He replaced the bomb cover. They eased the weapon down onto the carriage.

Mustafa moved it under the trailer.

On the creeper once again, Ramzi re-connected the hooks and operated the small air winches to secure the bomb up inside the submarine. After two audible clicks, indicating the bomb had locked into place, he plugged the bomb's external wire and jack assembly into a socket inside the sub. Then he tightened the bolts to the watertight compartment.

A few minutes later, with the carriage and creeper aside, Ramzi opened the conning tower. Mustafa climbed into the vessel, and sat down. He inserted the timer and set it to 25 seconds. As it counted down to zero, Ramzi listened carefully.

"There," he said when the relay clicked and the zeros switched off. "Try the meter."

Mustafa pressed the test button and the meter inside the cockpit indicated 20,000 volts. Ramzi smiled, nodded, and removed the key from around his neck. Mustafa flipped open a small cover and inserted the key.

Ramzi tightened his stomach and swallowed. *One wrong connection—one miss-wired circuit.*

He inhaled and clenched his fist while the young Arab turned the key. Three red LEDs began blinking.

"Good! All safety features work."

Mustafa removed and handed the key back to Ramzi, then climbed out of the sub.

The Snow Leopard dialed a number on his satellite phone. The other end picked up and Ali said, "Fifteen minutes." Ramzi closed the phone and proceeded to let down the jacks on the trailer.

"Move the charger and bomb carriage to the back Mustafa, so Ali can attach the trailer to his truck for the tow."

When they finished, the leader handed Mustafa Fakouri a wad of qat and placed a small amount in his own mouth.

Chapter 66

Las Vegas, Nevada

"At 3:25 a.m. you will all attack." Kareem Abu Bakr faced the seven *shuhada'a*.

He pointed to three. "One last check to make sure your clothes and equipment are ready, then we will leave." The chosen were helped by their comrades with their equipment. Rasool made sure the charges and initiating circuits were functional.

When they finished straightening their sweatshirts and jackets over the harnesses, Kareem glanced at his watch. "We go now to avenge Osama and bring down the infidels."

The first three *shuhada'a*, Fahd, Mohammad, and Kamal, indicated they were ready. The plans called for them to leave several minutes apart. Rasool went first to observe from near the Jacuzzi, watching for authorities or any suspicious activity, ready to give the abort signal if necessary. Kareem left next to bring the taxi around.

A few minutes later, Kareem turned onto Tropicana Avenue and they hit the downtown traffic. The three young Arabs were always amazed by the bright lights, even though they had ventured out several times before.

Fahd the Saudi was going to the Macao Bay's shark aquarium with the largest charge because he had the heaviest build. They calculated that he could take out the whole lower area and three other floors, including one casino.

It took them almost a half-hour to arrive. Kareem dropped Fahd off in a darkened alcove in the parking garage among a line of other taxis. There they aroused no suspicions.

Kareem next exited back onto Tropicana Avenue. They stopped for several minutes at two red lights. He stared at the Palestinian and the Egyptian while he had the chance to make sure they did not look scared. Both men had a wad of qat in their cheeks. They appeared ready to do their jobs. The narcotic would bolster their courage.

After some maneuvering to get into Hadrian's parking structure, he found another dark area to drop off Mohammad. He then headed for the Tuscan, Kamal's target.

The round trip back to the Consulate Suites took a little more than an hour. He noted that he could see Rasool from the taxi parking area. The man banged his fists together three times, the signal that all was okay. Kareem flicked his nose in acknowledgment that he was ready for the others. Rasool, the observer, would use his key to the apartment unit so as not to alarm the four remaining *shuhada'a*.

As the men arrived at the taxi, one by one, Kareem saw they were eager to go. He was surprised how calm the young Arabs were. The qat really worked.

From Tropicana Avenue again, Kareem turned left on Las Vegas Boulevard, then dropped off Ahmed at the curb near the Tuscan with its famous fountains and water displays.

A U-turn and five blocks further, he pulled into the Vienna parking garage. He found a dark parking place. Yessem waited until the foot traffic slackened, then got out. Kareem nodded to the Yemeni and said, "You know what to do."

Driving out of the parking garage, he doubled back to Las Vegas Boulevard then turned right on Sahara. He gestured for Abdul. "Bompensiero's is over there."

The whites of young Omani's eyes showed.

"Take several deep breaths before you get out, Abdul. Calm yourself." Kareem waited for at least two minutes before he let the Arab out.

Then he headed back to Paradise Avenue. Turning left, he worked his way through the traffic to Charleston Boulevard. He turned north again, then after a few blocks, turned back onto Las Vegas Boulevard.

Jamshid dipped his head and smiled, "My building."

Kareem pulled into the Galaxy parking structure. The young Somali's eyes blazed with fanaticism when he exited the taxi.

Returning to Sahara Avenue, then onto Paradise by the Trade Show building, Kareem arrived back at the Consulate Suites before 12:45.

Rasool had their carry-ons ready and jumped in. "The flight leaves in forty-five minutes. They got us first-class tickets on Delta."

"The Porsche is waiting?"

"In Los Angeles. We should be on our way to Mexico by the time the fireworks begin."

Chapter 67

East end of Lake Mead, Arizona

The Milky Way was at the zenith over the Grand Canyon when Ramzi bin Omeri gestured to Ali to turn left toward the new Smuggler's Cove boat docks. Two faint lights lit the area. Scanning around to make sure no one else was there, Ramzi spotted the top of a small tent beyond a knoll. A dog slept under one light in front of a small house.

Ali swerved left, then swung the truck around to the right to line up with the docks. Ramzi got out to signal him. Watching the side mirror, Ali backed into Lake Mead until the boat floated off the trailer. He continued until the truck's dual wheels were submerged, then locked the brakes.

Ramzi unfastened the cable hook from the trailer and gave the heavy boat a shove. Ali moved the truck forward while water poured off the trailer. He stopped for Ramzi to reconnect the trailer's turn signals and brake lights.

By now, the *shaheed*, Mustafa Fakouri, had gotten out of the truck to help. He grabbed lines and pulled the vessel toward the dock. After several minutes, the slender Jordanian managed to tie it off to a cleat.

Patting the truck fender with his hand, Ramzi said to Ali, "I will see you at the cove."

Ali swung the truck around to the right to exit the ramp area.

"You guys going fishing this early?"

Ramzi flinched. He turned slightly to see a blond young man and woman, probably the campers from the tent. Struggling to hide his accent, and turning his face away from the red lights of the truck, he said, "We want to get out there where the big ones are."

"Nice boat." The man ambled toward the vessel. "What I can see of it in the dark."

"Let me get it started and you can look around inside?" Ramzi motioned, turned his back to the couple and moved toward the dock.

"Sure," said the man. "I'm Josh. This here's Beth."

Ramzi raised a hand gesture for a hello.

The Jordanian, obviously seeing the three coming toward him, cast the line he held into the boat and jumped in. He went to the opposite side.

Ramzi, keeping his face away from the light, hopped over the gunwale. He pushed the starter and the boat engine started.

"Can you untie and hand me that line," he said to the blond man.

Josh bent over and undid the rope from the cleat. Turning, he threw the line in the boat. "Nice throaty sound."

Sitting on the gunwale now, Ramzi reached and put his hand on a knife. "Come onboard. I will give you a look around."

The woman held back.

In Arabic, Ramzi told Mustafa to load the crossbow.

"What's that language you're speaking?"

Ramzi waited several heartbeats until Mustafa could pull tension on the weapon and release the safety. They had discussed what to do in a situation like this. Ramzi tightened his grip on the knife.

"*Al-aan!*" he shouted. (Now!)

He heard the crossbow release and then a gurgling sound from the woman.

"What!" the blond man shouted.

Ramzi spun, saw the woman sink to her knees, and pounced. He plunged the knife up under the man's rib cage. The dog started barking. The man heaved a breath and collapsed.

"Quick, Mustafa. Get them onto the boat!"

Ramzi yanked the man over the gunwale. He sprang toward the woman who seized the bolt high in her chest, her mouth gasping for breath. He grabbed her under the arms and dragged her to the boat. Mustafa pulled her in.

"Let's go!"

It took only a few moments for Ramzi to recover and get to the helm, then he motored slowly in an arc. A voice shouted from the house for the dog to shut up.

Several minutes later, after passing the 5-mile-per-hour buoys, Ramzi accelerated toward the middle of the channel. "Put the teapot on." His own voice sounded calm to him, as if nothing had happened. The two campers lying on the deck stopped twitching and went silent.

He glanced at the water line in the darkness. Even with the heavy rains and snowpack over the last winter, the lake hadn't risen much. A white calcified strip a hundred-meters wide covered the rocky shoreline from the water line upwards.

"What are we going to do with them?"

"There are some lead diving belts in those side shelves." Ramzi pointed. "Put them on the bodies. We will dump them in the lake."

The young Jordanian seemed completely unfazed by the killings. Ramzi figured he'd seen plenty of dead people when the Jews ran his people out of the West Bank.

After he saw that the Arab had the weight belts attached to the bodies, he pointed to a depth gauge. "Keep an eye on this instrument, Mustafa. There are some underwater rocks."

Ramzi steered a course from the compass and chart that he had mapped out over the last two weeks. Heading first westerly toward California, he then shifted direction toward Hoover Dam.

Several minutes later, he glanced left over his shoulder at the Grand Canyon. Stars in the eastern sky revealed the shape of the massive cliffs.

"Okay, Mustafa. We're in deep water. Let's dump them."

They dragged the bodies to the back and pushed them over the side. The two campers splashed in and quickly sank out of sight.

"Now, wash that blood off the deck and pour me a cup of tea." Ramzi flicked on deck lights and gestured toward a hose.

Squirting water on the deck, forcing blood out of drain holes in the stern, Mustafa finished and poured two cups of tea, handing one to Ramzi.

The Snow Leopard blew across the top, then took a sip. "Your extra CD is in the packet?" he asked.

The Jordanian unzipped a case and held up the disk.

Ramzi took another sip of tea, glanced around at the reflection of stars on the glassy surface of the lake, and locked the boat on course.

Turning to Mustafa he said somberly, "We will make sure your family receives a CD. Al Qaeda will support them for the remainder of their lives."

In the low deck lights, the thin young Arab, no more than 20, stared into Ramzi's eyes without blinking. He had a full head of wavy hair, a cropped full beard, and an angular face. "I am proud to destroy the infidels. The directions for my funeral ceremony and property are here." He waved the CD.

Ramzi swallowed and blinked. "I have known hundreds of *Mujahedeen* who have died fighting Russians and Americans. You are as brave as any I fought with. This, what you are going to do today, will strike a blow against the Americans that they can't recover from."

"Are you sure the bomb has enough power to destroy the dam?"

"Easily. It will destroy the dam and flood the valley below 50 to 100 kilometers wide. One young Arab will bring the Americans to their knees." Ramzi put his hand on Mustafa's shoulder. "More Americans will die today than Arabs have been killed in Palestine in 61 years. It will avenge Osama's death."

In the dim deck lights, the young man's eyes glared with fury, obviously thinking about the Zionists.

There was a long silence. Finally, Ramzi asked, "Do you remember the instructions?"

"Yes. I trained on the other boat in Yemen. I memorized all the lessons."

"What if you are discovered? What do you do?"

"I will override the safety features and set the timer as soon I reach the proper depth. If anything goes wrong or I am detected, I will set it off early."

Ramzi raised his eyebrows. The zeal with which the Jordanian spoke reminded him of his former comrades, long since dead. "You know where the bomb is most effective?"

"I was told to go down to 180 meters, as near to the center of the dam as possible, and against the concrete. The 200 megaton blast will take out the dam, let all the water out of the lake at once, flood the valley to Mexico, and destroy the electrical power systems."

"The Americans have protective screens to keep big objects out of the lower water outlets."

"Yes, I saw the photographs and diagrams. The red light and photo will guide me around the east edge to the middle of the dam."

"You have been trained well, my comrade." Ramzi kissed Mustafa on both cheeks. He took the lanyard from his neck and handed the Jordanian the key to defeat the bomb's safety features.

Mustafa put it over his head.

Turning, the Snow Leopard throttled back on the power. He took a sighting on a peak to the east with his night-vision compass, then another on the left penstock intake tower near the dam. "Seven degrees further. Watch the depth gauge. When it reaches 400 meters, that is our drop off point."

Mustafa sat in front of the depth gauge. Ramzi throttled back on the speed. One more glance toward the Grand Canyon. Faint outlines delineated the ridges.

"Three-hundred meters," Mustafa said.

"More than half-a-klick further." Ramzi took another sighting on the peak.

Eight more breaths, and Mustafa said, "We have arrived."

Throttling back, Ramzi let the boat coast to a stop. "This is good. Let's put the top up. Then you get into the sub."

The young Arab closed the cover on the depth gauge. They pulled the green canvas top out of its well and stretched it tight over the support frames. Mustafa fastened the lines to the front of the boat and drew them tight.

Ramzi unlatched the cover over the submarine and flipped it over, exposing the vessel.

He opened the conning tower lid while Mustafa slid on thin diver's boots. The young Arab gave Ramzi one last defiant look, and said, "*Allahu akbar.*" (God is great.)

"*Allahu akbar,*" Ramzi repeated as he watched the man climb into the vessel. Mustafa held a plastic-coated check-off list. He flipped switches, tapped gauges, and turned on air valves, going through one test after another, finally putting a scuba mouthpiece in his mouth and inhaling a breath. He held up a thumb and removed the lanyard from his neck. Inserting the key, he turned it.

Ramzi saw the three red LEDs blink.

Mustafa removed the key and pressed the button to check the capacitor charge. The gauge surged to 20,000 volts. "It all works," he said. His nostrils flared as he blew air from around the ballast tanks and nodded that he was ready.

"Steer on heading 192 degrees for 2 hours," Ramzi said, setting the dials on his Aqualand eco-drive chronometer and dive calculator. "Then proceed on heading 178 degrees for one and a half hour. You will come to the edge of the eastern spillway. He pointed to the color photograph and map he had given Mustafa. Follow it around to this side of the dam. There is a powerful alcohol motor to use the last few minutes to keep you against the concrete, out of the strong currents."

The Jordanian found the switch for the alcohol motor. He held the photo and traced a line around the eastern side of the lake. Finally, he rotated and compared the plastic-encased photo with the map of the lake showing depth.

"The entire river flows through those four penstocks," Ramzi said, pointing to the four structures sticking up in the lake near the dam. "That is why you will need the motor. If you get too close, they could pull you in."

Mustafa nodded that he understood.

The Snow Leopard blinked. He had waited for this moment for three years. Exhaling deeply, he lowered the conning tower lid until he heard a solid thud, then turned a wheel to tighten the seal. He hit the lid with a wrench twice, the signal that all was ready.

It took a lot of force to release the levers that held steel cables around the submarine, keeping it tight while towing. They snapped loose. Ramzi watched it sink while he pulled the cables onto the boat.

A whirring sound commenced and air jetted from the sub. It went down, then slowly moved forward, trailing a stream of bubbles. The last Ramzi saw of the vessel was a small red light blinking in the conning tower window. Watching until the light disappeared, he replaced the fiberglass cover on the underwater boat cavity, then threw the steel cables into the lake.

The Snow Leopard started the boat engine and headed back toward the east, where Ali was waiting.

It took only twenty minutes or so to reach the small cove with a boulder near the entrance. Ali bin Khalifa must have spotted the boat in the dark. He flicked a red light twice.

Guiding the vessel around behind the rock, Ramzi weighed anchor. He flopped out the rubber raft that inflated itself, and headed for shore using paddles.

Ali lifted the front of the raft when it hit mud. They opened two air valves and shoved it toward the middle of the cove. Then they ran for the vehicle.

"We have two hours to reach the airport near Kingman, Ali."

The Arab drove up onto the road and headed for the Colorado River. He accelerated, throwing mud off the wheels.

"Drive slower, and turn the headlights on," Ramzi said. "Don't attract attention if we pass any vehicles."

When they approached the dirt road one mile east of the Ibrahams' former sign shop, Ali turned left. They bounced over ruts until Ramzi spotted the second boat, right where they planned for it to be. Ali approached it and wheeled the truck around. "Guide me under so I don't knock it off those blocks."

Ramzi got out, signaled Ali into position, and the Arab backed the trailer under the smaller boat. Motioning to stop, Ramzi hooked the safety cable and side latches.

Then they took the time to place the explosive vest on Ali. If the authorities stopped them, that would be it for them and anyone within 100 meters.

They pulled the vessel to the road and headed west toward the river and Highway 93.

When they reached Palo Verde Springs, a few nightlights were on, as well as two old mercury street lights. The lights cast a ghostly, bluish glow. The truck rose over a knoll, and roadside reflectors were visible for several curves.

"Okay, Ali, more speed. Don't lose the boat though."

Ali kicked the speed up to sixty miles per hour and the truck swooped down into two of the dips. The trailer created sparks and the Arab slowed the vehicle a bit.

Twenty minutes later, Ramzi dialed his satellite phone.

When the other end said, "*Buenos dias*," he asked, "*Libre*?"

"*No, Señor. Use el segundo.*"

"*Bueno.*" Ramzi put away the phone.

After a long pause, Ali asked, "Problem?"

"The highway patrol must have closed the road to Kingman. He said to use the second idea."

Ali looked at the Snow Leopard and frowned. "What other idea?"

"There is another small airport near a factory by Highway 95 on the road to Needles. Take the new bridge over the Colorado River.

Ali turned north when they reached Arizona Highway 93 and headed toward Hoover Dam. Several miles further Ramzi saw the lights from the enormous new bridge.

"There may be Highway Patrol on the other side in Boulder City." Ramzi said. "I will do the talking." He turned on the radio and scanned to find a news station.

Twenty minutes later, they topped the peak of the new bridge and headed down the long slope of freeway toward Boulder City. Ramzi spotted diesel truck taillights ahead. "Give me your passport and green card."

"You have a idea?"

In the reflected lights, Ali had a mean scowl on his face. "There is gun under seat."

Ramzi snorted. "I always have a plan. Put this cap on." He handed Ali an LA Dodgers ballcap and put one on his head, also.

Ali slowed the truck to fall in behind an eighteen-wheeler.

Almost a half-hour passed. Ramzi glanced at his Aqualand chronometer three times the last few minutes. The vehicle line moved slowly. Another look over his shoulder at the still dark sky on the eastern horizon. Under the bridge lights, he noted the boat had life jackets, fishing poles and lights. It was a good decoy that they rented on the spot from a lake resident. He turned the radio on.

"Homeland Security warns again that the nation is on Red Alert." The radio reported.

Ramzi translated and said, "That is why the police are stopping vehicles on the highways."

A separate line for big rigs formed as they approached the city. Flares and a woman police officer guided them into the left lane.

"Al Qaeda discovered that the border is easily penetrated." Ramzi said this with a note of sarcasm. "The authorities will be searching all the big trucks from Mexico for Muslims."

Ali slowed the truck as they approached the police roadblock. He fumbled with the trigger for the explosive vest, a short cable that he merely had to jerk on. Ramzi turned up the radio volume when two officers signaled them to stop, and rolled down his window.

The cop on his side ducked to look inside the truck. He was an enormous man with a solid build. Glancing first at the Dodger's ballcaps, then at the fishing boat behind the truck, he asked, "Coming from the lake?"

"Yes," Ramzi said with a Mexican accent. He turned down the news. "Why the Red Alert?"

"Routine," the burly patrolman said.

"Is Las Vegas safe?"

The man on the driver's side tapped on Ali's window.

The burly patrolman ignored the question and scanned the passports and green cards. He motioned and said, "Hurry along, Mr. Chavez."

Ramzi feigned worry. "There is no information, *Señor*?"

"Sorry," said the patrolman. He banged his hand on the hood and waved for them to go.

The other officer was going to ask Ali a question when Ramzi nudged him. "Go, *amigo*."

Ali stepped on the accelerator and the truck and boat trailer lurched forward. The Arab blew out a large breath. "We will not pass next time."

Ramzi glanced at the Aqualand again. "Two hours, thirteen minutes. The bomb goes off."

He called another number on the satellite phone.

"*Buenos dias.*"

"*Buenos dias. Que pasa?*"

"*El camino del sur está bloqueado. Hay viente autos y grande camiones in la linea.*"

"*Gracias.*" Ramzi folded the phone closed, and swore.

Ali frowned. "More problems?"

We have to go north, Ali. Turn right on Highway 95."

"To Las Vegas?" Ali sounded shocked.

Chapter 68

Boulder City, Nevada

Sheriff Bob Stroman jerked awake. "That's it!" He sat up and swung his legs over the edge of the bed. "Honey, wake up." He poked Carrie.

"What time is it? It's not daylight."

"It was a submarine!"

"What! Go back to sleep. You're dreaming."

"It was a submarine! The Arabs were building a submarine!"

Carrie raised her head. "Bob, it's 1:50 in the morning. We have a game tomorrow."

"The computer image. The image Ricardo had on the computer was a submarine."

"Oh, Lord. I don't believe this."

"I have to tell Kurt and Krysta."

Carrie beat her head on the pillow. "Not at two o'clock in the morning, Bob. Get some sleep!"

Stroman went to urinate. When he came back and laid his head on the pillow, he couldn't sleep. He lay wide-awake staring at the ceiling, examining all the various shades of gray.

It was a submarine. And they were secretive about it. Got to tell Kurt.

Chapter 69

Lake Mead, Arizona

The helicopter banked and Kurt Valdez pointed below. "There's the white boat the Global Hawk spotted with the night-vision. Drop us down on the bow, could you major?"

The chopper hovered long enough for Kurt and Casey Walinski to slide down the two-inch rope to the bow of the anchored boat. The pilot set the aircraft down near shoreline to wait.

Casey was surprisingly agile for a man who weighed at least 200 pounds and was less than six feet tall. He wore a Homeland Security ball cap, but in the chopper lights, Kurt could see his head was shaved.

Kurt jumped down onto the deck. He reached for Casey's hand. "Uhh! You desk jockeys get fat."

"Fuck you, James Bond!" Casey grinned and exhaled a large breath.

Kurt looked around and said, "Big boat."

"Yeah. Especially to be left out here by itself." He pointed. "Someone sank a raft, too. But it didn't have time to go under."

Kurt found a light switch, then scanned the deck and controls. He noticed the long, clamp-down cover in the middle of the boat. After he made a once around, peering over the bow, then the stern, he returned to the middle. "Engine's still warm."

Casey grunted acknowledgment and swung a Geiger counter from its shoulder case to his right hand. Switching it on and adjusting dials, he said, "There's a trace of radioactivity."

Kurt unlatched the middle cover and raised it. "What's this cover for?" For a moment he was puzzled.

"I don't know. But the Geiger is getting warmer. Hear the clicks?"

Casey turned the Geiger toward the cavity and it went ballistic. "Holy shit! They had a nuclear device in here."

Kurt frowned as he studied the hole.

His phone rang. "What's up Krysta? We're busy."

He listened to her for a moment. "The Global Hawk located that boat for us. We're on it as we speak."

She said, "I'm talking to the operator right now."

"Okay, ask her to play back her recorder and find out where this white boat came from during the night. It's nuclear! Here's our GPS reading." He read coordinates off the screen, then folded his cell phone.

Casey tested all around the cavity and took more readings. "They must have had a good-sized bomb under this thing."

Kurt's phone rang again. "Yes, Krysta?"

"Sheriff Stroman says the Ibrahims built a submarine!"

"A submarine! That's what this boat's for. Hell, yes! Gotta warn my boss."

Kurt immediately called Berkley at CIA.

"Hey, Top. Al Qaeda just put a submarine into Lake Mead. We're sure it has a nuclear bomb onboard!"

He was silent while the CIA deputy director panicked. "I'll arrange for the SEALs to make an air drop."

"No, no, Don. We don't have time. Get me a drop from Nellis Air Force Base, twenty minutes from here. A helium-oxygen breathing setup good for 1,000 feet. An underwater jet scooter with a passive Robertson Sonar. Some lithium-hydrochloride percussion explosives in C-4 clay. And a flat, strong magnet, less than two inches square or circular. Got that?"

Kurt listened to Berkley repeat the list.

"Yeah, in C-4 clay. And, get me a contact name at Nellis."

Kurt cut the phone off.

Casey looked at Kurt with narrowed eyes. "What the fuck you gonna do, Double-Oh-Seven?"

"I think we have a suicide bomber, down 500 feet, headed for Hoover Dam with a nuclear bomb! If I'm correct, he's got at least an hour on us."

Kurt signaled to the chopper to pick them up.

When they were buckled in, Kurt said to the pilot, "Fly us over Hoover Dam. The Arizona side."

Chapter 70

Henderson, Nevada

Ramzi bin Omeri gestured to the U.S. 215 offramp that also indicated McCarran Airport. As soon as Ali took the turn, Ramzi knew it was a mistake.

A line of vehicles were strung out down the hill to the intersection where a red light flashed. Several came in behind the truck and boat trailer.

"This is not good," said Ali. "We can miss flight."

Ramzi fidgeted and, after several minutes, opened the passenger door to step out. A few horns honked and drivers stuck their heads out of their windows and shouted. The line of cars and trucks stretched down to a traffic signal. Vehicles had been moving onto the shoulder, but were now jammed there also.

Glancing down to a frontage road on the right, a few motorists moved south, the direction they had come from. A six-foot fence with barbed wire on top ran alongside the offramp.

Ramzi swallowed and glanced at his watch: 0305 hours. The attacks would begin in 25 minutes.

Up to their left on the expressway, cars and trucks now slowed as they approached the overpass. Ramzi reached for his satellite phone, and then realized there was no one else to call. They were stuck.

He got back in the vehicle.

"What are we going to do?" Ali asked. "We can't stay here. The attacks in Las Vegas are going to...."

"I know!" Ramzi glared at him. "We have to leave the vehicle." He opened the door again. A police officer on a motorcycle slowly moved down past them on the shoulder. Ramzi slammed the door to turn off the inside light.

On the offramp, a quarter-mile ahead of them, a fire truck backed down, red lights flashing. Twice it hit the Siren for short blasts.

Ramzi stared at the blinking red light. For several minutes no one moved. His focus faded. His mind drifted.

Daybreak. Northern Afghanistan. Dug into hillsides. Overlooking a ravine down to the Panjshir Valley. Road snaking alongside stream.

Pre-dawn quiet. Screeching and clanking noise in the distance. Diesel smoke from T-72 tanks. The Russian 516 Armored Corp halted above the canyon.

Patience. Waiting.

Entire armored division. Narrow gorge. Narrow road.

Hind helicopter gun-ships last night. Radar and infra-red night vision. *Mujahedeen* hiding.

Waiting.

Tank column moving. Down the steep winding road. Around sharp curves. Stretching out ten kilometers. Squeals and diesel rumblings echoing in the canyon.

Battle seasoned warriors. Waiting. Heartbeats pounding.

Last sharp turn.

There it comes.

T-72 rounding curve.

"Now!" Ramzi commanded.

Bright flash. Rocket-propelled grenade. Tread blown off bottom tank. Last curve. Jammed in bank. Three more tanks explode. Direct hits. Tank plunging in river. Column jammed together.

Entire mountain erupting. Flashes everywhere. Ear-splitting volleys. *Mujahedeen* firing. At the top, two tanks plummet off the plateau.

Russian turrets. 155-millimeters fire. Afghan-Arab bodies flying.

Orange blast. Ears ringing. Hind gun-ships over the ridge. Rockets and RPGs exploding on their positions. Rapid-fire 50-caliber. Tracers lacing the hillside.

Unleashing sidewinders. One gun-ship explodes. Another gyrates into mountain.

"Don't let them clear the road!" Ramzi yells.

Two more tanks erupt.

Massive shock volley. Dozens more T-72s' big guns.

Coughing. Acrid smoke rising. Nostrils stinging from cordite. Another rapid volley. Ears ringing.

More gun-ships. Pummeling *mujahedeen*. Bodies littering hillsides.

Sidewinders screaming toward choppers. A fusillade of missiles. Hinds exploding.

A tactical retreat. Succumbing to overwhelming firepower. Swarming over peaks. *Mujahedeen* covering retreat. Fighting to the death.

Four Migs. Napalm.

An ambulance Siren blared, jarring him out of the memory.

"Wake up. Move," Ali shouted.

Ramzi blinked moisture away and snapped back to the moment. He watched a crane arrive from the crossroad on the right. Firefighters signaled and guided the rig to the underpass.

The Snow Leopard checked the time.

Three Minutes.

"I was remembering the battle of the Panjshir Valley with the Russians' 516 Armored Corp."

After a moment, Ali said, "356 mujahedeen died that day. More than a thousand Russians. It was beginning of end for them."

"You saved me that day, my friend. I would have died."

"And I gave you your name.

The Snow Leopard grunted and checked the time again.

Chapter 71

Los Angeles, CA

Kareem glanced at his watch and noted that it was 3:23. Their Delta flight had arrived at LAX three minutes early. "*Seven minutes until the shuhada'a meet Allah.*"

Rasool pushed the black Porsche up to 70 and accelerated around semi trucks. Kareem watched for highway patrol vehicles and aircraft. A sign came up ahead that indicated the 605 freeway.

"Take the south exit, Rasool."

The Porsche curved onto the ramp.

Kareem tapped his watch, inhaled a deep breath and let it out. "Very soon, my comrade. Why don't you drive slower. We do not want the police to stop us now."

For a moment Rasool glared at him, then the Saudi backed off the accelerator. When the vehicle slowed, he set the cruise control. Kareem switched on the radio and dialed for a news station.

Chapter 72

Las Vegas, Nevada

Jamshid tilted his head back and drained the glass. The Somali grimaced as the strong liquor went down. Scanning Las Vegas from the edge of the Galaxy balcony while the building rotated, he thought that it was somehow against Allah's dictates for so much wealth to be concentrated in so sinful a place. He pulled back the sleeve on his sweatshirt to look at his watch.

It is time.

He took one good look around and stepped inside. At least 200 people remained near the railing of the outside balcony and in the bar and restaurant. Perhaps another 1,000 people rode the elevators or occupied the building and casino directly underneath.

At the elevator, five people waited for a ride down. The door slid open, they entered, and a young man pressed the first-floor button. Jamshid briefly locked eyes with two of the passengers and smiled with a quick nod. The car accelerated down and he counted the seconds. The blast would be most effective after thirteen seconds. The entire top of the Galaxy would come down. The glass elevator on top, and the restaurant, bar and balcony would collapse onto the casino below.

Now he inhaled two large breaths. The time seemed to stretch into long moments between seconds. He had a quick vision of his brother and sister and himself playing as small children, then it was gone—eight … nine ….

The Saudi Fahd leaned against the railing and studied the sharks at Macao Bay. The magnificent fish never stopped swimming, living bundles of fluid muscle.

That was what the Caliphate was, too—an endless well of strength. The West had the weapons, the technologies, and the wealth. But the tide of history was changing. With all their expertise, they could not defeat the Muslim world's most effective and inexpensive weapon—the *shuhada'a*.

Fahd glanced at his watch—3:20. *Five minutes.*

Scanning the remaining crowd, he saw that most of the children had left at this time of the morning. He spotted one security guard. The man had given him only a cursory glance.

His gaze returned to the sharks. In a few minutes, they would all be flopping around together, or squashed dead in a mass of wet rubble. It surprised him how calm he was. The daily regimen of prayers had given him strength. The qat gave him courage.

He walked slowly toward the corridor and away from the aquarium. Water would dissipate the explosive force.

Yessem stood in line for more than an hour at the Vienna to get a choice seat for *Phantom of the Opera*. The Yemeni sat in the center of the theater, where his explosives would do the most damage.

He scanned the stage, the enormous chandelier directly overhead, and then the crowd. He sneered, thinking that in an instant it would all come down, along with at least two floors from above.

He performed a mental calculation, counting seats running across, and then rows from front to back. After a few minutes, he came up with a number of about 900. That was not counting the two balconies—probably an additional 1,500 people.

When the opera began, he didn't understand the music or singing voices, but the visuals were clear. The phantom must have been a handsome man when he was young. Due to an accident, his face became horribly disfigured. Disfigured to the point that he wore a mask. The man fell in love, and obsessed about a beautiful young woman. At this point Yessem had trouble following the story. But there was a locked gate to what looked like a prison, a graveyard, and a swamp with hanging vines and moss.

He pulled his sleeve back. The lighted hands on his watch showed it was 3:20. Glancing from left to right, he saw that the crowd was enraptured by the theatrics, music and voices. He reached inside his jacket and found the trigger.

Fahd counted the steps into the corridor. In spite of the qat, his heart now raced. His stomach muscles seized in tight knots. He breathed at least twice the normal rate.

Ten more steps.

He held the trigger tighter, rotating it in his grasp. His palms sweated.

Now!

He gulped and shouted, "*Allahu akbar!*" then squeezed the trigger.

A blast erupted. It instantly mushroomed in all directions. Three levels of the building plunged. The aquarium shattered. Thousands of tons of seawater burst through glass. Large predator fish twisted and flopped. Tons of concrete fell.

The main part of the building, arranged in three wings spread from a central tower, withstood the blast well. Three floors in the middle sagged and collapsed onto the aquarium. People screamed. They plunged into the abyss below. Columns buckled and followed the floors down. A billowing cloud of smoke and dust spread from the blast. Concrete slab pieces held by reinforcing steel dangled over the huge gap. Sharks, rays and smaller fish gasped for oxygen and flopped around among the rubble.

Large sections of floor broke and caved. Would-be survivors clung to rebar. They grasped carpet shreds. Some wailed to their deaths.

Jamshid reached thirteen in his count in the elevator. He shouted, "*Allahu akbar!*"

The others in the elevator looked at him with gaping mouths as he squeezed the trigger.

The explosion blew the central section apart. Two-thirds of the way up to the top of the Galaxy, the tower buckled. First the glass elevator slid down in slow motion. Then the balcony fractured and fell in large sections. Shortly the whole mass keeled over and collapsed onto the street and buildings.

A crowd on the street heard the blast and looked up horrified as the upper structure roared and came down. Huge sections of balcony careened onto vehicles. An air pressure wave, filled with glass, concrete chunks and dust, radiated out from the Galaxy. The tall edifice collapsed onto the main building.

Yessem flared his nostrils. He watched the phantom move through the swamps and vines. He was dead calm as he palmed the trigger switch. He inhaled two large breaths, knotted his jaw and shouted, "*Allahu akbar!*" He squeezed.

Less than a heartbeat expired before the immense chandelier came down. Seats sheared away from the blast center. People and debris soared with hot expanding gases. Concrete slabs from two floors above collapsed into the theater. Concrete and steel squealed and roared. The screaming lasted only seconds.

Chapter 73

Irvine, California

"I can drive if you want to sleep," Kareem said.

"Sleep! I cannot sleep. We should hear news any moment." Rasool lit a cigarette. His hand was shaking.

Kareem pointed, "Take the 405 east. One and a half kilometers."

The radio suddenly blared, "The Macao Bay in Las Vegas just suffered an enormous explosion."

"Yeah!" shouted Kareem and Rasool simultaneously. They slapped palms together. "Osama is avenged!"

A breathless commentator struggled to get the news out. "It is reported that three floors have collapsed in the center of the structure near the aquarium area."

Rasool turned the sound up.

"This also just in: The Galaxy has crashed down onto the street and casino." The two Arabs looked at each other with open mouths.

The radio announcer gasped. He sounded as if he were weeping. "There appear to be separate reports that there was a powerful explosion in the Vienna, too. It is believed that more than 2,000 people are trapped inside the theater where the *Phantom of the Opera* was playing."

Kareem yelled and drummed on the dash.

The radio blared again, "Hadrian's Palace has just reported that there was a tremendous blast in the magic show and mall areas. It is believed hundreds of people are trapped inside."

The two Arabs went wide-eyed and silent. Kareem felt his pulse race.

"In further news," the radio continued. "In the WBB hotel, a young man who appeared Middle Eastern, tore open his shirt exposing a vest containing explosives. As he reached for an activation device and yelled, *"Allahu akbar!"* a guard shot him in the forehead."

"They got Kamal!" exclaimed Rasool.

"It is too late for the infidels," Kareem said.

Chapter 74

Lake Mead, Arizona

Kurt Valdez sighed when he spotted the blinking red beacon and cockpit lights of the helicopter flying from the north.
About time.
It dropped elevation and came in low over the lake. The only other lights at this early hour were on a water filtration plant to the northwest several miles across on the California side, and a boat landing south of it along the same shore.
He aimed his light at the aircraft and flashed the standard military code. After a couple of minutes, the chopper veered in his direction. Three men inside the helicopter looked at him. He could make out a large raft hanging underneath. The pilot hovered side-on and Kurt signaled to a flat spot near the edge of the water to set the raft down, with space beyond to land.
The chopper flooded the area with light long enough to shed its heavy cargo.
Two people got out of the far side of the aircraft and handed out gear. When they finished, one gave a thumb-up to the pilot. The aircraft rotors speeded up, and it rose and headed north.
When the man in charge approached, Kurt was astonished to see that it was Lieutenant Menzies. Oops. A silver oak leaf. Lieutenant Commander Menzies, now.
The officer thrust his hand out and grinned, "Tiburon!"
Kurt grabbed him, drew him in and slapped his back.
Menzies gestured, "You remember Gilbert Espinosa from our Saudi mission? Master Chief Espinosa, now."
Kurt hadn't seen the SEALs in over four years. As the chopper noise faded, he held up a light. Both men were huskier than they had been in Saudi Arabia. Menzies still wore his dark hair cropped short. Espinosa's wavy black hair was now down on his neck. It looked good with his green eyes and light Latino complexion. He wore small gold earrings.
Finally, noticing the somber look on Menzies' face, Kurt asked, "Why so glum?"

"On the flight out we heard the news that some Las Vegas hotels have suffered simultaneous attacks."

"Attacks? Several attacks, like terrorists?"

"Yep. They shot two before they could explode. Radio said they looked Middle Eastern, had explosives strapped to their bodies. One yelled '*Allahu akbar,*' before a security officer shot him. The other yelled 'Osama!'"

Kurt assimilated this information.

"This something you're involved in, Kurt?"

He didn't answer right away while he considered the ramifications. "What are SEALs doing in this part of the country?"

"We're doing our annual jumps and dives into Lake Mead. I arranged for the Air Force Tech Sergeant to have our deep-water diving equipment ready to bring out today. He woke me when he heard the request for mixed-gas diving equipment."

"Wow! Lucky," Kurt said. "Those terrorist attacks in Vegas are probably a diversion."

"Pretty strong diversion."

"What we think we have here, commander, is a submarine with a nuclear device." Kurt paused to let that information sink in.

Menzies blurted, "Holy Shit! How'd you discover that?"

"We found a boat this morning that we'd been looking for. It had a hollow section under it large enough for a Kilo-class sub. We checked the space with a Geiger counter and it gave off a clear reading."

"Damn!" The commander gestured to the six-man raft in the dark. "Then we need to haul ass. Grab the other end of the raft, Chief," he said to Espinosa.

Kurt helped the SEALs roll the heavy six-man craft the rest of the way into the water.

"So you found that boat, and you think a sub's here in the lake?"

"That would explain a diversion, wouldn't it?" Kurt helped the men give one last heave on the raft. They loaded the remainder of the gear and jumped in.

"We're pretty sure the Snow Leopard planned this one, too."

The officer exhaled several large breaths. "Shit! We can't waste time. What's the plan?"

"I believe they have a suicide bomber in the submarine. He was probably trained on exactly what to do."

"The dam!" The officer blurted.

"That's right," Kurt said. "I've thought about this. The damage a nuclear attack would do, the target value, the propaganda value."

The three men climbed into the raft and Espinosa primed the motor. The Mercury outboard started. The chief backed the raft around, then steered for the exit from the cove. The commander flicked on a red light on a pole and checked over the gear. Kurt examined the C-4 explosive and fuse.

"This is a tricky mission. The entire Colorado River pours through four penstocks about twenty-feet in diameter, four stories tall, near the face of the dam. The currents must be terrific."

"I wondered why they asked for alcohol-powered underwater jet-scooters, Kurt. We only had two fueled and ready."

"We flew over and surveyed the dam with lights. There are two places on top to hook pulleys and ropes."

"That's what all the rope's for."

"And the mixed-gases for diving. I figure this is a deep mission. Rope will keep me from being sucked into the dam's generators."

They talked loud enough for Espinosa to hear the plans. Menzies said, "If we approach the terrorist, or he suspects something, he'll set the bomb off."

"The electrical generators in the dam make a lot of noise. He won't hear our raft or scooter. You brought a passive Robertson Sonar, didn't you?"

"Yes. Rescue Squadron 66 at Nellis Air Force Base had one available."

The commander helped Kurt stand so he could slip on the wetsuit. The raft had traveled several hundred meters close to the eastern shore when Espinosa said, "There's a boat fence."

It stretched across the lake, dimly silhouetted by the streetlights on the dam.

"That's what you wanted the bolt-cutters for?" Menzies said.

"Yeah," Kurt said. "After we flew over the lake, we saw that fence and decided cutting it would be quickest."

Espinosa said, "Why didn't you just have the chopper set us down on the other side?" he bumped against the fence.

"I thought the *shaheed* might hear the helicopter. Maybe he's approaching from shallows."

"Sounds hairy," said Menzies. "Hope that jet-scooter has enough power to keep you away from the vortex." He took the bolt cutters and cut the fence.

Espinosa eased the raft through the hole.

Kurt yelled. "Don't let the wire hit the raft!" He leaned over and pushed away from the sharp metal.

"Pull along the spillway to the left, Chief, out of the main current. We'll hang one rope pulley here on the spillway."

He gestured to a rocky section south of the spillway that sloped up to the road on top of the dam. "I'll climb that hill to the road to attach the other one to that railing."

The lake and dam were now visible under the streetlights.

The dam appeared different to Kurt from the surface of the lake. It looked smaller—only 400 meters across where the road passed over—and curved in a half-circle for strength. The four intakes protruded above water like giant rock spires, connected to the dam itself with reinforcing bridges. Openings around them allowed the river to pour through into central collection pipes. The concrete flood-overflow spillways spread out from both sides about a quarter-mile apart. Blacktop roads wound steeply up both sides away from the canyon and dam structure. Kurt heard that its generators produced as much electricity as a large nuclear power plant.

Menzies said, "I can feel the power of the currents from here."

"Yeah," Espinosa said. "I'm steering toward the spillway to keep from being pulled directly toward the penstocks." He guided the raft to port, then moved along the spillway at the edge of the lake.

"I see why you needed the rope and pulleys," the commander said.

"I figure we have to tie off at two places, then pay out the rope."

It took Kurt a couple of minutes to scramble up to the road and hang the second pulley. He connected it to a post for the safety railing. The SEALS pulled tension between the two attachment points with a loop and the other rope connected in the middle. The two tie-off points and loop would allow them to pay out the ropes connected to the underwater jet scooter, keeping it out of the intakes.

The SEALs had the scuba gear and one scooter ready when Kurt returned.

The three men donned the breathing apparatus. Kurt got onto the jet-scooter, with rope attached with a snap-hook to his front. Menzies adjusted Kurt's air supply, handed him the Robertson sonar, and the C-4 explosive packet. Finally, the commander pointed to the magnet Kurt requested, then snapped the communication helmet on him.

"This is the latest in underwater communications. Uses VLF—very low frequency modulation through the water."

Kurt nodded acknowledgment.

The officer gave him the thumbs-up and Kurt let himself sink. He immediately felt pressure and yawned to clear his eardrums. The oxygen and helium breathing mixture left an acrid taste. Exhalations boomed past his ears. Air cells in the wetsuit squeezed into smaller volumes, hastening his descent. He heard popping sounds that grew louder as he sank. Humming noise from the electric turbines below the dam permeated the liquid space. Kurt shook his head to keep from being spooked. He turned on a small infrared light so he could see the dials on the sonar.

It seemed like minutes passed. He looked back toward the raft. The attached blue rope appeared dull gray and barely visible in the infrared light. Nothing else. Merely black water. Frigid, inky water. He swallowed. His exhalations continued to boom. The popping sounds got louder as he went deeper.

His depth gauge indicated 60 meters. Chill and blackness bore in on him. He could feel the cold on the surface of the wetsuit.

Shortly, he passed the 100-meter mark. *Wow!* He jerked. A huge catfish flicked across the infrared. *Must be 250 pounds.*

"You with me, Kurt?"

Commander Menzies' voice in the helmet calmed him. "Still here. Passed 100. Turning on the sonar."

"Roger that."

The currents here were strong. They tugged him toward the intakes. He didn't dare think of a rope breaking or coming loose. Or the alcohol motor not starting on the jet-scooter should he need it. He would be sucked into the vortex and crushed in the blades of a turbine.

He swallowed again and flicked on the switch to the sonar. A low frequency moaned in his earphones for only a few seconds. *Shit! No moving metallic echos. Just fish.*

For a split-second, he wondered if this is how he would die. Vaporized by a nuclear blast. He shook his head to clear those thoughts. His depth gauge said 130 meters. He shivered. It *was* cold, very cold.

"Passed 140," he said, as much to calm himself as anything. "Nothing on the sonar."

"Acknowledged."

Mustafa Fakouri felt the current pull the submarine to the right. He gasped and widened his eyes. For a moment, he wondered if he could reach the dam itself with these powerful currents.

The fence across the lake was not as deep as they thought. He managed to adjust ballast and pass below it. Now he ejected water and the submarine rose. He diverted the red spotlight to the rock face on the right. The currents seemed less powerful there.

Glancing at the satellite photo of the dam, he calculated that he traversed about 100 meters beyond the fence along the eastern rock face. His instructors told him to expect calmer water on that side of the lake, but it was also shallower. He had to pay close attention and not scrape rock.

So far Mustafa didn't use the alcohol motor to power the vessel. Now the batteries were indicating half-charge. He realized that the dam's electrical generators were loud here as he approached the structure itself. The growl radiated through the lake. It seemed to resonate within the metal of the submarine. Soon it would be safe to start the combustion motor and quickly take the boat the last 500 meters to its target. He looked to where the red spotlight illuminated the rock once more. Then he glanced back at the photo.

It surprised him that he was so calm. He had no fear of dying. In fact, the thought of being able to destroy a major part of the crusader's power gave him immense pride—to be chosen for such an honor.

He saw the red numbers count down on the bomb's initiation circuit. Less than 15 minutes to get into position. His depth gauge read 100 meters. He checked the compass and steered seven degrees to the right. The planners thought the water was shallow to the left. Time to head straight across to the dam. He constantly repeated the instructions over and over again. The bomb would be most effective, he was told, if he was hard against the concrete, right between the intakes, at 170 meters depth.

Once he arrived at that point, he could turn the timer to zero and meet Allah and his seventy virgins.

Kurt Valdez spoke into the mouthpiece, "The sonar shows nothing, Commander. We must have arrived ahead of him."

"Roger that, Kurt. We'll draw you back up. Keep a slight negative buoyancy to create drag so as not to overrun the rope. Use the hydrofoil planes on the jet-scooter to stay off the rock like we discussed."

"Acknowledged."

A few seconds passed before Kurt felt the gentle tug on the nose of the underwater craft. He turned on the infrared light several times each minute to make sure he didn't collide with the rock.

As he rose, the lesser pressure caused his buoyancy vest to swell. He valved off air to keep himself from rising too fast. That concerned him, should the terrorist arrive. With all the generator noises and the popping and cracking sounds, the man wouldn't hear him. But he might spot Kurt's air bubbles.

He flicked on the infrared again to make sure he didn't collide with the rock face. Then he switched on the sonar. Still no indication of another moving vessel.

His depth gauge read 50 meters when Menzies spoke again.

"My light illuminated your bubbles. I'll slow your ascent."

"Okay commander. I just made it above 40 meters."

Kurt flicked the light on again and saw the face of the dam to his starboard side. It was amazing how black the water appeared out of the beam. He inhaled several slow breaths, trying to be aware of a breathing problem. The gas mixing apparatus worked perfectly. He wasn't dizzy, no spots before his eyes, no feeling of urgency for oxygen.

Just then he heard it. He held his breath. Sure enough, a combustion motor started. He turned north and flicked on the passive sonar. A dark-red image emerged onto the screen. No doubt about it. He saw a cigar-shaped object. It came toward him from 150 meters away. It cruised 60 meters deeper. Several shivers went up his back.

"Got that, Kurt?"

"He's here."

A faint infrared light shined far below.

Kurt said, "I'm going to settle right on top of him."

Chapter 75

Lake Mead, Arizona

Mustafa Fakouri flinched when the alcohol motor started. It was much louder than he expected. The submarine surged forward. For a moment, he fought panic. He knew the only means of control on this minimum vessel were control planes and a rudder at the prop. Or, he could control ballast by releasing air to descend, or blowing out water to rise. That was it.

Through the round, thick glass windows, he took one good look around where the beam of red light penetrated. Except for several fish and drifting plants, the beam reflected nothing except the rock face on the left. It had to be more than 40 meters away.

He rotated the light beam straight ahead and watched for the concrete dam to appear. The loud whine of the alcohol motor propelled the sub forward.

Kurt Valdez heard the motor start. He confirmed the shape of the submarine on the sonar. Swallowing, he wrapped the C-4 explosive around the magnet then inserted the fuse. He cut the fuse at one-and-one-quarter inch—six minutes and tested the striker. *Good.*

He inserted the materials in a plastic folder attached by Velcro on his chest where he could retrieve them with one hand.

It alarmed him that he had to start the motor on the jet-propelled underwater scooter. He winced at the thought the terrorist might hear it. The machine lurched when the alcohol motor came to life.

"Give me rope."

"Acknowledged," Commander Menzies said. "I can barely hear your motor over the other noises. His is a lot louder."

"Roger that." Kurt exhaled in relief with that knowledge. He felt the line tension release as his motor took over. He could see the light beam from the sub far below. It now dawned on him for the first time how clear the water actually was.

The tricky part. Staying ahead of the sub. Approaching from above. If there was a clear glass view window on the top of the vessel, the terrorist might spot him. He knotted his jaw at the thought of sudden disaster should the man set off the bomb immediately. For him, it would be instantaneous and he wouldn't know it. However, millions of Americans and Mexicans within 200 miles of the dam would suffer from the blast.

He banked to port and exhausted air from his compensator to sink. The scooter followed his guidance and came about. Kurt lined up parallel to the direction the submarine traveled and remained three meters off to its left while he descended.

A quick glance at the sonar. "Forty-five meters to target, directly below."

"Acknowledged," Menzies said. "Extreme caution."

Huh! No need to remind me.

"Coming up on the dam." Kurt said. He shivered.

That would divert the currents and make it more difficult to approach the submarine. For the first time, he could see parts of the vessel illuminated by an interior light emanating from four portholes. He realized there was no glass facing upward. Better yet, he could see there was a lifting eye near the prop.

The sub approached the dam and banked to starboard. The operator obviously did not suspect anything. He kept the light trained on the concrete.

Kurt banked right also. Now he felt the full power of the current. He knotted his stomach muscles. Time to act was running out.

As he went deeper, he could see into the back porthole. The faint red light silhouetted a man's head.

"He's at the dam, 140 meters down. Give me slack. I'm closing in."

Kurt tilted down and accelerated toward the craft. He unfastened the hook of his rope connection. Locking his jaw, he gained speed.

When he passed alongside the sub at a downward angle, he reached to fasten the hook and rope onto the sub's rear lifting-eye.

He missed. Fighting panic, he now ran ahead of the other vessel.

Kurt held his breath and tilted the dive planes upward to slow the scooter quickly. A couple of meters more and the man would have seen his bubbles. It required several lengths of travel to get back in position behind the submarine. Then, he had to accelerate once again to catch up.

Hurry!

Regaining momentum, he reached with the hook for a second try. The scooter speeded. *Now!*

Got it.

Kurt let the rope pay out through his hand. Slowing now, he yanked the Velcro strap and seized the shaped charge of C-4 explosive. The clay-like mass the size of his fist felt hard and cold. He had to hurry. He struck an arc and lit the fuse. Speeding to come alongside the terrorist, Kurt reached out for the sub again.

Mustafa Fakouri carefully maintained a five-meter space between the sub and the dam. He set the light and concentrated on not letting the vessel get any closer to the concrete. The current was powerful here. Indeed, it required all his attention to control the vessel.

He glanced quickly at the bomb timer. Six minutes. On schedule. He couldn't miss. He could pull it off. A 22-year-old *shaheed. He* would bring the crusaders down.

Ensha allah! The currents are powerful.

They diverted the vessel to starboard and almost pulled him off course. He squeezed the grips.

Must focus.

Kurt felt the current increase. Gritting his teeth, he worried that the terrorist would hear his motor. There was no choice. He must apply power. He was close enough now to touch the sub.

The back of the man's head was visible through the glass. This was it. Last chance. One-half the fuse had burned off.

Swallowing, he reached out with the C-4 and forced the wad onto the small circular window. He made sure the magnet attached to the steel rim. Then he backed off the power and tilted the planes upward. The rope streamed past him. For a moment, he almost lost control of the jet-scooter. He seized the grips. His stomach muscles knotted. The sub sank deeper.

Easy—Easy.

He applied power and banked sharply.

Damn!

Kurt cranked the throttle full on to come about. He flicked his light toward the concrete of the dam.

Backward!

He drifted backward, toward the massive suction. Powerful currents drew him toward the penstocks. He fought panic.

Struggling to maintain control, he tried to keep the machine level and rising. Slowly, the scooter fought the current, finally coming alongside the dam. Then it began to gain forward momentum.

Several breaths later, as the minutes ticked down, Kurt thought about the C-4. If he didn't get far enough away from it when it exploded, the concussion might break his eardrums. That would knock him unconscious. Sucked into a penstock. Down into the turbine blades.

Two or three minutes must have passed already. Another two minutes at most to get clear. In a moment of desperation, he turned 45 degrees to the left. The current pulled him out away from the dam. He injected lots of air in his compensator to rise as quickly as possible.

"The C-4 will explode any second, commander. The sub is on the rope. I may not make it far enough away from the blast."

It took several seconds for Menzies to answer. Apparently, he understood that the rope was no longer attached to Kurt's scooter, and that if Kurt were knocked unconscious, it would be certain death. "Discard your head gear, buddy. Cup your hands over your ears. Inflate your vest to the max."

"Roger that, Sir. I think the C-4 on the back porthole will take him out and disable the bomb circuits."

Kurt tore his headgear strap off. He figured he had gained as much momentum as possible from the currents. With the last seconds ticking down, he turned directly away from the submarine. He cupped his hands over his ears and braced for the worst.

Three more breaths from the scuba. The charge exploded.

Ouch!

Kurt felt the surge through his body even though it was a small one. The pressure wave passed through living tissue with almost no resistance. It felt like someone hit him in the stomach. His ears ached. They rang. He opened his jaw wide several times to ease the pain.

Now he turned the throttle full on again. He also switched on the powerful white scooter light and headed to where he thought Commander Menzies was.

Glancing at the depth gauge after he had gained some speed and elevation, he saw that it now read 60 meters. He breathed easier. Mimicking yawning again, his ears squeaked when they cleared.

Now Kurt spotted a light flashing at him. He diverted the scooter a few degrees to the right and headed toward it.

By the time he reached Menzies, Sergeant Espinosa was alongside him. Kurt held a thumb and forefinger in a circle indicating that all went well. He signaled for them to tighten the rope to the submarine.

The three of them cranked their machines full on and headed up the rope toward the raft. When Kurt's head popped above the water, he saw that the rope attached to the road was taut. Menzies saw it, too.

"Get the outboard going, sergeant! We'll take care of your scooter. And give me two grips."

Espinoza rolled into the raft. In moments, he had the Mercury outboard started. He handed Menzies two grips with short pieces of rope and snaphooks on the ends.

The commander turned to Kurt. "I'm gonna cut the rope to the road after we tie off the scooters."

Kurt understood. He watched Menzies secure a grip on the rope and attach Espinoza's scooter to a hook. The commander then connected the other grip and hooked on his machine. Kurt was right alongside him when Menzies fastened his.

They shut the motors off and pulled themselves hand-over-hand on the rope as the sergeant edged closer with the raft. Kurt rolled onto the craft first. The commander followed as soon as he was clear. They removed their scuba gear and pulled down the tops of their wetsuits.

Menzies then cut the rope to the road. The raft jerked and almost capsized as the tension released. It immediately moved backward toward the penstocks. Water poured in.

Espinoza revved the outboard motor, and after a couple of minutes, it made headway toward the eastern spillover.

"Okay." Menzies shouted. "While Sarge goes in reverse, we'll pull in the rope. Just like reeling in a big fish. We tie off every 50 meters and he moves forward pulling the sub."

Kurt reached for his satellite phone. "First I've got to call the office."

He dialed Berkley on his secure line. The counter-terrorism chief answered immediately.

"What's the latest, Tiburon?"

"We've got a dead terrorist here, Top, and a disabled bomb." Kurt heard cheers in the background. Berkley must have held a thumb up.

"We need a big chopper to lift this water-logged submarine out of the lake."

"They'll be there any minute. I had to fight them off to let you handle it. The navy was talking torpedo."

"If they'd succeeded, there would be no dam right now." Kurt shook his head. "Make sure they bring some heavy rigging. And tell them the bomb's probably active! I think I only disabled the timing circuits."

"Gotcha. It's not over yet. Just for your information, Kurt, Sheriff Stroman and Krysta Mazur are headed toward the Las Vegas airport. That's where they think the Snow Leopard is headed. He may have an explosive vest."

"Understood, Top."

"They can't make a move on him, until they determine whether he has accomplices."

"Roger, that."

The phone disconnected.

Kurt turned to help Menzies pull in the rope as Espinoza allowed the raft to move in reverse.

They had managed to draw the sub in about 60 meters, coiling the rope onto the raft, when the choppers arrived.

Menzies got on the radio and directed the helicopter crew as they lowered a cable and attachment shackle. As the commander talked them into position with the apparatus, Espinoza tied it to a loop in the submarine's rope.

Menzies said into the mike, "Take it easy. Don't lose it. There's a live bomb and dead terrorist in the sub."

After the chief had the connection made, he backed the raft to get some slack and Kurt released it to the aircraft. Finally the commander cut the loose coils free so the chopper could lift the load.

"You got it," he said. "Easy as she goes."

"Roger that," came the reply on the radio.

Dawn was still three hours away. Visibility came from the lights on the dam.

Kurt, Menzies and Espinoza watched as the helicopter revved its props and slowly tugged on the sub. It took at least 20 minutes to get the vessel to the surface with the chopper pulling at an angle over the Arizona side of the road.

Kurt held a light on the sub, and when it bobbed up, watched water mixed with blood pour from the blast hole.

"Hold it there," Menzies commanded on the radio. "Don't hit the spillway concrete."

A second helicopter approaching from over the lake now dropped a steel cable with two short cables and connecting shackles. Chief Espinoza moved the raft over against the sub. Kurt connected the shackles to both of the vessel's lifting eyes.

Menzies spoke into the radio, "Take some strain, Number Two."

The second aircraft, staying over the water to keep its rotors away from the rope, reeled in the cable until the submarine came level.

"Chief, move the raft around while the first chopper comes clear. I'm gonna cut his rope."

"Aye, aye, Sir."

Menzies keyed the radio's mike. "I'll cut the rope to Chopper One, while Number Two comes directly over the load."

Both helicopter pilots acknowledged.

Kurt winced as Menzies sawed it with the Bowie. The rope rang when the strands unraveled, then finally popped and flew away. The jet engine on Number One quickly backed off on power. The second chopper adjusted position over the sub and took the full load. The vessel righted itself.

Menzies exhaled a loud breath. "You got it," he said. "Remember, the bomb is still live. What's your destination?"

"We're headed 75 miles southeast to a remote location for an inspection. Eventually a C-5 from Nellis will take it to the Nevada Test Site. A crew will open the sub and remove the bomb. We're authorized to take Kurt Valdez."

"Roger, that," Menzies said.

Kurt nodded approval. The first helicopter hovered and dropped a harness for him.

He grinned. "It's in the hands of the military. Where you guys headed now?"

"Dhahran, Saudi Arabia." Espinoza made a face.

"Oh, please. Can I go?" Kurt asked.

The SEALs, laughing, hugged Kurt.

Menzies turned and pointed. "There comes our chopper to pick up the raft and jet-scooters."

Kurt dropped the wetsuit onto the raft, grabbed his clothes bag and climbed into the harness. He waved to the SEALs as the aircraft pulled him up.

The helicopters rose and headed away.

In the chopper, a sergeant helped Kurt out of the harness.

When he stepped into the cockpit, the three marines cheered.

Kurt smiled broadly. "How long to the remote site?"

"Thirty minutes," said the lieutenant colonel at the controls, tilting his head back. "That big pouch back there is like a beanbag. Bet you can be asleep in five minutes."

Chapter 76

Henderson, Nevada

Ramzi bin Omeri swore as he looked at his watch. "The attacks started." The big rig that was on its side was now fastened down onto a large tow truck. Two police officers directed cars onto the 215 freeway headed west and east or onto Highway 95 north. Ali sighed. "We finally move."

"Thirty minutes lost," Ramzi huffed. He clicked on the radio again.

A reporter shouted rapid staccato into his microphone. "This just in. Terrorists attacked four hotels in Las Vegas during the night. The damage and casualties have not been determined." His voice sounded terrified. "Two were shot. One by a security guard at the WBB, and another by a policeman at Bompensiero's. The terrorists appear to be Middle Eastern."

He gasped. "From the national newswires, it has just been reported that separate attacks were carried out in four other major cities." The man's voice now trembled. "They were all timed to begin at 3:30 a.m., our time."

He stammered. "It . . . it is expected that casualties will number in the tens of thousands. This is without doubt the largest-scale attack ever carried out by terrorists on American soil, dwarfing September 11."

"Good," Ramzi sneered. "The Zionists can feel what thousands of Muslims feel."

The radio continued reporting. "Further news on the attacks. Terrorists were killed in unspecified hotels in Houston and Saint Louis. It is reported that their explosives failed to go off."

Ali pushed on the accelerator and the truck and boat trailer moved.

"Take a right here on Lake Mead Drive." Ramzi pointed.

After they made the turn, several rescue vehicles with their Sirens blaring and lights flashing passed by in the left lane.

Ramzi turned up the volume on the radio.

"We have with us an eyewitness who was on Las Vegas Boulevard when the bombs detonated downtown. This is Amy Scott-Russell. Amy—is it okay if I call you Amy?"

"Of course."

"Where were you when the bombs went off?"

"I was in a taxi in front of that hotel when a blast occurred."

"Sorry folks, we have to keep the locations from the public for the moment. What happened, Amy?"

"I thought it was an earthquake. The street shuddered. Then there was this terrific blast. It felt like the taxi rose off the street." Her voice quivered.

The announcer said, "I know this is hard for you, Amy. It's difficult for all of us. Did you see any signs of buildings crumbling?"

"No … no I didn't. After several minutes, people ran away from the hotel. Smoke came from the top. Glass in some of the windows shattered."

"How long would you say it took for the police and fire trucks to get there?"

"Less than ten minutes. You know this just happened like—fifteen minutes ago."

"Thank you Amy Scott-Russell." The man's voice now cracked.

Ali drove by the hospital where the fire trucks and emergency vehicles unloaded casualties. "Six more streets, Ali. I am looking for a petrol station."

"Another news flash," the radio blared. "Cincinnati was one of the four cities bombed. The Grand Hotel was attacked by two terrorists at the same time. The hotel collapsed in the middle from explosions. It is unknown at this time how many injured and dead there are."

At this point, it sounded as if the announcer was almost in tears.

"There is the ARCO station I was looking for," Ramzi pointed. "Pull under the canopy closest to the street."

Chapter 77

Seventy miles southeast of Lake Mead, Arizona

Kurt Valdez watched under the floodlights as the other chopper eased the submarine to a bare sandy spot in a vast, arid, uninhabited area. As soon as his helicopter landed he was out and over to the vessel.

A marine and air force sergeant blocked the sub underneath and allowed slack in the lines from the helicopter. It leaned over. Bloody water with pieces of skull, brain and bones poured out through the blast hole. It spread out and soaked into the sand.

All six crew members from both choppers now knew that this was a live nuclear bomb. The nearby marine's face blanched. He trembled.

"Got to hurry," Kurt shouted. "We've got a big one here!"

Edging around the craft, he hyperventilated two large breaths. He first examined the bolts on the bottom where he thought the bomb was inserted. Then he peered into the blasted out window. Kneeling to see, his stomach lurched and he swallowed back bile. The terrorist's head and torso were missing from the mid-chest area up.

He stood and held his stomach. After several minutes, most of the blood, bone and tissue drained away.

The marine gave signals to the chopper pilot to take up slack and the vessel slowly righted itself.

"Hold it!" Kurt shouted. "Gimme some time. He shined his light through the blasted-out porthole, into the cockpit. It took a few moments to focus. Sure enough, the timer was similar to one he'd disabled in Saudi Arabia four years ago. There was no light coming from the device and the wires were blown away. A 20,000-volt meter had a broken faceplate.

"Come on, man," the marine shouted, "we gotta get this fucking thing outta here."

Kurt ignored him and saw that his measured charge had jammed the conning tower latch and the cover was crumpled. A split rubber gasket protruded. The cover would have to be forced open to get inside.

"You seen enough, man?"

Kurt glared at the marine. "Wait a moment." After a long pause, he turned to the air force tech-sergeant next to him. The man had been selected to accompany the ordnance all the way the test site.

"The bomb we dismantled before had a control harness plugged into the front of it. They used a very powerful capacitor to set off the fission triggering device. There's a 20,000-volt meter in this sub."

The sergeant looked at Kurt with wide eyes. "Holy shit!" He gulped. "Even a bump or shock could set off that capacitor!"

Kurt moved his face close to the sergeant. "They'll have to discharge the capacitor first to prevent setting off the bomb. It can easily kill a man."

"I'll pass that on," the sergeant said. His voice trembled and his eyes reflected his fear. It was obvious he was thinking vaporization.

"Furthermore, stay wide of populated areas. Have that pilot land softly. Warn the pilots of the C-5 what they're dealing with."

"Are you finished here, Kurt?" The marine growled at him with a disbelieving look.

"Yeah. Let's get this sucker to the Test Site."

The sergeant got into the helicopter and it lifted the submarine. The aircraft banked in slow motion then, as planned, would head toward the lower end of the Grand Canyon and Nellis Air Force base's runway where a C-130 Hercules cargo plane was waiting to take the weapon to the Nevada Test Site.

Kurt hurried toward the other chopper. His satellite phone buzzed and he looked at the display. *Stroman?*

"What's up, sheriff?"

"Krysta has been on the phone with NSA. They intercepted two suspicious calls, one from near Lake Mead and one from Boulder City. They came from the same satellite phone."

"Why were they suspicious, Bob?"

"They sounded coded, in Spanish. The first one from near the lake warned that the highway patrol had a roadblock set up on the highway heading south. It said to go to a second plan. The next call, from Boulder City, warned that the highway south—must be talking about 95 South—was also blocked."

"When were the calls made?"

"More than two hours ago, Kurt. If this is our terrorist, and he went north, he may have become involved in a traffic jam on the Highway 215 Alternate. A jack-knifed big-rig got sideways under the bridge and had vehicles backed up for forty minutes or so just before the terrorist attacks began."

The sheriff's radio announced that all flights in and out of McCarran were cancelled for the time being.

"You hear that announcement?"

"Yeah. McCarran's closed. Where are you now, sheriff?"

"I was stuck behind the rig for awhile also. NHP has all the main highways out of Vegas blocked off. If there are any terrorists left in this area, we'll get 'em. With all the flights stopped, roads and airports are jammed with people and vehicles. Take six to eight hours to clear it, Kurt."

"We stopped the submarine at the dam, Bob. That terrorist is dead. We're headed over the lake toward Nellis. A C-5 transport is taking the sub with a nuclear bomb to the Test Site to dismantle it."

There was a gasp, then a moment of silence while the sheriff considered that.

"Jesus! That *is* good news. I'll inform Krysta."

"This is not national news, yet, Bob. The bomb is not defused. Where is she, now?"

"She's at Nellis coordinating with the Air Force. They have three surveillance aircraft over Mojave County."

"Really." Kurt paused to think. "See if they have videotapes back to about 0240 hours. On the south side of Lake Mead, a white boat stopped in a cove. Tire tracks went up to the road and they turned toward Palo Verde Springs. We need to ID the vehicle. I'm gonna see if my people have anything from high-altitude surveillance aircraft. I'll get back to you later."

"I'll keep you informed, too," Stroman said.

Kurt got into the second helicopter and it lifted off.

In a few minutes, the noise of the rotors increased as the aircraft banked, heading toward Nellis Air Force Base.

Kurt straightened in his seat and looked out the window toward Las Vegas. Twenty minutes later, he saw the four plumes of smoke rising over the metropolis in the pre-dawn light.

"Those mother fuckers," growled the pilot.

Chapter 78

San Ysidro, California

Kareem ducked to read the brightly lit road sign that straddled the freeway. "What does it say?" asked Rasool.

"International border, five miles. César will be waiting for us in the parking lot on this side. Move to the right lane."

Rasool flipped on the turn signal, glanced in the mirror, and changed lanes. "What are we looking for?"

"One kilometer. A big parking area." Kareem glanced at his watch. "We are early. In an hour, it is daylight."

They went silent. The Porsche cruised almost noiselessly.

Kareem fidgeted as they approached signs advertising insurance and Mexican divorces. After they passed more than a dozen, he saw his landmark and pointed, "There it is. Go slow."

Rasool turned into a large dirt lot. He eased the Porsche to a tollbooth where Kareem paid and did the talking. They continued through lines of parked vehicles illuminated by tall parking lights.

Kareem leaned forward and searched for their contact. "Turn the lights down. Use smaller ones."

Several cars and groups of people moved toward the border. When they passed directly under a pole light, Kareem pointed to the far wall, "There."

A truck's lights blinked. "Park on that side and we take flight bags."

Rasool pulled forward and parked in an empty space. He shut off the motor and opened the door.

Kareem put his hand on the other man's arm. In the pre-dawn light, he handed Rasool a packet. He could see the whites of the man's eyes. His jaw appeared lighter where he had recently shaved off his beard.

Rasool took the packet and tore off the flap. He emptied two small, pink pills into his hand.

"If the Mexican police hold us, we bite the pill." Kareem leaned his face close to Rasool's.

Rasool replaced the pills and stuck the packet in his shirt pocket. "I do what I must do." He opened the door and grabbed his luggage out of the back seat.

Kareem seized his also. They got out and locked the Porsche. He waved to the truck, its engine started and lights came on.

The man pulled alongside them. The Arabs opened the passenger door. Kareem was surprised that there were three small children in the cab.

"For decoys," César said, looking at Kareem. "Put the baggage in back." The Mexican gestured with his thumb. Change to old clothes and boots.

Kareem and Rasool took the faded denims and boots out of their luggage, went over between parked cars and changed. When they returned, they slung their flight bags over into the bed with fishing equipment.

They got in the truck, Rasool next to the driver. One boy who appeared about eight got in after him.

Kareem got in the back middle of the crew-cab, a child on both sides of him. The girl on his right was no more than seven.

The noisy truck, with a muffler leaking, took off. "I am César. I will drive you to Ensenada to boat."

Kareem nodded.

The Mexican exited the parking lot and turned the old truck toward the international border, where a short line formed.

César eased behind another truck and said, "Don't talk to inspectors."

As they approached the agents, Kareem slid a pill out of his packet and put it into his mouth. He pushed it up to his gum line with his tongue. He tapped Rasool on the shoulder.

He saw the man do likewise.

"Have your passports ready, if they ask," César said.

"We have them in our shirts." Kareem was keenly aware of the pill.

César edged the truck forward and rolled down his window.

The agent leaned toward him under the bright quartz lights and examined the passengers. "*Adonde va?*" He motioned to the other agent to talk to Kareem.

The agent on the passenger side rapped on the back truck window.

The girl rolled it down.

César said, "*Nos vamos a pescar en Ensenada.*" He gestured to the fishing equipment in the bed of the truck.

The agent near Kareem glared hard into the Arab's eyes. "*Pasaporte?*"

Kareem reached into his shirt pocket and slid out the document past the packet with the other pill. In Spanish, he said to Rasool, "*Su pasaporte, señor.*"

Rasool took his passport out and passed it to the boy, who handed it to the agent.

The Mexican flipped through the documents examining them. He rattled off a long string of rapid Spanish to Kareem.

"*Hable despacio, por favor, señor.*"

The Mexican looked hard at the men's clothing and the fishing equipment in the back. He cocked his head, perhaps suspicious that the neatly clipped men did not fit the image of anglers.

"Get out of the car." He said in good English.

César stomped on the accelerator and roared out of the Port of Entry. He shifted and headed for a congested residential area. After three blocks, he made a series of turns and stopped in front of a house. He jerked the parking brake.

He turned the lights off. "Hurry, get inside."

Inside the small house, they all sat on low, worn out couches and chairs.

"Why did you drive off?" asked Rasool. "They have our passports.

César said, "They put me in prison. If they find you Arabs."

Cars pulled up outside. A gruff voice yelled, "*Abra la puerta!*"

César shook. There was a pounding on the door. "*Abra la puerta!*"

The door burst open and Mexican *federales* burst into the room with guns drawn.

Kareem looked at Rasool and nodded. He made a motion and bit down on the DZ-41 capsule. Within seconds his chest seized. He choked. His face felt like it was going to explode. He worked his mouth like a fish out of water. Froth gushed on his lips. His last vision was of Rasool's face beet red. Bright expanding circles spread on a black background. It went black.

Chapter 79

Fifty miles northeast of Las Vegas, Nevada

Ramzi bin Omeri downshifted the big Yamaha Virago and grumbled under his breath. This was the fourth rain gully across the road. And, they were getting wider.

Accelerating again, the machine straightened as it gathered speed. His dual headlights lit the road ahead revealing a high bank on the left side with large boulders. On the right side, a sharp drop-off plunged into an arroyo. From behind him, Ali's lights illuminated the road on both sides.

The Snow Leopard swallowed hard. He leaned forward on the powerful V-4 motorcycle as he approached a larger rain washout. He veered to the high side of the road near the embankment, and at the last moment accelerated to jump the gap.

Stopping fifty meters beyond, he looked back. Ali gunned the motor on his bike and leaped over the same spot, apparently following Ramzi's tire tracks. The Arab pulled his Virago up beside Ramzi and raised his face shield.

"That was worst one, my comrade. They become more wide."

"Yes. But, we must keep going while it is dark. The GPS shows ten kilometers to the paved road."

Ramzi dropped the bike into gear and took off again toward the Valley of Fire State Park.

To the east, faint traces of red sky showed on the horizon. The emerging light revealed a dark outline of mountains. Ruts had firmed almost as hard as concrete. When the motorcycle drifted into them, it jerked violently causing him to fight to keep from losing control.

He jumped across another gully and accelerated again. His light beams bounced around on the road ahead revealing a rise. The surface improved with the slight uphill tilt. He crested the top, went another half-kilometer, and skidded to a stop.

Gaping at the wide gully that stretched across the road before him, he swore.

Ali pulled alongside again.

Ramzi dismounted. He shut off the engine, took off his helmet and put the stand down. Motioning to Ali to do the same, they took out spotlights to examine the rain damage.

Directing the lights around on the gully, the Snow Leopard saw that it was four meters deep in places and two meters across.

Ali gaped at the enormous size of the chasm. "We cannot do!"

Ramzi grunted and walked toward the upper end where the gap was narrower. His light illuminated a small animal trail that looped up around boulders.

After considering it for several moments, he decided that the trail was impassable for a heavy motorcycle.

They both went to the lower side of the road. Their lights shined into the dry ravine strewn with boulders.

Ramzi swallowed hard. "We will jump the gully."

"Jump!" Ali sounded panicked.

"We will, or they catch us."

Ramzi looked at his watch again. An hour past detonation time.

No blast.

The realization that Hoover Dam did not explode infuriated him. It was well past the time for the nuclear explosion. That meant that Mustafa failed.

Four years wasted.

Again, he stared at the wide gap. First, the jack-knifed semi truck at the offramp to Interstate 215 that delayed them for an hour, now this.

The Snow Leopard shined his light behind onto the road toward the small hill. He saw that the tire-track ruts resumed when the road leveled. However, the road was solid enough to gain speed. He considered it.

He gritted his teeth and inhaled a large breath. Swallowing hard, he said, "I am going to go back and get a run for it. You hold the light on the gully right here." He shined the light on the narrowest part of the gap. "See the opposite bank is lower. The back wheel needs to land there."

"You cannot do! Your body break."

"The trick is to go fast enough, Ali." He mounted the motorcycle. Starting and revving the big V-4, he headed along the road, directing the headlight to where the smoothest part of the track was. A half-kilometer back, near the top of the knoll, he turned around and accelerated. He hung on tight through the dried-mud tracks. The motorcycle flounced and trembled.

One-hundred meters from Ali's light, Ramzi accelerated fully. He used all of the bike's power. As he gathered speed, he noticed that the machine was more easily controllable. It didn't wobble in the ruts. It drove straight.

Up shifting, he grabbed another handful of throttle and the one-liter engine roared. The bike headed straight for his comrade's light.

The Snow Leopard gripped the bars. He tucked in his knees. Fifty meters to go. Leaning back, he opened the throttle full wide. Time stretched. Every moment recorded in his brain.

He soared over the gully and slammed onto the other side. The back wheel hit hard. The big Yamaha jerked when the front shocks took the full impact of the landing.

Panicking, he held on with all his strength. The motorcycle shook. He backed off on the throttle. The wobble grew worse. He slid back and poured on the power. The bike rose in front with the surge and straightened.

After three deep breaths of relief, he circled and went back to the ravine.

"I cannot do," Ali yelled.

"Do it now."

Ali stared hard at the gap. He shined his light along the far side. "You fly at best place."

"I know what you are thinking comrade. But remember our battles with the Russians. *Mujahedeen* vomited before a battle. When the shooting started, everyone directed their attention to the enemy's defeat.

"Get on the Yamaha and follow in my tracks. Go fast. I'll hold the light right here."

Ali nodded and replaced his helmet. He cinched the chinstrap, started the motorcycle, and took off toward the top of the knoll. Circling and straightening out, he shined his headlight at Ramzi.

Ramzi heard the engine rev. He waited, directing the beam of his headlight where Ali should cross. The loud sound of the bike broke the desert silence. Ali moved up and down several times on the seat. He twisted the throttle and gunned the engine.

After a few minutes, Ramzi became alarmed. He pointed his light toward Ali, off to the side.

I must make the jump.

He flicked the beam rapidly back and forth. He shined the light on himself, raised a palm and waved for Ali to see.

The big Yamaha started forward and gained speed. Ali accelerated. A dozen meters from the gully, the Arab slammed on the brakes and came to a stop. He had to jump off the machine to keep it from falling over.

Ramzi yelled. "Stop!" and blinked his light rapidly at his comrade.

Ali raced the engine. He strained to get the bike back to a straight up position. In the dim light, Ramzi could see him struggling, and then hoisting a leg over.

The man returned to the top of the hill. Once again he moved up and down on the seat, leaned forward and twisted the throttle. The Yamaha came forward again. This time, when he was 100 meters from the ditch, he increased speed. Approaching the gully, he yelled and shut the throttle off.

The big machine went airborne. It slammed the front wheel on the opposite bank. The bike roared and flew high in the air. Legs and arms flailed.

The motorcycle flipped. Ali soared. He slammed to the ground. The Yamaha bounced on him. It continued flipping and bouncing another three-dozen meters.

Ali lay still.

Ramzi yelled and ran to him. He pulled off the man's helmet and unzipped his jacket. Ali was unconscious, made no sound. Ramzi examined his body with his light, first moving Ali's head back and forth, then each arm and leg. He bent over and listened to his shallow breathing.

Deciding he did not have a broken neck and no obvious broken bones, Ramzi swallowed hard and locked his jaw.

I should have stopped him.

He rose and went to the wrecked bike. The front forks were bent under the gas tank. The wheel was crumpled. He grimaced while he thought of the options.

He will have to ride behind me.

Walking back, Ramzi heard Ali moan and hurried to him. He stared hard at the injured man. In the Afghanistan War, the Snow Leopard had earned a reputation as a commander who did not let his men down.

"I cannot feel my feet."

Unfastening Ali's belt, Ramzi pulled down his leathers.

He grimaced.

Broken thigh bone.

He pressed hard on the injury.

Ali made no sound.

"Can you feel that?"

"No, my commander."

Ramzi elevated the man's knee from underneath.

Ali still made no sound. Finally, he asked, "The motorcycle?"

"Broke." Ramzi shook his head. Again, he swore to himself. "You will have to ride behind me."

"No!" Ali sounded distant. "You escape."

Ramzi stood. He squeezed his lips together. He had witnessed severed spinal cord injuries in the war.

He walked over to where the road overlooked the wash. The dim, predawn light illuminated the *wadi* and boulders. It reminded him of daybreak in northern Afghanistan. The desert ravine not unlike this one. The first time he met Ali bin Khalifa. He shut his eyes. Twenty-two years. Still vivid dreams. The great battle that changed the war. He blinked.

Entire armored division. Narrow road.

Hind helicopter gun-ships. Infra-red night vision. *Mujahedeen* hiding. Waiting.

Tank column moving. Down steep road. Sharp curves. Stretching out ten kilometers. Squeals and diesel rumblings in canyon.

Battle seasoned warriors. Waiting. Heartbeats pounding.

Last sharp turn.

There it comes.

T-72 rounding curve.

"Now!" Ramzi commanded.

Bright flash. Rocket-propelled grenade. Tread blown off.

Last curve. Jammed in bank. Three more tanks explode. Direct hits. Tank plunging in river.

Ear-splitting volleys. Flashes everywhere. Entire mountain erupting.

Mujahedeen firing. Two tanks plummet off the plateau.

Russian turrets. 155-millimeters firing. Afghan-Arab bodies flying.

Orange blast. Ears ringing. Hind gun-ships over the ridge. Rockets and RPGs exploding on their positions. Rapid-fire 50-caliber. Tracers lacing hillside.

Unleashing sidewinders. A gun-ship explodes. Another gyrates into the mountain.

"Don't let them clear the road!" Ramzi yells.

Two more tanks explode.

Massive shock volley. Dozens more T-72s' big guns.

Coughing. Acrid smoke rising. Nostrils stinging from cordite. Another rapid volley. Ears ringing.

More gun-ships. Pummeling *mujahedeen*. Bodies littering hillsides.

Sidewinders screaming toward choppers. A fusillade of missiles. Hinds exploding.

A tactical retreat. Succumbing to overwhelming firepower. Swarming over peaks. *Mujahedeen* covering retreat. Fighting to the death.

Four Migs. Napalm.

Shrapnel in leg. Ali grabs Ramzi. Over his back. Over the pass.

Hiding him until missiles take out Migs.

In a cave. Shooting a snow leopard. The mother of two cubs. Raising the little ones.

Ali bin Khalifa giving Ramzi the name Snow Leopard.

The yelp of a coyote snapped Ramzi back to the present.

Chapter 80

Valley of Fire State Park, Nevada

The Snow Leopard knotted his jaw and steeled himself. He pulled out his Beretta and chambered a shell. Turning slowly, he walked back to Ali.

Ali blinked his eyes. The whites were just visible in the early dawn. He swallowed, nodded, and turned his head. The man mumbled a prayer.

Ramzi whispered, "*Allahu akbar, sadiqque*," and squeezed the trigger.

He slid the gun back into his trousers and dragged Ali's body to the gully. Finding the deepest part, he flipped the corpse in. Finally, he hefted several large rocks and rolled them onto the body.

Mounting the big Virago and taking off, Ramzi was still three kilometers from the paved road in the state park. He sped up as fast as possible and jumped three more small gullies before he spotted the blacktop.

He stopped on the last knoll before the road, shut off the motor and put the stand down. Removing his helmet, he realized it would be full daylight in another hour.

The motorcycle made pinging and clicking noises as the metal cooled. A falcon screeched in the distance. Listening intently for small aircraft, he stood for several minutes, blinking, and thinking about Ali.

He walked a few meters and urinated. The distant rays of the rising sun blanked out the last bright stars. A planet and a quarter-moon remained visible. The landscape was now a mixture of ghostly boulders, with dark and gray patches of desert bushes. There was nothing more, no motor sounds whatsoever.

He could not make it.

He swallowed. Scanning the entire sky, he saw the contrails of an airliner, which he followed to the silvery craft made visible by the rising sun.

No spotter aircraft.

He mounted the Yamaha again and when he reached the blacktop, accelerated. Toward Lake Mead, the GPS indicated a good road that wound all the way around through the state park, veered toward the northeast, and then connected to Interstate 15.

On the paved road, he had time to think over a plan. Turning on the news again, he listened with earphones to the reports about the hotel attacks.

Most Americans would think that the bombings of the hotels were the main terrorist strikes. After all, they'd killed more people than on September 11. They were only sideshows. The dam was the principal target.

The bomb failed.

As he motored in between the state park museum and out buildings a vehicle came over a rise far ahead of him, its lights moving up and down as it went through low places and then over the small hills and around curves. It traveled fast.

Ramzi continued to cruise at a moderate speed.

An SUV passed by quickly. At the last moment, he spotted the Nevada Highway Patrol insignia.

His stomach tightened. He gripped the throttle and had the urge to hurry. Looking in his rear-view mirror, he saw that the patrol vehicle didn't slow. It rose on a higher elevation, then dipped out of sight beyond it. Ramzi increased his speed.

Originally, he had planned to turn near the small town of Overton to another dirt road alongside the Virgin River. Now he changed his mind. No more dirt roads and rain gullies. He would go immediately to Interstate 15 and take his chances.

Twenty minutes later, after he had run the motorcycle up to 120 kph, he took the last offramp to Mesquite, Nevada, and turned north. In the early dawn, he cruised by two casinos and through a residential neighborhood to the local airport alongside a golf course. He parked and locked the motorcycle among several cars. There were seven small aircraft and a fuel dispensing station, but no control tower.

Leaving his helmet, he grabbed his backpack and entered a large clump of shrubbery at the edge of the golf course. A meter-wide stream with moss growing in it wove through the course. The sun would come over the mountains in a couple of hours.

He removed and stashed his leathers, then put on a khaki shirt and trousers. Last, he donned the LA Dodgers baseball cap.

He set the alarm on his Aquameter for two hours and lay down.

Chapter 81

Mesquite, Nevada

The vibration on his wrist woke him. Ramzi shivered and blinked to see the sun was brilliant. He struggled to awaken. Two hours sleep was not enough.

Retrieving an American military food packet, he tore off the wire and poured water into the magnesium powder in the side pouch. It generated so much heat he had to set it down. While it cooled, he downed a protein drink and some water.

After a few minutes, he kneaded the food pouch and ravished a hot tuna-macaroni casserole with asparagus.

Revived, he took a circuit board radio receiver, hand transmitter and a clump of Semtex from his backpack. He plugged in one wire on the radio. Simulating an attack, he initiated the transmitter signal, then watched the Aqualand. Less than a minute went by before an LED flashed red on the circuit board.

Good. It would have exploded.

He switched off the transmitter to prevent accidental discharge. Then he plugged in a second wire to an incendiary charge on the radio and formed Semtex around it. The red LED blinked, indicating it awaited a triggering signal. Sliding it into its plastic case, he carefully inserted it in a side pocket of the backpack.

He swallowed. Many people would die if they tried to take him.

Next, he counted out $5,000 and $10,000, wrapped bands around the two packets.

Still hiding in the brush, he took out the computer, went online and opened the satellite imaging maps. Locating Mesquite, he ran through a simulated flight to his destination, writing down the coordinates and GPS readings where he would need to make course corrections. His chosen route bypassed military bases, no-fly zones and a bombing range. It also skirted the commercial airports' flight paths in order to stay far away from radar. Finally, he made sure there were no small airports directly in line.

Thinking like the master chess player that he was, Ramzi choose an alternate route. When he finished, he sent an email giving numerical codes for both destinations.

The computer beeped indicating low battery and Ramzi stowed the machine. He removed a small tee-shaped device. Holding it in his palm, a protruding stem stuck out from between two fingers. He carefully stuck it in his shirt pocket.

Then he grasped his pack and headed for the landing strip.

At the motorcycle, he turned on the radio. It gave periodic reports on the hotel attacks, concluding with, "Homeland Security has declared a nationwide Red Alert."

He nodded. *Complication.*

It was almost two hours before a man rode a small bicycle toward a four-passenger aircraft. As he dismounted with a bag of golf clubs over his shoulder, Ramzi ambled around near him and said, "Good morning."

The man started. "Oh, I didn't see you there!" He was a slim man with a thin gray mustache and wore a golfer's cap, slacks and an open-collar shirt.

"I have an emergency and I need a ride."

"Sorry. I have a tournament in Salt Lake."

Ramzi pulled one money packet from his trousers. "It is an extreme situation. I have $5,000 here if you take me to Tuk-son."

The man blinked. He seemed to think the request odd. Yet he eyed the money, took the bills and flipped through them. His eyes grew wide. A cheek muscle twitched. "What's the emergency?"

"My son is in critical condition in the hospital."

"I am entered in a golf tournament. The prize money is eight grand."

Ramzi squinted. "The commercial flights were booked. I am desperate. I may not see him alive again."

The man looked off in the distance. He shook his head. "How much more?"

"I will give you $10,000 more if you get me there."

He opened his mouth wide. "Ten thou ... show me the money."

Ramzi pulled the second packet out, and fanned it.

The man stared at the stack, twice as thick as the first. "That's a lot of money. You could buy a vehicle and drive."

"Too slow. I have to get there immediately. How fast will the aircraft travel?"

The man flipped through the first stack of bills again, and said, "180 knots."

Ramzi knotted his jaw. "This is easy money."

The man rubbed his jaw. He was silent for several breaths as if he were thinking. "What's your son's name?"

Ramzi almost answered, Ali, then caught himself. "Ricardo."

There was another awkward pause.

"How old?"

Now Ramzi glared at him.

The man raised his eyebrows.

"Seven."

He fanned the money again. "I really would like to help you out … and this is a lot of money." He shook his head.

Swinging the Beretta from the back of his trousers, Ramzi said, "I have to get there."

The man jerked back and put his hands out.

Ramzi chambered a shell and pointed the gun at him. He bore his stare into the man's eyes. "I won't harm you if you take me to Tuk-son."

The man's eyes were wide as he looked down the barrel of the pistol.

Ramzi gestured with the gun. "Remove those cables from the wings and tail."

For a moment, it appeared the man was about to run.

"Okay, you're in charge." Then he turned, opened the aircraft rear door and swung the golf bag onto the seat. He folded and set the bicycle in afterward. Removing the hold-down cables and opening the pilot's door, he climbed in.

"Hand me that radio headset and don't start the engine yet," Ramzi said.

He took the radio equipment and ducked under the aircraft to the other side. Climbing into the passenger's seat and setting his backpack between his legs under the co-pilot's steering yoke, he handed the headset back to the man.

"What is your name?"

"What? Oh—Tom."

"Okay, Tom. We are going to fly over those mountains over there." Ramzi pointed south. "Then over the Grand Canyon near Seligman. From there, we will head straight south. If you follow my instructions, you'll get the money."

Tom blinked and frowned.

Ramzi seized the steering yoke. "Do you have to ask permission to take off at this airport?"

Tom put on the headset, switched on the radio and started the engine. "No. I filed a flight plan yesterday. Only the fueling station guy is here during regular hours. He has not arrived yet."

Ramzi slid the gun in his trouser pocket. "Give me the flight maps and radio frequencies. Explain the controls."

The pilot opened a ring-bound book, took out a chart and unfolded it to Nevada and Arizona. On the console, he pointed to rods, levers, buttons and dials, explaining their functions.

"So this red lever controls gas mixture?" Ramzi squinted.

"Yes. And this black one is the throttle."

"How much fuel does this aircraft have?"

"Forty-two gallons. I filled up yesterday. I planned to make it to Salt Lake, to the golf tournament, and back here."

"How far can 42 gallons go?"

"About 800 miles."

Ramzi nodded. "How do you turn the transponder on?"

Tom raised his eyebrows. "This small black button activates it when the radio is on the correct frequency."

"What is the alarm frequency?"

Tom coughed. There was a long pause. "You mean an emergency signal?"

"Do not try to fool me. I know transponders give alarm signals."

Tom still hesitated.

Ramzi flared his nostrils and pulled the Beretta out.

Tom blinked. "There is a hijack frequency."

"Show me how to set it, Tom."

The pilot's bottom lip quivered. He pointed to the radio and said, "Seventy-five-hundred. Then press this black button."

"And what does that do? Give out an identification, friend or foe alarm?"

"Something like that," Tom said. "It would draw immediate attention to the aircraft."

Nodding, Ramzi said, "Show me where it says that in the manual."

Tom continued not to look into Ramzi's eyes. He perused the index of the flight manual and turned to a page for emergency landing and hijack procedures.

Ramzi studied it as if he could read English fluently. He saw the 7500 frequency listing and recognized the words *emergency* and *hijack*. "Good. Who do you contact when you want to take off?"

Tom pointed to the ATIS frequency for wind, weather and approach information where it indicated the Mesquite airport. "The UNICOM frequency on the chart allows contact with other pilots. After you check ATIS for all flying conditions, you dial 119.5 megahertz and any aircraft that wants to land here would use the same frequency. You would talk to the other pilots to stay out of each others' flight patterns." He set the radio and static came on.

"Any other settings we have to know about?" Ramzi clicked the radio up one channel, then back to 119.5 megahertz.

"There are two, 123.6 and 122.9. The first is the universal control tower communication frequency, and the second is the UNICOM, which connects us with fuel service at all airports."

"Okay, Tom. Good." Ramzi tapped a glass window. "And this is the GPS?"

"Yes."

The Snow Leopard wrote down the coordinates for Mesquite. He ran his finger down the Arizona map, and then pointed to Luke Air Force Base near Phoenix. "Is this the way they mark all important military bases?"

Tom leaned over and read the information on the chart. That's a special control base. There are only three like it in the US."

"What does that mean?"

"Aircraft must fly between 2,000 and 2,500 feet. Or," he pointed to another elevation, "stay above 4,500 feet. The base has special control and recording equipment."

Ramzi nodded. "Start the engine and take off."

Tom slipped on dark glasses, started the Cessna and taxied out toward the runway. He scanned the sky, flipped to two other channels on the radio, and then went back to 119.5. "It's all clear out there."

In a few minutes, they were airborne.

Ramzi said, "Turn to heading 135 degrees. Fly low. No more than 2,000 feet off the ground."

"That is unusual," said Tom. "We will use a lot more fuel."

Ramzi said, "Do as I say."

The Cessna gained altitude until they crossed over the Virgin Mountains. Two more ranges were visible to the east. Tom flipped the radio channel to 138.7 megahertz. "That will give us continuous weather information."

The radio squawked and reported, "Major thunder storms from 220 degrees out of the west have moved as far as Kingman, Arizona. The storms are accompanied by high, vortex winds in desert areas. A small aircraft advisory has been issued by the FAA."

Ramzi felt his stomach knot. He put the gun back in his pants. "You have done well, so far." He looked at the plane's license. "Tom Menke … Min-ke … Mink?"

"Menke. One syllable. You said it right the first time." The man seemed more relaxed.

"Okay, Tom Menke. How far away from that storm do we need to be?"

Tom thought for a few moments. "At least fifty miles."

It appeared that the man was now comfortable with the assignment. While he set the throttle and adjusted the fuel mixture, Ramzi removed the tee-shaped device from his shirt pocket and gripped it in his left palm with a stem protruding between two fingers. With his right, he unscrewed a stainless cap.

The Cessna cruised along at 180 knots. The engine droned at a rhythmic growl.

Ramzi said, "I am sorry I pointed the gun. This is an extreme emergency. My son is a severe asthmatic. A Mexican woman takes care of him."

Tom remained silent.

"I was desperate to get to him."

The aircraft dropped elevation and the Grand Canyon was visible on the left. Ramzi watched the GPS for a minute. He made a quick move and slammed his fist onto Tom's leg. The needle sticking out from the tee handle stuck.

"Ow!" He yelled. "What did you do?"

"Sorry, Tom. I have to put you out for awhile."

The pilot jerked, convulsed, and after a couple of minutes, his head flopped over against the seat.

Ramzi replaced the needle safety cap and unscrewed it from the handle. He slipped another charge from his pocket and twisted it on, making sure the safety cap was secure. Finally, he put the assembly back into his pocket and gripped the co-pilot's yoke. Turning to heading 110 degrees, he guided the aircraft toward a gap between three peaks. He flew low, weaving his way through the range. It had been two years since his last pilot lessons.

Chapter 82

Nellis Air Force Base, Nevada

Krysta Mazur sat behind a desk in the Nellis Air Force Base Flight Control Center. She scanned a computer screen, flipping between two views transmitted by Air Force Global Hawks from 55,000 feet. Her adrenalin level was too high to get sleepy at 9:10 this morning, despite the fact she'd been awake all night.

Several hours ago, NSA's satellite lost track of the vehicle that Ramzi bin Omeri was suspected of using to flee Lake Mead. After daylight though, an air force sergeant operating one of the Global Hawks spotted the tow vehicle and boat leaving a service station and tracked it to the west side of Lake Mead. The video replay showed the driver leaving the vehicle parked at a boat landing, then departing on a motor scooter.

She called her boyfriend, Randy, the deputy at Clark County, Nevada, for assistance. She also alerted Sheriff Stroman.

While the two law officers did their detective work, Krysta ran the NSA and air force surveillance videos back and forth several times. Among all the traffic that had accumulated after the semi-truck accident under the bridge, she finally picked out two motorcycles leaving from the alley behind the service station. They left less than twenty minutes after the white truck pulled the boat and trailer under a canopy at the station.

She managed to track the motorcycles to a narrow dirt road winding around the south side of Nellis Air Force Base, then out into the wilderness.

The sheriff called and told her Randy had viewed videos at the lake guard house and retrieved a license number on the motor scooter. Stroman visited the rider and the young man told him that he merely delivered the vehicle and boat. He also said that no one he spoke to seemed foreign.

Krysta, receiving images from Lieutenant Byron Miller, one of the Air Force Global Hawk operators, said, "We've got wreckage seven miles from The Valley of Fire State Park."

The lieutenant dispatched a helicopter. It went to the crash site and personnel discovered a wrecked motorcycle and a body.

"They said he looked Middle Eastern."

"Middle Eastern?"

"Yeah, like right out of Afghanistan. Except he wore expensive motorcycle leathers. And, get this. He was shot in the head and dumped in a ditch with big rocks rolled on him."

"Jeez!" Krysta said. "His buddy must have done him in."

"They think he had a broken back. Anyway, I just uploaded the latest from the Global Hawk."

"Thanks, Lieutenant."

She downloaded and spotted the area of the wreck. After several minutes of running back and forth in time, she tracked the other motorcycle to a golf course and small airport north of Mesquite, Nevada. There, the Global Hawk's lenses tilted away from the rising sun. She was unable to pick out the motorcycle.

During all the intense excitement, she had held it. Now she couldn't stand it any longer. She had to use the bathroom.

When she returned to the desk with a cup of coffee, she ran the videos back and forth for quite a while, unsuccessfully. Finally, out of frustration, she called the airport. All she got was a recording.

After several more minutes, she called the Nevada Highway Patrol. When they realized she was investigating the terrorist acts, they transferred her to the Mesquite office.

"This is Krysta Mazur with the Department of Homeland Security. We've been tracking suspected terrorists, and one ended up at your airport three hours ago. He's wanted for Murder One. Have you had any departing flights this morning? Anything suspicious?"

"Glad to help. Burt Reynolds here. Not the actor." He laughed. The voice was raspy, like a heavy smoker. "Murder One. Wow! We had one odd call about a flight this morning. This is interesting because Tom Menke filed a flight plan yesterday to go to Salt Lake for a golf tournament. His partner, I guess that's what they call each other now, Samuel, called and said he was suspicious. Everyone in town knows them. The pilot didn't call Samuel before he took off this morning. He said that's not like Tom. He *never* forgets to call."

Krysta pondered this information for a minute. "Tom Menke is the pilot's name?"

"Here, Ms. Mazur." A raspy cough. "Damn! These things are killing me. Gotta quit." He cleared his throat. "Why don't you call Samuel? That's probably the best I can do for you." He gave Krysta the number.

When she called Samuel, he answered immediately. When he heard she was calling about the flight, he became agitated. "I know something's wrong. He should be half-way to Salt Lake by now. He was going to take off at seven. Tom *always* calls me." Samuel's voice sounded near panic.

"Do you have any information on the aircraft? How fast and how far can it go without refueling?"

"Just a moment." The phone went quiet. More than a minute went by. Krysta heard him pick up the phone. "It's a Cessna. It can go 800 miles on a full load of fuel. And, Tom's meticulous about that plane." He read off the aircraft's ID and call sign, and told her it could travel 180 knots.

She jotted down the information and thanked Samuel.

Next, Krysta called the Salt Lake flight control. They had the flight control plan filed on computer, but the aircraft didn't show up and they hadn't spotted it on radar. "We can track them 120 miles out."

Krysta thanked them, called Sergeant Miller again and asked for the Global Hawk videos of Mesquite after 0600 hours this morning. While she downloaded, she apprized Sheriff Stroman of the latest events. Then she raided the refrigerator and heated a "Healthy Heart Microwave Breakfast."

Smiling when she took it out, she thought, *an oxymoron.*

She pushed her hair behind her ear. While she ate, she zeroed in on the Mesquite airport and replayed the computer starting at 6:30.

At first she had the same problem as before, sunlight in the lenses. Then she saw it. She had to replay the video several times. Two people got into an aircraft and the plane took off. It headed southwest over the Virgin Mountains. Then the video cut off.

She frowned and switched to the other Global Hawk that covered Lake Mead and south to Interstate 40. A huge storm cloud moved in, with lightning flashes at the leading edge.

Darn it!

Moving back to the Mesquite video, she reran it. No other aircraft departed for the next two hours.

Krysta called Sergeant Miller again. They had nothing more from the Global Hawk in a southerly direction.

Thanking him, she was about to hang up when Sergeant Miller said, "You know, I used to work at Luke Air Force Base near Phoenix. They know everything about that part of Arizona."

Miller gave her the number of the base's Control Tower. When Krysta spoke to a Sergeant Coleman at Luke AFB, the woman told Krysta that because of the Red alert, there had been no small aircraft out this morning. "And there were definitely no hijack alarms?"

"Hijack alarms?"

Sergeant Coleman explained how they worked.

"What if they flew near ground level?"

"Only a crop duster could get below our radar."

She thanked Sergeant Coleman and called Kurt.

She talked fast when he answered. "The Air Force Global Hawks tracked our terrorist to a city airport in Mesquite, Nevada. He probably hijacked a small aircraft there. They tracked the plane to the Grand Canyon and lost it.

Then they put me onto Luke Air force Base just west of Phoenix. No small aircraft have passed through Luke's airspace because of the Red Alert. And there were no hijack alarms."

"How does a pilot activate a hijack alarm?"

"If a pilot had a problem, there's a frequency and a button on the control panel. He would have sent an alarm code."

Kurt asked, "Could they fly just above ground level, and between mountains?"

"Sergeant Coleman told me it's possible a crop duster could get under their radar. And that kind of aircraft wouldn't have a transponder, either."

"So, all we have is he headed south from Mesquite?"

"I'm afraid so. I'll see if NSA has anything."

"Okay. What kind of aircraft?"

"A Cessna four-passenger with a cruising speed of 180 knots per hour. They left Mesquite at 0713 hours."

"Okay, thanks Krysta."

Chapter 83

Nellis Air Force Base, Las Vegas, Nevada

Kurt Valdez motioned the pilot to get the jet ready while he dialed Langley with his satellite phone. Don Berkley picked up immediately.

"Good news, Tiburon? I hope."

"Well, sorta, Top. DHS' Mazur and the air force might have located our terrorist. If she's correct, he should be flying south headed straight for the Mexican border, probably less than two hours away."

"Less than two hours! We don't have enough time!"

"He's in a white Cessna that has a max speed of 200 miles per hour. He can only cross into Mexico 100 miles or less east of Yuma, or down the New Mexico state line near Douglas, Arizona. Use all your connections, Don. NSA, air force. Mexican police."

"Damn short notice!"

"Remember, we need him alive. And he has DZ-41 capsules. Most surely, explosives, too. Whatever they do, don't spook him with fighter jets. If he's headed for the border, I'll get him."

Chapter 84

Central Arizona

After he passed between the mountains, Ramzi turned due east. The Cessna droned on. His head drooped and he shut his eyes. He immediately recovered and dug out some *qat*, inserted a plug into his mouth.

Manipulating his tongue around the mass, he chewed it until there was a large wad in his cheek. He flew close to the ground along the north rim of the Grand Canyon, testing his memory of the lessons from the flight simulator. The aircraft came out over the Kaibab Plateau and the Colorado River took a turn to the south. Ramzi veered northeast to skirt a peak.

The next 60 kilometers were tricky. Three airport radars scanned this area. He wrote down the GPS coordinates for course corrections. Those headings allowed him to weave between peaks and canyons without being detected. He set the radio on 123.6, the universal control tower frequency.

Ten minutes later, after transiting the peaks, he crossed the Colorado River and Highway 89. He flipped through the UNICOM and three other frequencies. He heard static and what sounded like the distant voices of pilots. He smiled in satisfaction.

A huge desert spread out before the aircraft. Tan, red, and blue-gray cliffs and ravines marked the Navajo and Hopi reservations. Inhabited areas had green patches and crop circles. Barren drainage deltas spread wide, revealing vast scars from previous flash floods.

He glanced at the GPS. The next marker was coming up in less than five minutes, Steamboat Canyon. The marker was twenty-five miles from Fort Defiance, another airport with a control tower, and potential trouble. He dialed the airport frequency and dropped elevation.

Flying 1,000 feet off the ground through a ravine, Ramzi turned right to a heading due south. He barely could see a highway far out to the left. He stared at it for several moments and thought he spotted two big trucks.

"Fort Defiance control tower. Small aircraft west of Highway 89."

Ramzi locked his jaw and turned up the volume.

He switched to the UNICOM frequency and listened. After several minutes, the radio blared, "Fort Defiance control tower. Small aircraft west of Highway 89."

Resisting the urge to increase speed, Ramzi gradually gained elevation. He would cross U.S. Interstate 40 in less than three minutes. He hoped that the control tower could not contact the military or highway patrol before he had a chance to get out of the state.

After ignoring two more requests, Ramzi heard another conversation.

"Control tower. Piper 23531."

"Piper 23531."

"What is your elevation?"

"I'm at 4,850 feet."

"Do you have a visual on a small aircraft at 2,000 feet at your eleven o'clock?"

Several seconds passed. Ramzi stared up at five o'clock. It took him a few moments to spot the other aircraft. Red against the brilliant sky. It would pass over him in less than a minute.

He held his breath. The radio was silent. The engine droned on.

"Piper 531. Affirmative. It will pass under me in shortly."

"Control tower. Thank you, Piper 531."

"Piper 531."

Ramzi swallowed hard and closed his eyes. Within minutes, the Cessna crossed Interstate 40. He changed course again, heading due southeast to New Mexico. The aircraft would be out of Arizona in ten minutes. Switching the radio between several frequencies, he remained up to the minute with the situation.

He dropped elevation into a barren ravine, crossed into New Mexico, and came around a mountain. Five minutes into the state, he turned due south. He flew low through a valley and entered an Apache reservation marked on the chart. A high range of mountains lay before him, with a couple of 11,000 peaks.

Veering southwest, Ramzi crossed back into Arizona, where he again changed direction to due south. He flew over the state lines for a few minutes, made a jog west for five miles, then turned south again so he could cross Interstate 10 between Bowie and San Simon, Arizona. Cochise Head Peak in the Chiricahua Indian Reservation was visible in the distance. The international airport near Douglas, Arizona was on the far side of the peak.

Twenty minutes.

Chapter 85

Nellis Air Force Base, Las Vegas, Nevada

Kurt hurried to the Lear jet. While he buckled in and the door locked shut behind him, Colonel Black flipped switches and the engine whined. She taxied out onto the runway. Pointing to a notebook, she said, "Those are the most current flight charts. Fold them out to Arizona. And don't talk while I take off." After she received flight clearance, the officer applied power and released the brake. Shortly, they were airborne.

"Nice aircraft, Colonel." Kurt said.

"Call me Karen. It's the base general's Lear. Cruises at 620 knots, Kurt."

He ran his finger along the designated flight path. The aircraft leveled and the pilot eased off to cruising altitude and speed. After studying the chart for several minutes, he asked, "Why is Luke Air Base marked differently?"

"It's a main military air base. There are three special ones in the U.S.: Kamchatka, Alaska; El Toro Marine Base in Orange County, California; and Luke. They have powerful radar equipment and special computer tracking systems."

"So it's safe to say our terrorist couldn't get through there without raising alarms?"

"We would know it by now."

Colonel Black held a hand up to answer a query from the Luke control tower and gave them the information they requested. She asked the flight controller, "Any suspicious flight activity this morning?"

"None. With the Red Alert, nothing whatsoever." came the response. "You have clear skies all the way to Fort Huachuca."

The commander acknowledged and signed off. She looked at Kurt. "There's your answer."

He nodded. "So assuming the terrorist read a chart similar to this, he would go wide of this area." After thinking about it some more, Kurt said, "He wouldn't go near *any* airport with a flight control tower."

"That's probably a good observation."

"How can I tell which airports have flight control towers?"

She pointed to the symbol at the Yuma airport. "Like that."

Kurt glanced out of the window. "Is that *Phoenix* below?"

"Yes it is."

"Wow! Already. How long before landing?"

"Less than twenty minutes."

"Good." He traced a finger on the chart from Mesquite toward the Grand Canyon. He noted the only path to get to Mexico around Luke AFB and Phoenix, was east, on the north side of the canyon, between peaks. There were flight control towers at the Grand Canyon lodge area and Page Arizona. Kurt traced a line between them through the Hopi and Navajo reservations. He spotted a radar symbol at Fort Defiance, near the New Mexico state line.

"Can you contact the airport at Fort Defiance, Karen, on 119.45 megahertz?"

"If anyone's there during a Red Alert." She switched to the listed frequencies, trying first the control tower, then the UNICOM frequency.

The radio replied, "Fort Defiance Flight Control."

After identifying herself, Colonel Black asked the man if they'd had any contact with small aircraft this morning.

"Affirmative, colonel. A small aircraft passed under a Piper Cub this morning. It was keeping radio silence and flying low, at about 1,000 feet. Get this. It was traveling at 180 knots with its transponder turned off."

Kurt felt his heart speed up. "That's our man."

The pilot asked, "Did you get a heading?"

"It disappeared out of radar range on a 135 degree course at 0831 hours when it crossed Interstate 40. I grounded the Piper Cub for the Red Alert."

She signed off. Then, contacting the control tower at Fort Huachuca, the colonel received approach and landing instructions for the army base airport.

Kurt traced a flight path between three small airports and Fort Defiance, crossing into New Mexico, then heading south through the Apache reservations.

"He chose a good course. The only radar that might be active today is in Lordsburg. He could have flown through the high mountains of the Apache reservations, down the state line then back into Arizona."

The pilot said, "There is a lot of illegal alien traffic through that area."

Kurt said, "Fort Huachuca and the international airport near Douglas wouldn't pick him up if he stayed east of Cochise Head peak. It's only forty miles through the mountains to Mexico."

Colonel Black held a hand up and took landing instructions from Fort Huachuca. She banked the aircraft to head south westerly. The landing gear popped and made a rushing sound. The jet engine slowed to a whine.

Kurt glanced at his watch. It was 1025 hours. It had taken less than an hour to make the flight from Las Vegas.

The colonel made a smooth landing with the Lear jet. They taxied toward the berth. Kurt scanned for his contact.

"I thank you very much Karen. You're a great pilot."

"My pleasure, Kurt. Get that son-of-a-bitch." She smiled.

Chapter 86

Southeast Arizona

Ramzi bin Omeri dropped elevation and glided through ravines and around mountains, staying below radar detection.

He took the explosive circuit board and transmitter out of the backpack. Making sure the transmitter was off, he activated the receiver, and slid it on the floor under his seat.

He reached into his pocket and pulled out the needle assembly again. Unscrewing the second medical charge, he fastened it on the assembly. He slammed his hand onto Tom Menke's leg. Then he turned his attention to flying again.

Seven minutes to Mexico.

Less than three minutes later, Tom moved his head around and popped his neck. It took him a while to come awake. "Whoa, what happened to me?"

Ramzi crossed the International Border. A highway appeared before the aircraft. He banked right to pass over the ridge of a north-south mountain range.

"You were asleep. I flew the Cessna. We are in Mexico."

"What?"

"That is correct. You are going to land this aircraft on that highway ahead of us, behind those two large trucks."

"You drugged me!"

"That is correct, also. Now, you will land this plane and get your $10,000." Ramzi slid out the other packet of money and flapped it in front of Tom's face.

The man glared at him.

Ramzi shoved the Beretta against Tom's groin.

The man flinched.

"Now," said Ramzi.

The Mexican highway lay before them. The two trucks cruised down from the mountains, arriving at a gentler slope.

Tom appeared ready to cry. After adjusting the throttle and fuel mixture, he grasped the yoke and lined up the Cessna on the highway. He eased off on speed and dropped elevation. The wheels folded down with a rush. In less than two minutes, they bumped down on asphalt.

"That was a good landing, Tom." Ramzi handed the $10,000 to the man. "I am going to take your bicycle."

He opened the door, got out with his pack and slid the bike out of the back seat. Gesturing northeast, he said, "Head back on 45 degrees. Animas, New Mexico is 70 miles from here."

He turned his gun around and, with the handle, broke the controls on the radio and the button on the hijack alarm. Then he slammed the door.

Tom Menke, open-mouthed, didn't wait. He immediately revved the engine, turned and was quickly airborne.

Ramzi watched the Cessna bank and head back toward the U.S. He pulled out the transmitter and activated it. Glancing at the Aqualand computer, he waited. The Cessna leveled off at a low elevation. Ramzi pressed the button and the aircraft exploded.

He smiled and made his brief phone call. He said, *"treinta-cinco,"* to give his contact his pick-up location and went off-line. Then, verifying that the DZ-41 capsule was still in his khaki shirt pocket, he took a map out of the backpack. He donned a Levi jacket and the back pack, and readied the bicycle. A long, gradual slope lay before him and *Agua-Prieta*, Mexico.

Ramzi took off on the bicycle. Several times he looked back when big semi-trucks and vehicles approached. Finally, a dark-green Chevrolet pickup came upon him from behind. At the right moment, he feigned a fall, tumbling onto the road.

The pickup swerved and passed him. The driver pulled over and backed.

Holding his knee, Ramzi made a face as if in severe pain.

The driver rushed to him. *"Esta bien, Señor?"* The man wore a straw hat with the edges rolled up and gray khakis.

Ramzi kept wincing and holding his knee. He grunted as a deaf-mute would and motioned to his ears, shaking his head. He pulled out the Mexican map with marked circles in the city and showed it to the man.

The Mexican looked at it and traced his finger along the streets. Nodding his head, he helped Ramzi up. While the man hoisted the bicycle into the bed, Ramzi limped to the truck. Two pigs in crates chomped corn in the back.

Several times on the road toward *Agua-Prieta*, the man, obviously a farmer, glanced at Ramzi's backpack. His eyes grew wide when he noticed the edge of the Aqualand dive computer under Ramzi's sleeve. He must have wondered about its diamond bezel.

It took them only twenty minutes to reach the streets where the circles were marked on the map.

Ramzi got out and retrieved the bicycle. He handed the farmer a 500-peso bill.

The farmer tried to refuse it, but Ramzi kept grunting and frowning and pushing it toward him. He indicated with gestures that he insisted the farmer keep the money.

As the green Chevrolet took off, Ramzi spotted the cantina, *El Lobo*, that advertized *Dos-Equis* and *comida*. That would be a good place to hide until dark. His handler should arrive by eight.

Chapter 87

Fort Huachuca, Arizona

Kurt Valdez paused for a moment to gather his thoughts. The Lear jet had made the entire flight, including takeoff and landing, in less than sixty minutes.

If they analyzed correctly, Ramzi bin Omeri was thirty-five minutes away. The man he had been trying to catch for five years was now within his grasp.

At this same moment, at the Nevada Test site, scientists and military weapons experts dismantled the nuclear bomb that they suspected Ramzi smuggled into the United States.

A voice shouted as he climbed out of the Lear jet, "Kurt Valdez!"

Kurt beamed when he greeted Timothy Barfield. "Hey, Tim! How goes the war?"

The African-American grinned wide. "Thanks for asking for me, *compadre*." He handed Kurt a cup of coffee. "Black, if I remember correctly?" The young man wore faded Levis and a tee-shirt with hiking boots. He had a worn backpack hanging from one shoulder. However, his build and haircut still marked him as military.

"You read my mind. Black is fine. We've had a busy 24 hours."

"Shawn is warming the chopper. About five minutes."

"Oh, no. Have to put up with him, again?"

Barfield laughed. "Afraid so. We got the equipment you asked for. It took some scrounging around. But we got it all."

Kurt blew across the cup and took a sip.

"Here are the weapons you asked for, Kurt."

Kurt turned and grasped Hector Navarro. "Hey, you crazy Apache."

The young Indian grinned ear to ear and handed Kurt two Tasers.

Kurt took one. He tipped the cup and took another drink of coffee.

Navarro looked past Barfield and held a thumb up. "The chopper's ready."

An electric vehicle pulled up. Navarro pointed to a duffel bag. "The other gear you requested."

It took only 18 minutes for the helicopter to transport Kurt, Barfield, and Navarro to the small airport in Douglas, Arizona, close to the international border. During the flight, Kurt went over the plan.

Shawn set the chopper down and they unloaded. The helicopter idled, its blades rotating slowly.

Douglas Commercial Airport, Arizona

Kurt Valdez' satellite phone buzzed and he saw Berkley's number. He clicked it on. "What's up, Top?"

"Hey Kurt. NSA tracked the Cessna to Mexico. It landed eight miles east of *Agua-Prieta* on Mexican Two."

"I'm twelve miles from there right now." Kurt smiled at Berkley's pronunciation of the Mexican city in his Baltimore accent.

"The Snow Leopard blew the small plane after it took off and almost reached the border."

Kurt clenched his fist. *Killed the pilot.*

Berkley said, "We think Ramzi rode a bicycle a ways then caught a ride to town. Ned Taggert is on radar at our office in Douglas. He tracked the suspected pickup to an area with hotels near a military hospital."

"A military hospital? Interesting." Kurt rubbed his jaw. "So I'll take Navarro to Mexico with me, without Barfield?"

"Yeah. That's why I sent Hector with his Mexican passport. He's as good as you are, Kurt. Remember, he got his ticket punched in Colombia in the drug wars."

"Yeah, I remember."

"Be very careful, Tiburon. Ramzi will kill you or Navarro like squashing a fly."

"An Apache and I are going downtown *Agua-Prieta* to smoke the Snow Leopard out of a hotel or bar?"

"Krysta Mazur had a contact with NSA. Fort Meade picked up a strange sat-call from near *Agua-Prieta*. In bad Spanish, all it said was, *treinta-cinco*. After washing it through the computer, we got a 95-percent confirmation it was Ramzi's voice."

"*Treinta-cinco*? A pickup location code?"

"Exactly. Navarro has a contact with the Mexican *federales*. Three of them are scouring the area looking for someone who looks different, with instructions to wait for you both."

"They know he has explosives and the DZ-41 capsule?"

"Do I always cover your ass, Tiburon? Yes… *federales* are leaving him alone. He's all yours. Get tracking."

Kurt grunted and clicked the phone off. *Killed the pilot.*

Barfield and Navarro pulled supplies out of a military duffle bag. They loaded the materials behind the seat of an aging Chevrolet El Camino along with several other items Kurt had requested. Then he hurried to the office to talk to the radar technician.

Scanning quickly, Kurt saw that the control room was ultra modern. He thought it resembled computer arrays in a big office. Large flat-screen displays showed views of different locations along the Mexican border and in the city of Agua-Prieta.

The only operator this afternoon was Ned Taggert, who weighed at least 300 pounds. He seemed nervous and darted around from one computer to another on an office chair.

Kurt introduced himself to the man and commented, "Wow! I'm surprised. Looks like a power plant or factory."

"Except for the panoramic views of the screens. We get them from hot-air balloons. Nothing happens around here that we can't watch." Taggert moved a joystick and a flat-screen display zoomed in on a downtown scene. "Your terrorist is in this area near the hospital. We were four minutes late or we would have videos. He'd already mingled with the crowd."

Kurt raised his eyebrows in surprise. "Where is that in the city? In the middle?"

"I'll show you. You want a coffee?" Taggert shoved his chair and rolled over to a counter, walking in a sitting position.

"I'm in a hurry." Kurt continued to scrutinize the downtown screen.

"Calm down. You hungry?" Taggert walked the chair to a small refrigerator, took out two burritos and popped them into a microwave.

Kurt shook his head. A box of pastries sat on the counter.

Back in front of a computer, Taggert said, "Watch this." A scene of the city zoomed back out and the horizon tilted. The operator moved in slowly so Kurt could take in all the area as if in a small aircraft. Using a light pointer, he said, "See the hotels and cantinas? We suspect that's where he was dropped off. The *federales* are looking for him in these three blocks." Taggert ran the pointer over the area.

"Busy place," Kurt said, shaking his head. "And he probably has explosives wrapped around his body."

Taggert took a big bite of burrito, spilled some on his shirt and swore. He wiped off the spot.

Barfield and Navarro came into the office.

Tim Barfield looked at the screens in amazement. "Jesus! Why do we grovel around in the bushes? We can see 'em squat to shit."

Kurt gestured to the downtown streets for Navarro. "This is where the hotels and cantinas are. They think he mingled with the crowds there."

Taggert continued to pan the street scene. "Right there," he guided the pointer. He pressed some keys and a printer began scrolling out a picture. "I'll give you a couple of overhead views, also."

He manipulated a second screen to a straight down shot of the same streets.

Navarro's phone rang. He unfolded it and answered. He repeated for Kurt.

"A guy in a khaki shirt and denim jacket and pants? Yeah, with a backpack? Could be our man. *Tenga cuidado, hombres. El tiene un explosivo. Lo necesitamos vivo.*"

When Navarro closed the phone, Kurt nodded. "Definitely. We need him alive."

"We're ready, Kurt." Navarro exchanged the El Camino keys for the jeep with Barfield.

The three men slipped earphones and lip-mikes over their heads and pinned the amplifiers inside their shirts. They tested them, Kurt and Navarro headed out to the Chevrolet.

Kurt Valdez' satellite phone rang again. He saw Berkley's number.

"Something else, Top?"

"I just got a call from the Test Site."

Kurt inhaled when his boss paused. "And?"

"They turned the sub upside-down, opened it, and found a nuclear bomb."

"Just as we thought. I presume they were in a deep, concrete-and-steel-encased cave?"

"Three-thousand feet down where they used to test bombs. Three techs volunteered. The others rode the elevator to the surface. Could've been booby trapped"

"Don't keep me in suspense."

"After they got it out of the vessel, they removed the top cover. Sounded like your experience disabling the Saudi bomb."

"They had photos of the Russian ordnance to work with?" Kurt asked.

"Of course. We figure Pakistanis copied the Russian bomb. Techs recognized the detonator circuit. They cut the high-voltage leads and took the capacitor out."

Kurt blew out a large breath. "How much yield is this bomb?"

"Are you ready for this?" Berkley cleared his throat. "They estimate 200 kilotons. If that sub had gone 300 feet farther and exploded, it would have taken out Hoover Dam. A couple a hundred thousand people would have died."

"God damn!" Kurt gritted his teeth. "We've got to squash those fuckers once and for all. I'm going to take out the Snow Leopard tonight."

"Be careful, Tiburon. He'll have explosives. And will most likely be in a crowd."

"I've been thinking about this for years, Top. He's not getting away this time." Kurt signed off.

Two hundred kilotons.

He looked at Navarro when he got in the El Camino. "We're going to get this asshole tonight, Hector, *amigo.*"

Chapter 88

Agua-Prieta, Mexico

Ramzi bin Omeri scrutinized the small city as they came to the commercial area, the people, the buildings, and the farmers markets. He took in everything. It reminded him of the dry, dusty towns of Iran and Afghanistan.

The farmer pulled the pickup into a marketplace stall. Ramzi paid him and gave the bicycle away. He immediately mingled with the crowd and scanned for *la policía* and the *federales*. Within the four blocks to the most congested area, he spotted two of them.

He had begun planning his evasive maneuvers after the flight control tower's radar at Fort Defiance, Arizona, detected the Cessna. He was sure the CIA and American authorities followed his flight and knew he was here. They probably watched the Cessna explode.

Ramzi picked out the third *federale* as the man talked on his phone. He sneered. *Amateurs.*

After spending several minutes memorizing the area, he counted the number of steps between several prominent places and three cantinas that he might have to duck into. He passed beyond them and dodged into a crowd. Meandering through it allowed him to retrace his steps.

The third *federale* frowned and stretched his neck, frantically searching the area. The officer glanced in Ramzi's direction once, which prompted him to kneel and tie his shoe. When he stood up, he saw the *federale* looking away. He worked his way along the sidewalk to a cantina, *El Lobo,* and slipped into the establishment.

Compared to the drab outside, the interior of the bar surprised him. Walls painted in bright red and yellow colors displayed menus. Paintings depicted Mexican beers, different chiles—poblano, serrano, ortega, and jalapeño—and murals of Mexican revolutionary scenes. A chest-high, knotty-pine bar stretched two-thirds the length of the back wall. It was covered with a small roof of palm fronds. Well-distributed lights and spots on a music stage created a nice ambience. Hallways on both sides of the bar led to the kitchen and the bathrooms.

A waiter gestured for him to pick a table, so Ramzi took a seat where he had a full view. There were only nine customers, two of them women. He scrutinized the faces. Satisfied they were locals, he checked the menu on the wall nearest him. He waved to the waiter and ordered a *chile relleno* with a *Tecate* beer.

Three musicians entered wearing black ensembles, large round Mexican hats, and polished high-heeled boots. They opened cases and took out a trumpet and two guitars.

Ramzi grabbed his small pack, went to the bathroom and locked the door. Removing his shirt and jacket, he pulled explosives from the pack, formed them around his midsection and duct-taped them firmly in place. He arranged a detonating switch that would slip out from beneath his shirt.

He put the shirt and jacket back on and adjusted the sheaths for the Beretta and knife, taking care with it because the weapon was the latest with an exploding point. The initiating switch for the explosive had to be switched on and squeezed firmly. Satisfied with the apparatus, he opened the envelope in his jacket pocket and fingered the DZ-41 capsules.

The bathroom was sparse with merely a wash basin and toilet, both in need of cleaning. He opened the window on the back wall to take a look. A wire fence stretched around the bare dirt yard with several overflowing trash containers in a far corner. A dirt alleyway ran beyond the fence, with houses on the other side. Nobody was in sight and he made sure there were no dogs. He turned backward and leaned his torso out. Reaching to the top window ledge, he decided that, in a hurry, he could pull himself out through the narrow bottom half of the window without disturbing the explosives.

He took one more look around and judged it was two hours before dark.

The door lock rattled. Ramzi quickly drew his head back in and spoke loudly, *"Esperé, hombre"*—wait. He flushed the toilet, turned on the faucet and closed the window.

Grabbing the straps on the pack, he opened the door.

"Gracias, señor," said the man, as he passed Ramzi.

"De nada." Ramzi heard the sound of a trumpet and guitars. He walked slowly through the short hall and scanned the cantina again before entering it.

The waiter had brought his food and now warned him about the hot plate.

"La quenta, por favor." Ramzi asked for the check right away.

When the man brought it, he paid.

He ate slowly, keeping an eye on street activities through slits in the window blinds. If a *federale* came in and headed in his direction, he would pull the Beretta and dispatch him. Simple as that. If American paramilitaries came through the door, as a last resort, he would set the explosives off.

One more couple arrived and sat at a table near a front window. Two more band members entered and added an accordion and a trombone to the Mariachi ensemble.

On the sidewalk, people walked by in both directions. One Mexican ducked into the bar and reminded a cook about a fiesta the following night. He made a lurid comment to one of the two women, and she giggled and told him to shut up.

Ramzi finished the *relleno* and beer while the band struck up *Adelita*, a Mexican favorite. Two guitarists sang along with the music. Several more customers came through the door. The light outside was beginning to darken. There was no sign of the law.

He considered this for a moment. He was sure the CIA warned off the Mexicans after they spotted him. His battle would be with the Americans.

Ramzi glanced at the Aqualand.

Ride will be here in one hour.

Chapter 89

Agua-Prieta, Mexico

Hector Navarro parked the Chevrolet in a slot.

Kurt Valdez checked the charge on the Taser. "You ready, amigo?"

"*Vámenos*." They retrieved the remainder of their gear.

After the two men got out of the car, Kurt looked over his comrade.

"Stop," said Kurt, holding his hand up. "Your boots look new. Go scuff them up."

"Fuck, man. I'm all psyched up."

"I know. He'll be scrutinizing everything, Hector. You're too cleanly shaven around your beard and mustache. Are you wearing cologne or deodorant?"

Navarro appeared shocked. "Both. I'll spill some beer on me."

"He still might suspect you. He probably won't get too close, in case you have a Taser, or are a martial-arts expert. But, he might try to get close enough for a whiff. I would."

"Why would he take a chance? With a gun and explosives."

"Just be aware. Oh, remove your wire and mike, too."

Navarro flashed a disgusted look and removed them. His phone buzzed.

The *federales* he talked to earlier apparently spotted their car when it pulled in. When Navarro signaled to the officer, the man gestured toward a crowd. "Over there, Kurt." Navarro pointed. "The target headed in that direction."

They split up. Kurt made a half-circle toward the sidewalk on the opposite side of the street. A tall building, the Mexican military hospital that showed on their maps, lay several blocks to the east.

Navarro headed away to the left. Kurt saw him mingle with the Mexicans on the sidewalk. The man wore tight Levis, work boots and a zip-up sweatshirt with a hood. Kurt also wore Levis with a light jacket to hide his weapons. Neither of them wore a Kevlar vest because they were so difficult to conceal.

The small border city reminded Kurt of Tecate, Mexico, where his family was, except it must have been three times as large. Most of the buildings were old. Raised cracks in the sidewalks made it easy to trip. Power and telephone lines sagged between wood poles. The blacktop in the streets had potholes and grooves.

Kurt hurried through the busy street scene. It was Saturday, market day. Taco vendors pushed small carts. Boys hawked chewing gum. People ducked in and out of the stores. Men sold *serapes* at stop signs.

While he proceeded quickly and cautiously, Kurt searched the crowd and found Navarro. The man talked on his phone again while scanning the sidewalks. He apparently spotted the *federale* and raised a finger. Navarro pointed across to Kurt's side of the street to the cantinas.

Kurt nodded. He coughed from dust and smoke as a loud truck passed by, exhausting a black cloud. A young man on a motor scooter sped past the truck while stray dogs scampered out of the way.

Kurt saw the three cantinas that were in the photos Ned Taggert printed for them—*La Bodega, El Demonio Colorado* and *El Lobo*.

He motioned a kid selling chewing gum toward him. The boy grinned at the mention of the money and scrutinized the drawing of Ramzi.

"Just offer everyone gum and go on, Kurt said. "This man is dangerous, so offer him gum and pass on quickly. You're playing spy. Be very secretive *como* James Bond."

The kid beamed, hustled along the sidewalk and entered *La Bodega*. Kurt and Navarro moved slowly forward scrutinizing everyone. After two or three minutes, the kid came out, looked at Kurt and shook his head. He gestured to the second bar.

The kid disappeared into *El Dimonio Colorado*. Several minutes later he came out and shook his head again. He then turned toward *El Lobo*.

Navarro hurried across the street to meet Kurt near the edge of the cantina. Mariachi music came from inside.

Several minutes passed while they waited anxiously for the boy to come out. Finally, he exited and looked around. Navarro motioned him over and then nodded to Kurt.

Navarro signaled that he's at a back table in the right corner and that there was a bar along the back wall."

In the car, they had talked about the fact that Ramzi knew Kurt.

However, he didn't know Navarro. The man volunteered.

Kurt told him, "Go to the bar and order. Speak your best and fastest street Spanish, *hombre*. He'll shoot you in the blink of an eye. And he probably has enough hi-tech explosive to take out three buildings."

"If I have to think of all that, I won't be able to act natural."

"Okay. I'll shut up."

Navarro paid and sent the kid off, looked at Kurt and nodded. He clenched his fists three times, breathed in and headed toward the entrance.

He stepped through the door of *El Lobo* immediately following another man.

Chapter 90

Agua-Prieta, Mexico

Ramzi bin Omeri spotted the boy entering the bar selling chewing gum. His tray was held by a strap over one shoulder. The kid made a once around, bearing harsh insults from some of the patrons. He headed in Ramzi's direction.

Glowering at the boy, Ramzi shook his head.

The boy cast his eyes downward and skulked out of the bar.

A few minutes later, Ramzi saw two men enter the club. The first man, a small, thin Mexican, ambled over to the women and began talking to one of them. The second man walked to the bar and ordered a *Corona* beer in rapid Spanish.

While he was served, Ramzi scrutinized him. He wore an oversized forest-green sweatshirt and Levis. His boots were fairly new. There was something about him that caught Ramzi's attention, but he couldn't put his finger on it.

Even under the sweatshirt, the man appeared solid. His thighs and buttocks looked thick. He either worked hard, was some kind of athlete or had military connections. *That was it.* He didn't slouch like a construction worker or farmer.

Soldier. He labeled the man to keep himself on high alert.

Soldier took a long drink of the beer. The bottled foamed over and spilled onto his sweatshirt. He quickly rubbed it off, then turned around to face the band. He stood straight, between bar stools and didn't put his boot on the chrome foot-rail.

Ramzi saw through the blinds that daylight was beginning to fade. He searched and found the trigger of the bomb. Then he grasped the Beretta with his right hand under his jacket. He rose from his table and strode to the bar. "*Dos Equis*," he ordered.

The bartender popped the cap off the beer and slid it to him. He dropped twenty-peso and ten-peso notes on the counter.

Soldier stood so he could see Ramzi move and conversed in rapid Spanish to the man next to him. With Ramzi's limited understanding of the language and the noise of the music, he had difficulty following the conversation. He inhaled deeply. From a meter away, he was sure the faint odor under the beer was of *English Leather*.

Several minutes passed. The band finished the number and took a break. Soldier tipped back the beer and finished off the bottle. He turned around toward the bar in Ramzi's direction and set the bottle on the counter. Ramzi shot a quick look at his hands.

Too soft for a physical worker.

Soldier asked the bartender, *"Donde esta el baño, señor?"*

The bartender pointed toward the hall to the bathrooms.

Soldier stepped out two steps around another man as he passed so as not to not face Ramzi directly. Definitely an unusual move.

While the man was away, Ramzi moved back to his table in the corner. His satellite phone vibrated. He glanced at the readout, and a faint smile spread on his face.

This changes the balance of the whole battle.

After several minutes, soldier returned to the bar.

Scrutinizing him carefully for weapons, Ramzi noted that he took a quick scan around when he returned. He was certain soldier watched him out of the corner of his eye. There was no bulge in his sweatshirt, nothing visible in his hands.

A man on the far side of the bar tripped and knocked over a metal bar stool. It slammed to the floor with a loud crash. Soldier spun and reached, as if for a gun.

Ramzi clenched his jaw. Flaring his nostrils, he slipped out his knife.

The Mariachi band played loud. A man and woman rose to dance. The woman in the far corner leaned forward, exposing ample breasts. Soldier leaned back with his elbows on the bar. He seemed to be inhaling deeply. His eyes darted. Ramzi was sure the man could see him.

Ramzi narrowed his eyes. Soldier knotted his jaw. His Adam's apple bobbed up and down as he swallowed.

He turned slowly in Ramzi's direction, keeping his hands visible. Dropping money on the bar, he took two steps toward the front door.

Under the table Ramzi held the Beretta with his left, the blade of the knife with his throwing hand. He rose, twisted his torso to gain leverage and hurled the knife. Soldier jerked in a fast reaction. The knife sank into his kidney. It exploded and blew a section out of his body. Soldier pitched forward on his face. People screamed. The band stopped playing. Glasses crashed off the bar.

"Silencia!" Ramzi jumped up and yelled. *"Al piso!"* He waved the gun. People got on the floor. The bartender held his hands up.

To the band, he shouted *"Musica!"* One after another, they played again.

A Mexican yelled and ran out of the door.

Grabbing his backpack, Ramzi headed for the bathroom. He shoved the window open and dropped the pack out. He turned backward, slithered out and dropped to the ground. He grabbed the pack and ran for the trash cans. Bounding up over a short can, he put a hand on the fence and leaped over.

He looked in both directions, turned left and ran hard. Passing three houses, he saw an opening between the next two, going away from the bar. He took it. Before he came out to the street, a large brown pit bull with a white face rushed him. It lunged for Ramzi's throat. He saw the wide mouth coming, the bared teeth.

At the last instant, Ramzi swung the gun up to the dog's chest and blasted it. The animal made a raspy noise and fell to the ground with a thud.

Ramzi backtracked to the rear door of the house. He rushed it and crashed through to a short hallway. A woman and small boy screamed.

He held the gun on them and shouted, "*Quienta!*" They moved to the front room. An old man and two pre-teen girls cowered.

Still waving the gun, he commanded, "*Sientanse!*" He stared at them until they were all sitting and told them he wouldn't harm them if they remained quiet. The girls wept.

In a few minutes, he took several plastic ties out of his pack. With the gun he motioned the mother and grandfather together so he could cinch them to table legs. The boy, sobbing, asked if Ramzi killed his dog.

"*Lo siento mucho. El me ataco.*" He made the boy sit by the table and snapped another tie onto his wrist.

Ramzi's phone buzzed on silent. He glanced at the message. In Farsi, he told his ride how far he was from the original pick-up point.

Chapter 91

Agua-Prieta, Mexico

Kurt Valdez heard a shot and the music stopped. It began again after a few breaths. Then a Mexican man ran out of the cantina yelling.

Pulling out his gun, Kurt ran to the door and looked inside. He saw Navarro on the floor in a pool of blood. The hair rose on his neck. His gut tightened. He jumped inside, quickly covering the room with his Uzi. Everyone was speechless. The band stopped playing. A woman cried in the corner, her head turned away from the body.

"Adonde va?" Kurt yelled.

The bartender pointed to the hallway, *"Atra. Tenga quidado, señor!"*

Just then, Kurt heard a shot. There were screams. This shot was louder.

The bartender motioned that the shot came from the direction of the military hospital.

Kurt had noticed the taller building earlier. He examined Navarro and saw the hole from the exploding knife. *"Llame la policía."*

Then he hurried out of the bar and caught a glimpse of the hospital between buildings.

His phone buzzed on silent. He answered and Krysta told him to listen to a recorded conversation. "It's in Farsi. And they determined the approximately coordinates. It's the next street away from the border and from the tall building."

Listening to the playback, Kurt was enraged. It was Ramzi's voice.

After a moment, he said, "Those are directions, Krysta. Probably from the original coordinates." Kurt memorized them. "Keep me posted. He killed Hector."

"Oh, no! Dammit, Kurt! Be careful."

He ran to the corner and around the block, turning right twice. He slowed after he passed the first house. Several Mexicans peeped from half-opened doors. In the faint remaining light, a man stepped out and pointed to the fourth house opposite him. Kurt nodded to him.

Now he hurried along the street dodging from behind cars and trees. He started when he saw another body, then realized it was a dog. The Mexican pointed toward it.

Ramzi was close. Kurt could sense it. He pulled out four pieces of a dart gun from inside his jacket and screwed them together. While he inserted a dart, he heard a Siren approaching from several streets away. Transferring the dart gun to his left, he crept forward pointing the Uzi with his right.

A flickering light came on in the house beyond the dog. It took him a moment. *Candles.*

Kurt stood behind a tree where he could view the dog. The candle lights came from behind window shades.

He eased toward the corner of the house. Crouching, he silently moved along between shrubs and the dead animal. Two paces around the back, he saw the smashed door. He tightened his fist on the Uzi. The Siren stopped on the other street.

A car's headlights bounced along the alleyway, then went dark. Kurt quickly moved back to the side of the house and waited. The car stopped. He heard voices and crying. He switched the blowgun to his right, his gun to his left. He brought the blowgun up.

Inhaling three deep breaths, he held one and listened. Young female voices, pleading. Then he heard a woman screaming for mercy inside the house. Ramzi came out with young girls on both sides of him.

From behind the side of the house, Kurt put the blowgun to his mouth. Ramzi half-dragged the girls toward the car. For a brief moment, Kurt thought of rushing them. The light was fading.

When they were near the car, Kurt yelled, "Ramzi!" and fired the Uzi into the ground. Immediately, he aimed and blew a dart. He saw it hit Ramzi in the neck.

The man turned, snapped his gun up and fired twice.

Kurt felt a hot pain in his shoulder.

Ramzi thrust both hands up, fingers splayed, the gun flying. His mouth opened wide. The girls screamed. He collapsed onto his face. The car's gears growled and it spun its wheels in reverse.

Kurt could barely make out the front of the car now. He aimed and pumped three rounds into the radiator, another into a front tire. The driver's door opened and a man ran. Kurt dropped the blowgun and directed the girls to go inside the house.

Moving to Ramzi, he saw the man was still convulsing. In the near darkness, the man's eyes showed white.

Dialing his phone, when it clicked, Kurt said, "Hi Krysta. I've got him. How far away is the sheriff?"

"He's in *Agua-Prieta* now. Give me your GPS coordinates."

Kurt read them off along with the street name. He grabbed the gun and dragged Ramzi into the house. The man breathed shallowly. It took Kurt a few minutes to calm the family, cut them loose and explain the situation.

He gave the backpack to the grandfather and told him to carefully remove the contents. He ejected shells from the Beretta. Then he opened Ramzi's shirt and jacket.

The family panicked when they saw tubes taped to the man's chest.

"*Cuidado! Cuidado! Explosivos!* He took his knife and deftly sliced the tape. Stripping it off of Ramzi's body, he lifted the assembly and eased it onto the large table.

Then he turned and checked Ramzi's body for more weapons. The old Mexican handed Kurt plastic ties from the contents of the backpack and he cinched them on the terrorist's wrists and legs.

He gave the boy a small light to signal with and told him to watch for a car in the street.

"*Pinsas?*" Kurt asked the old man.

The Mexican brought him rusty pliers. Kurt worked it open and closed several times. He told the family to go outside and two houses away.

Working slowly and carefully, Kurt cut one after another of the wires to each explosive cylinder. There were two small tanks that he figured were acetylene.

Would have taken out two buildings.

Kurt was aware of a car arriving out in the street. He heard a door close. Sheriff Stroman came in the front door with the boy.

Stroman glanced at Ramzi on the floor and the remains of the explosives, now spread in pieces on the table. Kurt dropped the wires on the floor and grasped the clay-like *Semtex* with detonators inserted. "The most delicate part." He slid out the fuses and laid them on the table. Seizing the batteries, he set them on the opposite end.

"That does it. The bomb squad can take it from here. Let's get that asshole to the States."

They dragged Ramzi to the sheriff's car and pushed him into the backseat.

Stroman said, "Gotta get him across the border before the police figure this out."

Kurt told the old man to keep the family away from the building until the *federales* got there. He waved to them as Stroman took off.

As they sped toward the international crossing, Kurt dialed Langley.

Berkley came on the phone, he immediately told Kurt that it was set up so U.S. forces would meet him at the border crossing and take charge of the prisoner.

"We are less than five minutes from there right now."

"Kurt?"

Uh, oh. He didn't like the sound of Berkley's voice.

"Kurt? The Gallegos Cartel has your family."

"What!"

"Far as we can tell, they're unharmed."

"What the fuck is going on?"

"A hostage exchange."

Kurt fairly shouted. "The U.S. doesn't negotiate with terrorists!"

There was a long silence. Finally, Berkley asked, "Is he still unconscious?"

Kurt sneered at the terrorist and growled, "Yes."

"Insert your XC-99 into his body in a good place. We'll get the bastard again, even if we have to blow up his aircraft."

Kurt sputtered. "I'll kill him."

"No, Kurt. Don't harm him. We'll track him."

Shutting the phone off, Kurt set it on the dash. He knotted his jaw.

"What's happened?" Stroman sounded alarmed. You've turned white."

"The Gallegos has my family. Hostages."

"Goddammit!" Stroman shouted. He turned toward the international border.

The U.S. soldiers parked and stood waiting. The border inspectors waved the sheriff through. Further on, they motioned the car toward a building.

Strong arms seized Ramzi bin Omeri and laid him on a table. A woman medic began injecting a locating device with an air gun. She planted it into the back of Ramzi's neck, below the collar line.

Kurt handed her the advanced XC-99 chip and pointed to where he wanted it inserted.

Several minutes passed, SAPs and soldiers slapping Kurt on the back, men banging fists together. Kurt was numb to what was going on around him.

Ramzi finally blinked several times. He shook his head. His vision apparently cleared and he gazed horrified at the figures around him.

Kurt told the group that the Gallegos Cartel had his family. The men dragged Ramzi to a standing position, and propped him up against a table for him to regain complete consciousness.

"Give him your best shots, Tiburon."

Kurt drove his middle knuckle into Ramzi's solar plexus. The terrorist doubled over. Kurt flipped him over his shoulder onto the floor. He popped a fist into both kidneys. Then he grabbed Ramzi's hair and flopped him over onto his back. He kicked him in the testicles as hard as he could.

The man lay doubled up in the fetal position, moaning.

Kurt flared his nose and heaved several deep breaths.

The medic placed her hand on his arm. "Let me fix that shoulder wound."

Chapter 92

International Airport, Yuma, Arizona

Kurt Valdez glared at Ramzi bin Omeri and said in Farsi, "I'm still going to kill you. Even if I have to go to Afghanistan to do it."

Ramzi stared back at Kurt for several breaths, unblinking. He said. "*Koja man mitivonam bekaram yek goushte kar?*"

Kurt knew the expression well: Where can I buy some donkey meat? It was an idiom in Afghanistan that implied that you will starve trying to find me. He snarled, "You have made this personal by bringing my family into it. And, killing my comrade." Kurt nursed a sore and taped shoulder where Ramzi's bullet grazed him.

"I am truly sorry for that my worthy adversary. It was the *last* resort. Not my choice."

Krysta Mazur had been listening to the conversation from the front seat. Her phone buzzed. Glancing at it, she said, "It's the sheriff." After listening a moment, she said, "Okay," and turned to Kurt, "They're ready at the border crossing." She started the engine and put the white SUV in drive.

Kurt sat in the back seat half facing Ramzi, who now stared out the window.

The news was partially good this morning. Don Berkley from Langley had negotiated an exchange—Kurt's family for Ramzi.

Kurt had been nauseated with the thought. They were releasing the world's *most-wanted* terrorist, whom he'd been trying to capture for six years. He wondered how they kept the deal secret from the government and the press.

Krysta took the vehicle through the west airport exit, passing the control tower as previously arranged, and onto fortieth street. In the early morning dawn, buildings were now becoming fully visible.

It was a mile to Highway 95 where she made a left to head toward San Luis, Arizona, situated twelve miles away on the Mexican border. The small city of San Luis Rio Colorado was across the international line.

Flat farmland along the highway lay in various stages of growth, fed by several irrigation canals from the Colorado River. A pungent odor came from rotting vegetables and ripening crops ready to harvest. Some fenced squares were freshly plowed or burned off. Others grew maize or hay. Large tractor-trailer-sized rectangular blocks of hay bales, covered with tarpaulin and ready for transport, were stacked next to access roads on the edge of the cultivated sections.

The Chevrolet SUV rumbled onto a bridge over an irrigation canal. They made two 45-degree turns and crossed over another bridge over the same canal. The road turned south, made two ninety-degree turns, and continued south again. A sign indicated five miles to the international border.

Kurt spotted it and clenched his jaw. He studied the Snow Leopard in the gathering light. The man was at least fifty now. He looked different from the CIA photos. Surgical scars showed faintly under his skin. Gray hair sprouted at his sideburns. Even handcuffed to the door ring, Ramzi had poise, a professional military composure. He could be a high-ranking officer in any country's army.

Since their verbal exchange, the man had not made eye contact with Kurt. He knew it was because Ramzi was ashamed that the cartel had kidnaped his family—a severe breach of their code of ethics.

Krysta pointed. "There's the immigration building where we make the exchange." She pushed her hair behind her ear.

Several military tanks parked in a defensive perimeter. Their big guns pointed toward the border.

Turning into a driveway, she acknowledged a man in uniform signaling them. She swerved over into the far left lane, eased forward slowly against the direction of the parked cars and stopped.

Border Protection had cordoned off the normal lanes and directed going-to-work traffic to a re-opened former port-of-entry an eighth-mile to the east. All six of the inspector booths underneath a gray roof and the connecting lanes to Highway 95 were closed. Even the Mexican port-of-entry 100 feet to the right was cordoned off. No allowance for an accident or for failure.

Sheriff Stroman came out of a building toward them with an immigration official. His name tag said Jimenez. Krysta opened the rear door and Kurt cut the prisoner's wrist tie. He pulled Ramzi up for the sheriff.

Stroman, almost a head taller than the terrorist, glowered at him. He seized Ramzi by the arm, and with Officer Jimenez, hustled him toward the middle of the platform near the border.

From the same door Stroman exited, a female officer motioned Krysta Mazur and Kurt inside toward her. She introduced herself as Nadine Vickery and warned them to remain hidden. "The cartel has 50-caliber automatic weapons aimed in this direction from the other side."

They followed her to an office with a view window facing the border. Down to the right, the six vehicle lanes were visible. Several armored vehicles were visible from where they stood.

Vickery rapped her knuckles on the window. "One-inch-thick bulletproof glass. The walls have steel plate inside the concrete block." She handed them binoculars, then pointed out four flat-roofed buildings with a clump of trees surrounding them. Narrowing her eyes, she said, "We spotted men with automatic weapons on those buildings earlier with night-vision."

Kurt studied the port-of-entry area for several minutes. He spotted two gunmen. His stomach muscles tightened. He felt his anger surge.

He gestured and growled, "We have those shooters covered?"

"Absolutely," Vickery said. "They will be blown off the roofs, if they open up. There are two armed Predators with a Global Hawk watching and directing events from high above."

"Do we know how the exchange is going to be made?"

"The cartel has your wife's cell phone. The sheriff has already talked to them and they will make the swap at six o'clock."

Kurt glanced at his watch. It was three minutes to six. He had an empty feeling in his abdomen. "So we're only spectators on this one?" He heard the strain in his speech. He coughed, scanned with the binoculars and refocused.

Stroman's voice came over the speaker. "We just received a call, Nadine."

Kurt tightened his grip on the binoculars.

The speaker reported, "Watch in the direction of those trees straight ahead. The semi-trailer."

Officer Vickery pointed, "Next to the long gray building."

The trailer door swung open. Kurt saw his four children climb down steps led by what looked like a dark Mexican woman. Baderi came next, helping Raisa, Kurt's mother-in-law, down to the pavement. He focused the binoculars on his second wife, who was leading their three-year-old. Behind them, but still in the trailer and barely visible, was Siamarra with two other women.

Kurt swallowed hard, suppressing anger and relief. Leaning forward, he saw Ramzi below and on his right, slowly moving away from the building. Sheriff Stroman and Officer Jimenez held both his arms. Stroman spoke into a phone mike. They stopped 25 feet from the street.

After several breaths, Kurt's family, without Siamarra, walked across the street holding hands. The dark woman released them, they passed the three men and continued on into the building where Kurt was. They cried out when they saw him. He grabbed them and hugged them, then gestured to some benches. "Now calm down. Sit there, while we rescue your mother."

Returning to the window, Kurt watched Siamarra approach with the two other women. The sheriff cut Ramzi's tie, released him and he passed them by.

I'm gonna get you, asshole.

Handing the glasses to Officer Vickery, Kurt ran to Siamarra. When he ushered her into the building, the remainder of the family rushed to them.

After the wives and children settled down, Kurt returned to the window to see Ramzi fade from view among the trees on the far side of the street and parking lot.

Sheriff Stroman and Officer Jimenez were to remain in view until the Snow Leopard got out of sight.

Kurt asked Krysta if she would take his family to the Yuma airport for him. He said he had unfinished business and would ride with Sheriff Stroman. She agreed and Kurt explained it to his family.

After watching their sad looks, he promised them they were going to have lots of time together the next few days. Krysta rounded them up and took off.

Chapter 93

San Luis, Arizona

Kurt Valdez and Sheriff Stroman headed back north into the U.S. on Highway 95. The sheriff made the jogs in the road and when it straightened out, he accelerated.

"That's the most difficult thing I've had to do in my entire life," he said. "Turning a major terrorist loose. Especially after what happened in Las Vegas!"

"I know," Kurt said. "I've been chasing him for six years. You wouldn't believe what he's involved in."

His phone buzzed. He saw the CIA's identification and turned the sound up so Stroman could hear.

"You got him, Top?"

"Yeah, Tiburon. They must have discovered the first transmitter. But the XC-99 is sending out a clear signal."

"Good. They didn't find it. The medic inserted it under his crotch, next to his prostate. And I kicked him hard. He'll think the pain is from the kick."

"It's working great. So is the camera on the Global Hawk. He just took off in a black SUV, headed west on Mexican Two. The soldiers of the Gallegos Cartel are escorting him. There's an international airport near Mexicali. We figure he'll catch a flight from there."

"I know the place well. What now, Top?"

"If we confront Ramzi at the airport, a lot of innocent Mexicans could get shot up. Or if the *federales* get him, the Gallegos' soldiers may target their families later."

After a long pause, Kurt said, "So we are just going to let him go?"

"Sharpshooters will try to take him out, on the tarmacs when they land. If they miss, hopefully he'll feel safe enough to go back to Iran. We'll pinpoint him there, if they don't discover the XC-99."

"So what now?"

"Take three weeks off with your family. We doubled the surveillance to protect them. Have Sheriff Stroman take you to them at Yuma International."

"They are there already?"

"Ms. Mazur is there with them. We booked a flight to San Diego for all of you."

Kurt glanced at the sheriff. Stroman nodded.

Signing off, Kurt heard an inrush of air as the Jimmy surged. Within seconds they were going eighty. Stroman slowed quickly when they came to a right turn, then turned on the flashing lights to pass through Somerton, Arizona.

"XC-99?" the officer asked.

"The latest nuclear-battery-powered chip we implanted in Ramzi. Gives out a homing signal. We can turn it on remotely to make it hard to detect."

When Stroman arrived at the airport, Krysta had gathered Kurt's family at the baggage check-in area.

Kurt turned to the sheriff. "This might be the last time I see you, Bob. You did one hell of an investigating job to get the leads on the submarine."

"We were too slow, Krysta and I. We should have obtained warrants or something to investigate the Ibrahim brothers much sooner."

"Nevertheless, we'll get Ramzi. The story of how we prevented the terrorists from using the nuclear weapon to destroy Hoover dam will come out. The government will award you and Krysta Presidential Citations."

"You're the one who put the final pieces together and stopped them. You risked your life." Stroman extended his hand.

"We did it together, Bob. Don't diminish your role." Kurt reached to shake the sheriff's hand. "Take care. We'll get together after all this is finished."

The lawman returned the handshake. "My family and I would like that."

Kurt exited the SUV and headed for Krysta and his family. His boys spotted him and shouted.

"The government booked us a flight to San Diego, Krysta. Did my family talk your ears off?"

She beamed. "They are wonderfully polite and respectful." She pushed her hair behind her ear.

Kurt signaled to Siamarra to hold his family back. He pulled Krysta aside, told her what an excellent job she did, and how valuable she was to the country.

"We did it together, Kurt. All of us. It took everyone to put the puzzle together."

"In a sense, I feel like we were too slow," he said. "Maybe they could have stopped the hotel attacks if the big picture had been assembled sooner."

She said, "I've been doing this for eight years now. There is simply too much data to analyze quickly, and too much useless 'noise.'"

He nodded. "The on-the-ground efforts and interrogations take too long, also."

Mohammad and Misha'il called out that their flight was ready.

Kurt waved acknowledgment.

He turned back to Krysta. "This might be the last time I see you. I want you to know I think you did a very professional job with the analysis and tracking Ramzi."

"I wish we could've stopped the bombings and the cartel."

"Like I told the sheriff, we'll get Ramzi. And the story of the nuclear weapon will come out. You and the sheriff will receive Presidential Citations." He reached to shake her hand. "We will all get together again."

"I just wanted to stop them." She took his hand and shook it.

Chapter 94

Arabian — Persian Gulf

Kurt Valdez scanned the desert below through the porthole of the Lufthansa flight to Dhahran, Saudi Arabia. He was in a somber mood after spending a pleasant three weeks with his family in Tecate, Mexico, thinking it hadn't been long enough.

It was his own fault. NSA tracked Ramzi bin Omeri to the small mining village of Sarcheshmeh, Iran, and he'd volunteered to go in after the man.

Why do I do this?

He shook his head.

'Cause they know I've been there three times recently.

That's why he'd volunteered. No one else could do it. No one who could handle the Snow Leopard, that is.

Stupid. Suicide mission.

Even Don Berkley, his contact and boss at CIA, considered the mission extremely dangerous. The man was seriously conflicted in agreeing to allow Kurt to go. However, they knew it was only a matter of time until Iranians discovered the XC-99 chip. They had to move quickly while they had time.

I was the only one.

Kurt reasoned that he had the language skill and had rescued another agent, Akmad, four years ago in Iran. He had the physical abilities and endurance. His knowledge of the country made him one of the few remaining choices. The government and military would cover his ass, with a fly-in rescue if necessary.

The Airbus 300 landed and Kurt passed through customs at the airport. He wore slacks and a white *ghutra*. Kurt searched for the SEALs, spotted them and waved. Commander Menzies and Master Chief Espinosa searching the crowd, finally saw him. They approached and laughed at his Arab headdress.

"What's with the disguise, Tiburon?" Menzies asked.

"Incognito."

"Right," Menzies said. "No one will spot you." The SEALs laughed again.

"I'm starved," Kurt said. "When do we eat?"

Master Chief Espinosa gestured to a white SUV. "How about a Big Mac?"

The men got into the vehicle and cranked up the air conditioning, even though it was March.

This McDonald's looked exactly like the ones in the states, except the sign and menus had both English and Arabic lettering. Taking bites from a chicken sandwich, Menzies filled Kurt in on the military aspects of the plan.

"We'll have the C-130 Hercules ready with everything you need at 1830 hours."

After eating, they had been on the highway only several minutes when Kurt's satellite phone buzzed and flashed a code.

Glancing at its view window, Kurt thought, *What's up with Berkley now?*

"Can you pull over to that station, Gilbert?"

Espinosa swerved behind the red Chevron-Texaco gas station. Kurt slipped out his phone. Searching for a satellite connection until an LED confirmed it, he dialed the necessary eleven digits, then entered his seven digit password.

Berkley came on the line. "Are you sure you're ready for this, Kurt?"

"Of course. We gotta get that son of a bitch before he tries another attack."

There was a long silence. Then the deputy counter-terrorism chief said, "They have your top secret orders at the base. Commander Menzies is taking care of your backside, making all the military preparations."

Kurt acknowledged. "I'm with them now."

He glanced beyond the station. There were small sand dunes with thorn bushes on the other side of a curb leading to distant high-rise apartments. He could see a bathroom for the station, a door slowly closing after an Arab left it.

"Your homing device is sending out a signal. But, a warning. Pasdaran has located some of them with electronic gear the Russians sold them. Need I tell you to keep your pill ready at all times."

"I've been through all this before, Top, in Orientation. I'm less than a mile from the base now."

A long pause. "I guess I just wanted to talk to you while I have a chance, Kurt."

"If something goes wrong, you have my instructions."

Another long pause. "Okay. Good luck, Tiburon."

Kurt slid the antenna into the satellite phone and slowly slipped it into its pouch.

Huh. Don's getting sentimental.

After traveling three kilometers, Espinosa turned onto the military base and came to a gated complex. A marine checked their IDs and waved them through, gesturing to a parking area.

Entering the Officer of the Day's building, Kurt was met by a lieutenant who handed him a diplomatic pouch and gestured to another small office.

Kurt grasped the wire on the packet and tore it open. He read the brief at the beginning of the communiqué, and noted the designation: "Operation Yellowjacket," and shrugged. Then he frowned at the first part of the message.

Figured that's why they're getting the Hercules ready.

He read through, then slipped more information out of the packet. Unfolding a map that covered the southern half of Iran, he saw that there were temporary designated coordinates marked: "Eyes only."

He moved his finger to the landing zone, the LZ, Sierra-victor-forty-niner. Right in the desert hills. There were seven recent aerial photos which he lined up in an overlapping arrangement.

LZ is sand dunes and arroyos. Break an ankle, I land wrong in the dark.

It took two hours to study the information, maps, and photos. Kurt finished and returned the materials to the pouch.

When he left the office and met again with Commander Menzies, the officer said, "A very dangerous mission, my friend. Pasdaran and the Revolutionary Guards are treacherous in Iran. They'll torture you if they catch you."

Kurt waved him off.

Chapter 95

Strait of Hormuz, Persian Gulf

Kurt Valdez pulled the sleeve of his jump suit back to glance at his watch. 2343 hours. Twenty-eight minutes to target. He signaled to Commander Menzies from the seat of the Hercules. The SEAL officer acknowledged. They wore oxygen masks in the de-pressurized and nearly dark aircraft.

The officer's eyes were barely perceptible with the headgear. Menzies' six-foot height and athletic build were folded and buckled into the not-made-for-comfort seat.

Military planners had worked all day to prepare for the jump. They'd gathered a list of gear for Kurt, including the black non-glare suit, pack, and chute. Then they'd grounded a commercial Gulf Air flight and inserted the C-130 in its scheduled time and flight path. Kurt wondered how they could get away with slowing to the 150-knot jump speed he needed, but he didn't ask. He figured they'd planned for that, too.

He had also checked the equipment himself. Currency: 700,000 Iranian rials, survival gear and med-equipment in case he was injured during the jump. He packed a modified Tiawanese cell phone, two of the latest tiny GPS devices, and a radio. The radio would be used to listen only, so Menzies could talk him down to the LZ during his free fall, and after his chute opened. He was going in with no gun, naked.

Unzipping a pouch, he fingered a cyanide capsule. They wouldn't take him alive.

Behind his lenses, Menzies' gaze flicked to the capsule and pouch. He probably wondered what Kurt was thinking at the moment.

Going through the details of the mission helped keep his mind off the jump itself for the next few minutes.

An engine cut off. He knotted his fists. His heartbeats pounded at his temples.

The aircraft slowed and plunged. Kurt grabbed his shoulder straps. The Hercules then banked hard to starboard and leveled out, the signal for final approach. He recalled that, as part of the decoy plan, the pilot would report to flight control in Isfahan, Iran, that they'd lost an engine. The simulated Gulf Air flight was to change heading to Dubai for repairs.

The loudspeaker announced, "Target minus ten minutes."

That was the signal for the commander to help Kurt into his jump gear. They unbuckled their seatbelts and hurried to the back. At the rear of the aircraft, the SEAL grabbed the parachute pack and Kurt slipped into it. Menzies pointed down and Kurt cinched the straps tight, making sure they cleared his testicles. Three inches to the right or left and a strap would catch one, knock him unconscious when the chute opened. He could go into a spin that could kill him.

Menzies handed him fresh oxygen gear. Kurt had run out several minutes ago. He slipped it on, then tightened the side straps. He was already getting tunnel vision after inhaling without it. The officer turned on the valve. A few quick breaths cleared his head and satisfied Kurt that the gear worked properly. He slid his goggles over his head and adjusted them, then pulled on two pairs of gloves. The oxygen mask, goggles, and gloves reminded him that he was jumping from 32,000 feet.

Sixty below out there.

The SEAL officer slapped his back hard two times, meaning he was ready.

Loud pops. The back ramp of the C-130 opened. A rush of frigid air entered. The loudspeaker came on again. "Target minus fifteen seconds."

Kurt sauntered to the back ramp. He hyperventilated four breaths of oxygen.

Walking to the edge of the ramp, he counted to himself: Ten ... nine ... eight .... Three ... two ... one ....

He leaned forward and plunged into the darkness. Turbulence hit his body. He twisted around to a face-down, spread-eagle position and flared his arms. Spreading and rotating his hands to control his direction, he bent his knees so that his feet pointed upward. Then, he cocked one leg slightly to turn toward the moon. The inside of the aircraft had been kept almost dark so his eyes would be fully adjusted for the faint glow from the new crescent.

Air rushed by. Hurtling downward at 200 miles per hour stretched the fabric tight on the jump suit. It fluttered on his arms and legs. Other than that, he had no sensation of falling. The lights from the city of Bandar 'Abbas and on ships in the Gulf fifty miles away, along with blinking red lights on television towers, seemed to rise toward him as he plummeted toward earth.

He blinked tears away. The desert surrounding the city to the north and east reflected almost no light. It was invisible, a huge dark area. Kurt concentrated on keeping his body aligned with the moon. He watched for the faint, green chem-glow lights that would mark his landing zone.

It seemed as if several minutes had gone by when he heard Menzies' voice in his earphones, "Adjust to ninety degrees."

Good. That meant he was sending out a homing signal, and his radio was working. He pulled his right foot toward his back and spun 45 degrees. Plunging downward, he picked up speed. He couldn't perceive it, but he knew his body corrected rapidly.

"Check descent," came the voice on the radio.

Kurt arched his back and sensed more air resistance. The correction must have worked, as the radio went silent.

A glance at his timer and the luminous dial of the altimeter showed 11,000 feet.

Four miles in a minute.

His body grew comfortable. The lower elevation and friction from falling warmed him.

The moon appeared at a different angle. Kurt could now make out the faint glow of the desert far below. For the first time, he felt the sensation of falling. The ground appeared to rise toward him.

The commander's voice spoke again: "Check altitude."

Kurt repeatedly watched his altimeter. He now passed below 3,000 feet. Moving his hands and left foot, he made an adjustment. The ground now came into clear focus.

He pulled the parachute cord and quickly felt two jerks, one, a slight one when a small chute opened. In turn, it yanked the main chute out, causing sharp pain where the straps crossed his shoulders and thighs. Jolted to a slow drift, he tugged on the chute lines to steer, then slid the oxygen mask down around his neck.

He was vulnerable now. If Iranian forces had detected his dive from the aircraft, they might spot him with night-vision scopes.

Menzies' reassuring voice said, "93 seconds to target; 48 degrees."

Kurt checked his watch and pulled on the lines to rotate his drift. He now took a few seconds to remove his goggles.

When his watch showed 28 seconds, he spotted the three chem-lights set by his comrade from Afghanistan.

Good. Hakim made it.

Only a slight correction on the lines. He passed over the triangle of lights and spun 180 degrees into a slight breeze. The chute slowed his descent almost to a stop. His feet plopped into soft sand.

Perfect.

Kurt quickly gathered in the chute. In his earphones, he heard Menzies break the radio squelch twice. It was the signal that they could see him moving. They would maintain radio silence well out over the Gulf.

His old comrade from Afghanistan, Hakim Jamahalien, came over the rise. Kurt laughed. "*Shikar!* Long time, no see!" He hugged his close friend.

The two men shared a quick, happy reunion.

Then taking out his knife, Kurt cut the map off the parachute. The fabric of the map also doubled as a sun blanket. Over the next few minutes, the two men dug a hole and dropped in the remaining parachute, jump suit, and pack. Kurt also dumped the oxygen equipment, knife, radio, watch, and goggles into the hole. They covered it and hid the shovel.

He was fully warm now, even in the cool March breeze.

Hakim handed him summer Afghani clothes, a *shalwar kameez*, to wear. They would change again when they got to the mountains and snow.

Donning the clothes and a gray turban, Kurt drank some water and hoisted his pack.

"How far to the car?"

"Three klicks. I brought a used Shikar. They modified it with compartments and packed the equipment from the list."

"A Shikar for Shikar." Kurt laughed heartily for the first time in days.

"We need to be 500 klicks past Bandar 'Abbas to Kerman by daylight."

"He's in, DO," said Don Berkley. "Got a signal from his homing device."

The director of operations nodded. "Both of them are good men. Make sure we don't lose 'em."

Berkley ran a hand over his bald head. "A Global Hawk's been circling at 56,000 feet. *Papillon*, Colonel Wisneski, is controlling the remotes. She worked with Kurt in Pakistan on Operation Cobra where we took care of "Headfake," and those Pakistani generals."

"How long before he reaches the Snow Leopard's twenty?"

"Eight, nine hours."

"Anything goes wrong, don't leave them hung out with their dicks in the wind in that stinking hell hole. Send in the choppers, and get 'em out fast!"

"Got an evacuation plan and a frigate in the Gulf, Sir, ready to go on my word."

The DO closed the door behind him as he left the office.

Chapter 96

Kerman, Iran

Shortly after daylight, Kurt Valdez guided the Shikar around the first traffic circle in Kerman, a large city in the center of Iran. The highway ended abruptly into a maze of streets.

Rolling the window down, he heard the high-pitched chanting of the religious muezzins reciting the suras of the Koran on loudspeakers. "I actually missed them," Kurt said.

Hakim smiled and pointed. "There, the spire on the mosque."

Kurt spotted it, too. "Warn me if you see the police." They had both experienced several anxiety attacks when revolutionary guards gave them hard looks in the small villages they passed through, and at one accident they stopped for.

Driving three-quarters around a roundabout to turn west, Kurt went two more blocks. Then he swore to himself and slowed the vehicle as they came to a congested area.

The street ran between old buildings with narrow sidewalks and broken hexagonal-tile streets.

A rivulet of putrid water trickled alongside curbs. Bluish exhaust from trucks and buses mingled with dust and lay heavy in the air. Horns blared. Cars and motorcycles whizzed by less than a meter from the driver's door. Cables stretched diagonally above busy intersections with four-way traffic lights dangling in the middle.

When a pedestrian trotted across the street a few cars ahead of them, Kurt tightened his stomach. He couldn't decelerate because of the flow but diverted the car a few inches to the right to miss the man, who turned side-on to make himself a narrow target.

"Son of a bitch! We gotta get outta this section of town."

Hakim exhaled loudly. "It's going to be like this everywhere. If we get in an accident, it is over for us."

They fought the traffic for another tedious 45 minutes, all the while moving in the direction of the huge mosque. They rounded another traffic circle, and a pond surrounding the religious monument came into view.

"Beautiful!" Kurt said, his mood suddenly changed. "I'm always amazed how stunning the mosques are."

The structure was covered with turquoise tiles and had three domes with spires on top. Beige tile with black patterns was laid throughout the arched passageways. The pond wound through trees, beautiful flowers and shrubs. Several types of waterfowl swam near the edges.

Hakim read a sign in Arabic script and made mental calculations. "According the Hijri calendar, it was built in 406. That is 1028 in our date system."

Both men stared in awe at the sight.

Finally, Hakim gestured to a man wearing a maroon turban signaling them. "There's our petrol."

Kurt drove behind the mosque to a mud-brick wall. A small white truck was parked beyond. The men filled the Shikar's two gas tanks and put four extra gas containers in the trunk.

"It will save you two hours waiting in line," the driver said.

While Hakim paid the man for the contraband and conversed with him, Kurt checked the oil and started the vehicle. The Irani waved and drove off.

Hakim said, "He drew a map for me and said to drive around the main part of the city on Imam Khomeini Highway. That will avoid the police. It takes an hour to connect to the main road to Tehran, then another 90 minutes to Rafsanjan once you leave the city."

Kurt felt a hand grab him.

"A checkpoint!" Hakim sounded alarmed.

Kurt awakened, startled. Glancing around, he saw a sign in Arabic and English that said: Rafsanjan, 40 kilometers.

"They will catch us!" Hakim blurted.

Kurt seized the man's wrist. "Calm down! They're not going to get us."

Hakim's eyes were wide with fear. Kurt surveyed the situation.

Blue and white buildings on both sides of the highway were joined by an overhead truss structure fabricated of large-diameter pipes. Lights and signs faced opposite directions. Four revolutionary guards inspected vehicles.

"Just a routine checkpoint," Kurt said. "Nothing to get alarmed about."

Hakim applied the brakes too hard and jerked the car twice, skidding the second time. He stopped behind another vehicle. The man hyperventilated.

Two guards searched a vehicle three ahead of them. One patrolman had the trunk open, the other a back door.

Kurt clenched his jaw. "Get a hold of yourself."

Hakim put his hand to his mouth and frowned.

"We rehearsed our story." Kurt glowered. "Now calm down! I'll do the talking."

One guard eventually closed the back door of the car. The other guard nodded and allowed the driver to get in and drive away.

The next vehicle in line was a red Nissan truck. The inspector on Kurt's side scanned underneath with a mirror. He moved along to three different places when he shouted to the other. They forced the truck over into a side parking area.

"May have had opium," Kurt said. "Might work out to our advantage."

He took out a pack of strong Turkish cigarettes and lit one.

The car ahead of them took off when an inspector waved them on. Kurt rolled down the window as the guard motioned to them.

He blew a puff of smoke toward the officer. "*Ala shoma koubai,*" Kurt greeted him.

The uniformed man asked where they were headed.

Kurt offered him a cigarette. "*Man mikahim be Sar-Cheshmeh, be Murdan.*" Kurt told the officer that they were headed to the village of Murdan, situated in the mountains near a copper mine.

Hakim, finally calmed, answered the other officer's questions. Two additional inspectors tore apart the Nissan truck thirty meters away.

The officers looked inside the workbag of masonry tools in the backseat and examined both Kurt and Hakim's visas and work papers for the dam at Shahrbabak.

When it seemed they were satisfied, Hakim asked the inspectors where the turnoff was for *Sar-Cheshmeh* and how far up in the mountains it was.

The officer pointed to a cloud of gray smoke tinged with green, and told them to head toward it. He told them Shahrbabak was 120 kilometers past Murdan, which was just beyond the copper mine at *Sar-Cheshmeh*.

"*Kheili mahm nun. Khoda ha fez.*" Hakim thanked the inspector and said goodbye.

He started the engine and pulled away.

"Whew," Kurt said. "One more to go. We get past it, we can hide in the mountains."

A half-hour later, Hakim stopped near *qanaats* where they both urinated and stretched. Kurt took over driving.

"The *qanaats* here are bigger than they are in Afghanistan," Hakim said. "I didn't realize Iran had them, too."

"The Persians invented them about 2,500 years ago. I read in *National Geographic* that work was begun under the early kings, Cyrus, Xerxes, and Darius. Some are 400 meters deep tapping underground streams. They run for thousands of kilometers throughout Iran."

Kurt slowed for a curve. "Iranians manufacture their own water pumps. That's why the gardens and orchards are so green in Kerman. There are no major rivers, but it's lush."

The two men went silent as the Shikar cruised comfortably at 120 kilometers per hour. It was cool and dry outside, and with the car's air vents open, the temperature inside was pleasant. Both men were more relaxed now. There were almost no vehicles and they hadn't passed police or military vehicles, or guard stations for a while.

They came to another *qanaat* where a man stood next to a large drum. It was a flat-topped mound 25 meters in diameter and four to five meters high.

Kurt pointed. "There are one or two men down in the hole cleaning out the water channel. Must be a deep well, judging by the size of that mound. I'll bet there are 400 meters of rope on that drum."

"Four-hundred!"

"More than 130 generations of families have maintained them—father to sons keeping the water channels open."

"Praise Allah."

Kurt scanned the arid desert wasteland on both sides of the highway. The pediment stretched at least 100 kilometers to the southwest, gradually rising to peaks. Several had small snow patches. Grayish-green smoke boiled up from between the mountains. To the north, it was at least 200 kilometers to an escarpment that ran parallel to the highway. An occasional green belt filled the valleys where there was always a small village.

After almost an hour of silence, Kurt started to say something but saw Hakim was asleep. He slowed for a curve through a barren gorge. The smoke from the copper smelter was straight ahead. They came to a large flat area with green fields. Villagers in the fields loaded produce into baskets borne by donkeys.

Immediately beyond the Sar-cheshmeh smelter, Kurt shook Hakim awake. "Another government checkpoint."

The Afghani bolted upright.

Kurt held his breath and then exhaled slowly. This checkpoint might be worse. These guards were army and were not in a hurry. "Remain calm. I'll do the talking."

A short man in a green uniform, with heavy, dark eyebrows, glared and motioned them to stop. He told them to get out. No friendly greeting here.

Another soldier, a tall, thin man, came from across the street. The two inspected visas and work papers, looking suspiciously at Kurt and Hakim, grilling them harshly, asking them about their accents and why their hands were soft. They set the tool bag on the ground and removed tools.

A yelling match over the implements began. For at least twenty minutes the soldiers shouted at Kurt and Hakim, and the two shouted back. The tall man was going to keep some of the tools. Kurt got in the his face and argued with him, glaring him down.

Finally, Kurt demanded to see the base colonel. "We were hired to work at the dam at Shahrbabak!"

After several more minutes of shouting, pulling back and forth on tools, Kurt grabbed the tool bag and threw it in the back seat. He yanked a trowel out of the tall soldier's hand. "They can get other workers for the dam!"

He got in the car, started the engine and started to turn around. "We will leave," Kurt yelled.

"Wait!" the short man ran toward them and shouted. The look on his face turned to fright. He visibly swallowed twice, raised the steel bar gate and waved them through.

Kurt accelerated, shifted and sped away. "Assholes."

"What happened?" Hakim looked stunned. "They changed their minds."

Kurt was silent for a few moments.

"They got scared. They thought we were actually going to leave." He tapped his chin. "You know what that tells me. They need skilled workers up here and can't get enough. They thought we really were going to leave. They'd have to answer."

"Our papers must have no mistakes. They fooled them."

"Maybe they couldn't read very well. Anyway, we were lucky, Hakim. For now."

They passed the power distribution facility. Kurt felt the hair on the back of his neck stir. He shivered. "We're getting close to him, saddique. I can feel it. We're probably passing him."

They continued on toward the village of Murdan. Kurt spotted a dirt road heading off in the direction of the barren mountains to the south. He turned and followed barely traveled tracks for several kilometers where it divided.

"We need to set up the satellite antenna," Kurt said.

They got out, pulled the three parts of the antenna from a slot in the trunk. They had to traverse several snow patches to scale a barren peak. Then, finding a large rock where there was no vegetation and could not be seen from the main road, they mounted the antenna. Hakim attached a solar battery and energized the circuitry. He aligned a directional dish to coordinates they had been given.

Kurt finished the job by setting up explosives and a self-destruct device. A motion detector was connected to the initiating mechanism. "I hope there's no curious wildlife around here."

Back on the highway, they had traveled 15 kilometers when Hakim pointed to a sign in Arabic. "Murdan. We are here."

Kurt drove through the small village set in a bowl. It was cleared of snow, but the surrounding peaks had patches. Shops and stores lined both sides of the main street. Twelve kilometers beyond, he pointed. "The turn in the satellite view."

He veered north onto a rough road. Kurt stopped so they could get the GPS from under the wheel well. Continuing on, the Shikar bounced over rain ruts and tracks overgrown with brush.

Passing through a wet patch where the snowmelt had soaked in, Kurt said, "No tracks. No one travelled this road for a while. You watching the distance?"

Hakim read the coordinates. "Another three klicks."

Kurt memorized turns, brush, and large, protruding rocks so they could drive back in the dark.

"Here," said Hakim. "Turn right. Half a klick."

The vehicle eased over a small rise and dropped elevation. Kurt spotted the trees he saw in the satellite image. He pulled the car among them, they unscrewed a panel in the trunk and unloaded all the equipment. Finally, they covered the car with a camouflage net.

Turning to the ancient ruins of a hamlet nearby, they searched through what remained of small huts. Shaped like igloos, but narrower and taller, they had entrances that one person could crawl through to a sunken floor. Most had caved in, and rain had leveled the mud-clay mixture that originally covered frames of branches and grass matting. It took the two friends a few minutes to find one that was hidden enough, but still intact. A dank, putrid smell came from within.

"This one will work." Kurt pointed.

Hakim wrinkled his nose. "I pray we are not remaining long."

"Better than Afghanistan." Kurt grinned at his comrade's disgusted look.

"This village was occupied 3,500 years ago. I read about it. No one has lived here since."

Hakim raised his eyebrows.

"Archeologists stopped digging after the shah was overthrown in 1978."

The two friends set their equipment near the chosen hut. Kurt took a branch and stirred the debris inside. "I don't think there are any asps at this elevation. But let's not take a chance. They could be hibernating."

I was thinking, "Rats and snakes."

For several minutes, they stirred the brush inside nearby huts. Satisfied, Kurt hung a light and began shoveling out chunks of rock, branches, mingled dirt, and rat droppings. It took almost until darkness to make the space livable.

"Not bad," said Kurt. "This will do until we finish business."

Chapter 97

Murdan, Iran

It was 0200 hours when they parked the Shikar in Murdan and pedaled two small fold-up bicycles through the residential area. To Kurt's surprise, buildings looked like a group of apartments in Switzerland. The tiny GPS he wore around his neck kept them on track to Ramzi bin Omeri's residence. This first reconnaissance was to locate guards, dogs and possible alarms.

The two comrades avoided the few streetlights and stayed in the darker areas. Using night-vision headgear, they spotted two guards on patrol. The sentries ambled around in haphazard fashion, stamping their feet frequently. Kurt decided they were tired, bored and cold.

They had pedaled two kilometers from the Shikar when the red LED on their GPS blinked. The hair rose on the back of Kurt's neck. He shivered.

Right there.

It was a center apartment in a row of five units. He took his Minnie-cam and zoomed in on the front of the apartment, the garage door and front door, and the two windows.

Kurt got Hakim's attention and blew lightly on a high-frequency dog whistle. No response. He blew it three more times, waiting in between. A dog barked in another section of town. Then another. Good. No dogs nearby.

Kurt signaled to hide the bicycles. They found a hedge in a dark area.

On foot, they eased around behind the apartment. A narrow alley for trash containers, gas meters, telephone pedestals, and electrical transformers lay between concrete block walls. They sneaked the 126 paces to where the back of Ramzi's yard should be. Once again, Kurt blew the dog whistle softly. After three blows, there were still no answering barks.

Relieved, he straightened and cautiously peeked over the back wall. With the night-vision, he surveyed the area and tried to determine if there were any electronic detectors.

A sliding glass door on the back of the house led to a covered patio. A very small yard of grass came to the masonry wall. Two floodlights were mounted on the corner posts of the patio cover. Kurt spotted motion or infrared sensors. He scanned the yard down below.

Aha.

Two more sensors. All of them probably controlled six lights.

Another door, a meter wide wood or composite door with a glass window and adjustable blind, was over to the left. It had a standard brass lock. A hibachi sat on a ledge near the door.

Kitchen?

With the Minnie-cam, he zoomed in on the sensors, the door-lock, and several points on the sliding door. He shot a wide angle of the whole back of the house.

Kurt eased down and the two men retraced their steps back to the bicycles. It took 15 minutes to return to the car, and another 40 to drive to the ancient village. By way of the remote antenna, Kurt sent an 18-second communication burst, complete with photos, to Langley.

"Can they locate us now?" Hakim asked, shivering.

"We have at best three days. I'm sure with the electronic equipment Pasdaran has, they could determine that a message was sent. More likely they'd discover the antenna."

"So, three days to move on him?"

"A good guess," Kurt said. "Let's sleep and get everything ready for a rapid getaway. Each time we leave may be the last."

They set up motion detectors and infrared sensors around the area, then slept. When Kurt awoke in the late afternoon, there was a message.

He knew that twelve days before, Langley had pinpointed Ramzi's residence. They'd recorded the patterns of his movements each day when he returned to work at the power distribution facility.

They also determined that his wife or partner worked at a hospital, and her hours were irregular. The power plant was a 25-minute drive, the hospital twenty minutes farther. Since there were no large metropolitan areas within a three-hour drive, the two were easy to track with satellites.

Kurt assimilated this information then read down. Yesterday, Ramzi drove to a reservoir for the city of Khafunabad, a one-and-a-half-hour drive. His vehicle was still parked at the dam parking area. His woman left home at 1700 hours and turned toward the hospital for an apparent twelve-hour shift.

"Let's go!" Kurt said. "It'll be dark in half an hour. Grab your equipment."

They dressed for cold weather in heavy, winter, *shalwar kameez,* and headgear. Kurt seized his pack, set the incendiary devices for twelve hours to destroy evidence of their occupation, and folded the camouflage net. He pulled the car out.

The timing was good. On the road, they could still see the larger rocks and brush. They went over the plan again. Last night, they found a place to leave the car among trees one kilometer from the nearest apartments, and about three kilometers from Ramzi's residence. Hakim drove by the apartments twice. Each time, people gawked at them under the dim streetlight.

They waited for a while in the grove. Kurt's satellite phone paged silent. He read the message.

"Ramzi left the reservoir," Kurt said. "We've got ninety minutes."

This time when they passed the apartment, the street was clear. Kurt grabbed the equipment and crept to the front door. Hakim left. It took several minutes to pick the lock. When it clicked, Kurt pushed the door open and saw a motion detector blinking red and beeping.

Flashing his light around, he ran through the rooms searching for people and animals. In a bedroom, a large black cat jumped on the bed, arched its back and hissed, yellow eyes wide. He found what he was looking for in the nearby closet. He yanked a cover on an alarm panel open and pulled the leads off a battery. With the light in his mouth, he began unplugging wires while a timer counted down. Ten … nine … eight—three … two ….

There!

The LED went dark.

Done.

He searched the closet and the bedroom. The cat scampered off into another room. He looked under the bed and in all the drawers for weapons. In the nearby bathroom, Kurt spotted a large, old-fashioned straight razor and leather strop.

Returning to the front room, he noted the positions of a large-screen TV, a divan that pulled out into a bed, a fold-up computer table, and three cabinets. The fireplace adjacent to the TV filled the opposite wall. There were alabaster lamps on two exquisite, ivory-inlaid tables, and a matching coffee table. A striking red Persian carpet with blue, green and gray patterns covered the entire tile floor. Thick and obviously hand-woven.

Expensive.

Locating the alarm pad, he noted that the red LED was off. He didn't find a gun in any drawer or shelf.

An arched passage led to a dining table and chairs, then to the rear sliding glass door. Centered on the left wall, a large hutch was full of china and crystal glasses. The kitchen was opposite the hutch.

Kurt eased through, making sure not to touch anything. The powerful odors of garlic and curry were familiar. Everything within was neat and clean and put in its place. A tile counter contained a mortar and pestle, an electric can opener, six knives in a rack, a coffeepot, and a stainless sink with a dishcloth draped on the faucet. Two small drawers held large cutting utensils and metal and plastic spatulas. A refrigerator and a gas range-oven combination shared one electrical outlet.

Huh, automatic lighter.

The appliances were small.

At the back door, remembering there were motion detectors, he twisted the knob and eased it open for a look. Another alarm keypad was mounted on the wall near a telephone. He turned, slipped a knife out, and after testing its edge, put it back.

No guns.

Returning to the front room, he checked a short hall with a laundry room off to the side, a main bathroom, and another bedroom. Still no weapons, except for brooms and mops.

The bedroom smelled stale and looked unused except for a worn path in the rug leading to the garage door. The far wardrobe closet was half-open and empty. There was no bed. He opened the garage door and saw an automatic opener and the segmented, roll-up door in front. Closing the door, he spotted a small piece of cardboard on the floor.

Kurt picked it up and stared at the neatly-trimmed rectangular strip, turning it over in his hand. Either it had been placed in the door and fallen out or had merely been dropped. He pushed the door all the way open and saw no other pieces. The door on the garage side had been unlocked. For a moment he stood and looked at the doorjamb. A gray, rubber weather-strip ran along the contact edge. One step into the house, another keypad for the alarm system was mounted to the wall.

Kurt's phone vibrated on silent.

Holy shit! Four kilometers!

He hurried to the kitchen and picked out a plastic spatula. Back at the garage door, he took the small piece of cardboard, held it inside the jamb with the spatula, and pulled the door closed on it. He slid the spatula out at the last instant and returned it to the kitchen.

Gotta work fast.

He went to the main bedroom closet and turned the light on. The alarm panel had a label written in French. Locating the proper color coding, he plugged the power supply wires in, then held his breath while he plugged in the alarm wires. An amber LED went out and two tiny green lights alternately flashed.

Near the front door, Kurt activated the alarm system. There was a short beep and a red LED began blinking.

One minute.

In the bedroom, he lay down on the far side of the bed. Sliding the Taser out of his trousers, he made sure the electrodes were fully loaded against their springs. He shifted the drug darts taped on his chest.

Kurt swallowed hard. *Last chance.*

Several minutes went by. Kurt breathed evenly, taking a deeper breath every so often.

It seemed like a long time passed when he heard the garage door roll up. Then the alarm beeper sounded. It shut off. At least half a minute went by.

Cardboard, in correctly?

He heard noises from the kitchen: The refrigerator closing, ice in a glass, a cabinet door slamming shut. Ramzi came into the bedroom. Kurt heard ice cubes swirling and clinking. Ramzi smacked loudly. He went into the bathroom. The glass made a noise when it was set on tile. The shower door opened and squeaking handles adjusted the water temperature. Kurt heard the faint noises of clothes coming off, of a hamper closing. More faucet squeaks. Another drink.

The shower door closed.

Kurt eased up. The bathroom door was half open. Between the gap, he could make out the form of a naked body through the translucent pane. He rose to a standing position and crept around the bed.

The shower faucets squeaked again and the water went off. Ramzi toweled off. The shower door opened. For a few breaths, he disappeared into a hollow behind the wall. In a moment, he stepped back out in shorts, undershirt, and slippers, pulling on a robe.

Kurt tightened his jaw. Eyes wide, he breathed steadily. He raised the Taser and lifted a foot to step and position himself.

The cat made a loud screech and bolted from under the bed.

"Shit!" Kurt started. He pulled the trigger.

Ramzi gawked and yelled, "Valdez!"

The darts missed.

Ramzi jumped. He seized the razor.

Kurt pulled a towel free and held it tight before him.

They went back and forth, twisted and parried. Ramzi slashed. Kurt jumped and flicked a foot toward his arm. The Arab yelled and swiped again at Kurt.

Kurt spun and thrust a foot toward Ramzi's crotch. The man flicked the razor. Kurt felt a sharp pain in his leg. Another kick. It hit the wrist of the hand holding the razor. The implement flew.

Ramzi spun and flipped out a foot. It caught Kurt on the upper thigh as he twisted. Kurt shoved the man back against the basin.

Backing, Ramzi grabbed a hair dryer. He shouted and flung it hard. It hit Kurt above the eyebrow. He reeled backward.

A square box came flying. Vials and tiny glass bottles broke against the wall and door. Ramzi grabbed a jar. It crashed above the door. A flurry of powder burst in the air.

Kurt coughed and blinked. Fanning his hands back and forth, he choked on the talc. The Arab rushed him. Kurt flicked another kick, aiming for the crotch.

Both men wheezed from the billowing powder. Kurt charged and rammed an elbow into Ramzi's chest. Ramzi twisted, seized Kurt and slammed him against the tile.

Kurt was stunned. For a moment, he was immobilized with a pain on the hip blade.

Ramzi ran out.

Kurt heard a drawer jerk open. He hobbled rapidly to the living room. Ramzi flipped a gun around and racked the slide.

Kurt dove. He grasped Ramzi's wrist, twisted, and bent it backward.

The man yelled and dropped the gun. Kurt kicked it into the hallway.

The Arab came at Kurt's eyes with fingernails. He flicked a foot at Kurt's crotch. It missed but gave Ramzi a moment to retreat into the kitchen. He came out with a cleaver.

Kurt dove for the gun. He grabbed it and turned it toward Ramzi.

A powerful kick sent it flying. Kurt spun. The Arab slashed with the cleaver. Kurt lunged back. The blade missed. Another slash. It caught Kurt on the forearm. He yelled loudly.

Both men breathed in gasps. Kurt kicked and caught Ramzi near the crotch again. The man yelped. He spun with the cleaver. Kurt flicked a foot out hard and the weapon flew against the hutch. Glass crashed to the floor. Kurt bounded for the gun.

Ramzi jumped on him as he twisted back. The gun bounced off the floor. Kurt came around to face the man again.

The Snow Leopard gasped, eyes wide. He backed away and looked around. Seizing a large piece of glass from the hutch, he lunged back at Kurt. Kurt parried. He felt a sharp pain in his shoulder.

Ramzi raked the glass down Kurt's forearm. Kurt grasped the man's testicles, yelled, and flung him over his shoulder. The Arab crashed through the coffee table. Kurt drove a knuckle into his kidney.

Ramzi shouted. He flailed with the glass.

Kurt dodged and drove his knuckle into Ramzi's kidney again. The Arab finally lay immobile, his mouth working for air.

Kurt ripped the tape off his chest and gripped a drug dart. Exposing the needle, he stuck the man and watched as the entire vial emptied.

After he caught his breath and looked at his wounds, he peeked outside and looked around. Stepping out to the porch, he sent a message to Langley: *Package secure*. Then he went back inside and glanced at himself in the mirror. He had a deep cut above his eyebrow with blood running down his cheek.

Guards will wonder about this.

However, the shoulder was worse. In the bathroom drawers, he found first aid materials. He grimaced and cleaned the wounds with antiseptic and towels, then bandaged himself.

His satellite phone buzzed. He glanced at the message. Ramzi's mate was coming. She was five kilometers away.

Not again!

Langley added that they told Hakim to stay put.

Kurt checked Ramzi. The Arab was breathing steady. Kurt pulled him around to the front door side of the couch, hidden. Returning to the inside garage door, Kurt looked in. A brown Mercedes was parked on the right side. Oil spots and chunks of mud where tires had rested were on the left side.

He closed the door and turned. There on a small shelf was the piece of cardboard.

It was a warning signal.

He went to the dining area and retrieved the gun, a Beretta. The clip was full. He stashed it near Ramzi, under the edge of the couch. Next, Kurt kicked the visible broken glass under the hutch and shoved the broken table so it couldn't be seen from the hall. He wiped blood spots from the floor and off of the cleaver, and returned it to a drawer. Taking the bloody towel to the bathroom, he rinsed it and wiped the powder off the bottom of his boots. He saw the cat's yellow eyes peeking from under the bed.

Heading back to the living area, he noted that powder tracks were clearly visible from the dining area, but not from the hallway to the garage.

The sound of the garage door rolling up startled him.

Running to the shower in the far bathroom, he turned the water on. Then he hurried to hide in the wardrobe closet of the small bedroom near the garage.

After several seconds, the inside door opened while the big garage door out front rolled shut. A woman came through.

"Honey, I'm home," she called out in Farsi. She must have heard the shower running, stopped and went into the nearby bathroom.

Kurt pulled out another drug dart. He inhaled several breaths and waited by the door.

The toilet flushed. Water came on in the bathroom. A door opened and closed. Three footsteps.

Now!

Kurt stepped out quickly. The woman had dropped something, started to bend over, and saw his boots. She screamed and stood up.

Seizing her, Kurt spun her around and placed his hand over her mouth.

She grabbed at his crotch. Jerking wildly, she tried to bite his hand.

She was his height and stocky. It took all his remaining strength to subdue her. He finally flipped her to the floor and got a knee in her back. He jabbed in the drug dart in her neck and pressed his thumb. She stopped moving after several deep breaths.

He dragged her into the bathroom, locked the door, and pulled it shut.

Hurrying to the other bathroom, he turned off the shower. Then he went out front and notified Langley.

Before Hakim arrived, he dragged Ramzi to just inside the roll-up door and took the controller from the Mercedes. He retrieved the Beretta, then making a once-around, opened the front door a slit.

Hakim arrived. Kurt motioned for him to back up the Shikar to the garage door. Kurt operated the remote when the vehicle was in position, locked the front door, and helped Hakim push the body into the car. While Hakim eased forward, Kurt verified that the garage door closed.

"Whew! What a battle, *saddique*." Kurt looked around. "The police?"

"I saw them over on the other street." He pointed.

"Okay. Take it easy until we get out of the village."

Within fifteen minutes, they turned on the side road where they had set up the antenna. They put Ramzi in a net bag and shoved him behind a panel in the trunk. It wouldn't be readily noticeable if the revolutionary guards took only a quick look inside. Kurt then sent a burst communication informing Langley. In a half-hour the antenna would self destruct.

Before they took off, they put the masonry tool bag on the backseat and Kurt changed into his *shalwar kameez*. When they passed through the guard station at the far side of the copper mine, Kurt got out the pack of Turkish cigarettes. He feigned smoking one when he drove up to the swing-open gate. He chatted and offered both soldiers cigarettes.

The guards had a different attitude this time. Kurt pretended to be relaxed. The soldiers exhaled and waved the men through the gate.

Pulling away, Kurt said, "Now we have to hurry. I'll drive to just past Kerman. Then you drive to the turnoff near Bander 'Abbas. I want to be near the Gulf an hour before daylight."

Chapter 98

East of Bandar 'Abbas, Iran

Seven hours later, Hakim said, "Wake up, Kurt. We are one hour from the LZ."

Kurt blinked, sat up straight, and looked around. "Wow! I must have been tired. Smooth sailing after we went through that revolutionary guard station near Rafsanjan, eh Hakim? Except for that 5-ton driver with no lights."

"We were lucky. If you had not spotted him, we might have been killed when he crossed over the highway."

"It *was* close. Sure jarred us awake. The man didn't even hear our horn."

"That is why you see so many trucks on the sides of the road." Hakim slowed as they approached a small village.

Kurt exhaled. They had driven 120 kilometers per hour most of the night. But there were several dicey moments when they approached other vehicles. There was another incident when two wild camels crossed the highway. Hakim had to slam on the brakes.

"We're coming up to our turn." Kurt gestured left. "Highway 91."

Hakim made the turn. "I am getting tired."

"Pull over. I'll drive the last 90 kilometers. We need to check our passenger also."

Kurt's satellite phone paged him. He glanced at the readout. It said, Papillon now tracking to LZ XL39.

Kurt smiled and said, "Papillon. Lieutenant colonel Diane Wisneski. She's tracking us. Together we took out 'Headfake,' a Pakistani general high up in the ISI who helped Osama bin Laden plan September 11. The Pakistanis refused to arrest him, so we took action ourselves."

Kurt worried that the Iranian Pasdaran could possibly intercept these messages, now. They might suspect that intelligence operatives were operating in Iran.

The landing zone, LZ X-ray-lima-three-niner, was less than a half hour away.

The eastern horizon was just turning a lighter blue by the time they approached the end of a tile road that led to the landing zone. A cloud of dust rose from behind the Shikar as it dropped down onto rutted dirt.

"Very fast for this road, saddique."

Kurt ignored Hakim's warning and drove with the high beams on. After several minutes of bouncing on the road, which became narrower and more rough the farther they traveled from the highway, Kurt's pager came on again.

He slowed to read the message. "Hostile chopper pursuing. Two more following, 10 min. Will brief. Papillon."

Fuck!

Kurt pushed the small car to the limits of its suspension system. They sped over rises and fell into dips that caused the springs to bottom. Several times the car bounced so hard that he almost lost control. Each time, Hakim looked at him, panicked.

They must be approaching the pick-up point. It seemed like they had been on the road for more than twenty minutes.

Hakim held up the lighted display on his GPS. "Three clicks from the LZ."

"Good," said Kurt.

Suddenly, a white flash burst near the right front of the vehicle. The car lurched off the road from the shockwave. Hakim yelled.

A chopper streaked past them, banked, and headed back toward them with full lights on. Kurt shoved the brake pedal to the floor. Jumping out, he swung the Beretta around and shot at the lights.

Another rocket disintegrated off to the other side of the vehicle. The chopper hovered, rotated its lights. All Kurt could see was intense white glare. All he heard was the whine of the jet engine and the steady pops of the rotors.

So this is how it would end. On the Iranian desert. In the middle of no man's land.

A stream of automatic fire raked the ground around Kurt. A loudspeaker blared in Farsi, "Throw away your weapon."

It took a few seconds for Kurt to realize that they didn't want to kill them.

Interrogation!

They wanted answers. After he thought for a moment, Kurt held up the Beretta and threw it several meters onto the sand. Deftly slipping a cyanide capsule into his mouth, he raised his hands.

The helicopter hovered level 40 meters away, the lights now aimed straight over the car. Kurt was aware of a rope falling out of the chopper. Several men in combat boots and holding automatic rifles slid down. They shouted as they approached him.

His mind raced. He worked the cyanide pellet between two molars where a tooth had been. He wondered if Hakim also had his pellet at the ready.

Kurt knew that the Pasdaran and the Revolutionary Guards had methods to make anyone talk. Or die in the worst imaginable pain. Head in a vise. Air bladder inflated through the ass. Boiling oil on the testicles!

The Iranians came forward, one man taking the lead while the others covered him. They advanced a dozen paces. A speaker directed any other occupants of the car to come out of the vehicle and throw their weapons down.

Hakim opened his door. He held up his hands and showed them to be empty. He walked toward the chopper, hands up. Then he fell forward, kneeled in prayer fashion, and touched his head on the road.

The chopper rose and came forward slowly, its rotors popping louder. Over the noise, Kurt heard a screaming sound. At first he thought it was Hakim. But it was mechanical. It screamed louder. Time slowed to a series of jerks. His mind registered what the sound was. He remembered that sound from combat. One of the soldiers shouted.

Kurt immediately translated the command: *Incoming!*

He dove into the deep fold of a tire rut and covered his head.

A blast shuddered through the ground. The roar and shockwave rushed over his head. Molten metal flew in all directions from the spot where the chopper had been. Rotors sailed through the air with a warble. The Shikar flipped upside down. It came down with the sound of broken glass and crunched metal. Four military jets screamed by overhead.

Kurt's eardrums rang. He yawned to control the pain. It took several seconds for him to realize what had happened.

He ran to the gun. He was aware of a sharp pain in his leg and fell toward the Beretta. Yelling, he rolled over. In the dwindling flames of the destroyed helicopter, he saw blood gush from his thigh. He moved his hand to the pain and winced when he found a piece of glass protruding. He shouted, jerked it out and rolled to his knees.

In the now ebbing flames, he saw two soldiers moving, shaking their heads, rising to kneeling positions. One looked around at the others, lying sprawled, smoke rising from their bodies. Another stood and stumbled.

The Iranian brought his automatic weapon to his shoulder. Kurt could see the curve of the weapon's banana clip silhouetted by the flames. The barrel of the gun swung around toward him. For a moment, everything went silent. The jets had banked and headed south. Popping and crackling noises came from the smoldering remains of the chopper. Cooling metal from the upside-down Shikar pinged.

Kurt pointed his Beretta at the soldier. In Farsi, he yelled, "Drop your weapons!"

The startled man made a quick movement with the barrel. Kurt blasted him with shots in the throat and neck. He quickly turned the gun on the other man, who fell forward on his face. His weapon lay underneath his body.

Kurt jerked his head when he heard the sound of more helicopters coming.

Shit! Here we go again.

Two choppers banked and swept into an arc toward him. He remembered that Papillon had warned that more choppers followed the first one. He squinted to try to see markings. Finishing their banking move, the aircraft came on, menacing. He stumbled toward the dunes. He dove and lay motionless on the sand.

The helicopters' lights swept in an arc toward Kurt.

Those are hostiles, we haven't gotta chance.

He lay in the rut, his face turned toward the oncoming aircraft. With his tongue he located the cyanide capsule to make sure it was still in place.

A chopper made a sweep of the terrain, flooding its spotlights on the scene of the downed Iranian helicopter. And the bodies of the soldiers. It shifted its lights onto the upside-down Shikar.

Kurt could not make out any insignia. He remained motionless.

The second chopper revved its rotors, set down, then slowed the engine to an idle.

A wave of sand blew over Kurt and Hakim. Kurt coughed and choked. He covered his face with his turban.

He was aware of men jumping out of the craft and heard voices. He couldn't make out the language.

If they were Iranians, he would rise up, shoot Hakim, then bite the cyanide. That would be it. Finished. End of mission.

He strained to hear the communication above the sound of the choppers' idling engines. The helicopter above hovered. Several commands came from the advancing soldiers. Kurt gritted his teeth from the pain in his thigh.

Voices moved closer. It was now or never. He raised his head to look at the oncoming personnel. Sliding his gun hand around, he aimed it toward Hakim. The Afghani lay flat on the sand, face down, probably unconscious. Kurt could barely see the back of his head. It would have to be a good shot. Moving his finger to the trigger, he checked the cyanide capsule once more.

He saw quick motions as three men dove to the ground. They must have seen him move his gun hand.

"Throw your gun away!" came the command in English.

Americans!

"Don't shoot! We're Americans!" shouted Kurt. He rose, dangling the Beretta by the handle between his thumb and forefinger. He spit out the cyanide capsule. "Man, am I glad to see you guys."

"Who's with you?"

"My partner. I've got the only gun."

A new voice came from behind the group. "Anyone injured, Kurt?" It was Lieutenant Commander Menzies.

"Yes, Sir, Commander. We've got our package in the car, if he survived."

The SEALs moved toward them.

Wincing and holding his leg, Kurt smiled at Menzies. "Thought you guys were gonna be too late."

Kurt heard a high-pitched scream from jet aircraft. He recoiled as a flash, then a muffled explosion, came from the direction of Bandar 'Abbas.

The commander shouted, "Get those men on stretchers and outta here! The Iranians have scrambled some jets."

Kurt said, "Roger that." He limped to the back side of the Shikar. He had to jerk on the deck lid several times to free it from the space between the backseat and the crushed roof.

"He's alive, commander."

"Give Kurt a hand!" shouted Menzies.

Kurt heard the jets banking for a turn.

Hope those are ours.

The aircraft circled and came toward them.

Kurt tried to run to the chopper with the solders dragging Ramzi. The pain in his thigh slowed him as he stumbled over the ruts of sand.

Inside the chopper, the pilot revved the rotors. The jets screamed by, their U.S. flag emblems glinting in the lights. The helicopter rose, and Kurt felt his weight shift to his stomach as the craft banked toward the Gulf and accelerated.

They flew close to the ground to avoid radar detection. It was not light yet. Kurt could see nothing in front and wondered how the pilot could control the aircraft so precisely. He knew that sometimes they didn't. Choppers frequently crashed or collided when flying with night-vision.

Within minutes, they were heading out over the Gulf. Kurt could make out a reflection of the waning moon on the water. Shortly, the helicopter banked again, and he spotted the red and white lights on a ship. He blew out a large breath, smiled and nodded to Menzies, who regarded him with awe. Glancing at Hakim, he saw that a medic had given him a shot. The man lay unconscious, breathing heavily.

Kurt's satellite phone vibrated. He glanced at the readout. It said, "Nice work. Papillon."

Menzies said, "The Snow Leopard's coming around. Man, does he have a surprise coming. There's a jet waiting for him in Dhahran. Headed to Langley. And the Farm."

Glossary: Arabic and Farsi

Abaaya: A long black cloak worn over the clothing of Arabic women.
Alaikum salaam. Response to **Salaam alaikum?** Good, how are you?
Ala shoma koobai? (Farsi; Iran and Afghanistan) Hello, how are you?
ANSWER: Kheili mahm nun: thank you very much.
Allahu akbar: God is great.
Al Qaeda (the base or foundation).
Baksheesh: Bribe or deal sweetener.
Baleh: (FARSI) Yes.
Bazaar: (Iran and Afghanistan) Marketplace.
Bedouin: The ancestral tribes of the Arabian deserts.
Burqa: A garment that completely covers a woman, with a gauze-like aperture to peer from.
Caliph: Holy man.
Chadore: (Iran and Afghanistan) A large cloak worn over the head of women so they may hide part of their faces.
Chai: tea.
Ensha Allah: God willing.
Fatwa: Order issued by Caliph. (Osama bin Laden recieved one to attack Saudi Arabia)
Ghutra: The head covering worn by men. May be white or light colors, or checkered red-and-white or black-and-white, (called a **kaffiyeh** in some areas). Held with an **igaal**.
Hajj: Pilgrimage to Mecca, Saudi Arabia, the holy site established by Mohammad, that Muslims yearn to make.
Hawala: Money handlers who transfer $250 billion throughout the world each year, faster than a wire.
Igaal: a cord that was traditionally used to hobble camels.
Imam: The leading holy man.
Islam "submission" (to God's will) (a way of life) **Adherent**: a **Muslim (Moslem)**
Jambiga: An Arabic sword. In Yemen, a small curved sword with jewels in the handle.
Jihad: A struggle, a fight, a mission.
Kheili Koobai (FARSI): Very good.

Kheili mahm nun (FARSI): thank you very much.
Khoda ha fez (FARSI): Goodbye.
Koran, Qu'ran: Inspired by mystical revelations of **Mohammad** as recorded by scribes. The approved canonical text was set down after his death in **Suras,** the 114 chapters of the Koran.
Madrassa: a religious school.
Mahram: The male escort who must accompany all Saudi women when they ride in vehicles or go to public places.
Majli: judge.
Mohammad (b:570 d:632): Believed to be a prophet through whom God spoke.
Muezzin: religious criers (on loudspeakers).
Mujahed, mujahedeen: Warriors participating in a jihad
Mullah: (Iran and Afghanistan) A leading holy man.
Mutawa, mutawaeen: Harsh religious police who enforce the holy laws of the Wahhabi.
Naan: (Iran and Afghanistan) Delicious whole-wheat bread the size of a pizza, cooked in a kiln. (pronounced noon)
Osama or Usama (young lion)
Pasdaran: Iran's intelligence agency
Qat: Bitter grass that Yemenis chew each afternoon. Effects are like strong coffee *and* aspirin.
Ramadan: the holy month of fasting from sunup to sunset that occurs approximately every 13 months or so by the modern calendar. (Began after Mohammad's first revelation)
Rials: (IRAN) currency.
Saddique: friend.
Salaam: peace.
Salaam alaikum: Greeting: Hello how are you?
Answer: **Alaikum salaam**. (I'm fine, thank you).
Shalwar Kameez (Pakistani areas): Loose fitting shirt and pants, usually gray.
Shia, shi'ite: Minority sect (Believe Caliphs are God given and are descendants of Ali, Mohammad's son-in-law).
Shuhada'a, Shaheed: Martyr or martyrs. Suicide bombers.
Shukran: Thank you.
Shukran a saddique: Thank you my friend.
Shura, Sharia: Holy council.
Sunni: Largest sect of Islam (Believe Caliphs must be elected only from the tribal descendants of Mohammad).

Thobe: The long shirt-like garment worn by men, usually made of white cotton, but may be of darker colors in the winter. (Also known as a **dishdasha** in some countries.)

Ulema: clergy.

Wahhabi: A severe form of fundamentalist religous observances practiced in most of Saudi Arabia.

CPSIA information can be obtained at www.ICGtesting.com
Printed in the USA
BVOW071216280812

298784BV00001B/1/P